"Why do you hate him so?"

"You see me as I am," he said simply. "Look at me. This is his fault." He stood up and turned before her, like a model, raising his arms, pointing his feet as though about to dance.

She stared through blood-rimmed eyes at the tall, green-haired, white-skinned mockery of a man, whose twisted mouth flowed across his face like a skein of blood. He seemed invented, like something dreamed up by a bad artist during his final drink. He looked mythical, demonic.

He was all too real.

"Will killing me bring you back to yourself?" she asked wonderingly. "Will torturing me change you?"

The Joker laughed, softly. "No, but it will change him, when he knows what I've done. He'd grieve even without knowing who you were, but when I tell him you were his sister, when I send him the tapes of you twisting and writhing, the sound of your screams, of your voice, pleading. . ."

"I haven't pleaded with you."

"Oh, but it's early days. You will. Sooner or later. Before the end. . . ."

—*From S. Tepper's* Someone Like You

The Further Adventures of The Joker®

™

Edited by

Martin H. Greenberg

BANTAM BOOKS
NEW YORK • TORONTO • LONDON • SYDNEY • AUCKLAND

*To David R. Silvers, who
roots for the Caped Crusader.*

THE FURTHER ADVENTURES OF THE JOKER

A Bantam Book/February 1990

Cover and interior art by Kyle Baker.

Designed and Produced by M 'N O Production Services Inc.

ISBN 0-553-28531-9

Published simultaneously in the United States and Canada

PRINTED IN THE UNITED STATES OF AMERICA

0 9 8 7 6 5 4 3 2 1

Contents

The Further Adventures of The Joker

Belly Laugh
or
The Joker's Trick or Treat

Joe R. Lansdale

BATMAN'S JOURNAL

(Entry, October 28th)

Sometimes I start to believe my good press.

In my mind, late at night, before sleep claims me, I actually think of myself as the Caped Crusader, the Dark Knight, and all those ridiculous names the tabloids give me. I am fast and sure and perfect. The world's greatest acrobat, the world's greatest detective. There's nothing I can't do.

Then I awake and the world sets me straight. Creeps like the Joker step out of the light and into the shadows.

The Joker escaped from Arkham Asylum two weeks ago, and I've been looking for him without success. Waiting for him to strike. Dreading whatever craziness he might have planned this time out.

And last night it happened.

Judge Hadley's dead.

I wasn't there when Hadley died, but Jim told me what he saw, and I can imagine how it must have been for the Judge last night. He's walking along, feeling all right, fresh from a quick dip in the pool, then he becomes aware of the trouble as his feet turn to goo in his shoes. He falls down and flops, his ribs poke through his skin, turn to paste, and flow away. His heart and lungs push through his chest, throb inside his robe, go to mush. His brain oozes out of his ears like oily oatmeal, then there are no ears and no skull, just a blob of white and gray.

The mess pops and gurgles momentarily, makes the robe in the midst of the puddle pulse as if full of rats. Then all movement ceases. The moonlight catches the goo and a little moon-made rainbow rises above it. A white-gloved hand reaches out and drops a party hat into the mess. Painted on the hat is the green-haired, red-lipped, white-skinned face of the Joker.

And the Joker laughs.

Spare me a vivid imagination.

Here's how I found out. It was yesterday, just after noon. Gordon's office.

Jim got word to me, and I went over there, sat in a chair with a loose spring, and looked at him. It was a bad view. His clothes were rumpled, his face unshaven. The corners of his mouth drooped like crumbling masonry. His hands clutched the arms of his chair as if he were strangling small throats. There was a drop of sweat dangling from the end of his nose. His forehead was wet. The room wasn't hot.

I didn't feel so good myself. Felt small and worn and ancient inside my cape and cowl. Even a little foolish. It had been that kind of year. My last case, the mess with Subway Jack, had taken a lot out of me. And now Gordon had something to say to me, and I knew what it was before he said it.

"The Joker."

Gordon got a tape recorder out of his desk drawer, took a tape from the plastic evidence bag, slipped it into the machine, said, "Listen."

(click)

Well, pilgrim, that old wind is howlin' around the asylum, and the rain is hittin' the nuthouse walls like whips. Lightnin's popping outside the windows like six guns, but it isn't botherin' me, nosirree. Day I get bothered, well, that'll be the day, pilgrim.

I'm sittin' here lookin' just the way Batman made me. White-faced, green-haired and red-lipped. No Stetson. No pony. Sittin' here in the hoosegow, right where Batman put me. And I been looking at the rain and lightnin' through barred windows. And I'll tell you, Mr., I'm tired of it. And know what, darned if I don't get me a plan to break out of this here hoosgow, like in the cowboy pictures.

Gonna break out and ride away.

Hear me, Sheriff Batman?

Pretty soon there's gonna be a showdown at high noon, and you and me and are gonna slap leather, and when the smoke clears, you and your bat ears are gonna be laying in the middle of the big trail like so much dust.

Okay, that's all for the John Wayne impersonation. I also do a mean Humphrey Bogart and the best Sidney Poitier in the world, outside of Sid himself.

But now, I'm going to talk like the Joker. And pardners, the Joker's wild.

Wild as Dorothy's tornado. Madder than a liberal democrat with a budget cut.

And guess what, Bats? By the time you hear this, I won't be in Arkham Asylum anymore. In point of fact, I'm not there now. There's no wind and rain and lightning outside my window. That's just a bad memory, but one I wanted to share with you.

What I'm saying here, Cowl Head, is all the world's a stage and Heavens to Mergatroit, I've gone stage left on the Asylum. I'm in a new suit under a new spotlight. Crime's spotlight.

(long pause)

I'm calmer now. Shall we talk?

Good. Let us call this Joker Notes. Let us call this the first serial installment. Let us call it a brief history of my parentage. Let us call it a game. Let us call it entertainment and a clue.

(pause)

My. We're calling it lots of things, aren't we?

Okay. Here goes.

I was born in a small vat of chemicals. My mother and father was Batman. He's strict.

I'd like to talk about him. I'll keep it short and sour. I hope to kill the sonofabitch.

But there are others that come first. I'm starting at the bottom of my hate list and working to the top. If you were a movie, Batman, you'd be five stars. And I'll save the best fun for last.

And Gordon, I give you four stars—make you fourth on the list. Don't be disappointed you didn't get top billing. You're an ache in my heart, but Batman, he's a pain in my soul.

Right now I dream of Judge Hadley. You remember Hadley, don't you? He's the one said I was mad that last time and that I should never be released from Arkham Asylum, no matter what. He called me homicidal. Wrecked. Ruined. He made fun of my wardrobe. He's one on a list of five, and I think I've made it clear where you two are on that list. But for now, let me say I'm drawing a line through Hadley, and I'll add this:

Check his house, out by the nice, heated pool. And don't get him on your shoes.

(maniacal laughter and a series of coughs)

Excuse me. Almost choked.

Now I'll find a couch and lie down. Relax. Analyze my life. Next time, I'll shoot the works.

(click)

"The tape came in about three hours ago," Jim said. "No one knows how it was delivered, or who delivered it, but it was found at the front desk. We've theorized someone dressed as a cop brought it in during a shift change. The Joker or one of his thugs, probably.

"When I heard the tape, I got some blue coats and we went out to Hadley's, and it was quite a mess. It looked like an army had puked out there by the pool. All that was left besides the goop was his robe, swimming trunks, and house shoes. You see, Hadley always took a late-night swim before bed. Told me he started doing it when his wife died, because after that, he couldn't sleep unless he was worn out. Why, he has a heated pool, so he can do it year round."

"It's the sort of thing the Joker would know," I said. "Leave it to him to have all the right bad connections."

"Yeah," Jim said. "He's probably had a better crime business and information center going from the asylum than some crooks got on the street. He's got enough money stashed away to pay for the contacts and to get things done. Anyway, one of the boys spotted something in the bottom of the pool, a gold coin about the size of a half dollar. We fished it out with a pole and a scoop. It had the Joker's face on it. Lab boys say it has pin-size holes in it, and when it hit the water, it released a color-less, odorless chemical that mixed with the water and turned it into an acid. It won't do a thing to cloth, plastic, metal, any of that. Just works on flesh and bones. It's major bad business. Stuff in that coin—and it was just a few drops—could have dissolved a killer whale and had enough left over to mush-out an aquarium full of fat guppies. That's it. You've got the low down and you've heard the tapes. Any thoughts?"

"Just one," I said. "Wish that tape had been three minutes of music."

Fifteen minutes later, I'm in the so-called Batmobile, roaring along past fine downtown skyscrapers with cop-per-colored glass reflecting sunlight bright as a promise from God; buildings with show windows full of orange and black crepe paper and ceramic pumpkins and holi-day floral arrangements and mannequins decked out in masks and costumes that make them witches, Casper the Ghost, the Werewolf, the Frankenstein Monster, Dracula . . . or, Batman; darting through thick traffic, past gooseneck pedestrians trying to catch a view of me, as if they thought by will alone their eyes could cut through the smoke-colored windshield of the Batmobile and the sight of me were truly worth something.

Then I'm roaring out, into the older sections of Gotham where trash blows across the streets like urban tumbleweeds and sad eyes look out of dirt-colored apartment doorways and dust-filmed windows; apartments whose tenants are not only people, but cat-sized rats and thumb-sized roaches and enough despair to put on pants and take a fast walk; sections where in one sense it is Halloween everyday, minus the festive.

I drive down streets I have no need to travel. Drive down them because they put me in touch with what I do and who I am; drive past the wreck of the once majestic Gotham Theater, formerly at the center of downtown, now part of the urban dead, and I turn my head to look . . . and review my past in an instant, as if it is all inside my head on a very short reel of black-and-white film.

My mental projector rolls and the film is fast and silent with dialogue cards. There is a SERIES OF SHOTS where I, Bruce Wayne, am young again, and inside the Gotham Theater with my parents, sitting in a middle row between them, sharing a bag of popcorn, watching the rereleased classic, *The Mark of Zorro.*

Scene OVERLAPS AND DISSOLVES to me and my parents taking a shortcut home, foolishly walking down the alley out back of the theater.

There is one streetlight in the alley. Its light is dirty amber and is currently the only true color introduced into this otherwise black-and-white scenario.

OVERHEAD VIEW. The three Waynes look like ants crawling through filthy maple syrup.

CAMERA SWOOPS DOWN, goes CLOSE on a MAN coming out of the shadows. He's carrying a revolver, wearing a slouch hat, oversized coat, and too-long pants. He walks like a man with a monkey on his back.

He points his revolver at the three of us, opens his mouth, and a DIALOGUE CARD fills the screen. It reads: GIVE ME YOUR GOODS OR I'LL SHOOT.

Card goes away. My dad steps protectively in front of my mom. Man panics, FIRES. (Gun Burst is BRIGHT ORANGE.) Dad goes down.

Man FIRES again. (Another burst of ORANGE.) Mom's pearls take the shot before her throat does. The necklace snaps. The pearls pop away, hit the alley, and bounce in all directions.

Mom falls.

CAMERA FOLLOWS as Man flees into the darkness and the darkness closes like a mouth and we DISSOLVE TO CLOSE UP of me on my knees between my dead parents, my fists bunched into little white knots, my face lifted to the streetlight as if it is some god I can appeal to.

The COLOR of the streetlight becomes more distinct, more GOLDEN. It highlights the tears on my cheeks, makes them look like cold, wet gems.

Hold a beat.

Streetlight DIMS gradually, and—

—FADE TO BAT-WING BLACK

My mental projector clicks off and the reel automatically resets for another time, and I'm alone in my skull with gray space aplenty. I turn my head back to the street and drive on between worn-out, soulless buildings as if they are ancient mountain ranges and the car is a dark cloud full of thunder, rain, and lightning, going get-up-and-get-it toward the graying horizon of a bad October day. And inside that cloud is me, a single drop of captured rain, on a course I can't control, ready to spill at nature's decree.

(Entry, October 29th)

Today, I come to you to write that I'm a failure and a fool.

Here's the news, straight from the October twenty-seventh edition of the *Gotham Gazette*. I'll paste it on the page.

FAMED PSYCHIATRIST AND
POODLE DISSOLVED

Marilyn Chute, famed doctor of psychiatry, noted for her work with such infamous psychopaths as the Joker, was victim to a bizarre and unexplained murder yesterday morning. She was found partially dissolved along with her poodle, FiFi.

The body was discovered at approximately ten o'clock

by her day maid, Tuppence Calhoun. Mrs. Calhoun said she let herself in with her key, and when she didn't see Dr. Chute, assumed she had gone shopping or out to answer a call from her office.

In preparing to clean the tub, Mrs. Calhoun discovered the shower was on and that the tub was full of a gelatinous mess containing a rhinestone dog collar, a shower cap, a mass of blond hair, white fur, pink dog toenails, and a purple party hat with a clown's face on it. Mrs. Calhoun is recorded as saying, "It was a damn silly way to die, wasn't it? Whatever happened to stabbing and shooting people?"

Police have refused to release details of this peculiar case, but Police Commissioner Gordon is calling Dr. Chute's death murder, and the Joker, who recently escaped from Arkham Asylum, is suspected. He was under the psychiatric care of Dr. Chute.

Critics of Commissioner Gordon and Batman, claim Dr. Chute was an obvious target, but was overlooked by both the police and Batman, who many criminologists claim, has been much overrated as a detective.

Dr. Chute is survived by a sister, Carolyn Holt of New Jersey, and a brother . . .

The Joker told me what he was going to do, and who he was going to do it to, and I failed to see it. Now Dr. Chute is dead and something of a joke, even to her housekeeper, and, of course, that is the Joker's way.

He once said he got a belly laugh out of his crimes, and especially out of baffling me, and that's why he did them, and I'm sure his belly is rolling now.

He said he was going to get even with five people, and though there are literally hundreds of people the Joker might hold responsible for real or imagined ills, I should have considered his psychiatrist to be tops on his list. But I was too close to the matter. I was looking for people who had actually done something to him. Jim and I put him behind bars, Judge Hadley convicted him. Seemed logical that he would next go after the prosecutor. Possibly the cops who took him to the asylum. Attendants at the asylum. And thinking that, Jim and I decided to put twenty-four-hour surveillance on those people, others like them. The obvious choices.

But the doctor who was trying to cure him? The one person who thought there was a seed of humanity in him somewhere? The one who thought he could be rehabilitated? It isn't logical he would want to do her harm.

But the logic of a madman is a sane man's confusion.

I should have suspected. No, I should have known.

He said next time "I'll shoot the works." And it was a clue. Shoot for Chute, and by the works, he meant his chemicals. And he said he was going to lie down on a *couch*—as in a psychiatrist's couch—and he said he was going to *analyze* his life, as in analysis. . . . It was all there.

He must have known she showered with her poodle. She probably told him during one of their sessions. Something to humanize herself and make the Joker comfortable, draw out his humanity.

But the Joker has no humanity. He filed it away. Found out where she lived, put the coin in the showerhead when she was out, or had it put there, and when she turned on the water for her morning shower, it activated the chemical, and . . .

The Joker merely had to wait and read about it in the papers.

When he said the tape was a clue, he didn't mean for Hadley, since he spelled that out. He meant it was a clue who his next victim was going to be, and I missed it. I thought it was merely chatter. A general warning that four others would die.

Now I have to ask myself the question: Who's next?

(Entry late October 29th)

Earlier tonight the Bat Signal struck bright against the night sky; a gold and black invitation to go downtown.

Alfred brought in my costume and I dressed and drove over to Jim's office.

When we were alone, I said, "Putting in a twenty-four-hour day, Jim?"

"Twenty-eight," he said. "The tape arrived an hour ago. They called me down to hear it. Thought you might like to hear it, too. Besides, if I can't get any rest, I want someone else to suffer with me."

"No rest for the wicked, and the good don't need any," I said.

(click)

Sung by the Joker: I'm an ole cowhand, from the Rio Grande . . .

Enough music culture. Let's talk. Ah, here we are again with yet another clue. I suppose that now, after the fact, of course, you have figured out the clues in the last tape. Shoot, Batman, you should have got that. I really thought this would be tougher.

Now, here's my report, and I'm your reporter. If you can find where I'm holding court with a handful of stooges, then come and get me. In the meantime, I have to eat my lunch. Quite good actually, legumes and rice.

But, hey, you guys didn't turn this tape on to hear me discuss my lunch, now did you? You want to know who's next? Well, I've told you. Complicated, I assure you, but seems to me a smart detective like yourself, Batman, and you, Commissioner Gordon, his erstwhile companion, should be able to tap it all out. If you do decipher my little code, it best be before tomorrow, fiveish. If you don't have it by then. Too late!

Hey, my food's getting cold. I'm outta here.

(click)

(Entry, October 30th)

I listened to the two tapes repeatedly, came up with nothing. The minutes were ticking away for some poor soul and I had no idea who.

I took out the list Jim and I had made of possible victims. Jim had arranged for everyone on it to be given police protection, but we couldn't be sure the Joker's next victim was on the list. And even if we hit on who he planned to kill, it didn't mean police protection would help. The Joker is wily.

"Your lunch, sir."

I looked up. It was Alfred carrying a covered silver tray. "I didn't hear you come in."

"No, sir, you were quite involved. . . . Excuse me, perhaps it's not my place, but don't you feel just the wee bit silly sitting here wearing your . . . Batsuit?"

"You wear a butler's uniform."

"It doesn't have a cape and ears, sir. This bat stuff, it's a little ridiculous, don't you think?"

"Truthfully, yes. But, it's my job to wear this suit. I'm a crime fighter. I don't want my identity known."

"I quite understand that, sir. Criminals are a cowardly lot and all that. A disguise to strike fear into their hearts, etc., etc. But, sir, around the house, here in the cave? It's like when you were a youngster and wouldn't take off your Zorro outfit. You slept in it. And then that dog you made wear a mask. I have to say, Master Bruce, this outfit stuff, it makes me nervous. A grown man and all. Wearing it out in the dark while beating up on people, that I can understand, but at home . . . quite disconcerting."

I pushed back my cowl. "Feel better?"

"Somewhat better, sir. I much prefer seeing your smiling face."

"Put the tray down, Alfred."

He set it on my desk, removed the lid. On the tray was a glass of milk and a sandwich.

"Jelly on this?" I asked.

"Of course, sir, isn't there always? I've made enough of those miserable peanut butter and jelly sandwiches to remember the jelly."

"Well, there was that one time . . ."

"I didn't feel well. I forgot. Please have me shot for that one failure. . . . Would you like me to eat it for you, sir? Not that I'm particularly fond of the mess, but you do seem a bit helpless at times."

"I can manage. Hey, this chitchat is great, Alfred, but

I'm really kind of pressed here. We're talking about peanut butter and jelly sandwiches, and I'm trying to solve a riddle that could mean life or death. And I tell you, I haven't got the mind for it these days. What should be obvious isn't. I need a vacation in the worst way."

I began to eat. He had remembered the jelly.

"The Joker, sir?"

"Yes."

"What's this list?"

"It's too complicated to explain. . . . You wouldn't understand."

"Of course not, sir. . . . But what is it?"

"It's a list I've made from the two tapes the Joker sent me. Words from them that struck me as possible code words. That sort of thing. I'm trying to deduce from it who his next victim will be."

"Of course, sir. Might I see it?"

"If it will make you happy, Alfred. I'm going to eat."

Alfred looked at the list.

"I can't tell a thing from this."

"Didn't I tell you?"

"It's your penmanship, sir. Very messy. Might I listen to the tapes?"

I set up the tapes, turned them on, sipped the milk. Alfred picked up a pen, wrote in the margins of my list.

"Don't mess that up, Alfred."

"Hush, Master Bruce. I'm trying to listen."

When the tapes ran their course, I said, "Happy?"

"Well, sir, I don't have the mind for these things. Not like you. But seems to me the use of legumes is a bit out of place. Rather formal. Isn't that a bean or pea?"

"Yes, it is, Alfred. You're up on your agriculture. You'll note I've dissected the word and tried to spell numerous words with it, without success. Nothing that strikes a chord, anyway."

"Of course, sir, I'm quite sure you're the expert here. But isn't this Joker one to take offense at odd things? My understanding of him, sir, is that he doesn't have both his oars in the water. Correct?"

"Correct."

"He makes a point of saying he's giving you a report,

says he's your reporter. He talks about holding court. About you and Commissioner Gordon tapping it all out, and that's what a court reporter does, taps keys. So, it seems to me he's talking about the court reporter. Perhaps he dislikes the idea of his madness being recorded. The Judge sent him up, as you like to say, and his psychiatrist stated in court he was mad, in much nicer and more conservative terms, of course, and the reporter made a record of that to be permanently placed on file. If we knew the court reporter's name . . . ?"

I put down my sandwich, punched up the trial transcripts and the court reporter's name.

"Bean," I said. "Jack Bean."

"Your legume, Master Bruce?"

I was uncertain if I should be happy or embarrassed. It wasn't the first time he'd done that to me. "Alfred, would you like to wear this suit and let me wear yours?"

"What? And look as ridiculous as you? I think not, sir."

I pulled on my cowl and got out of there.

So I went to stop a murder, tried to find Jack Bean. I told Jim my suspicions (though I felt guilty that I couldn't mention Alfred gave them to me), and he got the police in on it, of course.

Zip.

No Jack Bean. He wasn't doing any court reporting that afternoon. The trial he was working had been closed for the day. Lawyer recesses, something like that.

We had officers combing all over for Bean. Had people calling around. He didn't answer the phone at his apartment, so we went over there, afraid of what we might find. Me and Jim in the Batmobile, followed by a pack of uniforms and detectives. That wasn't my idea or Jim's, but the city council has been big on police involvement in my cases lately. They want to be sure their officers are on the scene of anything big that goes down. So I had to play mama duck, let all the little ducks follow.

Jim showed the building superintendent his search

warrant, and he opened up Bean's apartment. We went in and looked around.

No Bean, dissolved or otherwise.

I went next door and talked to a neighbor. A Mr. Monteleone. He was old and gray and wore knee-length shorts that revealed calves with varicose veins like hoses. He said he had lived in the apartment long enough to know Bean, and, "We have a drink together now and then, because you got to drink with someone so you don't drink with just yourself, know what I mean?"

He said he was confident enough about Bean's schedule to say he'd be in at four o'clock. He was always in at four o'clock.

"Think the Bean drinks a little too much," he said. "Know what I'm saying? They mostly give him the little stuff these days. Traffic violation trials, that kind of thing. See, the Bean does everything around the drinking. Likes to get home at four so he can have a little snort before the TV dinner is ready, then he watches the news and throws another one down his neck. After that, he watches some of the sitcoms, ones with the young girls on them, know what I'm saying here? Drinks while he watches. Whole bottle of Scotch, nightly. I been over there some. Had a few snorts myself. He don't hardly go out after he gets home. Lonely kind of guy. Know what I'm saying?"

I thanked him and he asked me if my cape got caught on stuff when I was running and jumping, and I said, "Sometimes."

I went back to Bean's apartment and Jim got all the cops to stand out of the way, and I started going through the place. The cops had already done that, but they hadn't found much. I didn't either. Some empty Scotch bottles in the kitchen trash. A few girlie magazines under his mattress. A nightstand with an alarm clock, a computer dating magazine, and coffee cup rings.

The bathroom was a nightmare. Greasy mirror, stained toilet. Tub with a crust instead of a ring, and a drain strainer full of lint and scum. If the Joker didn't get him, whatever was growing in that strainer might.

I kept looking.

Four o'clock, Bean came through the door.

He was short and stout with a few tufts of brown hair on the sides of his head. His dome was slick as the bottom of a china bowl. His nose was a drinker's ruin.

To say that he was a little surprised to find us there, puts it mildly. He almost dropped the sack of groceries he was carrying.

We explained he was on the Joker's hit list, and that his apartment was being searched in case the Joker had rigged it with his dissolving chemical.

When he heard that, he went limp, sat down in a soft living room chair, and stayed there. His face oozed sweat. His blue shirt got so wet with it, it looked black. His eyes bulged. He leaned forward, looked like a toad ready to flex his legs and spring to the center of the room. He chattered like a squirrel: "You got something yet? Why me, huh? I got nothing personal against this Joker fella. I'm a court reporter, not a judge. I write down what's said by everybody. You check in the light fixture there? Might have hid something in the light? If I was going to hide something, I might put it there. What about it, huh?"

Jim leaned against the wall with his arms crossed. He looked at me, said, "Well? Find anything in the light fixture?"

"One more look about," I said, and I started with the bedroom again. As I searched, I took a nervous glance at the alarm clock on Bean's dresser, watched as the time crawled toward five.

We could get him out of the apartment, but I wasn't sure that would help. The Joker might expect that. He could be waiting somewhere with a high-powered rifle loaded with a pellet full of the chemical. Then again, he might not know we'd figured out who the next victim was. No matter how you went, with the Joker it was a crapshoot.

I checked the clock again. . . . Then it hit me.

The clock. Bean was the kind of guy whose schedule would be easy to learn. You could time him like the sunrise.

The Joker had made us aware of the time. The clock was in plain sight. . . . It added up.

I went over and picked up the alarm clock and pulled the miniature tools out of my utility belt and worked the back off.

There was a small explosive device attached to one of the Joker's coins and that was attached to the alarm. Pretty simple. I easily disarmed it. The alarm had been set to go off at five. It was now 4:45.

But what about the water? There had to be water to mix with the chemical. It had to be planned in such a way that Bean would get both the chemical and the water.

I went back to the bathroom. Looked in the tub, under the sink, in the commode. I lifted the back off the commode, looked in there. Attached to the float was a plastic explosive and a miniature clock. It was set to go off at five. It was a small amount, but it was powerful stuff. If it blew, the entire wall would come out, on both sides, and the water pipes would shatter and the apartment would be flooded with water. The water would mix with the chemical.

Bean would get wet, then dissolved.

I disarmed the explosive.

I called Jim in and showed him what I'd found. "It's harmless now," I said, "long as we treat the explosive with a little respect."

"It's got my respect," Jim said. "I'd give it a wedding vow if it wanted it."

Jim and I shook hands.

Five o'clock came and went.

Then the phone rang.

"Do I answer that, or what?" Bean called to us.

We walked into the living room. The phone rang again. Jim said, "Yeah, go on. You're in the clear. We found what we were looking for."

The phone rang a third time.

Bean let out a sigh. "Thank God. Hey, I owe you guys, big time. I was afraid things were all over for me, you know?"

The phone rang a fourth time.

He answered it and a stream of water sprayed out of the receiver and hit him full in the face, making his flesh steam like fresh dog dung on a cold morning.

Bean screamed and went down.

Jim dove for him, but I grabbed him, pulled him back, yelled for the cops to stay away.

Bean's head wobbled like a fat lady's thigh, spread wide, went soft. His ears eased down his face as if they were flags being slowly lowered. He collapsed to the floor, squirmed. His head went from soft to liquidy. His eyes floated on the mess like grapes on vomit. His teeth sank into it like seeds. His head flowed slowly under the couch. The rest of his body was solid. It flopped once, went still.

The Joker's chemical, of course. The coin in the clock, the explosive in the commode. I was supposed to find those. The Joker had replaced the phone with one of his own. A coin in the receiver. Water pressurized inside. When Bean answered, all the Joker had to do was activate the device electronically, and Bean got a faceful of the chemical.

There was nothing we could do. It was over in instants. We stood there like idiots. A roomful of cops and the great Batman, the Fool Detective.

Then there was a snap and the base of the phone exploded sharply and something popped to the ceiling and drifted down.

A purple party hat with the Joker's face on it, floating to the floor with the help of a green paper parachute. It came to rest near the goop that was Bean.

Jim slammed his fists against his legs. "I thought we had him beat this time. It was after five."

"He said fiveish, and it's fiveish."

"I think we both need a long rest," Jim said. "Maybe retirement."

I didn't argue with that. There was something else to consider now. Jim and I were next.

I could almost hear the Joker laugh.

(Entry, October 31st, Halloween Night)

I had to stop the Joker before it was Jim's turn. Since we knew he was four, there might not be a tape, and though he had good men, I didn't believe they could protect him.

And for the moment, neither could I. I was too exhausted. So much, in fact, that if anything were to happen, I would have been useless. My muscles trembled. Spots swam before my eyes. The contents of the Joker's tapes reeled through my brain and blended into mental white noise.

It was better that I chance some rest, then refreshed, go and stay by Jim's side. And once I made that decision, laid myself down, my mind let go.

First I thought of the Joker; thought of when he was part of the Red Hood Gang and I had accidently caused him to fall over a railing and into a vat of toxic waste that transformed him physically into what he was today.

Had it been an accident? Or had part of me wanted to do him in even then, before I knew what he was capable of? Do we sometimes sense our greatest adversaries? Taste the bitterness of past life experiences? Or is it something else? Something even more primitive, like a sense of smell that tells us that here is a predator. Beware!

All I know is that, in a sense, I had created him and was indirectly responsible for every murder he ever committed. Perhaps, without my interference, he would have become nothing more than a petty thief.

But I was too tired for guilt. I began to sink down, down, away from it all, and . . .

The dream is technicolor and I'm wearing my 3-D glasses and holding my Scratch and Sniff card. I am the camera eye and the CAMERA goes CLOSE ON the JOKER sitting in a huge chair as if it is a throne. The chair is upholstered in regal purple and there is a series of great, green gems screwed into the top of the chair's backrest. They glow as if filled with phosphorescent puss.

He's wearing a green, ruffled shirt trimmed in bright yellow, a deep-purple dress coat and pants, highly polished green shoes with purple laces, and socks with purple and green clocks on them.

He looks as he always looks. Skin white as flour, hair heaped high, the texture of seaweed, the color of fresh lettuce. His lips are blood-red and he's smiling, as he is always smiling: a wide, ugly smile showing plenty of nice, white teeth.

He laughs suddenly. Wildly. Quits.

He's a happy kind of guy.

Behind him, a heap of corpses percolate with rats and maggots and decay. I recognize many of the bodies as his victims.

One of them appears to be a huge bat.

The Joker JERKS FORWARD SUDDENLY, and the 3-D glasses make it seem as if he's coming out of the screen. He merely pokes his head into my space and says softly, "Boo."

SLOWLY, he resumes his restful position, continues to smile.

FLASHING LOGO at the bottom of the screen says for viewer to SCRATCH CARD. I do. I sniff, and am overwhelmed with nausea. The card lets forth ODORS of DEATH and ROT and CORRUPTION.

CLOSE ON THE JOKER. CAMERA FILLS with his smile.

HOLD THAT FRAME

(beat)

Edges of frame start a SLOW BLEED of BRIGHT RED BLOOD, and gradually it flows toward the center of the dream screen until the screen is FILLED and the dream darkens and—

FADE TO THE DEEP DARK PURPLE OF THE JOKER'S COAT.

I awoke knowing I had discerned a truth, even if I was unclear what that truth was. Exhaustion had allowed me to rest for an hour, and I felt better. An hour's sleep to me is like eight for some.

I sat on the edge of the bed and put my head between my hands and went over everything I could remember about the dream. It had been presented as a film, and I felt that that presentation was my subconscious trying to tell me something. Trying to alert me that I had been looking around the answer to all this, instead of right at it.

I pulled on my robe and went down to the Batcave and played his tapes again. They were riddled with film and stage references. I had noticed them immediately upon hearing the tapes, but deduced they were there for the purpose of surrounding the nonfilm references so that they would stand out and provide clues. For those of us (Alfred) who had the savvy to perceive clues, that is.

I was thinking of waking Alfred up, putting him on the case, when I decided to run it all through my head again: the John Wayne routine, the cowboy movie talk about six-guns and hoosegows and ponies and Stetsons and jail breaks. Titles like *High Noon* and the *Big Trail* slipped in. Humphrey Bogart, Sidney Poitier, Dorothy's tornado, "All the world's a stage," a handful of stooges, four and five star ratings, serial installment, spotlight, call it entertainment, a cowboy song . . .

"Heaven's to Mergatroit," as that cartoon mountain lion Snagglepuss says, it hit me.

Obvious.

My subconscious had known the answer from the very first tape, but it had somehow been hidden behind a wall of hate for the Joker. I was trying too hard. I knew now why I had seen my last moments as a child in the form of a film when I drove by the Gotham Theater. The hind brain was trying to tell me something. It was giving me yet another film reference, telling me that all these things the Joker mentioned had one thing in common (and the second tape should have made this even clearer). A place where once upon a time they were all represented.

A place that had played revival films like *Birth of A Nation* and *Gone with the Wind*. Cowboy movies had shown there by the hundreds and cowboy stars had visited the stage and popped blanks into the air and twirled ropes. Some like Rex Allen, Gene Autry, and Roy Rogers had sung songs. Horses had even been on that stage. The screen had shown the Three Stooges, cartoons, and feature movies. Even *The Mark of Zorro*.

A strange and horrible warmness came over me.

I knew where the Joker was hiding.

*   *   *

Outside the Gotham Theater a shadow stepped out of the darkness, and the shadow was me. The October wind rose up as if surprised and blew a clutch of papers and leaves down the street. A soft-drink can rolled and clattered.

I soaked up the night and remembered when the theater was still brightly painted and brightly lit and there were gaudy posters behind the poster glass; posters like *The Mark of Zorro* with a man in black wearing a mask, cutting down the bad guys with a long, sharp sword. I remembered my dad's hand on my shoulder, my mom's hand holding mine. I remembered Zorro. I remembered gunshots that echoed in the alley out back.

I eased up to the door and tried it. It wasn't locked. I opened it and went in.

The lobby was surprisingly clean and there was a dim light and a mannequin in a clown suit standing behind the concession counter. The clown's hand was outstretched. It held a playing card. Above and behind the clown on the wall was a long orange banner with TRICK OR TREAT, BATMAN written in black.

Cautiously, I went over and took the card and turned it over.

It was a Joker. Written in the margins was: Happy Halloween. You are expected. Compliments of the Joker.

I went straight for the doors that led into the theater proper, pushed them open boldy, walked on in.

It was dark in there except for the light of the projector shining on the screen, showing it to be yellow and stained from age, tossed food, and drinks. The huge stage where performers and stars had strutted their stuff had gone gray. The crimson curtains on either side of it had turned the color of rust. There were shadows at the ends of the aisles and they hung like black crepe paper and wove their way between the rows and rows of seats. Due to water damage, the ceiling drooped like an old woman's bosom and cobwebs dangled from it like rotting gauze. The aisle carpets, once red, were blackened in the centers by years and years of spilled soft drinks and tracking feet. The blackness fled to the edges in little dark forks that looked like a sewage leak. The smell of mildew, rot, rat dung, and history hung in the air.

A film flickered to life on the screen. A section from *The Man Who Laughs*.

I sensed movement, glanced over my shoulder at the sagging balcony. A skeleton was gliding down from it, catercorner, floating through the darkness toward me, squeaking as it came.

It was the sort of gimmick William Castle might have used to sell *House on Haunted Hill*. But this gimmick was holding revolvers and the revolvers were lifted and even as they spat fire, I dove between a row of seats.

The skeleton continued to squeak down the wire, snapping off gunfire. Slugs slammed into the aisle carpet, followed me, smacked the backs and seat cushions of the chairs. One bullet tore through the heel of my boot, clean as a hot needle through a blister; I could feel the heat through the sole, but it didn't touch me.

I sprang up from between the seats, put a boot on the armrest of a chair to get leverage, and leaped back toward the wire that held Two-Gun Bones.

As he touched the carpet, I grabbed the supporting wire with my gloves and used it to swing myself around and whip both legs into his face. He took it with a grunt and a discharge of teeth, dropped the revolvers and went loose.

It was, of course, one of the Joker's goons dressed in a hood and black outfit with a glowing skeleton painted on it. The wire and the harness he was wearing continued to support him, even though he was unconscious.

I kicked the revolvers into the dark between the seats, turned back to the screen.

The film had changed. Excerpts from the 1930 *The Bat Whispers* stuttered across the screen. I guess the film segments were the Joker's way of showing how he envisioned himself *(The Man Who Laughs)* and how he envisioned me *(The Bat Whispers)*. Maybe he saw life as a movie. That might be an easier way to take it. As something without real substance. Flickering light and sound, nothing more.

The wall to my right was rigged. A portion flopped open and two men rushed out. They were wearing masks, ghoulish glow-in-the-dark things. When I was a kid some of the movies had ushers dressed like that as a gimmick. When you're eleven or twelve, it's pretty spooky.

These days I was the one who played dressed up, and I was a lot spookier.

I moved, fast, incredibly fast. No brag, just fact, and met them halfway.

They were quicker and better than the Joker's usual muscle. For all his intelligence and stashed, stolen money, he has a hard time recruiting the right guys. No one wants to work for a homicidal clown.

But these two . . . better than normal.

But not that much better.

I slid to the left as the closest one threw a short, snappy punch at my head, and the punch slid over my right shoulder and I slammed him with a forearm in the solar plexus so hard, blood spurted through the mouth slit in his mask.

I kicked him in the face with the top of my foot, changed the looks of his nose. He went down.

Two seconds gone. Maybe three.

The other guy saw this, of course, and even though he had an automatic, he didn't look too confident.

Which was smart.

I dropped low and used my hands to support myself, twisted around and swung my legs at his knees and knocked his feet out from under him. His gun popped once and off-aim, then I was on top of him. I snatched the automatic from him as easy as taking a rattle from a baby, tossed it away, popped two sharp punches into his face, and he took a siesta.

I estimate it took about five seconds for all that. I must be getting old.

On the movie screen was the Joker. He was sitting in a replica of the time-traveling device from the movie *The Time Machine*. It was little more than a Victorian chair with a wheel at the back, decorated with colored lights. The wheel was spinning, the lights were blinking. In front of him was a control panel and a lever. He was wearing a purple suit and a shirt of canary yellow with a scarlet scarf tied loosely in a bow around his neck. His smile was wide and white.

His voice came through the speakers cold and high and crazy:

"You were a bit slow this time, Bat Sap. Getting too old to cut the mustard? I assumed you'd work out my little riddles eventually and I've been ready for you all along. Kept a constant welcoming committee on alert, and laid my little plans. I had hoped to go through my victims in order, however. Gordon will have to be number five. It's bothersome. But hey, I'm a flexible kind of guy."

I started moving cautiously down the aisle, ready for whatever.

"This time, Bats, my theme is the movies, and right now Kung Fu movies."

More of his men appeared. They came from the front of the theater, from the back, from the balcony on ropes. They wore black Ninja outfits with swathes of black cloth across their faces. They carried poles and swords and knives and chains. There were ten of them. They surrounded me.

That made it almost even. I was warmed up and not in a good mood and needed the exercise.

I dodged a whirling blade, swept my attacker's feet from under him, and side-kicked him out of the aisle and through a chair. He didn't get up.

Good. I was a little busy.

I left-jabbed another, took his chain, hit him with it and he was out of the picture. I tossed the chain away, avoided the thrust of a *bojitsu* pole, then the pole was mine and I showed its former owner how to use it. A couple of times. He didn't enjoy the demonstration. He went down and I broke the pole on the side of another thug's head.

Things blurred after that. I stunned some nerves, broke some bones, and when the dust cleared, the Ninjas had all taken a trip to the Land of Nod.

I turned toward the stage and saw the Joker's image frozen on the screen. A spot in the stage floor opened up and the Time Machine replica rose out of it and locked into place. The Joker was seated in the chair. His teeth flashed like neon.

"Did you ever see the film *Mr. Sardonicus?*" said the Joker.

I paused, wary. He wouldn't show himself like that unless he felt protected.

"Near the end of it, William Castle paused the show and appeared on screen to let the audience choose the fate of the ghoul, Mr. Sardonicus, who, by the way, was a man with a very nice smile. Not too unlike my own. But alas, a sense of humor is not always appreciated. The audience was asked to show a card with a thumb on it— you got this when you got your ticket—and to turn it up for Sardonicus's survival, or down for his extermination. Those plebes voted he should be eliminated. I was quite crushed. I thought he was the hero of the piece."

I had to make my play sometime. Had to get him to show his hand. I started to ease forward.

"Ah," said the Joker, "not so fast. You see, I lied. Your friend Commissioner Gordon is here with us, and you might say he's a little wired."

A light attached to the ceiling came on, shined brightly on a seat in the front row. I could see the back of Gordon's broad shoulders and silver-haired head. He was slumped forward, but I could tell he was wearing one of the Joker's party hats.

"He's unconscious at the moment, Batsy, but quite all right. But soon, the lights in Gotham will dim, and Commishy Gordon's skull will light up like a jack-o'-lantern with a big candle inside. Ah, not another step, or I throw the switch."

I froze, tried to come up with a plan while the Joker talked. It was his biggest weakness, talking.

"Ever see the movie *The Tingler?* That's where I got the idea. It's the one about this thing that latches onto a person's spine and stings them to death, or perhaps it would be better to say, tingles them to death, and . . . no, haven't seen it? Oh, and now you never shall. Too bad.

"But, as I was saying, when the movie came out, one of the promotional gimmicks was the seats in the theaters were rigged with a mild electrical charge and a voice on the screen would announce—the Tingler's in the theater, and bam, all the chairs in the place got a harmless dose of Ready Kilowatt. Nice idea, don't you think? Scared the piss out of me when I was a boy.

"Commishy, however, will not only get a dose of Ready, he'll get the old boy's lifeblood. I flick this switch all the way, and bam, you get to see Gordon's head fly off smoking.

"Isn't this something? I enjoy our chats so much, I stray. Movie history is such a fascinating thing. However, the thing for me to decide now is the fate of our Commissioner Gordon. And this brings us back to Mr. Sardonicus and the Thumbs Up, or Thumbs Down cards. What shall it be?"

"Joker," I yelled. "Don't do it. Let Gordon go and I'll let you strap me in the chair."

"I'm going to get you anyway, Bats. Now, about Gordon's fate. I'm afraid there's no audience to do it. You've beat them all up. And since Commishy is out for the count, and you have a definite bias, and I so much prefer my own bias, I'm afraid that the burden is left to me. Or rather, my image on the screen will decide."

The screen Joker came unfrozen and lifted up a large card with a fist and extended thumb on it. The Joker smiled and turned the card so the thumb pointed down. The screen froze again.

"There you have it," said the Joker. "Say good-bye to the Commissioner."

I knew then he was going to do it and there was no reason to try and stall. I started running, and he hit the switch. There was a crackling sound and Gordon's head jerked and smoked and a lick of flame flashed off the side of his head and his hair and party hat caught fire.

I yelled, "Bastard," made the front row of seats, put a boot on the back of a chair, and sprang for the Joker, just as he pulled back the switch and threw it again.

Kilowatts sizzled and more flames jumped from Jim's body. He *was* dead. No one could take that kind of voltage. I could still feel the electricity crackling in the air, and could smell . . . plastic?

Even as my hands grabbed at the Joker's coat and I

jerked him from the Time Machine, felt how light he was, I realized, too late, the Joker had once again made me a fool.

He had used my rage against me.

The plastic replica of the Joker with the mechanical mouth and switch-pulling hand, exploded. It was filled with assorted Halloween candy and a nerve gas.

The explosion blew me off the stage.

An armrest struck me in the back, knocked what air I had left out of me. I lay crumpled on the floor between the stage and the front row, amidst Halloween candy and the burned replica of Jim. The electric shock had melted the plastic Commissioner and burned its clothes and hair off. The head had melted off at the neck and lay under a seat near my hand.

I was weak as a second-night bridegroom, but the explosion hadn't done any real damage, and I hadn't gotten as much gas in my lungs as I feared. I could feel its numbing effects, but it made me feel more slow than incapacitated.

But that was bad enough. It looked as if the Batman, who was born out back of the Gotham Theater, was going to die inside it. The real Joker appeared at the edge of the stage and looked down. He was dressed the same as his replica had been. He held a large, air-compressed gun in his hand.

"Trick or Treat, Bat Sap. I knew you couldn't resist getting your hands on me," he said. "Especially if you thought I had done Gordon in. And I will. Out of order, unfortunately. But, that's life."

I tried to breathe slowly, deeply, regain some strength. I eased my hand farther under the seat and touched the plastic Gordon head.

"I could have filled that model of me with my dissolving liquid, you know. But I wouldn't have had time to gloat, and I gloat so well. . . . See, I've already turned thumbs down on you. This pressurized gun holds one large pellet of my dissolvent and water, and all I have to do now is squeeze the trigger, and splat, you're bat guano. So, before my gas wears off and you climb up here and knock knots on my attractive green-haired head, I will, for all the unhappy years you've given me, bid you *adieu*."

He laughed that insane laugh, and it went up my spine and kicked around inside my head, and just before he pulled the trigger, I grabbed the plastic head, twisted and tossed it. It hit the gun on the tip of the barrel just as the Joker pulled the trigger. The plastic head took the blast I would have gotten, and the chemical splashed on either side of it and on the Joker.

He yelped, jumped back, and dropped the gun. The mess had splattered on his coat and pants, but hadn't touched his flesh.

I was still weak, but I managed to pull myself over the edge of the stage. It seemed to take hours.

The Joker was screaming with rage. He ran at me as I came up on my knees, and he kicked, and as he did, a thin blade sprang from the bottom of his shoe.

Normally, I could have blocked it with time to spare, but I was still weak from the gas, so I only managed to twist partially out of the way. The blade tore into my side like a nuclear missile.

I grunted, slammed his shin with my forearm, and the Joker went stumbling back.

I was on my feet now, and the Joker slapped at me with his right palm. Again, too slow. His hand hit my shoulder, and he had one of his souped-up joy buzzers strapped to his palm, and when it hit me, a shock like a lightning bolt went through me.

For a moment, I thought I'd go down.

So did the Joker, and he got in too close.

I snapped out a lazy left jab and grazed his cheek and he went back a foot and his hand went inside his coat and came out with a deck of cards. He threw them at me. They were metal cards with razor-edged sides. I tried to dodge them, but it was like trying to move out of the flight of a flock of geese. A number of them hit me and stuck, the worst being one that tore through my cowl and cut deeply into my forehead.

I yanked it free and shook like a dog and the others flew out and away from me like panicked pigeons.

I smiled at the Joker.

He, of course, was smiling back. But there was nothing mirthful about his grin.

The effects of the gas had worn off, and I charged him with a yell.

He knew the bloodlust was on me and he tried to run for it.

I caught him by the shoulder and spun him around and hit him with a left hook in the midsection, and he blew out his breath and went skidding across the stage. He got up, wobbled toward the screen, put his hands on it, touched the bottom of his image, tried to get his breath back.

I calmly strolled over and took him by the shoulder and turned him around. I smiled at him. A nice, big smile.

He could hardly find his voice. "I give."

"Okay," I said, and hit him with a hard right cross that connected with the side of his jaw and knocked him through the screen and onto the floor of the room beyond.

The rip in the screen went from top to bottom, splitting the Joker's film image as if it had been halved by a giant cleaver.

I went through the split into the darkness and the light from the projector followed me in. I took hold of the Joker's lapels and pulled him to my height and let him dangle in my hands. He was unconscious. A bruise the color of my cloak was forming on his paper-white cheek. He looked like nothing more than a pathetic clown puppet. I thought of all the people he had murdered, all the lives he had shattered and haunted, including mine, and I thought how easy it would be to snap his neck, to make certain it all ended here.

Then I remembered where I was. The Gotham Theater. The place I had last been a child and my parents had sat on either side of me and I had felt loved. And moments later I had felt dark and empty because that love had been taken away from me.

I was a crime fighter, not a murderer like the Joker, and I hoped that's how I would always be. Still, I hoped

Arkham Asylum held him this time, because next time around I couldn't be sure of the color of my soul.

I dragged him through the split in the screen and onto the stage, over to the Time Machine. I set him in the seat, unfastened the air hose from the gun and the compresser behind the curtains, and used it to bind him to the chair.

I stared at the projector light, watched dust ride down its beam. That beam had held all kinds of dreams and that night so long ago. I had shared a dream with my parents. A dream where a man in black fought the bad guys and always won and got the girl in the end.

I took in a deep breath, climbed off the stage, and checked on the Joker's men. A few of them were moving. I unfastened my cloak and used the pen knife in my utility belt to cut it into strips. I used the strips to tie the hands and feet of the thugs.

I used the rest of it to bind my wounds, then I went out of the theater and out to the Batmobile, used the phone inside to call Jim.

I put a hand to my injured side, walked down the alley and out back of the theater, stopped where my parents had fallen.

I glanced up at that one lonesome streetlight. Certainly it was not the same light of long ago, but it was in the same place. I looked at it the way I had that night when my parents lay on either side of me.

It occurred to me that maybe I, too, had been shot that night, only wounded, and that I lay in some hospital somewhere in a coma, dreaming all I thought I had lived. Living in a permanent dark world where a man can dress like a bat and fight a criminal who looks like a psychotic clown.

Sirens wailed in the distance.

—For Kasey Lansdale

"Definitive Therapy"

F. Paul Wilson

ARKHAM ASYLUM

Medical History

NAME: *"The Joker"* DATE OF BIRTH: *Unknown* MR# *20073*

ATTENDING PHYSICIAN: *Dr. R. Hitls & staff*

CHIEF COMPLAINT: *Committed to life internment by court order. Returned to this facility after the most recent of his periodic escapes.*

HISTORY OF CHIEF COMPLAINT: *A career criminal with a long, well-publicized, well-documented history of antisocial and sociopathic behavior in the guise of a self-created public persona known as "The Joker." Convicted of multiple murders. Multiple escapes and readmissions to this facility. See old charts.*

PAST HISTORY: *Little available besides what is in the public record. The patient relates a history of juvenile delinquency, which meets the criteria for Severe Conduct*

Disorder, undifferentiated type (312.90).

ALLERGIES: *None known.*   MEDICATIONS: *On no meds.*

PREVIOUS HOSPITALIZATIONS: *Many to this facility. See previous charts.*

FAMILY HISTORY: *Unknown. Patient uncooperative as historian.*

SOCIAL HISTORY: *No external stigmata of alcoholism or drug abuse.*

SYSTEMIC REVIEW: *According to what little history can be gleaned from the patient, he has been in generally good health for most of his life. He has a past history of facial trauma combined with toxic chemical exposure resulting in permanent disfigurement of the facies, the integument, and its appendages. No history of hearing loss or visual impairment. No thyroid disease or diabetes. No asthma, emphysema, or chronic lung disease. No heart disease or hypertension. No history of ulcer or colitis. No GU infections or past disease. No seizures or strokes. His psychiatric history has been exhaustively explored and documented at this facility. His facial/chemical trauma was once posited as the source of his psychopathy, but the patient relates a long history (undocumented) of criminal antisocial behavior since his early teens, long predating the trauma.*

DICTATED BY: *Harold Lewis, M.D.*   SIGNATURE: *Harold Lewis*

Physical Exam

NAME: *"The Joker" (legal name unknown)*   MR# *20073*

ATTENDING PHYSICIAN: *Dr. R. Hills & staff*

VITAL SIGNS:
  BP: *122/78*   P: *82*   R: *10*   T: *98.6*

PHYSICAL FINDINGS: *A thin, facially disfigured Caucasian male, apparently in his midthirties, alert, well-oriented, in no distress. The head is normocephalic with slight evidence of proptosis. Neuromuscular paresis and cicatricial disfigurement of the facial tissues have resulted in a permanent rictus. Ears, nose, and throat are negative. The neck is supple, the thyroid is negative to palpation. The chest shows a moderate pectus excavatum. The heart is normal in size and rhythm with no murmurs. The lungs are clear to auscultation and percussion. The abdomen is soft, no masses, no organomegaly, no tenderness. Normal uncircumcised male genitalia. The lymph nodes are negative. The limbs are intact and freely movable. The deep tendon reflexes are +2 bilaterally, the pupils are equally reactive to light and accommodation. The skin is markedly pale. Its appendages—the hair and nails—are green. This does not appear to be factitial since there is no sign of natural color under the cuticles or at the roots.*

PROVISIONAL DIAGNOSIS:

1. *Antisocial Personality Disorder (301.70)*

2. *Probable Delusion Disorder, grandiose type (297.10)*

3. *Rule out Bipolar Disorder, manic, mood congruent with psychotic features (296.44)*

4. *Rule out Intermittent Explosive Disorder (312.34)*

DICTATED BY: *Harold Lewis, M.D.*   SIGNATURE: *Harold Lewis*

SESSION ONE

He was painfully thin, and taller than I'd expected.

I remained standing as the guards led the gaunt, manacled figure into the interview cell.

The Joker's appearance is positively shocking at close range. I'd seen his face before. Who hasn't? But to find myself standing across a small table from the man, to have his eyes scan me from a distance of only three feet as if I were some kind of insect, was a jolt. The smile . . . that was what did it. We've all seen that soulless, mirthless grin countless times, shining at us in black and white from the front page of the *Gotham Gazette* or in never-quite-true color from the TV screen during the evening news, but nothing in the media prepares you for the original. The smile . . . the corners of the mouth are drawn up and back, fully halfway into the cheeks. And the teeth—so big and white. Bigger than Morton Downey Jr.'s. But they're not as white as his skin. So pale. Not so much in the bleached, albino sense; more like a white stain. I could not help feeling that with a little cold cream on a cloth I could wipe it off. But I knew that had been tried many times. The seaweed green of his hair and fingernails were the garnish on this bizarre human concoction.

During my five years of psychiatric residency in New York's Downstate Medical Center, and in various maximum security facilities about the country, I have encountered mental illness in its most violent manifestations. But I could not remember actually *feeling* madness as I did in my first seconds in the room with the Joker. Nothing in the media prepared me for the power of the man. In fact, the never-ending stream of stories about him in the press only serves to trivialize him. We've become used to the Joker; we've become almost comfortable with him. We all know that he is a career criminal and a multiple murderer, to boot, yet his face is so familiar that he has become part of the background noise of Gotham. His latest outrage does not stir us to as much anger as it would had it been perpetrated by a stranger. Better the devil you know . . .

My task was to get to know this devil.

With two armed guards watching closely, I thrust my hand across the table.

"I'm Doctor Lewis, Mister Joker. I'll be—"

"Call me 'Joker,'" he said in a surprisingly soft voice as he stared at me, ignoring my hand. The contrast between his grave tone and his grinning face was disconcerting.

"But that's not your real name. I'd prefer to address you by that."

"That name is gone. Call me the Joker if you wish to have any meaningful communication with me."

I was reluctant to do that. The patient's Joker persona

appeared to be the axis upon which his criminal career turned. I did not want to reinforce that persona. Yet I had to communicate with him. I had little choice but to acquiesce.

"Very well, Mister Joker. I—"

"*Just* . . . 'Joker.'"

I thrust out my hand again.

"Joker, I'm Doctor Lewis. I'll be handling your therapy."

He ignored my hand and appeared suddenly agitated.

"When did you arrive? I've never seen you before. Where is Doctor Hills? Why isn't he treating me?"

"Doctor Hills sent me. I'm new to the staff since your last . . . escape."

I could read fury in his eyes, but the grin never wavered.

"I want the head man. I *always* get the head man. I deserve it! I'm not just another petty crook, you know. I'm the Joker. I'm the king of crime in this burg and I want Doctor Hills!"

Grandiosity and entitlement. I considered adding Narcissistic Personality Disorder (301.81) to my list of diagnoses.

I shrugged and tried to be disarming.

"Sorry, Joker. He sent me in his place. Looks like we're stuck with each other."

Suddenly he relaxed.

"Okay."

Emotional lability.

For the third time, I stuck out my hand. This time, to the accompaniment of small clinks from the chains on his manacles, he took it. As we shook, I heard a buzz and felt a sting in my palm. I cried out in surprise and snatched my hand away. The Joker began to laugh.

That laugh. His speaking voice had been so soft, almost soothing. But the laugh—a broken, high-pitched keen that makes the small hairs rise.

The guards leaped forward and thrust him into the chair. He laughed maniacally as they ripped something from one of his fingers. The older of the two guards handed it to me, then they searched him for anything else he might be carrying.

I stared at the object in my hand. A joy buzzer. A simple, corny, old-time practical joke.

"He's clean, Doc," the older guard said as they finished their search.

I stared at the buzzer.

"He was supposed to be 'clean' when you brought him in here."

They said nothing but took up new positions, closer now, flanking him on each side.

I held up the buzzer.

"How did you get this?"

"I had it sent in."

"You can't just have things 'sent in.' Inpatients are severely restricted as to possessions."

"You mean *other* inpatients," he said. "I'm the Joker. What I want, I get. Security here is a joke." His eyes lit. "Get it? A joke!"

The guards looked uncomfortable as he laughed. And they deserved to. He should never have arrived at this interview carrying something like that. What if the prong had been poisoned?

He seemed to read my mind.

"All in good, clean, harmless fun, Doctor Lewis. I'm as harmless as a pussycat."

I gave him a level stare.

"I believe Colin Whittier might take exception to that . . . if he could."

The Joker snorted and waved a hand in dismissal.

"Whittier! A fraud! A charlatan posing as an artist. He left his mark on the art world—like acne. I put a finishing touch to his work—a match. Get it?"

He began to laugh.

"You murdered him!"

"No loss. He deserved to die. A destroyer of true art. The world is far better off without him."

Complete lack of remorse or guilt.

I remembered his latest atrocity so well. I'd joined the staff shortly after the Joker's last escape and it wasn't too long thereafter that he raided an art gallery that was showing the work of an immensely talented young artist named Colin Whittier. The Joker pulled all of Whittier's work from the walls and burned the canvases in the center of the gallery floor. Then he replaced them with a collection of dark abstracts, each signed, *The Joker*.

The next morning, Whittier flew into a justifiable rage. He yanked all the Joker's paintings and ripped them to shreds. An eye for an eye. And that should have been that. But it wasn't. Whittier was found in the gallery two days later, dead. Murdered. But not by any means so simple as a bullet or a knife. No, his mouth and nose had been poured full of thick green paint, asphyxiating him. And then he was nailed to the gallery wall within a large, ornate gilt frame. On the wall next to the corpse was written:

Colin Whittier
RIP
An artist who really
threw himself into his work

The casual brutality of the crime still blew an icy wind through my soul whenever I thought of it. And the perpetrator was sitting not three feet away from me. Grinning.

Grinning . . .

I'd quietly admired Whittier's work for years. His paintings spoke to me. I'd even bid on one or two of his early works a few years ago when they were still within reach, but lost out to deeper pockets. Now they were permanently out of reach. Well, at least there were posters. But when I thought of all the paintings he would never do, I felt a rage seep through to my very soul—

Stop!

This was no good. I was becoming emotional. I couldn't allow that. I had to help this man, and I couldn't do it if I remained angry. I terminated the first session then and there.

SESSION TWO

"He's clean this time, Doc," said the older guard as he sat the Joker in front of me.

"You're sure of that?" I said.

"Yeah. Pretty much."

I did not offer to shake hands with the patient.

"Good morning, Joker," I said, cheerily addressing him by the name he preferred.

The Joker stared at me, his eyes twinkling as I took my place on the far side of the table.

"I've decided to accept you as my physician for this stay, Doctor Lewis."

"Be still, my heart."

"I was getting tired of Doctor Hills, anyway. Such an egotist—an I-sore. Always letting off esteem. Get it?"

"Unfortunately, yes."

"But seriously, folks, if I am to cooperate in therapy, we must have privacy." He glanced at the two guards who flanked him. "I can't have a couple of screws eavesdropping on the intimate details of my life."

He had a point, of course. But I wasn't about to take any chances. I had the guards manacle his wrists and ankles to the arms and legs of his chair, then had them wait outside the closed door.

"Your credentials are impressive," the Joker said when we were alone.

Concern began to nibble at the back of my neck.

"You know nothing of my credentials."

"*Au contraire,* Doctor Lewis. I have a complete dossier on you."

He then proceeded to recite my *curriculum vitae,* ticking off one by one the schools I'd attended, the awards I'd received, my class rank in medical school, my appointment as chief resident on Downstate's psychiatric service, even my starting salary here at Arkham.

"That's an insult," he said, shaking his head in disdain at the last item. "You're worth far more than that."

I knew my jaw was hanging open and slack.

"Where did you—?"

My expression must have been hilarious, for the Joker burst out laughing.

"I told you—I'm the Joker, the Clown Prince of Crime! Nothing goes on in this city without my knowledge."

Persistent grandiose delusions. But how did he . . . ?"

I shook off my shock and forced myself to focus on the matter at hand. Namely, interviewing my patient. He was uncooperative, giving nonsense answers to my questions about his childhood, and purposely bizarre responses to the Rorschach blots I showed him.

I tried probing his past history again.

"Ever been in love, Joker?"

"Always. I'm girl crazy—girls won't go out with me, and it makes me crazy! Get it?"

I pressed on: "Ever been married?"

"Doctor Jekyll, I believe you're getting under my hide."

"Answer the question, please."

"Married? Me? No. I prefer to stay single and un-altared. Get it?"

For the second time, amid wild laughter, I terminated the session early.

CONFERENCE

Later that day I had a clinical conference with Dr. Hills, the chief of psychiatry at Arkham. We discussed my two disturbing encounters with the Joker.

"Be extremely wary, Hal," Dr. Hills told me. "He's a diabolical creature."

I'd never heard Dr. Hills talk like this. It was so unclinical, so . . . unscientific.

"I know he's an incorrigible, but—"

"He's worse than that. He's a master manipulator. He makes it extremely difficult, almost impossible, to stay in command of your therapy session. He turns everything around on you. If you're not careful, he'll reverse the therapy process. Instead of you treating him, he will be influencing you, making you question yourself, your values, everything you believe in. . . ." Dr. Hills's voice trailed off and a far-away look seeped into his eyes. "Everything."

I didn't know about that. What I did know was that he would not be manipulating me—although he had managed to unsettle me. That would not happen again.

"What I would like to know," I said, "is how he manages to have such easy access to outside sources from which he should be completely cut off."

"I know, I know. We don't know how he does it. But don't let that distract you. Stay on course. This is your trial by fire for Arkham Asylum. If you can weather the Joker, you can handle anything."

"You make him sound like the devil himself."

Dr. Hills looked away.

"Sometimes I wonder . . ."

SESSION FIVE

I tried to hide my agitation as the session began, tried to pretend that nothing untoward had happened. The Joker, for his part, was less cooperative than usual. Despite the fact that we were alone, he said not a word. Just sat there staring at me. Grinning.

Finally, I turned off the tape recorder, ready to terminate the session.

Then he spoke.

"Don't you like your new car?"

I bit down on the insides of my cheeks to keep from shouting out my anger. I couldn't let him see how shaken I was, how he'd gotten to me.

It had happened that morning. I'd been running late and so it was especially frustrating when I couldn't find my car in the Gotham Gardens parking lot. At first I'd thought I'd simply forgotten where I'd parked it, for there was a Mercedes in the spot I usually used. Soon it became clear that my car was gone. But who would steal that old junker?

Agitated now, I walked over to my usual spot and checked out the Mercedes. It was new. A brand-new 560 SEL. Royal blue. My favorite color. I thought about how

I was going to own one of those someday and I wondered which tenant in a low-rent apartment complex like Gotham Gardens could afford such a beast.

Then I saw the keys in the door lock.

I peered through the driver's window. There was an envelope on the front seat. With my name on it. I yanked open the car door and tore open the envelope. Inside was the registration card—in my name—and a sheet of purple stationery.

*For the exclusive use
of Dr. Harold Lewis.*

A playing card was attached. A Joker.

"Well?" the Joker said now from the other side of the table. "Aren't you even going to say thank you?"

No. I wasn't going to say thank you.

"How'd it drive?"

I'd been running late already and had no choice but to drive the Mercedes to work. How'd it drive? Like piloting a cloud. But I'd been too angry, too unsettled by this arrogant intrusion into my life to enjoy it.

I steadied myself. Finally, I felt able to speak calmly. "Where is my old car?"

"Gone. Dead. Kaput. Junked. Pounded into a neat little cube of twisted steel and sent back to the melting pot from which it came."

"Listen, pal," I said, "if you think such a blatant attempt at bribery will get you special treatment from me, or turn me into some sort of clandestine ally, you're sadly mistaken. I'm not for sale."

Not ever. I thought. *Especially not to the murderer of Colin Whittier.*

"Of course you're not. Do you really think I'd be so clumsy as to try to bribe you with a car? A *car*? Good gracious me, no. It's just that I simply couldn't bear to know that my personal physician was driving around in public in that 1982 Toyota. A *Celica*, no less! I've got a reputation to uphold. How do you think it looks to my organization when they see their leader's doctor driving a Jap junker? It was an intolerable situation that required an immediate remedy."

"I won't stand for it!"

"I'm afraid you have no choice, Doctor Lewis. The deed is done. Your old car is no more. You might as well use the new one. Why not enjoy it? Your conscience is clear, your ethics are unsullied. I ask nothing in return, only that you drive it. My image, you see."

"Guards," I called. I wasn't about to listen to any more of this.

"Dina will love it, too."

Dina? What did he know about Dina?

Weak and numb, I watched the guards unlock his restraints and lead him out.

SESSION EIGHT

The session was going particularly well. The Joker was opening up about his troubled, turbulent childhood. I still had no insight as yet into the mechanisms of his behavior, but we were just getting started in therapy. The important thing was that I felt that we were beginning to make progress toward a viable physician-patient relationship. Then he started with the crummy one-liners again.

"You know, Doctor Lewis, I was the kind of student who made my teachers stay after school. Get it? I was an honor student—I was saying either 'Yes, your Honor,' or 'No, your Honor.' Get it? When I was a kid I was so tough, I got thrown out of every reform school in the country."

"Can we try to be serious? Just for a moment?"

"Don't worry, Doc. I know you're trying. In fact, you're very trying. Get it?"

That did it. I made a final note prior to ending the session. But when I looked up, I saw that his hands were free. He was holding out a deck of playing cards.

"Pick a card," he said. "Any card."

Terror jolted through me. I shouted for the guards. By the time they reached us, the Joker's hands were back in the manacles. The deck of cards remained between us on the table.

"Never mind," I told the guards. After all, he hadn't tried to harm me. Maybe this was an opportunity to gain his confidence, which might put us on the quickest road to meaningful therapy. "False alarm."

As they returned to their posts outside the door, the Joker looked at me curiously. I picked up the deck and shuffled through it. All Jokers.

"How do you get these things smuggled in?"

"I've told you: I'm the—"

"'Clown Prince of Crime.' I know. A regular modern-day Mabuse."

"Ah. The doctor is a movie buff. Yes, I suppose I could be compared to Doctor Mabuse on a superficial level, but I am his superior in every way. Doctor Mabuse was a piker compared to the Joker."

More grandiosity. It was wearying.

"But you're real," I said. "Mabuse was fiction. He didn't have to worry about running up against Batman."

I knew immediately that I'd struck a nerve. Something changed in the Joker's eyes and demeanor. The airy, bon-vivant pose vanished. I felt a chill worm across my shoulders as cold hatred flashed from his eyes and hung like rank smog in the air between us. And then as suddenly as it had come, it was gone. Blown away by a gust of laughter.

"Batman! Talk about crazies! They put *me* in here while they let *him* run around loose in his cape and tights."

"They could have put you in the electric chair for murdering Colin Whittier," I said softly. I'd almost said *should* instead of *could.* I'd have to be careful.

"But they can't!" he said with another laugh. "Because I've been classified as insane! I'm not responsible. Isn't that wonderful? Oh, it's so good to be mad in America. I can do unto others, but they can't do unto me!"

As he giggled on, I said, "Don't you feel any remorse for the hurt you've caused people? For the artistic riches you've robbed from society by killing Colin Whittier?"

"Society? What has society ever done for me?"

"Well, you might have a point there, but you've caused untold harm in your lifetime—the deaths, the grief, the pain. Don't you feel any impulse to make reparation?"

"Not the slightest. I put the Joker first. If I don't, who will? I. Me. *Moi.* Society, the public good, the little man, they can take my leavings. And I'd prefer you not mention Batman in my presence again."

Remembering how quickly he'd gotten in and out of his manacles a moment ago, I nodded.

"And by the way," he said, "how does the lovely Dina like the new car?"

I was suddenly boiling on the inside, but I remained cool without.

"Just as you do not wish Batman mentioned, I do not wish anyone from my personal life mentioned."

"She's very attractive."

"I hope you're not thinking of threatening her."

"Threaten?" He laughed. "That sort of thing is for gunsels and dime-a-dozen desperadoes. *Fratellezza* swine. I like you, Doctor Lewis. I have no interest in threatening anyone dear to you. Besides, why should I? What can you do for me?

"You might think I can help you escape."

Another laugh. "I can escape any time I wish."

"Really? Then, why are you still imprisoned here?"

"Because for the time being it amuses me," he said without missing a beat. "Just as I can smuggle in anything I wish, I can leave anytime I wish. And when I decide that it's time to take my leave, I shall escape with *elan,* dear doctor. Without your help. No crude, petty jailbreak for the Joker. The Joker will not sneak out, nor will he crawl or tunnel out. He'll either fly or walk—at the time of his own choosing."

"We'll see."

"Yes. We will. And when are you going to ask that woman to marry you?"

"None of your business!"

"Ah! Business! I wish we were in business! Building and loan—I wish you'd get out of the building and leave me alone. Get it?"

"Good day, Joker," I said, rising.
"Good day, Doctor Lewis."

SESSION TEN

I could barely contain my rage. As soon as the guards left, I exploded.

"This time you've gone too far, Joker!"

"Whatever are you talking about, Doctor Lewis?"

"The ring, damn you! The goddamn ring!"

"You mean that little bauble I sent Dina? Think nothing of it."

"It wasn't 'just a bauble,' and you know it!"

When I'd answered my doorbell the night before, I'd been shocked to find Dina standing there with tears in her eyes. She threw her arms around me and told me how beautiful it was, and what a romantic way to propose. And then she showed me the ring—a huge solitaire, flawless, at least three carats. It was perfect, she said, the engagement ring she'd always dreamed of, and to think I'd sent it to her nestled in a bouquet of roses with the note: *Dina—Make my life complete. Marry me. Hal.*

I'd been planning to ask her to marry me as soon as I got on my feet financially, but I'd had nothing to do with this. I knew immediately who was behind it, though. I should have told her right then. But when I saw the look in her eyes, the joy in her face, I couldn't. How could I take that ring off her finger and say it wasn't from me? I wrapped my arms around her and said nothing.

"I won't have you interfering in my life!"

"Who's interfering?" he said through that grin. "I like you. I don't want to see you settle for second best. In a few years you'll be able to afford all these things on your own. But for now, it gives me pleasure to help you out. What's so wrong with that?"

"You're trying to compromise my judgment! And it won't work!"

"Of course it won't. We both know you've got too much

integrity for that. By the way, there's an engagement gift waiting for you in your apartment."

That did it. I stormed out of the examining room.

But deep within my gut was a strange new feeling, a growing awareness that it was my duty to render this . . . this *Joker* incapable of corrupting or harming anyone again.

CONFERENCE

"A pre-frontal lobotomy?" Dr. Hills said. "You must be joking!"

The irony of his choice of words was lost in the shocked silence around me. I'd gone directly from my session with the Joker to the psychiatric conference where I'd blurted out my recommendation. The rest of the psychiatric staff—Drs. Hills, Miller, and Bolland—were there, and I believe I stunned them all.

The solution had occurred to me as I'd entered the room. A pre-frontal lobotomy—surgical invasion of the frontal lobe of the brain. It had been used briefly with great success in the 1930s. Violent, agitated patients had become pussycats—gentle, placid, physically and emotionally in low gear. But the procedure had fallen out of favor because it was deemed too extreme. And because it was irreversible.

"Yes, I'm aware that it's a radical suggestion," I said, "but you've got to admit that this particular case warrants a radical solution. *Demands* it, I should think. Lobotomy is definitive therapy in the case of a patient as incorrigibly violent as the Joker."

Dr. Hills said, "We'll come under heavy fire from the patients' rights groups merely for suggesting it. The ACLU, all the—"

"What about the rights of the people he will harm in the future when he escapes again?" I replied. "And we all know he will escape again. Let's be honest, gentlemen: modern psychiatry has failed society in the case of the Joker. I know. I've gone through his past records. The man seems to escape at will. Then he goes on a rampage of murder and robbery, is caught, is returned to us, only to escape again for another rampage. No matter how we chain him, drug him, psychoanalyze him, he escapes. And he never pays a price for the harm he does! Between rampages, he's given a clean, comfortable cell, three meals a day, and free medical care. For life!"

"But a lobotomy—?" Dr. Hills said.

"We've failed to contain him, we've failed to change him with therapy or control him with drugs, and the courts won't send him to the chair. As physicians charged with treating the so-called criminally insane, I think we have a duty to consider the definitive therapy for his sort of behavior disorder."

There was a long silence. Finally, Dr. Hills said, "I'll take it up with the State Board of Medical Examiners."

I left the conference room in a state of wild exhilaration. I might have been the new man on the staff but I was making my presence felt in no uncertain terms. And beyond that, I knew that my recommendation for lobotomy would prove to the Joker once and for all that Harold Lewis, M.D., was not for sale.

SESSION NINE-A

Numb, speechless, I stared across the table at the Joker. That smile . . . if only he'd stop smiling.

"Well?" he said. "Do you like your engagement gift?"

"Where—?" My mouth was dry. "Where did you get it?"

I'd come home last night to find an original Colin Whittier hanging on my wall. An *original!* An abstract of swirling blues and greens that made me think of the depths of the ocean . . . the eternal cycle of birth, life, and death . . . cold, ghastly, unutterably beautiful.

The cost of a Whittier had gone through the roof since his death at the Joker's hands. Each was worth millions now. I'd never be able to afford a Whittier. Never. And the Joker had given me one.

I owned a Whittier original . . . a Whittier . . .

The monetary value meant nothing to me, for selling

it was out of the question. I'd sell my soul to the devil before I'd part with it.

"I have a bunch of the things," the Joker said. "From his show at the Gotham Gallery."

"But the papers said you burned them!"

"Don't be silly. They're far too valuable for that, although for the life of me I can't imagine why. The man showed not the slightest trace of talent. I burned some old canvases of my own that I was unhappy with."

"Then . . . you still have all those Whittiers?"

"Yes. Stacked up in one of my warehouses. I forget which one, actually. I had one of my men dig that piece out for you."

A stack of them . . . I felt weak.

"Well? Do you like it? You haven't told me."

"I—I can't accept stolen goods," I said, forcing the words past my lips.

"Too bad. I was going to give the rest of them to you as a wedding present." The Joker shrugged. "Very well. I'll have my men remove it and—"

"No!" I said—almost a shout. "I mean, not yet. Let me live with it a while."

The Joker's smile seemed to broaden. "As you wish, Doctor Lewis."

CONFERENCE

Whittiers . . . a stack of Whittiers . . . sitting in a warehouse . . . collecting dust . . . rats nibbling at the canvases . . . clawing at the paint . . .

The image roamed my mind at will as I sat at the conference table and waited for Dr. Hills to arrive. Finally, he burst in.

"They approved it!" he cried. "The State Board of Medical Examiners approved a pre-frontal lobotomy on the Joker! Any other patient and they would have said no, but the Joker—yes! Within weeks Arkham Asylum is going to be in all the medical journals!"

As excited chatter swept the table, I felt my blood run cold. The paintings. The Whittiers. A lobotomized Joker would be so passive and tractable that he'd tell the police the whereabouts of all his stashes of loot. The Whittiers ... *my* Whittiers ... they'd be returned to the gallery ... to be sold for millions apiece.

"When is the surgery scheduled?"

"Tomorrow morning. Doctor Robinson is flying in from Toronto tonight."

"Maybe we should give electroshock a try," I said.

"ECT has failed already. What's the matter, Hal? The lobotomy was your idea. Having a change of heart?"

I hesitated. How could I protest the implementation of my own suggestion?

But that had been before I'd known about the Whittiers.

"Maybe. I think ECT deserves another chance. It could be we're rushing this too much."

"We have to move quickly. It was the Board's opinion that delay will only allow opposition to organize and cause legal obstruction. They feel that if we present the world with a lobotomized Joker as a *fait accompli,* there will be far less protest. And we will have discharged our duty to the public. As you so eloquently stated Hal, we need definitive therapy in the Joker's case. And that's just what we're providing."

What could I say? I decided to risk everything.

"I'd like to go on record right now as being opposed to the surgery. At least at this time. I think we should explore other options first. And I'd like to call for a vote."

They all stared at me in shock. I didn't care. I had to stop the surgery—at least until I got my hands on the Whittiers. They were all I could think of. Even if I could only delay the surgery, it would give me time to convince Dina to move up our marriage so that the Joker could make good on his promised wedding gift. After that, I'd push again for the lobotomy.

But when the vote came, mine was the only hand raised in opposition.

SESSION NINE-B

That night I arranged another session with the Joker. I didn't even bother going through the motions of turning on the tape recorder.

"Did you really mean what you said about giving me the other Whittiers as a wedding gift?"

"Of course," the Joker said. "Have you set a date yet?"

I clasped my hands together to keep them from trembling. I'd always been a terrible liar.

"Yes. Tomorrow. We've decided we can't wait any longer. We're getting married before a justice of the peace in the morning."

"Really? Congratulations! I'm very happy for you."

"Thank you. So . . . I was wondering . . . could you tell me where you've stored those stolen Whittiers? I'll pick them up tonight, if you don't mind."

"No. Of course not. Do you know where Wrightson Street is?"

I could barely contain my excitement.

"No. But I'll find it."

"Here," the Joker said, casually freeing his hands from the restraints and picking up a pencil. "I'll draw you a map."

As he began to draw, I leaned forward. Suddenly his other hand flashed forward. I felt a sting in my neck. As I jerked back I saw the dripping syringe in his hand. I opened my mouth to shout for the guards but the words wouldn't come. A roar like a subway charging into a station filled my ears as everything faded to black.

A voice, faraway, calling me through the blackness. I move toward it, and come into the light.

A bizarre, twisted face, half Joker, half normal, floating before me.

"Time to wake up, Doctor Lewis," it says in the Joker's voice. "Time to rise and shine."

I try to speak. My lips feel strange as they move, and the only sounds I can make are garbled, unintelligible.

I try to move, but my hands and feet are cuffed to the chair. I can only sit and watch.

And as I watch, the Joker stares into a mirror and fits pieces of flesh-colored latex over his chin and left cheek. I only see him in profile, but as each piece is affixed, he looks less and less like the Joker, and more and more like someone else. Someone I know.

"You gave me some very bad moments there, Doctor Lewis," he says. "For a full twenty-four hours you had me believing I'd misjudged you, underestimated you. Self-doubt is most unpleasant, even in a minuscule dose. I don't know how other people put up with a lifetime full of it."

I try again to speak but the result is still gibberish.

"Don't bother," he says. "One of the effects of that injection is a disorganization of the speech centers of the brain. But let me get back to the story of my brief episode of inner turmoil. You see, all through these past few weeks I've been thinking that I had you, really had you. For instance, you kept the Mercedes. I mean, if you'd really wanted to show me up, you could have sold it, bought another old Toyota junker, and given the balance to charity. That would have put me in my place. Same with the engagement ring. Oh, I know I put you in a tough spot then, but if you really had the courage of your convictions, you'd have told the lovely Dina the truth. But you didn't. You were willing to let the very first step of your marriage be a false one. Oh, I was sure I had you."

He pauses as he begins brushing makeup over his latex mask, then continues:

"Then you go storming into the staff conference and drop your bombshell. I was shocked, believe me. A prefrontal lobotomy, Doctor Lewis? How audacious! It would have worked, I'm sure. I was almost proud of you when I heard. None of the other incompetents here had the brains to think of it, or the guts to suggest it. But you charged right in and told it like it was. I like that. Reminds me of me."

I try to speak again, with the same results.

"What's that?" he says. "You're not like me? Oh, but you are. A while back you took me to task for being indifferent to the consequences of my actions, their tragic effects upon the individuals directly involved and upon society at large. And I told you, quite honestly, that I didn't care. You were so self-righteous. And then what did you go and do? When you discovered that I had something you wanted, you tried to turn the staff away from your 'definitive therapy.' Up to that moment, I'd planned simply to disappear and, as usual, leave you all wondering how. But now I see that you weren't concerned with what was best for society; you weren't concerned with the responsibilities of your position here. You were concerned only with what Doctor Harold Lewis wanted. And you weren't even honest with yourself about it."

He lifts the mirror and holds it before his made-up face as he turns toward me. Hidden behind the mirror, he says, "See? Didn't I say you were just like me?"

And in the mirror I see the pale, distorted features of the Joker grinning back at me.

Horror rips through me. I try to scream but it's useless.

"That injection contained a nonlethal variation on my tried-and-true Joker venom," he says, staying behind the mirror. "So, besides scrambling your speech areas, it has also pulled your lips into a handsome smile. I've completed the picture by bleaching your skin and dying your hair and fingernails green."

Then he lowers the mirror.

I gasp as I see my own face on the Joker's body.

"How do I look?" he says.

I struggle frantically with the manacles, trying to pull free, trying to break the arms of the chair so I can get my hands around his throat.

"Guards!" he calls in my voice. The two uniformed men rush in and the Joker says, "The patient has become violent. I think it best to carry him back to his cell as is, chair and all. I'll order a sedative that will hold him until his surgery tomorrow morning."

The lobotomy! Please, God! Not the lobotomy!

As they drag me from the room, I hear his soft voice behind me.

"And I'll be sure to give Dina your best tonight."

On a Beautiful Summer's Day, He Was

Robert R. McCammon

a boy.

Junior was smiling, and the sun was on his face. He was fourteen years old, it was the middle of June and summer looked like a long sweet road that went on and on until it was out of sight, swallowed by the hills of autumn a hundred miles away. Junior walked along the street two blocks from his house, his hands in the pockets of trousers that had patched knees, his fingers clenched on bird bones. The warm breeze stirred through his shock of brown hair, and in that breeze he smelled the roses in Mrs. Broughton's garden. Across the street, Eddie Connors and a couple of his buddies were working on the engine of Eddie's red, fire-breathing Chevy. They were big guys, all of them eighteen years old, already getting beer guts. Junior lay in bed at night and listened to the racket of Eddie's red Chevy roaring up and down the street like a tiger looking for a way out of a cage, and that was when the shouting rose up from the Napier house like the wrath of God and—

Eddie looked up from the work, grease all over the front of his sweat-soaked T-shirt, a smear of grease across his bulbous nose like black war paint. He nudged the guy next to him, Greg Cawthen, and then the third of them, Dennis Hafner, looked across the street and saw Junior, too.

Junior knew what was coming. His feet in their

bright blue Keds stuttered on the broken pavement, where bottle shards caught the summer sun. He was a tall boy for his age, but gaunt. His face was long, his chin pointed. His eyebrows merged over a thin, sharp nose. *Know why your nose is in the middle of your face?* his father had asked him once. *Because it's the scenter. That's a joke, Junior. It's a joke. Get it?*

Smile, Junior!

SMILE, I SAID!

The corners of Junior's mouth upturned. His eyes were dark, and his cheeks strained.

"Hey!" Eddie shouted. His voice came at Junior like a freight train, and Junior stopped walking. Eddie nudged Greg in the ribs, a conspiratorial nudge. "Where ya goin', gooney?"

"Nowhere," Junior answered, standing on shattered glass.

"Yes, you are." Eddie tapped his beefy palm with a socket wrench. "You gotta be goin' somewhere. You're walkin', ain't you?"

Junior shrugged. In his hands he worked the bird bones deep in his pockets. "I'm just walking."

"Gooney's too stupid to know where he's goin'," Dennis Hafner spoke up, from a mouth that looked like a puffy red wound. "Skinny little fruit." His ugly lips spouted a sound of disgust.

"Hey, Gooney!" Greg Cawthen said, his face square and ruddy under a crewcut of red hair. "Your old man home?"

Junior squinted up at the sun. A bird was flying in the sky, alone in all that stark blue expanse.

"We're *talkin'* to ya, numb nuts!" Eddie said. "Greg asked if your old man was home!"

Junior shook his head. His heart was beating very hard, and he wished he had wings.

"Yeah, right!" Dennis nodded, and punched Greg on the shoulder. "They've got Gooney's old man in the crazy house again. Didn't you hear?"

"Is that so?" Eddie stared balefully at Junior. "They got your old man in the crazy house again? They got him locked up so he can't hurt nobody?"

Junior's mouth moved. "No," he answered. He felt cold inside, as if his guts were coated with ice.

"Why'd they let him out, then?" Eddie Connors went on, his eyes narrowed into fleshy slits. "If he's crazy, why'd they let him out?"

"He's not . . ." Junior's voice was weak, and he stopped speaking. He tried again: "My dad's not crazy."

"Sure!" Dennis let out a mean yawp of laughter. "They only put sane people in the crazy house!"

"It wasn't . . . wasn't a crazy house!" Junior said; it came out louder and harder than he'd wanted. "It was a hospital!"

"Oh, yeah! Big difference!" Eddie said, and again his elbow found Greg's ribs. Greg was grinning, his teeth big and white. Junior wondered if Greg Cawthen's bones were as white as his teeth. "So they put him in a *hospital* for crazy people!"

"My dad's not crazy." Junior looked back the two blocks to his house, the one with a big elm tree in the front yard. All the houses in the neighborhood were alike: wooden structures with narrow front porches and small, square lawns, most of the houses in need of painting, the grass dried and burnt, the trees throwing blue shadows that moved with the sun. Clothes hung on backyard lines, garbage cans stood dented and beaten, and here and there stood the hulks of old cars waiting to be hauled off to the junkyard. Junior returned his gaze to Eddie Connors, as his fingers played with the bird bones—the bones of a blue jay, to be precise—in his pockets. "He had a nervous breakdown," Junior said. "That's all."

"That's *all?*" Eddie grunted. "Hell, ain't that *enough?*" He walked out into the street, still popping his palm with the wrench, and he stopped about ten feet from Junior. "You tell your old man it's a free country. You tell him I can drive my car anytime I want, day or night, and if he wants some trouble he ought to call the cops again. You tell him if he wants some trouble, I'll give it to him."

"Nervous breakdown," Dennis said, and he laughed again. "That's just another way of sayin' *crazy,* ain't it?"

"Get outta here!" Eddie told the boy. "Go on, Gooney! Move it!"

"Yeah!" Greg added. And couldn't resist another, sharp shot: "I'll bet your old lady's crazy in the head, too!"

"MOVE IT!" Eddie shouted, king of the block.

Junior began walking again, in the same direction he'd been going, away from the house with the elm tree in its dried-up yard and paint peeling in strips from its front porch. His father's voice came to him, and he remembered his father sitting in front of the TV, scribbling on a yellow pad and saying this: *Know what a nervous breakdown is, Junior? It's what happens when you spend half your time keeping your mind on your work and the other half keeping your work on your mind.*

That's a joke. Get it?

Smile, Junior.

Junior did.

"Skinny little fruit!" Dennis Hafner shouted at Junior's back. And Eddie Connors called out, "It's a free country! You tell him that, you hear me?"

Know what normal is, Junior? It's somebody before a shrink gets hold of him.

Smile, Junior.

He walked on, along the street layered with sunlight and shadows, his fingers grasping the bones in his pockets and his heart dark as a piece of coal.

But he was smiling, on this beautiful summer day.

Junior turned right at the next block. Ahead of him, shimmering in the heat, was the last remaining wooded hillside in this suburb. It was green and thick and held secrets. It was a wonderful place, and it was his destination.

Before he reached the end of the street, where a rugged trail led up the hillside, Junior heard the noise of sneakers on the pavement behind him. Somebody running. His first thought was that Eddie Connors had decided to chase him down, and he spun around to face his attacker and try to bluff his way out of a bloody nose. But it wasn't Eddie Connors, or any of his ilk, at all. It was a gawky, frail-looking boy with curly brown hair and glasses, a dumb grin on his face. The boy wore a T-shirt, short pants that exposed his skinny legs, black socks, and sneakers, and he stopped just shy of running into Junior and said, "Hi, Junior! I saw you from over there!" He pointed at a house further up the block, near the intersection where Junior had turned. The boy aimed his dumb grin on Junior again. "Where you goin'?"

"Somewhere," Junior said, and he kept walking toward the hillside.

"Can I go with you?" Wally Manfred began to lope alongside. He was ten years old, his blue eyes magnified behind his glasses, and he needed braces in the worst way. Junior thought of Wally Manfred as a little dog that liked to chase cars and follow strangers, eager to be petted. "Can I, huh?"

"No."

"Why not? Where you goin'?"

"Just somewhere. Go on home, Wally."

Wally was silent. The noise of his sneakers on the pavement said he was still following. Junior didn't want him to see the secret place. The secret place was his alone. "Go home, Wally," Junior repeated. The beginning of the forest trail was coming up pretty soon.

"Aw, come on!" Wally persisted, and he darted in front of Junior. "Lemme go with you!"

"Ixnay."

"I can if I want to!" Wally said, a note of petulance in his voice.

Junior stopped. This wouldn't do. It wouldn't do at all. "Go *home,* Wally!" he commanded. "I mean it!"

Wally had stopped, too, and he looked as if he might be about to burst into tears. Junior knew Wally lived with his mother, in a house even smaller than his own, and Wally's father had gone out for a pack of cigarettes a year ago and never come home. Or that was the story, at least. Junior had overheard his parents talking about it, when they thought he was asleep. Parents had their secrets, just like kids. "I mean it," Junior said. "I don't want you to go with me."

Wally just stared at him, as the summer sun beat down on both of them.

"Go find somebody else to bother," Junior told him.

Wally took a backward step. His eyes looked wet behind his glasses. "How come you don't like me?" Wally asked, and something in his voice was terrible. "How come nobody likes me?"

Junior strode past him, and began walking alone again.

"I like *you!*" Wally called out. "How come you don't want to be friends?"

Know what a friend is, Junior? It's somebody who has the same enemies as you.

Smile, Junior!

He went on. He started up the path, and about fifty yards into the woods he hunkered down and waited to see if Wally Manfred was following. "I don't care!" he heard Wally shout from the street. "I still like you!"

Junior waited for about ten minutes, there in the underbrush. When he was sure Wally wasn't coming after him, he stood up and continued on his way.

The trail led through the last of the neighborhood's woods. Trash and bottles littered the ground, proof that others had followed this path, but Junior's secret place was up higher on the hillside and about a quarter of a mile away. The trail steepened and became a rough climb, and Junior had to struggle up by grasping onto tree roots that emerged from the dirt. He left the last of the trash and bottles behind, and climbed up through green woods. The secret place was well-hidden, and he'd only found it himself by accident, a couple of years before on one of his long solitary treks.

At last, there it was. A rusted, brown water-tank that rose about sixty feet from the crest of the hill and was all but obscured by trees. A ladder led up, and Junior began to ascend with a quick, easy grace. The ladder took him to the top of the tank, where he stood up and looked to the northeast.

The gray towers of Gotham City loomed before him, and in the valley below were thousands of houses and buildings that radiated out from Gotham City on its maze of streets. There seemed to be nothing green in there, nothing but concrete and brick and stone. Factories stood between him and the central city, and the haze today was a pale, shimmering brown that clung close to the earth. One of those factories was the chemical company where his dad used to be a shift manager, last year, before his nervous breakdown. His dad still worked with the company, but now he was a salesman and he was on the road a lot. The factory was the one with the six tall chimneys, and today white streamers of smoke were rising from them into the brown air.

Junior felt like the king of the world, looking down from this height. But he had the bones in his pockets, and there was work to be done.

He went to the tank's hatch, where there was a flywheel. The flywheel had been tough to crack open. He'd had to bring a can of Rust-Eater—one of his dad's products—and a hammer, and even then it had been a hard task to loosen the wheel.

Junior bent down and began to turn the wheel. It was still a tough job that he had to put his shoulders into. But the hatch was coming open, and in another moment he lifted it and looked down the hole. Another ladder led into the empty tank. Hot, dry air rose into Junior's face. He let most of the heat out, and then he eased down into the hole and began to descend the ladder, eagerness working in his brain like a hot little machine full of oiled gears.

He was happy for a while, industrious amid his toys.

He emerged when the afternoon had cooled. His pockets were empty. He resealed the water tank, went back the way he'd come through the woods, and headed for home.

Eddie Connors and his buddies were no longer in sight, but the red Chevy was still there. Junior stopped at Mrs. Broughton's and leaned over her fence to smell a rose, and his gaze ticked back and forth, looking for Junior or the others. A few beer cans lay on the street near the car. Junior stared at them, and began to shred the petals from a yellow rose. Then he crossed the street to the Chevy, took a handful of dirt and grit from the

Connors' yard, and opened the Chevy's gas portal. In went the dirt, quick as you please. He washed it down with some beer left in a can, and then he closed the gas portal and returned the beer can exactly as it had been.

He went home smiling.

And there he found his mother, on her knees in the front room, scrubbing the threadbare carpet around the easy chair that faced the television set.

"He's coming home!" Mom said, and her eyes were wild in her pallid face. "He called! He'll be home by six o'clock!"

Two hours. Junior knew the routine. There was no time to be lost. He shoved down the terror that threatened to rise up within him, and he caged it. Then he hurried past his mother into his small dark room, and he began to straighten his shelves of books and put them all in alphabetical order. If there was one thing his father demanded, it was order in this chaotic world.

Oh yes: and one other thing, too.

Smile, Junior! Smile, Wifey!

SMILE, I SAID!

When Junior was finished with his books, he worked on his closet. Blue clothes together, white clothes together, garments with red next, then with green. Laces tied in all the shoes. Socks balled up, just so. A place for everything, and everything in its place. "Help me!" his mother called, her voice getting frantic. "Junior, help me mop the kitchen floor! Hurry!"

"Yes, Mother," he said, and he went into the kitchen where his mother was working on the yellow linoleum tiles that would never fully be clean, never, never in a hundred years of scrubbing even with Stain-Away.

At four minutes before six o'clock, they heard his car turn into the driveway. They heard the engine stop, and the driver's door open. They heard him coming, and mom said to her son, "Daddy's home!" She clicked on an awful smile, and went to the front door.

"Darling!" she said, as the tall, slim man in a dark brown suit came into the house, carrying his briefcase of samples. She hugged him, stiffly, and drew away as soon as she could. "How was your trip?"

"It was," Dad answered. "Thank you. This is the only job I know of where you can have breakfast in Lynchton, lunch in Harrisburg, and indigestion in Fremont." His eyes, darker than his son's, searched their faces. "That's a joke," he said. "How about a couple of smiles?"

Mom gave a bright, forced laugh. Junior stared at the floor, and smiled with aching jaws.

"Come give me a hug," Dad said. "Know what a hug is? The freedom of the press."

Junior walked to his father, and hugged him with labored arms.

"Good boy," Dad said. "Know what a boy is? An appetite with a skin pulled over it. What's for dinner, Wifey?"

"I was going to put some turkey dinners into the oven."

"Turkey dinners." Dad nodded. "Okay, that's all right. It's a good night for the funnies. Turkey: that's a bird who'd strut a lot less if he could see into the future." Their smiles weren't quick enough. Dad slammed his briefcase down into his easy chair, and the noise made both mother and son jump. "Damn it, where's the happiness around here? This isn't a funeral home, is it? I've seen bigger smiles on dead people! That's no wonder, since the dead don't have to pay taxes! What's wrong with you two? Aren't you *happy?*"

"We're happy!" Mom said quickly. "We're real happy! Aren't we, Junior?"

Junior looked into his father's face. It was a tight face, with hard, sharp cheekbones. His father's eyes were dark and deep-set, and down in that darkness there was a rage coiled up and waiting. It flew out without warning, but most of the time it lay inside Dad's head and simmered in its stew of perpetual jokes and gritted-teeth smiles. Where that rage had been born, and why, Junior did not know, and he figured his father didn't know either. But jokes were its armor and weapons, and Dad wore them like metal spikes.

"Yes, sir," Junior answered. "I'm happy."

"Remember what I told you." Dad placed a finger against his son's chest. "People like to smile. If you can make people smile, you'll be a success. People like to hear a joke or two. They like to laugh. Know what a laugh is? It's a smile that's exploded." The finger moved to one corner of Junior's mouth and hitched it up. Then to the other. "There," Dad said. "That's what I like to see."

Mom turned away and walked into the kitchen to put three turkey TV dinners in the oven. Then Dad began his weekly inspection of the house—a wandering from room to room as he spouted off jokes and comments he considered funny, punctuated by the opening of drawers and cabinets. The rest of the evening would be spent with John in front of the TV set, watching the sitcoms and scribbling down on his yellow pad jokes and rep-artee that particularly caught his interest. *Grist for the grin mill,* he called it.

That's a joke, Junior.

Smile.

Sometimes between the third and fourth comedy show of the night, Junior opened a door and went down the stairs to the dirt-floored basement. He switched on the light bulb, picked up a flashlight, which was always in its proper place, and went to the far corner at the rear of the basement. He lifted a cardboard box and watched roaches scurry in the flashlight's beam.

The ants were swarming. They'd done a good job. The chipmunk was almost down to the bones, and most of the kitten's bones were showing now, too. It wouldn't be too much longer. But Junior was impatient for his toys. The basement was very damp, the walls mildewed. He won-dered if he'd have skeletons faster if he put the dead things in a dryer place. He lifted a second box, looking at his newest acquisitions. He'd found the dead bat in the abandoned house near the church three blocks away, and the robin had been snatched from a cat's jaws just yesterday. They weren't going to smell very good soon. The smell would rise into the house, as the beautiful summer days got hotter. Junior had been wanting to kill a full-grown dog or cat and watch its skeleton come out, but that smell would get up into the house for sure and his mother might come down here and find everything.

His father he didn't worry much about; nothing pulled his father away from the comedies and the yellow joke pad.

But if he was going to start finding bigger playthings, maybe he needed somewhere else to keep them.

At nine-forty, Junior was sitting in the living room watching his father snore in his easy chair. His mother was on the telephone in the kitchen, talking to her friend Linda Shapona, who lived a few streets over. They'd gone to high school together, and Linda owned the beauty shop on Kerredge Avenue. Mom was usually on the telephone most of the evening; it was her only route of escape. The television was on, the last of the night's comedies. The yellow pad had slipped to the floor, and Junior picked it up to see what his father had written there.

It was hard to read the writing. The pen had attacked the paper. Junior could only make out a few of the mass of scribbled jokes and puns, the writing running together and overlapping like a nest of thorns.

Boss. A big noise in the office but at home a little squeak.

What's a diplomat's favorite color? Plaid.

Heaven's where God pays all the bills.

A father always no's best.

Middle age is the time in life when a girl you smile at thinks you know her.

"It's late."

Junior looked up. His father's eyes were swollen, and he was peering at his wristwatch under the dim lamplight. "Gosh. I went to sleep, didn't I?"

"Yes, sir." Junior put the yellow pad down beside his father's chair. His father stretched, and his joints popped.

"I get tired early, I guess. I didn't even know my eyes closed."

"Yes, sir," Junior said.

Dad picked up the yellow pad and examined it. The way the light caught his face made him look very old, and the sight made Junior think of the collection of skulls at the Gotham Museum, one of his favorite places to spend a Saturday. "People like to smile," Dad said, in a quiet voice. "They like a man who tells jokes. A happy man." Junior suddenly tensed, because he heard the sound of a car's engine racketing. Dad stared at the front door, as if he expected Eddie Connors's red Chevy to come roaring up the porch steps and into the house. Eddie revved the engine a few times, getting ready to lay rubber on the street right in front of the house—and then the car began to pop and sputter, and after a few seconds of that the engine died.

"Thank God," Dad said, and let out the breath he'd been holding. "I can't stand that noise. It makes my head hurt."

Junior nodded. Eddie Connors wasn't going to be tearing the street up tonight.

Dad was looking at his son. They stared at each other, their faces similar constructions of flesh and bone. The people in the situation comedy prattled on, and the canned laughter filled the room. "You're my boy, aren't you?" Dad asked.

"Yes, sir."

"My boy," Dad repeated. "And you're not going to be one of those people who think the world owes him a giving, are you?"

"No, sir."

"That's a joke. Smile."

Junior did, on command.

His father leaned toward him. Closer. And closer still. Junior could see pinpricks of sweat glistening on his father's cheeks and forehead. His father's skin had a sour smell, and the man's eyes were like black glass. "Junior?" his father whispered. "I want to tell you a secret. Know what a secret is? It's anything a woman doesn't know. But I want to tell you, because you're my boy." His father's face floated before him in the dim light, half of it in shadow like a waning moon. "I'm afraid," Dad whispered. He swallowed thickly, as the canned laughter swelled. "I'm afraid I'm getting sick again."

Junior didn't speak. A small vein was beating very hard at his right temple, and his lips were bloodless.

"Sometimes," Dad said, "I feel like the world is spinning so fast it's about to throw me off. Sometimes I feel like the sky is so heavy it's crushing me down, and I can't get a breath. They gave me a second chance, at the company. They said I was good with people, and I could make people smile so I ought to be able to sell things." A grin flickered across his mouth like quicksilver, but his eyes remained black. "A salesman. That's somebody with two feet on the ground who takes orders from a person with two feet on a desk."

Junior did not smile.

"I feel like . . . the wind's about to take me away, Junior. I feel like I can't get steady. I don't know why. It's just . . . I can't stay happy."

Junior didn't move. He could hear his mother, talking on the telephone. He thought of the toys in the basement, slowly being whittled down to the bones by ants and roaches, a little more hour after hour.

"I can't go back to that hospital," his father whispered, right in his face. "I couldn't stand that place. They don't know how to smile there. That's what Hell would be for me, Junior. A place where people wouldn't smile. If I had to go back there . . . I don't know what I might do."

"Dad?" Junior's voice cracked. "I . . . wish you wouldn't . . . talk like this."

"What's wrong with wanting to be happy?" his father asked. The whisper was gone. "Is it a sin to be happy? Is it a damned sin?" His father was getting louder, and he drew his face back from Junior's. "You know, that's what's wrong with this world! They take everything away from you, and then they try to cut the smile off your face! Well, I won't let them! I'll see them in Hell before they break me down! They broke down my old man, and he was crying with that bottle in his hand and I said I'll make you smile again, I will, I'll make you smile, I'll do anything to make you smile, but the world broke him down! Because a man who smiles is a dangerous man! They want to cut the smile off your face, and make you weak! But I won't have it. I swear to God I won't have it! And you're part of me, Junior, you're my boy, you're my flesh and bone!" One of Dad's sinewy hands grasped his son's shoulder. "The world's not going to break us down, is it?"

"No, sir," Junior said, lifelessly, but in his chest his heart was pounding.

"Junior?" It was his mother. She was standing in the doorway between the front room and the kitchen, and her hands had seized the wall like white spiders. Her eyes tracked back and forth from the boy to his father, and over the noise of the television laughter Junior could hear his father's harsh, slow breathing. "Why don't you get ready for bed? All right?"

A silence stretched. And then Dad said, "Mom's the word," and released his son. As Junior walked toward the hallway that led to his room, his father said, "Know what a mother is, Junior? It's a woman who spends twenty years making a boy into a man so another woman can make a fool of him in twenty minutes." Junior kept going, his insides quaking. He had taken three more steps when his father said, easily, "Lock your door tonight."

Junior stopped. Terror had crippled him. Those words were not said very often, but Junior understood them. He looked at his mother, who seemed to have diminished in size, her skin turned a sickly gray.

"Lock your door," Dad repeated. He was staring at the television screen. "Say your prayers, will you?"

"Yes, sir," the boy answered, and he went to his room and locked the door. Then he lay in bed and stared at the ceiling, where cracks riddled the plaster.

In the morning, he could pretend he had had a particularly terrible nightmare. He could pretend he had not heard, as the clock's hands crept past midnight, the muffled noise of his father's voice beyond the wall, speaking stridently—commanding—and his mother's weak begging. He could pretend he had not heard his father shouting for her to laugh, to laugh, to fill the house with laughter. To laugh and laugh until she screamed. And there was the slapping noise of the belt and a lamp going over and the bed creaking savagely and his mother's sobbing in the silence that followed afterward.

Smile, Junior.
SMILE, I SAID!

His teeth gritted in a rictus, he lay with night pressing in on the house and darkness coiled within.

When he got out of bed, the sun was shining again. His father was gone, and so was the briefcase and the yellow pad. His mother made him breakfast. She had a split lip, but most of her bruises never showed. She smiled and laughed, a brittle sound, as she moved around the kitchen, and when she asked Junior what he was going to do today he said he had plans.

He left home early, bound for the secret place. He passed Eddie Connors's red Chevy, a deballed stallion at the curb. It would take more than a wrench to get the fuel line unclogged. He continued along the street where sunlight and shadows intermingled, and he went his way alone.

Atop the water tower on the high hill, Junior stood staring toward the spires of Gotham City. The chimneys of the factories were pumping out smoke, the arteries were clogged with traffic, and life went on whether your old man was crazy or not.

Junior opened the tower's hatch, and that was when he heard the voice.

"Hey, Junior! Hey, I'm down here!"

He walked to the edge, looked down at the green earth, and there stood Wally Manfred in his T-shirt and shorts, this time wearing purple socks with his sneakers. Wally was grinning, and the sun sparked off his glasses. Wally waved up at him. "I see you!"

Junior felt his eyes narrow. Felt his face tighten, around the bones of his father. Felt rage open inside him like the unfolding of a dark flower, and black seeds spewed forth.

"I followed you!" Wally said. "Fooled you, huh?"

Junior trembled. It was a quick trembling, over and done with, but it was like an inner earthquake and left cracks in his foundation.

The secret place had been found. His haven of solitude was no longer his. And what did he own on this earth, except the toys that were stored within?

"What're you doin' up there?" Wally called.

Junior made his face relax. He made a smile rise up, through the hot flesh. He opened his mouth, and he said, "Climb up."

"Is this where you go all the time? It sure is high!"

"Climb up," Junior repeated. "The ladder's strong."

"I don't know." Wally kicked at a stone with the toe of his sneaker. "I might fall."

"I won't let you fall," Junior said. "Honest."

"Maybe I can come up halfway," Wally said, and he started up the ladder.

What he was going to do about this, Junior didn't know. Sooner or later, Wally would tell somebody else about the secret place. Wally might even come up here alone, open the hatch, and see what was inside. Wally might go tell his mother, and then his mother might tell Junior's mother, and then . . .

They might get the wrong idea. They might think he was like his father. They might want him to go to that hospital where his father had gone, and where his father would be returning to soon. They might think something was wrong with him, and that something had been wrong with him for a long time but he'd been very good at hiding it.

"I'm halfway up!" Wally called out. He sounded scared. "I'd better stop!"

Junior was staring toward Gotham City, a garden of stones. "Come on the rest of the way," he said quietly. "I've . . . got a joke to tell you."

"I'd better get down!"

"It's a good joke. Come on up, Wally. Come on up."

Silence. Junior waited. And then he heard the noise of Wally climbing the rest of the way up, and Junior said, "That's a good boy. Know what a boy is? An appetite with a skin pulled over it."

Wally reached the top of the tank. There was sweat on his face, and his glasses had slid down to the end of his nose. He was shaking as he got off the ladder and stood up.

"There's a good view of Gotham City from here. See?" Junior pointed.

Wally turned to look at the city. "Wow," he said, his back to Junior.

One push.

Sixty feet down.

Drag Wally into the bushes. Hide him. Who was Wally, anyway? He was a little nothing, and he should never have sneaked up here to the secret place. One push, and the secret would be a secret again. But Junior didn't move, and then Wally turned around again and saw the open hatch. "What's in there?" he asked.

And it all came clear to Junior, what should be done, like a burst of brilliant light in his brain.

"Want to see?" Junior asked, smiling. He was cold, even standing in the sunshine, and he trembled though he could feel sweat on his back.

Wally walked carefully to the hatch and looked in, but it was dark in there and he could see nothing. "I don't know."

"I'll go down first. I've got a light in there. Want to see?"

Wally shrugged. "I guess."

"Just come down the ladder slow and easy," Junior told him. "Wally? You like me, don't you?"

"Yeah." Wally nodded, but he was looking at the open hatch.

"Follow me down," Junior said, and he slid into the hatch and descended the ladder.

In another moment, Wally Manfred followed. Junior reached the bottom and picked up a flashlight he'd brought from home. He didn't switch it on yet, and Wally said nervously, "Where's the light?"

"I've got it. Just come on down."

"It smells bad in here. It's hot, too."

"No, it's not," Junior said. "It's just right."

Wally reached the tank's floor. His hands found Junior's arm. "I can't see anything."

"Here's a light," Junior said, and he switched it on. A heat was building in his skull, and his temples were pounding. "See my toys?" he asked, as he swung the light slowly back and forth. "I made them, all by myself."

Wally was silent.

Wires dangled from pipes overhead, and from those wires hung the bones.

There were over a hundred. Constructions of wire and
small skeletons—birds, kittens, puppies, chipmunks,
squirrels, lizards, mice, snakes and rats. Junior had not
killed all of them himself; most of the carcasses he'd
found, on his long solitary treks. He'd only killed maybe
forty of them, the kittens, puppies, and some birds with
broken wings. But the skeletons had been reformed,
with wire and patience, into bizarre new shapes that did
not resemble anything that had ever lived. There were
birds with the skulls of kittens, and kittens with wings.
There were comminglings of rats and puppies, squirrels
with beaks, and other things with eight legs and three
heads and ribcages melded together like strange Siamese twins. There were things freakish and hellish, constructed from Junior's imagination. And here, on these
wires, was the result of the only thing that excited
Junior and made him truly smile: Death.

"I . . . think . . . I'd better go home," Wally said, and
he sounded choked.

Junior's hand closed on the boy's wrist, and held him.
"I wanted you to see my toys, Wally. Aren't they pretty?"
He kept moving the light, going to one grotesquerie
after another. "It takes hard work to do this. It takes a
careful hand. Do you see?"

"I've gotta get home, Junior! Okay?"

"I do good work," Junior said. "I make things that not
even God can do."

"Junior, you're hurtin' my arm!"

"You like me, don't you?" Junior asked, as he moved
the light from monster to monster.

"Yeah! I like you! Lemme go, okay?"

Junior swallowed thickly. His face was damp with
sweat, his heart racing. "Nobody who likes me," he said,
"is worth anything."

He let Wally go, and he picked up the hammer that
lay near the bottom of the ladder, next to the coil of wire,
the wire-cutters and glue and the can of Rust-Eater.
Wally was pulling himself up on the first rung of the
ladder, but Junior grinned and swung the hammer and
as the hammer crunched into the back of Wally Manfred's skull, Junior was filled with a blaze of joy.

Wally gave a little cry, and he fell backward off the ladder. In the wind of his passage, the freakish skeletons danced. Wally tried to get up to his knees on the floor, and Junior watched him struggle for a moment. The red was coming out of Wally's head.

Junior thought of his father, scribbling fevered jokes on the yellow pad. He thought of his mother, and how she sobbed through the wall on the nights when Junior locked his door.

Smile, Junior.

SMILE, I SAID!

Wally was mewing, like a wounded kitten.

"Know what a laugh is?" Junior asked.

Wally didn't answer.

"It's a smile," Junior said, "that explodes."

He hit Wally with the hammer again, in the back of the head. Again. And again. Wally was on his stomach and he was making no noise. Junior lifted the clotted hammer to strike Wally Manfred once more, but he stopped himself.

There was no use breaking the skull anymore.

Junior sat down beside the corpse, making sure not to get any blood on his clothes. He listened to the rustling of his toys overhead. The secret place was a secret again, and all was right with the world.

After a while, he prodded dead Wally with the hammer. Poked him all over, seeing how much meat there was on the bones. Wally was a skinny kid. It wouldn't be long. Wally had never known he was a walking Erector Set, with so many different neat parts.

Junior switched off the flashlight and he smiled in the darkness.

He was a happy boy.

He left the hammer in its proper place. Atop the tank, he sealed the hatch good and tight. Maybe he'd come back in a month and see how things were going. It would be like opening a Christmas present, wouldn't it?

Junior stood up and stared toward Gotham City with dark, hollowed-out eyes.

The chemical factory's chimneys were spouting a mixture of white, reddish-brown, and pale green smoke. The haze filmed the sky between him and Gotham's towers, and it shimmered like a mystery on this beautiful summer's day.

Junior descended the ladder to the earth and started walking home through the woods. The replay of a hammer striking flesh reeled itself over and over in his brain, and it got better every time.

On the way home, he came up with a joke of his own that he'd have to tell his father: *Why is a dead person like an old house?*

Because they're both morgue-aged.

Smile, Dad.

The Man Who Laughs

Stuart M. Kaminsky

Delicious. There they stood watching my raised right hand, their faces frozen in that wonderfully comic rictus grin of fear and horror. It was a moment to be savored, remembered. If Gideon had been there, I could have had him take a photograph to carry in my pocket, but Gideon was dead. Ah, ah, I'm getting ahead of my story. In my desire to get to my moment of triumph when all attention was focused on my performance, I neglected to tell you how this magic moment came to be.

Gideon, as we drove into Florida down Highway 41, suggested that we should never have left Gotham. The F.B.I., the Georgia and South Carolina State Police were somewhere behind us. The pitiful pack of clowns who considered themselves the Joker's gang was dispersed or dead. But it had been great fun. A vacation. A series of banks visited and withdrawn from to finance my triumphant return to Gotham.

Disaster. Disaster? I had surrounded myself with incompetents with no sense of humor. One must have a sense of humor, I reminded Gideon as he drove. I sat deep in the night shadows in the backseat of the recently stolen automobile. My face is a bit distinctive and has been known, for what reason I cannot imagine, to frighten rather than amuse small children. Gideon could do one thing well. He could steal automobiles. He couldn't drive them, but he could steal them.

We moved cautiously down the highway through the heart of Tampa and then St. Petersburg. The night-caws of pelicans sounded like fingernails against pitted glass. I closed my eyes and enjoyed the moment, forgetting the blue and mufti figures behind us.

"They'll spot us," Gideon mumbled as we crossed over a long arching bridge. "They'll spot you." Gideon wore a wide-brimmed hat of some distinction. He pulled it down further over his eyes.

I tried to ignore him. I sang dirges.

"Did you know, Gideon," I informed him, "that the nursery rhyme, 'Ring Around the Rosey,' dates back to the plague years? The children danced around bodies and when they sang 'Ashes, ashes, all fall down,' they were referring to the death and burning of the victims. That has always been my favorite nursery rhyme."

Gideon grunted unappreciatively. I admit I need an audience. What great performer does not. But this uncultured twig barely qualified.

"Pull over," I said.

"Why?" asked Gideon.

"Because the Joker says," I replied leaning out of the shadows, putting my face next to his. I could feel him hold back the urge to recoil. "We are going to play Joker Says. Joker says pull over."

Gideon found a place on the side of the road beyond the bridge. Traffic was light. It was well past midnight. He parked about twenty yards away from the highway, but kept the motor running.

"Joker says, turn the engine off."

Gideon turned the engine off.

"Joker says, get out of the car, but leave the key."

Gideon might have let out a sigh. I felt it deep within him as I touched his shoulder, but he contained it and got out. I followed him closing the backdoor as I got out. The car had been air-conditioned. The night was hot and moist.

"Joker," Gideon said, full of false bravado, "what's this? You need a toilet?"

"Sadly," I said, "we are no longer friends. Remember that wonderous moment in *Whatever Happened to Baby*

Jane? Blanche lies dying on the beach and Jane, beautifully made up, says, 'You mean that all this time we could have been friends?'"

"Joker, come on," Gideon said backing away. We were on a bay, the vastness of dark water catching glints of the half moon beyond the railing toward which Gideon was moving. "You can't get anywhere without me. You'll be spotted the minute the sun comes up."

"Joker says, let me worry about that," I said. "It will be more fun solving that problem than enduring another minute with the humorless creature you have probably always been."

A car breezed past behind me and in its headlights I could see the frightened eyes of Gideon. His hands were against the rail almost as knuckle-white as my face.

"Okay," he said, his voice quivering. "That's the way you want it. No hard feelings. I'll just stay here, walk to town." He looked around to see which way a town might be. Little lights danced across a curve in the bay.

"Joker says," I whispered, moving close to him, "it doesn't work like that. You know too much."

"Know too much," Gideon bleated like a lamb sensing slaughter. "I don't know anything."

"True." I sighed, grinning into his face, hoping the light of the moon from the water cast an appropriate macabre shadow, "but it seemed like the right thing to say. It suggests motive, albeit sinister, for what is about to transpire."

Gideon tried to duck under my arm, but I grabbed him. He lost his wide-brimmed hat. He punched at my face but I did not evade him. I took the punch and laughed. I let him punch me again and laughed even louder.

"Joker says, take a moonlight dip." And with that I threw the gurgling Gideon over the railing. I heard the splash, heard him come up gasping. I leaned over and covered my mouth to keep from laughing.

"Can't . . . swim," he gasped.

"Can't . . . swim," I mimicked. "But you must. Swim," I commanded.

"Can't . . . please," he gasped and thrashed.

"Swim, Gideon," I ordered, but all I got back was a burble. "Oh," I said with small laugh, "I forgot to say 'Joker says.'"

I found Gideon's hat. It fit surprisingly well. I got back into the stolen vehicle, turned on the air conditioner and proceeded on my pilgrimage heading south, knowing that I was running out of gas, knowing they were behind me, knowing the dawn was coming. Only the Joker could truly appreciate the aesthetic joy of this instant.

I drove listening to a predawn preacher on the radio foretelling the end of the world, the decline of morality. I prayed to my own demons that he was right and I encouraged him with amens. Dull road, hat pulled down, gas gauge dancing the *Danse Macabre,* I encouraged the preacher and pulled off the highway at a sign which told me that here I would find both Bradenton and coastal beaches.

I did not get as far as Bradenton and I never reached a coastal beach. As the car sputtered along the two-lane road, I found a turnoff in the headlight beam, a narrow stone-covered road along a thick growth of trees. As the last sputum of gas died, I turned the car toward a break in the trees and found myself going down the embankment of a creek. A pair of startled masked raccoons caught in the beams scuttered away from the lurching metal beast. When the car stopped, I turned off the lights and leaned back with a massive sigh.

"What a day," I uttered aloud.

The air-conditioning had, with the engine, failed, and the night heat oozed through the pores of the car like boneless fingers of the dead, but I was comfortable, the result of a day well spent. I slept.

The sleep was brief. The Joker requires little sleep, for he needs no dreams. My life is an elegant nightmare. Dreams are for those whose lives are dull. When my eyes opened, they opened on a wondrous sight. On the opposite shore of the small creek, up the slight embankment, stood a Ferris wheel. I reached into the backseat for my purple carpetbag, pulled Gideon's hat over my eyes at a jaunty angle, and stepped out into the ankle-deep water of the creek.

"Life," I announced to the hiding wildlife, "is a brief adventure."

I climbed the embankment, turned, and looked down at the car. Unless someone came across a thick patch of weeds, inched through tightly packed trees, and walked to the very lip of the creek, they would not see the car. I could have covered it, but that would not have been sporting, and I was impatient to see what the Ferris wheel promised.

When I crossed the weeded field, I found that the wheel promised much. I was at the edge of a small, traveling circus. I knew they still existed, had read about them; usually they had a dozen or so people from some South American country who doubled at everything, changed their names for each act. The tiger tamer doubled as bareback rider and catcher in the trapeze act. Back in Gotham, I had a wondrous collection of clippings about circus disasters. Nothing compares with a good cat-mauling in front of a full tent.

I quickened my step and found the peanut-torn ticket-and-cigarette-butt-strewn entrance to the traveling circus. It was even smaller than I had thought—three trucks and two trailers. The Ferris wheel was the only ride. There was a single cage and inside the cage slept a tiger.

The only person awake besides the Joker was a lean man in gray work clothes who worked on the mechanism of the Ferris wheel with a massive wrench. I moved toward him. He was, perhaps, forty years old, though the world had worn him badly. He was a walking set of contradictions. One could see the unsettled morning eyes, the thin body of the recently reformed alcoholic. But he also had the wry, long muscles of a laborer, not uncommon in a carnival or circus. He wore a gray baseball cap with faded lettering, and his face was stubble covered.

As I approached, he looked at me with eyes the color of his cap and clothes. I lifted the hat from my face and watched him. No reaction. None. Not even a blink. Was he blind? Nearsighted? Acting?

"What can I do for you?" he said.

"Surprised?" I asked moving closer.

He didn't even grip his wrench more tightly.

"Take more than you to surprise me," he said, removing his cap to show short gray hair. He wiped his forehead with his sleeve. "Had a lifetime of surprises. Seen every kind of person and creature there is, from three-headed cows to men who look like pigs."

"I'm a clown," I said.

"Yes," he agreed.

"I need work," I said.

"Not much work here," he said.

"I'll work for almost nothing," I said. "Life has been hard for me recently."

"Been hard for me all my days," he said. "But you're talking to the wrong man. You want McCoy. This is his show. You'll find him in the first caravan." He pointed to the proper van and he went back to work, ignoring me. I am not accustomed to being ignored. This had started as a good morning but the gray man had put me in an ill humor.

The van, with a neat row of beer bottles on the step, was marked: ORSINI CIRCUS, HOWARD McCOY, Prop. The lettering was fresh though the paint cheap and already showing signs of the moist weather. I removed my hat and knocked. Something grunted inside. I knocked again more loudly and grinned at the rising sun. The door opened and a small, red fat face with no hair beneath the nose or on the head emerged. He looked like the old carnival bumpkins who stuck their heads through tent holes so other bumpkins could try to hit them with baseballs. I considered the comic image of this head upon the impact of a steel baseball and I felt better.

"No clowns," he said. "I'm the only clown."

"You are McCoy?"

"The real McCoy," he said wearily.

"I work for meals and I eat little," I said.

This interested McCoy who opened the metal door with a creak and examined me with one hand held up to shield him from the sun. He wore a wine-red and food-stained woolen robe. His feet were bare with little tufts of red growing on the knuckles of his toes.

"You don't look funny," he said.

"That is my beauty," I said putting down my purple bag. "I fascinate children. They don't know whether to like me or to be afraid. This has been true of clowns since they were first conceived. There is a cadaverous aspect to the best of us, a challenge. We are forbidden and each laugh is a laugh of guilt."

"I wouldn't know about that," he said, scratching his plum belly. "You funny?"

"People have been known to die laughing from my jokes," I said.

"I don't know," McCoy said. "You look . . ."

"I am Gwynplaine," I said. "I can see you are a man of letters."

"I don't know," said McCoy again.

"You are familiar with Victor Hugo's classic tale of the man who laughs," I said. Something stirred behind him inside the van and another head emerged, the head of a beautiful, dark-haired girl of about twenty, who wiped sleep from her large eyes and looked at me with what I like to assume was admiration.

"I know it," said the girl.

"My daughter, Diedre," McCoy said. "Her mother's been dead some . . ."

"The man who laughs," said the girl. "They took this little boy and cut him so he grinned all his life, even when he was sad, and they showed him off like a freak."

"I know him well," I said. "I am him and he is me."

"Give him a job, Pa," she said, tugging at McCoy's sleeve.

"We can't afford . . ." McCoy began.

"I work for meals, the satisfaction of making children weep with laughter, and the occasional smile of a pretty girl," I said, looking up at Diedre's wide black eyes.

Ah, thought I, what magnificent evil could I play with this girl. Be still my bleeding heart.

"No pay?" McCoy asked cautiously.

"Not a *sou*," I said. "I have my own limited means and resources and my wants are few." I want, I thought, the world within my closing white-gloved fist.

"Bunk up with Hector," said McCoy. "He runs the wheel, rousts the show, rigs, drives. You'll have to do a

little of that. And you don't have to wear makeup during
the day."

"I must," I said sadly, picking up my purple bag. "I
have a skin condition that is not pleasing to the eye."

"Suit yourself," said McCoy. "Just so it doesn't stop
you working."

The girl smiled and the door closed.

Life, with one notable exception, went swimmingly for
two weeks and a day. The tent was a leaking sieve in the
Florida summer. The rotting wooden bleachers were seldom full. The circus consisted of an overworked family of
Brazilians who were all the acts, the award-winning
Flying O'Haras, the internationally known Malanati
Brothers, and Samson Grieff and his killer tiger. The
tiger was lazy and the Brazilians stupid. I tried to prod
the tiger at night into a frenzy in the hope that he would
develop a taste for humans and rid the earth of a Bra-
zilian in front of the rain-drenched evening crowd.

McCoy was a pitiful clown, a grouch, a grumbler who
went through his act with Diedre in a cloud of discon-
tent. Diedre was quite lovely, especially as a clown, and
I was careful to keep her from seeing my interaction
with the children. I snuck up on the little rats, frightening them, letting blood capsules ooze down my chin
when I caught a few of them alone after the show. And I
was a hit. I knew I would be. The kids told other kids
about the frightening clown. The crowds grew, the parents complained, but the children sought me out.

"You love children, don't you," Diedre said one night,
while she took off her makeup.

"I do," I acknowledged, wondering what one of the
scruffy little things would taste like.

She looked at me in the cracked mirror of the caravan
and smiled.

I have only one wonderfully communicative expression. I beamed it at her and imagined her falling from
the top car of the Ferris wheel when it was at its peak,
whirling around at a breakneck pace, perhaps the pair of
silent raccoons from the creek bank, masked observers
applauding my creative moment.

"You look at me strangely," she said.

"A line worthy of the poor girl in *Phantom of the Opera* or *Beauty and the Beast*," I said, leaning against the wall, holding my purple bag to my chest.

"You're funny," she said. "What do you keep in that bag? It's none of my business really, but you keep rinsing the same clothes and . . ."

I put my finger to my lips and said softly, "Secret things live in this bag. It crawls with clacking minute monsters that slither. Listen."

I held the bag to her ear. She hesitated and then put her delicate head next to the canvas, listening as if to the sea in a slime-covered shell.

"Hear it," I said.

The urge at that moment was irresistible. As her head rested, listening, I began to open the bag. I had a surprise for her indeed.

Remember, I said there was an exception to my happiness with the Orsini Traveling Circus. It was at the moment I began to reach a gloved hand into my bag, as I smelled the greasepaint still on Diedre's cheeks, that the exception came through the door. Hector knocked and entered without waiting for an invitation. He looked at me with suspicion. It was the only look he had for me. We had exchanged little about each other. I told him great lies of tragedy and he grunted. He told me no lies. His life story came in a short monologue on the first night, after which we spoke hardly a word.

"I had a family once," he had said. "Greensboro. Was a lawyer. The bottle got me. Lost the family. Lost my license. Wandered for maybe six years, killing myself, and then latched onto this circus. Been with it two years. Haven't had a drop since. This is as close to family as it gets for me."

"I appreciate your sharing confidences with me," I had said.

"No confidences," he had answered, sitting on his bunk across from me in a trailer not cooled by the open windows. "Warning."

"Warning? Me? I'm the most innocent . . ."

He didn't answer. Just looked me in the eye.

Since that night, I had left out a bottle on the rusted

space that served as a shelf above my bed. The bottle
was half full of bourbon. It had been willed to me by
Gideon along with his hat and a few other uninspired
objects. Hector had not touched the bottle. Neither had
he mentioned it.

And now he walked into the caravan unannounced.

"Father's looking for you," he said to Diedre as I
snapped my bag closed.

Diedre gave me a shrug.

"Later," she said, patting my hand, pulling her robe
around her, and hurrying out of the caravan.

I looked at Hector and he looked at me.

"Her father is not looking for her," I said.

"I lied," Hector admitted, his eyes unblinking.

"I mean her no harm," I said innocently, showing my
upturned hands.

"I think *you're* lying now. I've seen enough liars in
court," he said.

"That was long ago," I reminded him.

"Yes," he admitted. "But liars haven't changed."

"Perhaps," I said, moving past him to the door, "your
judgement has changed. Drinking does that. Do you
have nightmares? I'm concerned about my bunkmate."

"I can live with my nightmares," he said, our faces
inches from each other.

"Some nightmares are real," I said softly, holding
onto each tasty word like Bela Lugosi.

"I keep something hard under my pillow and I sleep
real light," he said aloud.

I left him standing there and went about my merry
mischief. I know. I know. I should have contained myself, waited till I was sure I was not pursued, lived an
exemplary existence, but there is so much fun to be had
and missing a day, nay even an hour of it, is offensive to
me.

The Brazilians were named Sotto. Though I had to
put in long extra hours to do it, I managed to get the
young brothers fighting over which was the superior
flyer, to get the daughter to think she was pregnant, to
get the father to take more than an occasional drink,
and to get the mother to determine that McCoy was

practically using them as slave labor. McCoy, himself, was easy. I told him Hector was back on the bottle and showed him the bourbon. I told him the Sottos were plotting with someone to ruin the circus and take it over. Diedre I managed to convince that she was letting life pass her by. I told her of the bloody show of the *Grand Guignol* in Paris, the cockfights in Mexico, the pit-bull battles in Texas, the cobra kissers of India. I made her long for the outer world, but it was long and hard because Hector was ever present, ever likely to come through the door or around a corner. In frustration, I poisoned the tiger with the digitalis I carried in my purple bag.

The Sotto brother who helped Grieff handle the cat took it hard. We all wept for him and the mangy creature. I helped to bury it not far from where I had left the car.

All this was hard work. At night I was exhausted. I even slept. I never saw Hector sleep, at least never when I was sure he slept. At night I would sit up quietly, ever so quietly. And Hector would have his head turned toward me, his eyes open. I would offer him the bottle, take an imaginary drink from it, and lie down again.

When your life is committed to, dedicated to a principle, a task, it is very difficult to suffer uninformed intrusion. I determined to renew my efforts to destroy this piece of traveling trash, especially Hector.

The next day went well. Pamphlets had to be changed removing the "Wild Tiger" act. I volunteered to distribute the pamphlets in town, headed down the road, threw them in a ditch, and spent a few hours in the woods stalking and frightening a pair of overweight, nearsighted hunters.

The crowd came that night to see me. I took tickets, told three or four early comers that the tiger was really mean tonight. It went perfectly. The Sottos glared at each other and McCoy. Papa Sotto missed a catch and one of the boys, the one who lost the tiger, almost tumbled out of the safety net. McCoy tripped on a prop bucket and couldn't finish his act. The crowd began to call for the tiger.

And Hector. Hector held the rigging and his fixed melancholy stare. If he had to have only one look, why couldn't it be a smile? He was beginning to really annoy me.

And then it happened. It happened on the night of a full moon. Hector was not to be seen. He had been sent by McCoy, at my suggestion, to town to pick up a few bottles of fine bourbon for which I gladly would pay.

The Sottos were brooding in their van. McCoy was curled up with a nice bottle, and Diedre was free to accompany me to the Ferris wheel with the promise that I would finally show her the mysteries of my purple valise.

"Too hot around here," she said.

"Not as hot as Calcutta," I said. "You sit in one of the million marketplaces and you can watch the old people dying of the heat with no place to go for shelter."

"That's awful," she said as we paused near the base of the wheel.

"Awful," I said dreamily remembering that wonderful torrid day I spent in the marketplace. I had daydreamed of that marketplace over the years knowing I'd have to return just once more before I died.

"You like the wheel?" I asked.

"Haven't been on it in years," she said with a little laugh. "I thought you were going to show me what you've got in that bag."

"I can run it," I said. "I've watched Hector."

"We can't afford to run it when we've got no customers," she said.

"I'll pay for it," I said, reaching into my pocket, pulling out a handful of bills, and handing them to her. She took them, looked around for someplace to put them and stuffed them into the pocket of her dress.

"It's too much," she said, and pulled some of the money out.

I covered her hand with mine and said, "I have much money and there isn't enough fun in the world. Get in."

She smiled and climbed into the waiting gondola. I smiled as I have always done and threw the switch. I even turned on the lights and music. I threw the switch full power and as the wheel ground into action I leaped onto the gondola with Diedre.

"You're crazy," she said, laughing. "Who's going to turn it off?"

The wheel picked up speed. I felt the wind blowing through my green hair and watched her.

"Wouldn't it be fun," I said, "to leap off into the night like a bird when we get to the top?"

"We're not birds," she said, smiling.

"More's the pity," I said into the wind, which took away heat, time, space, and night, leaving only the shift from star-filled sky to darkened circus grounds surrounded by the recorded calliope music of the "Colonel Boogie March." "But how do we know we can't fly unless we try?"

"You are funny," she said, holding tightly to the bar in front of her.

"I know," I said with a sigh. "You want to see what's in my bag now?"

"Sure," she said.

And I opened it.

When I pulled out the red scorpion in the clear plastic vial and held it before her, she pulled back only slightly. This was a girl who had seen much.

"Beautiful, isn't she," I said. "I picked her up after she had killed a gas station attendant in Waco."

"I am not partial to crawling creatures," Diedre said.

"I know," I said. "Let's let her go for a little walk."

I opened the top of the vial and shook the scorpion onto the floor of the gondola. Diedre lifted her feet.

"This isn't so funny, Gwyn," she said. "I mean. I know you wouldn't let a really poisonous scorpion . . . but it's not funny."

I looked deeply into her eyes. They were alert, bright with the exhilaration of the spinning wheel in which we rode, tinged with just the first blush of fear.

"But wait," I shouted. "There's more."

I pulled out the fer-de-lance in a plastic Tupperware box with air holes punched by the Joker personally using the ice pick that killed three lonely widows in Northern Wisconsin just two years ago.

"It's a fer-de-lance," I announced proudly.

She kicked at the floorboard, and I could see the red smudge of the scorpion go sailing into the Ferris wheel lights below.

"You're going to tell me it's poisonous, right?" she asked.

"The richest kind," I said, starting to open the box.

"I think I want to get off," she said evenly. She was admirable. Beautiful. In a moment she would be almost petrified with fear, and believe me, there is no greater beauty in the human face than that universal and eternal look. Beyond that terror is a human history of horrors locked in the collective memory.

"Can't stop it," I said opening the lid. "You might try flying. Or when we get near the bottom, you might want to open this bar and leap."

"If you're trying to frighten me," she said over the blaring music, "you're doing a good job."

The snake crawled over the lip of the plastic and looked around. Diedre pressed herself into the corner. I laughed. There are few moments in one's life as precious as that moment was to me. I vowed to carry a little videotape recorder with me as soon as I could steal one. The snake dropped to the seat next to me.

"He'll bite you," Diedre cried.

I reached into the purple bag and pulled out a small bottle of greenish liquid.

"Special antibite venom prepared for herpetologists in Argentina," I said. "I take it periodically. Never know when it will come in handy."

The snake had curled into and under the imitation-leather cushion of the seat.

"Now," I said, "you want to see the really interesting things I have in this bag?"

"No," she said, starting to stand, looking over into the night—and then she shouted. She did not scream, which was a pity. She shouted for her father, Hector, the Sottos, even for God.

"No help for you, my sweet," I said gleefully. "Look at this."

I pulled out the dark bottle of acid and held it up to the sky.

"Isn't it beautiful," I said with a sigh.

"You're crazy," she said, looking down at the seat, wondering where the snake would emerge.

"You are not well-read," I said with a sad shake of my head. "Madness is a social construct to identify the deviant. If you're not like other people, you're strange or crazy. Using that definition, I suppose I am crazy; but I'm very happy, which almost no sane people can honestly say for themselves. Now, I would suggest you either jump or watch me open this very potent bottle of acid."

"It'll get on you," she squealed, looking down into the darkness for help.

"So?" I shrugged. "Would it scar me for life? I can live with that, but don't worry. I'll be careful."

I began to open the jar as I watched her rise, watched the wind blow into her face, watched her dark hair flow backward like the masthead on a ghost ship I had the good fortune to board a decade earlier just off of Cape Town.

And then it happened. One of the great disappointments of my life just at the apex of one of my greatest triumphs. First, the music stopped. As we sped around, the lights of the wheel went out. I looked for someone in the darkness and thought I saw a figure as we swept past the ground. I hurled the bottle of acid toward the figure, heard the bottle clatter, break and hiss against something hard as we rose.

"All out," I said to Diedre. "It's time to see if some vestige of wings will magically appear."

The wheel was definitely slowing down but it would make at least two more turns because it was going so quickly. Plenty of time to play out my scene. We swooshed down once more and Diedre gasped. The snake had appeared at the top of the seat. I turned for an instant to enjoy the sight, and that is when the figure rushed out of the darkness and leaped onto the back of the gondola.

A hand came out and swept the snake into the darkness. I imagined but did not see it twisting like a piece of thick cord. I hoped it would survive and breed. Was it a fertile female? One could only pray, so that her offspring could prey.

The hand that grabbed my sleeve was gnarled. It was, as I knew, Hector's. I put my hands around his neck and pushed. The wheel slowed and Hector began to lose his grip. I felt something on my neck as I laughed. Oh, the drama of the moment. I let go of Hector with my left hand and reached for the thing on my neck, an enormous mutant spider, the prize of my collection, bred by a voodoo master in Haiti, guaranteed to have no antidote. I loved this creature as if it were my own offspring. I could not let him go into the night. I let go of Hector and gently returned the spider to my valise as Diedre pounded at me with her fists. I ignored her, but I couldn't ignore the thud of Hector's wrench against my skull.

I tumbled forward, breaking the bar of the gondola. We were about ten feet over the ground and stopping. I landed in the dirt in front of the wheel and rose, ready to take on Hector. I had to retrieve my valise before I set fire to the circus, stole one of the vans, and headed into the night.

"No," came a voice from the darkness, and the lights of the Ferris wheel came on. Surrounding me were the Sottos and McCoy. Hector had dropped from the wheel. In one hand, he held my valise. In the other hand, he held his great wrench. Diedre sat above us in the gondola, looking down. I blew her a kiss, laughed, and rushed for Hector with a shout of glee.

"Tonight," I whispered in his ear as I ducked under his swinging wrench and grasped him around the waist, "prepare to meet the devil."

I pulled, trying to crush his chest, but he was surprisingly strong.

"Beelzebub, I love this," I whispered, turning him around to face the watchers. The wrench hit me in the back of the head, not a full blow but enough to make me lose my grip. I didn't care. I grabbed the valise from Hector's hand and opened it as the Sottos and McCoy advanced on me.

"Watch," I called up to Diedre. "I dedicate the ears of your father to you, *querida*. If only you had a flower to throw me, a blood-red rose."

A hand touched my shoulder. Hector on the ground grabbed my pants leg. I pulled away, removed a round object from my valise, and held it over my head. I laughed. Into the night I laughed. Loud enough for Gideon to hear me fifty miles away in the bay I laughed.

"Don't go near him," Diedre screamed.

There they stood, their faces frozen in that wonderfully comic rictus of fear. If only that instant could last forever. They were beautiful. And then it passed. Hector was on his knees and then standing before me. I threatened him with the object in my hand. A thin trickle of blood came from the corner of Hector's mouth as he spoke.

"You're a liar," he said.

"Let me through," I warned.

Hector shook his head no.

I shrugged. It hadn't worked for Lon Chaney's Erik, either, but he had had the last laugh and so too would I. I threw the crystal sphere to the ground. It burst sending out a spray of liquid that sent the small crowd back a step. Some of it landed on Hector's arm. He did not move back. He touched the liquid, put it to his lips calmly.

"It's water," he said.

I reached down for my valise, but Hector's wrench hit my wrist sending the valise skittering along the ground. Then they moved in on me.

Ah well, I thought. I had survived much worse situations than this. I would, I was sure, live to laugh again.

Someone Like You

S. Tepper

Have I told you how happy I am to have found you," whispered the Joker as he tightened the thumb screws on the woman's hand.

She screamed, unable to control the sounds that came pouring from her throat. Each time he stopped his manipulations, she felt that she would be able to be silent the next time, but each time the pain took her by surprise, more intimate and horrid than she had remembered. Memory was not reliable. The torture had been going on for more than a day now, but it seemed forever. Like weeks, months.

"Think of it! Batman's sister!" whispered the Joker in her ear. "I never knew he had a sister. Does he know who you are?"

She had told him before. He seemed unable to hear it often enough. "He knew he had a sister. But he thinks she died," the woman gasped.

"Tell me. Are you his full sister? Half sister?" The Joker licked his red lips, as though they were rimmed with honey.

She choked on the words, words she had said over and over. "Half. His mother had been married before when she was very young. Her husband ran off, taking the child with him. She never saw either of them again."

"Why do you say, 'her husband' when you mean, 'my father?' 'Why say 'the child,' when you mean, 'me'?"

She gasped again, unable to answer. He watched her agonized face for a moment, then, realizing she could not speak, he loosened the devices on her hands.

A terrible throbbing replaced the immediacy of mutilation. She could speak once more. She could think once more, could search her mind for a reason for what she had said.

"I got into the habit of thinking of them as other people," she whispered through a dry mouth. "I've always spoken of them in that way. My father always spoke in that way. In the third person. He and she. When he went out to get us something to eat, he would say, 'He is leaving now.' If I did something he didn't like, he would say, 'She has been a bad girl.' As though we were characters in a drama, playing parts that had been written for us. Not as though we were real ourselves."

The Joker regarded her thoughtfully. "Almost a pity," he said. "I like perception. I'd almost like to let you live. If it weren't that you are Batman's sister, I would. . . ."

"Why do you hate him so?"

"You see me as I am," he said simply. "Look at me. This is his fault." He stood up and turned before her, like a model, raising his arms, pointing his feet as though about to dance.

She stared through blood-rimmed eyes at the tall, green-haired, white-skinned mockery of a man, whose twisted mouth flowed across his face like a skein of blood. He seemed invented, like something dreamed up by a bad artist during his final drunk. He looked mythical, demonic.

He was all too real.

"Will killing me bring you back to yourself?" she asked wonderingly. "Will torturing me change you?"

The Joker laughed, softly. "No, but it will change him, when he knows what I've done. Very complacent, Batman. Very pure. But also very sentimental. He oozes compassion. He'll ache over your demise, pretty lady, believe me he will. He'd grieve even without knowing who you were, but when I tell him you were his sister, when I send him the tapes of you twisting and writhing, the sound of your screams, of your voice, pleading . . ."

"I haven't pleaded with you."

"Oh, but it's early days. You will. Sooner or later. Before the end."

"I know someone like you," she whispered. "A woman. A woman exactly like you."

His eyebrows went up in astonishment. "Someone like me?" He laughed, a tumbling cacophony of sound. "Oh, that's unlikely!" He posed, pranced, looked at her over his shoulder. "Like me?"

She shook her head slowly, setting off waves of pain. "Not in appearance. No. In the way she is. Inside, she's just like you."

"What's her name?" he asked, interested despite himself.

"Delice Demain," she said. "She used to love jokes, painful ones. She loved hurting people. She thought it would lessen the hurt and loneliness she felt, but it never did. Still, she went on hurting others. She did it well. I don't know how many people she destroyed."

The Joker grinned, the shark-gape grin that made him look like a sliced melon, red lips slashing his head virtually in half. Still, there was something almost plaintive in his voice as he said, "She sounds interesting. I'll make you a bargain. Let's play Sheherazade. You tell me about this woman, keep me interested, and as long as you do, I won't play with my toys." He gestured toward the instruments mounted on the wall and scattered on the bench near her, the knives and electrical appliances, the branding irons, the devices of pulleys and clamps.

"And when I can't keep you interested anymore?"

"Why then, we'll proceed, of course. I'm only offering a delay, not a reprieve."

His victim laughed, a low, humorless laugh, with as much pain in it as a voice could hold. "I should be able to talk about her. I know her well. I was one of her victims."

"No, my dear, you are my victim. Believe it. Anything else you have experienced will pale beside this."

"Before I was your victim, I was hers." The woman sobbed, cradling her crippled hands in her lap. "I met her when I was only a child."

"Delice Demain," the Joker said.

"Yes. Delice Demain. She was my father's . . . acquaintance. Perhaps I should say his nemesis. My father was handsome, virile, amoral, impatient, still quite young. Thirty, perhaps. I was only a child, around ten. I can't remember exactly. We moved around so much, I didn't go to school. He taught me everything I knew. Then he met Delice."

"Not very interesting thus far," commented the Joker, toying with the thumb screws.

"Delice manufactured drugs. She was clever. No, she was brilliant. She was self-taught. By the time she reached her teens, she read chemistry books as though they were novels. She had a complete laboratory in a trunk, and she moved it around with her, wherever she went. At first he . . . my father . . . helped her. Then there came a time she used . . . used my father to test her drugs. Drugs to make men passionate. Drugs to make men happy. I have seen him lying on the bed beside her, his eyes staring into nothingness, full of ecstasy or empty fury or bottomless despair. Often he did not know where he was or who he was. Soon he stopped knowing anyone. He stopped knowing me."

"Ahhh," murmured the Joker.

"When she needed money, she would sell the drugs, to anyone. She liked to sell something very good to someone, get him hooked, then give him one of her specialties. She had a drug she called the purgatory pill, one that went on and on forever. The nearest thing to hell. . . ."

"Oh, I like her," whispered the Joker.

"Sometimes her victims came out of it. Often they didn't. I was with her once when she visited someone she said was a friend, laughing when she said it, sniggering, really. The man was one who had spoken to her, only once, in a manner she hadn't liked. Now he sat in a hospital ward, staring at the wall and screaming. He thought his flesh was burning and falling off his bones. He felt it. The doctors said he would be that way until he died. Of course, to him, it seemed forever. Delice laughed when we left there."

"Why were you with her?" the Joker asked suspiciously. "Why you?"

"Why not me? She'd half killed my father. I was there, a kind of leftover. I was an audience. She needed an audience. That's another way she's like you. . . ."

"Go on."

"She liked to slip her purgatory pills into candies and give them to children. She'd watch while they jerked and flopped and howled and sometimes died. Her favorites were little girls. She liked to give them to little girls."

"Scarcely worthy opponents," sneered the Joker.

"No, but they were innocent, you see. It was her way of striking out at innocence. She had lost her own; now she would destroy others."

"I do see," he mused. "Well, it has a nice symbolic thrust to it. Speaking of little girls, why didn't she give the pills to you?"

"Because I was her audience, I tell you. I was the one who saw what she did. I was the one who watched and judged and looked at her afterward, trying to find the real person inside her. She needed me."

"Did your father die?"

"I suppose he did, eventually. She left him staring at the walls in a hotel somewhere. I remember she had a suitcase full of money and she was wearing a long, spotted fur coat. She said a whole species of jungle cats had died so she could wear that coat. She loved it."

"What next?" the Joker asked, yawning.

"She got involved in assassinations. She was very beautiful. Had I said that? Very beautiful. There was an ultimate mystery about her, like death itself. Terror and longing, all mixed up. She could look in a man's eyes and mesmerize him, make him want her, make him give up anything for her. Then, when she had him alone, she could kiss him with poison on her lips and watch him die."

"And you watched?"

"I always watched. She always let me watch, wanted me to watch."

"Wasn't she afraid you'd betray her? Turn her over to the police? Help trap her?"

"Why would I do that? What would I have done without her. She was my whole life."

"She mesmerized you, too, then." The Joker laughed. "Rather nice touch, that."

"The deaths were always listed as heart attacks. They really were heart attacks. Induced heart attacks. She moved through politics like the angel of death, selling destruction to the highest bidder. She became rich. Very rich."

"Where?" The Joker licked his lips. "Where did she live?"

"She had a penthouse in Paris, and a villa near Rome, and an estate in Malaysia. She had a vast wonderful mansion in San Francisco, and a townhouse in New York. She had a pied-à-terre here in Gotham City. I came here with her. Otherwise I would not have been here for you to capture."

"Came to see your brother?"

"Oh, no. No. After my association with Delice? How could I? He would have detested me. He might have felt he needed to do something, bring her to justice. I came with her, but I did not come to see him. No. I couldn't risk that."

"You risked a good deal, getting drunk in the Wild Card. Didn't you know the place belongs to me?"

She turned her face away. "Perhaps I didn't connect your name to his. Perhaps I wasn't thinking."

The Joker snorted. "Sat there, getting drunk, telling one of my own men that you were Batman's sister? Everyone knows the Wild Card is my place. You couldn't have been more stupid if you'd tried."

"I suppose it was stupid. Yes. I know it was."

"So. Is there more to this story, or should we fire up some of the implements. I have an hour or so to spend yet tonight. We can always continue tomorrow."

"There's more," she whispered.

He yawned again and arranged several knives on the bench in order of size. "Yes."

"She decided she wanted to involve herself in the ultimate evil."

The Joker sat up, his brow furrowed, staring at the woman before him.

His victim nodded. "I knew you'd appreciate that. The ultimate evil, the one before which all other wickedness would shudder. She began to spend all her time in libraries, doing research. Evil wasn't defined anywhere. No one knew precisely what it was. The ultimate evil."

"Yes?" encouraged the Joker. "Yes?"

"The theologians defined it as the absence of God. Delice didn't believe that. That was too passive, too empty. She thought of evil as an active principle."

"Oh, it is. She was right, it is. An active principle. Powerful. With its own logic, its own ethics." He stood up and strode around the dungeon, his feet clacking on the floor as though he had been hoofed, his long, angular arms gesticulating, his fingers snapping. "She sought what I have always sought. Sometimes I have thought I came close. Innocence betrayed. Love shattered. Pain inflicted, mercilessly. I haven't tried genocide, yet. It takes a large organization to attempt genocide, but I've considered it. What did she think of genocide?"

The woman chained to the bench shook her head. "That wasn't it. She learned there is more evil in wiping out a species of animal or plant than there is in wiping out any subgroup of mankind. Mankind is capable of infinite schism, she used to tell me. Mankind splits into groups and languages and cultures at the drop of a hat. No, genocide wasn't the ultimate evil, for even if she had wiped out one group of man, nine others would have sprung up in its place, hydralike."

"Was it desecration? Blowing up churches? Wrecking temples? Is that it? I've done that, of course, on a small scale. How about instilling racial hatred? How about bigotry?"

"Evil, yes, but not the ultimate evil. Men are born fearing strangers and hating them. It is part of their old animal heritage. It is evil as many primitive things are evil; evil in that we should have overcome it by now but have not."

"Then what?" cried the Joker. "Surely she found something more than mere negatives! Surely she found an answer!"

"Oh, yes, oh, yes," moaned the woman on the bench. "She did. She found it."

"How! Where!"

"She looked in a mirror."

"What?" he screamed leaping at her with his claws extended. "What do you mean, she looked in a mirror!"

"It was an unusual mirror," admitted the woman. "When she had no luck in the libraries, she decided to go to a witch. The witch gave her a recipe. She could find what she sought in a mirror of a certain type, a cursed mirror. It had to be washed with the blood of a newborn babe and dried with the hair of a murdered bride. It had to be silvered thrice beneath a waning moon and framed with the wood of a yew tree, uprooted in its prime by a condemned man."

"Magic," sneered the Joker. "Superstition! I don't believe in it."

"Neither did Delice," said the woman quietly. "Not really. Still, she had tried everything else. She followed the ancient recipe word for word, almost entirely out of mockery. But, nonetheless, when she was done, she looked into the mirror and demanded to see ultimate evil."

"What did she see?"

"Her own face. What she had become. She saw what I see when I look at you. I told you she is someone like you. So alike."

He stood up, his face full of wonder, almost expectation. He turned around, thinking. "Where is she?" he demanded. "Right now, where is she? I want to meet her."

"Nearby," the woman said. "I was always with her when she traveled, so she must be nearby."

"What happened," he demanded. "When she saw herself?"

The woman was silent for a long moment. He started toward her threateningly, and her head came up as she said, "She had a religious experience."

He laughed, the laugh rising to a roar, the echoes tumbling between the walls like stones rolled in an abyss, the room shattering beneath the sound. "A religious experience!" And he laughed again.

"You laugh," she sobbed, "but it is true."

"She was born again," he cackled. "No doubt."

"No," the woman shook her head. "Oh, she longed to be born again and put away that face she had seen. She longed to be new and clean and not see that face again. But she could not be born again. The weight of evil was too heavy. She could not lay it down or overcome it. It hung from her in chains and ropes of guilt. It tied her feet with snares of horror. It confronted her eyes with terror. It filled her nostrils with rot. It sounded in her ears, like the cries of the damned. She could not get out from under it. I said she was like you."

The words took him in a place he had thought long sealed away. Like him. Someone like himself. Someone who could appreciate what he was, who he had become. Of all the pains he felt since his transformation, the pain of loneliness was the worst. How many times he had longed for someone like himself, someone to understand the desire to be born new, out of his own skin, out of his own self. . . .

"Where is she? Where? I want to meet her!"

"Perhaps she will come here. She has a habit of finding me, wherever I am hid."

"You, Batman's sister?"

"Me. Whatever I am."

He licked his lips, almost afraid to ask. "What did she do, when she had this experience?"

The woman sobbed and cradled her hands, rocking to and fro. "She decided she must expiate the evil she had committed. She decided she must somehow pay for everything she had done. She could not destroy herself, for self-destruction would only add to the evil. She had to find a way to sacrifice herself. A way to die without killing herself. Perhaps she thought you would do it. Perhaps that's why she came here, to Gotham City."

The Joker frowned and shook his head in abrupt negation. "She's a fool if she thinks I would destroy her. Why would I? Destroy someone like me? She would be my helpmeet, my delight. Together we could rule the world. If I had that poison of hers, that purgatory pill, do you know what I could do with it?"

"What? What would you do with it that she has not

already done? What assassinations? What terrible fates wished on the kindly and the innocent? What would you do?"

"Something," he mused, staring at the cobwebby ceiling far above their heads. "Something she never thought of. We would think of it together. We would build upon the foundations we two have laid. We would become more than the sum of our parts. We would shine in the firmament of darkness like black stars. . . ."

"She thought you would destroy her," said the woman after a long time. "Even now, she is probably waiting for you to do it. To destroy her, so that she may expiate her sins."

"Not a chance," the Joker said with a laugh. "Do you have any idea how lonely I have been? How I've longed for someone to understand me? To work with me? The very thought of her fills me with feelings I haven't had in decades. I'll find her. I'll convince her of the glory of our future together. You say she is like me! I've longed for someone like me. Is she still beautiful?"

"When I saw her last, she was beautiful. She was sitting before the mirror, brushing her hair. She was beautiful, yes."

"Is she shapely? Strong?"

"Yes. When I saw her last she was."

"Where did you see her last?"

She did not answer. Instead, she asked, "Will you let me live, for her sake?" She looked him in the face, her eyes wide, the burns on her face crusted red against her white skin.

He stared at her for a long moment then laughed, shrilly. "You tried to trick me, didn't you? Of course I won't spare you for her sake. Goodness would spare you, but evil would not. Evil would kill you, as I will kill you, without even staying around to see how it goes." And he capered around her, connecting this and connecting that, throwing a switch here and another there, barely noticing the quivering flesh, the howling lips, the blood that oozed thickly and more thickly still. "What I will do is let it end sooner than otherwise, if you'll tell me where she was staying!"

"In the hotel," she cried. "Just across the street from the Wild Card, where we met. In the Gotham Hotel."

"Ahh," he whispered, licking his red lips, running his bony hands through the stiff green foliage of his hair. "It's only half an hour or so from here, through the tunnels. What room? Tell me what room!"

"What room? Fourteen-oh-two, I think. Yes. Fourteen-oh-two."

"Then I'll find her there. I'll find her there. I want her more than I have wanted anything for years. Everything you tell me about her excites me."

He threw a final switch as he left the room. Behind him the woman's voice rose in a gurgle of final destruction.

From a pay phone in the street, he called the Gotham Hotel and asked for Delice Demain's room. The phone rang. A voice said, "This is room fourteen-oh-two, Gotham Hotel. Miss Demain is away at the moment. Please leave a message." The voice sounded odd, as though someone had been speaking through a distorter.

So she carried an answering machine with her? Well, why not? Why trust hotel operators to convey important information. People couldn't be trusted. He liked even that in her, that lack of trust. And how delightful that she was out, that she would return and find him waiting for her!

Room 1402 was almost adjacent to the firestairs. He slipped into the corridor as soon as he was sure it was empty. He knew a great deal about locks and was prepared to pick the room lock, but it wasn't necessary. The door was open.

A pleasant room. One light on, beside the phone. The green light blinking on the answering machine, to show there had been a call. No one in the room.

He mused, beside the door. Where should he wait? In plain sight, where she would see him when she came in? Hiding behind a curtain or in the closet? Or, perhaps he would leave a message, on her machine.

Perhaps, first, he would see what message was already there.

He pressed the button.

"Hello, Joker," the voice said. It was a familiar voice. It was a voice he knew.

He ran, all the way down the stairs to the street, down the alley, into the ramified passages that would eventually lead him to the underground torture chamber. He had been gone only a little more than an hour. Only a little more. Surely not too long. It couldn't have been too long.

But it had been too long. The woman was dead.

He stood looking down at the bloody, contorted body, at the face which, somehow, despite the terrible death it had suffered, seemed to be at peace. The loneliness rose around him like fouled water in an underground sewer, drowning him, and he still heard the words of the recorded message ringing in his ears.

"Hello, Joker, this is Delice Demain. The joke's on you. Batman never had a sister."

Help!
I Am a Prisoner

Joey Cavalieri

All I ever wanted was to make people laugh. I wanted to take everybody on a trip with me to the places in my head. I had so many imaginary lands charted in my daydreams, topsy-turvy principalities that rivaled the ones I admired as a lonely child: the depths of the Okefenokee Swamp; the untamed snowdrifts of Lower Slobbovia; the shifting desert sands of Kokonino County; the crisp, brittle atmosphere of the planet Mongo.

When I was young, I walked down the shadowy streets of Caniff's China. I drank mead with Val, protected by Foster's lofty turrets and stone battlements. The foreboding mists surrounding Eisner's Wildwood Cemetery were just as inviting to me as a sunny day in Barks's Duckburg.

The thing I wished for, strove for, when I grew up was what I nearly achieved. I wanted to draw a comic strip that people made a part of their day, every day, a strip that guaranteed them a laugh in a newspaper that often proffered nothing but bad news and bad weather. One ray of light among the murky tabloid shadows. A strip that could stand alongside "Peanuts," or "Calvin and Hobbes," or "Gasoline Alley."

Now my comic strip kills people.

It's all because of the Joker.

I have this theory that one can get into any building on Gotham's Upper West Side by leaning on a doorbell, af-

fecting the right accent and saying "Chinese food" into
the intercom.

I didn't remember ordering, but it didn't matter. I'd
fallen behind on my strip and hadn't left my atelier in
days. It reached the point where I was ordering cold noo-
dles with Szechwan sauce or moo shu pork practically
for breakfast. Tipping the delivery kid was the high
point of my social life.

I swung the apartment door open wide without bothering to consult the peephole. No delivery boy. I saw no one,
until a fist the size of a bowling ball knocked me back
across the living room. I collapsed in a heap on the floor.

My vision was blurred. I imagined that somehow my
eyes had been knocked out of alignment. Through a haze
I saw a massive man, more like a mountain, with arm
muscles as big as my head.

The burly man-mountain stood over me, preparing to
hit me a second time. I had enough presence of mind to
envision my head bursting apart like a garbage bag full of
red paint, spattering my ink-stained wall-to-wall. He
cocked his arm back. I looked up, speechless, as much in
appeal as to see my attacker. His black marble eyes
stared back, cold and expressionless, like windows in a
deserted house. Nobody home. No appeal, no pleading, no
begging, nothing I could say would stay a second blow.

But *someone* stopped him.

Another man strode into my apartment, looking the
place over as if he were going to buy it. His purple spats
sank into the thick carpet in slow, measured steps. He
paused to admire some of the artwork on my walls, trea-
sured pieces I'd collected over the years. "Barney Google
. . . with the goo-goo-googly eyes," I heard him say.
There was no greeting, no explanation of who he was, or
why he was here. He took his time, frosting the framed
artwork with his breath and wiping it off with a purple
glove. "Terry and the Pirates!" he said, "Bonnnnnnng!"
intoning an imitation of a Chinese gong from an old
radio show.

"Bonnnnnnng" was exactly how my head felt. Then,
my eyes readjusted from their haze. When I got a good
look, I nearly swooned again. I saw his face, as white and
final as moonrise. His smile came right from the label of

a poison bottle, a Jolly Roger. Both of those were warnings that what resided within could kill you. This grin was no different.

He placed his hand on the man-mountain's shoulder and spoke with a breezy familiarity, like he'd known me all my life, or he was just finishing a conversation we'd begun a short time ago. He didn't even look at me during his monologue. "So, I says to Punch here, I says, 'Punch, do you want to spend the rest of your life sucking back Thorazine in your OJ three times a day? No, of course you don't.' I says, 'Punch, I've been in and out of Arkham Asylum so many times that they're thinking of installing a revolving door just for me. But there's one thing, Punchline, ol' pal. Once we hit the open air, we'll be hotter than a Gotham sidewalk in an August heat wave. You'll be able to fry eggs on us. You can come with me,' I tell Punch, 'but I won't be able to rejoin that ol' gang of mine for a while. I'll only be followed and . . . what's that awful word? . . . . *apprehended.*'"

The man-mountain picked me up by my shoulders. He held me that way, rooted to the spot, while the Joker sat on the couch. "'We'll need a place to cool off for a little bit. And *this,*'" he said as he ran a purple-gloved finger through the dust on the end table, "'"must be the place."'"

Why did the Joker pick me?

I'm his favorite cartoonist.

A lot of people I respect, other artists, writers, critics, you'd be surprised, say they don't like "Boomertown." They say it's a hollow comic strip based on a demographic, not on any real experiences from my sheltered life. They say that baby-boomer humor is on its way out. The folks who don't like it don't think I draw all that well either. But it's got me a couple of awards from the American Cartoonists Federation, and it's got me into a couple of hundred papers.

It's also got me this place, a duplex apartment on Gotham's Upper West Side. I use the upper floor as my atelier, my studio. It's a new building, and the real estate market being what it is, it's expensive, so I don't have many neighbors.

Right above the drafting board is the skylight. "Natural light," the real estate lady said, "Perfect for an artist." That skylight cost me at least twenty-five percent more in rent, but it's worth it. I see the sun overhead in the morning, and the moon at night. Often, when I'm behind in my work, they're my only companions.

I gained two more companions, unwanted ones.

Two massive hands gripped my arms to my sides. The sullen giant had a narrow focus to his attention, but I took up all of it. He was eager to toss me to the floor at the slightest indication of movement, even an exhale. "We have quite an aficionado here, Punch," said the Joker, pulling down framed Sunday comic strips on my walls. The original art from the old days was particularly rare, since comics syndicates seldom returned drawings to the artists, but discarded them after use. "Winsor McCay's 'Little Nemo in Slumberland' . . . Crockett Johnson's 'Barnaby' . . . 'The Kin-der-Kids' . . . 'Polly and Her Pals' . . . 'Alley Oop' . . . You've got good taste, fella." The Joker smashed the glass frames against the coffee table, raining shards over a thick artbook collection of "Thimble Theatre." "And if there's one thing I can't stand, it's good taste." He shredded the heavy drawings to confetti. He danced about the room and tossed the paper tufts everywhere, giggling.

I fought against the restraint. "That . . . that stuff was irreplaceable!"

He stopped. "Irreplaceable?" He walked toward me. I tried to get away, but the man-mountain held me still. "You don't know the meaning of the word." There was hardly an inch between us when he pulled his lapel flower up close to my face. "Your miserable life is irreplaceable." It squirted.

"My eyes! They're burning up! Acid!"

"Not acid, you big sissy. Lemon juice. Packs quite a wallop, though, doesn't it?" He produced a walking stick, seemingly from nowhere, and twirled it like a drum majorette. The tip of the cane had a fist-sized replica of the Joker's head. "Now Punch and me, we're guests here. So you could at least show us a little. Damn. Hos. Pit. Al. Lit. Tee." He punctuated each syllable by jabbing me

hard in the stomach with the cane head while Punch
held me fast.

They made themselves at home on the lower floor of
my duplex. The man-mountain stationed himself at the
door as my "receptionist." He ordered food, accepted art-
supply deliveries, took in packages, dealt with Chinese
food delivery boys. "You might try to slip out a fortune
cookie message," explained the Joker. "'Help! I am a
prisoner!' I can't have that!" He laughed.

He also ordered a few things from a hardware store
for extra security. A large padlock kept me in the atelier
during my working hours. He caulked every window in
the place with that super adhesive they advertise on the
late movie. That was so I couldn't open them and yell out
to passersby. He put up wire mesh over the windows so I
couldn't break them and drop out a note. He needn't
have bothered. I was too intimidated by his pal Punch to
pull either stunt. In the elapsed time between such a
stunt and its discovery, I could be a dead man.

I remained upstairs, working. Business as usual, going
on inside. I have so few friends, and my schedule is so
demanding, that my becoming cloistered had little effect
on the strip. Since childhood, my closest friends have
been products of my imagination, penciled and inked in
by me. As I spent the hours drawing, I nearly forgot who
was living downstairs. I lost myself in "Boomertown."

Until the Joker began to make suggestions.

One evening, we had settled down to yet another Chinese delivery meal, one of the few things for which the
Joker would plug the phone back in the wall. "Siddown,"
he said. "It's not poisoned . . . yet."

Wiping the sauce of the General Tso's chicken from
his chalky face, he leaned across the dinner table at me.
"I want you to put something in your little strip for me.
It's not a big deal, I don't want it plastered all over the
place. Just work it into the background."

"What is it?"

"Some waves. You know, a cartoon representation of
the open sea. And a row of figure eights. Just do it."

"Why?"

The man-mountain stood up, knocking his chair backward.

"Just do it."

Some nights later, another helpful hint. The Joker paused between picking up prawns with his chopsticks. "Here's another background scene for you. Draw in some animals in cages. Next to 'em, there's an automobile parked, with a man getting out of the car door."

"You want me to draw practically a whole circus coming to town? But . . . 'Boomertown's' an urban strip! How can I possibly work that in?"

Punch reached over and grabbed my wrist so tightly I thought it would snap off. He dragged me and threw me against the couch. He hit me in the stomach so hard I thought the barbecued prawns would come up. In the next moment, they did.

"You're a creative genius," said the Joker. "You'll find a way to do it."

I get the *Gotham Gazette* delivered, not only for the news. I like to see how "Boomertown" looks reproduced in an actual paper, not just in the syndicate proofs.

One story caught my attention. Two men had been murdered in town, several days apart. One named Barry Cates, the other a Jeffrey Zuckerman.

The killings bore little relation to one another. The men were dissimilar. Cates was the headwriter on a soap opera. Zuckerman was a waiter in a deli.

The only possible connection the two men had was that they had both served on a jury together. That jury sent a man known publicly as the Joker to Arkham Asylum, supposedly for life.

Was there some link between these men . . . and what the Joker was doing in my apartment?

I would daydream out the studio window, see people on the sidewalk below passing by. I didn't dare yell out to them.

I would never have tried to make contact with them even if I weren't a prisoner. Left to my own devices, I'd stay here among my books and my drawing board.

I'd see them all drift languidly in and out of my window's range. Giggling young girls that I'd be too shy to ask out. Mothers leading their children by the hand as they scurry across the street. Men in tank tops bouncing a basketball on their way to the playground courts. Their infectious laughter floats up to my window. But it's a laughter I never shared. I wasn't good at sports or socializing. I was off in my own little world, too busy making my first attempts at drawing. What money I had I never spent on going out with girls or with friends. I saved it to buy collections of "Little Nemo" or "Little Orphan Annie." I could never share their camaraderie if I wanted to.

I was a prisoner long before the Joker got here.

The Joker looked at the art for another daily strip. "I did what you said," I told him. "See? There's the desert tree and the boating dock."

"Palmarina. Vito Palmarina," I thought I heard the Joker say under his breath.

"I had to put a picture frame around it, make it look like it was something hanging on the character's apartment wall. Otherwise, in 'Boomertown,' that would be really noticeable."

"Noticeable?" said the Joker. "*I'll* tell you what's noticeable. What do you call this?" He held the drawing about an inch from my face as he raved. "Did I ask for bats? Did I specifically call for bats? Punch, did you hear me ask the man to draw little bat symbols as a wall-border design?"

The man-mountain grunted, rising. I was cooked. I had tried to plant a hidden picture of my own. When the strip was held upside-down, a familiar silhouette symbol could be seen, repeated over and over again, the way a sinking ship telegraphs an S.O.S.

I could not imagine where Punch's fists had flesh on them. They felt like two massive clubs of solid bone.

How does Buz Sawyer roll with a punch, can you answer me that? How does Secret Agent X-9 withstand a
blow to the jaw that approaches knocking the head off
the small, thin bones of the neck? How does Dick Tracy
stand the ringing in his ears afterward? How does Steve
Canyon get up again to paste the bad guy with such an
uppercut that it knocks the villain over a cliff? What are
they made of that they can do that?

Not flesh and blood, that's for sure.

The *Gazette* came. There was a story about another
murder. The victim's name was Vito Palmarina.

It struck a chord. I got out some newspaper clippings
I'd hidden away on the murders of Barry Cates and
Jeffrey Zuckerman. Then, I looked back on the dailies of
"Boomertown" that I'd done the day before the murders
were committed.

I remembered the things the Joker made me draw in.

"The open sea. And a row of figure eights."

"Animals in cages . . . a man getting out of the car
door."

"Desert tree . . . boating dock."

Sea. Eights. *Cates*.

Zoo. Car. Man. *Zuckerman*.

Palm. Marina. *Palmarina*.

I surmised that the Joker was using my strip to send
secret messages to his well-hidden gang, giving them orders. They'd killed Cates, Zuckerman, and Palmarina.
Over the weeks I'd been following the Joker's directions,
they killed a mother of two not six blocks from here.
They murdered a Gotham U. film student on her way
home from an editing session. They slit the throat of a
social worker who specialized in treating people with
eating disorders. They garroted a cello player in the
Gotham Symphony Orchestra while he was walking his
Pomeranian one night. For good measure, they strangled the dog. In each case, the gang got its instructions
from "Boomertown."

*   *   *

I kicked against the padlocked door of the studio, slamming against it until Punch and the Joker had to respond.

I heard the click of the key in the padlock. I confronted them with the clippings, with what I had deduced. "I know what you're doing," I said, "and I'm not going to do it anymore." I was so worked up I forgot to be frightened.

"'I'm not gonna dooooooooo it anymore,'" the Joker mimicked in a playground nyah-nyah voice. "You know what you are? You're a no-good, lousy, stinking, rotten . . ." He searched for the most despicable thing in the world he could call me. ". . . *killjoy!* Punch, show the man what we do to killjoys."

I couldn't sleep that night, for the pain.

"Whitehall. Veronica Whitehall," the Joker mused aloud while looking at another week's dailies. "You think the yuppies in your cunning little continuing adventure series could do some decorating? Maybe provide us with an off-white foyer?"

"The whole strip is nothing but black-and-white," I countered. "How can I represent the concept of white in a rebus when there's no color in the strip?"

The Joker sat back in my leather easy chair. He'd spray-painted it purple. "Wait till the Sunday strip. That's in living color, isn't it? If you call that living."

"I . . . I'm running out of some art supplies. Ink. Paper. I'm going to need another delivery soon."

"I'll have Punch reconnect the phone and do it for you. Just tell him what you need and I'll . . . what's this?" The Joker shot forward in the chair. He pointed at one panel with anger. "Look at this dialogue balloon! You've got this ugly little potato-head character saying, 'But Andy, tell me, anything new?'" He ripped my work in half. "There's nothing new about *that* trick. It's so old its *beard* has a beard!

"Now there's someone I don't like very much. And I don't appreciate your attempt to contact him with the initial letters of that balloon! Punch!"

The walking mountain of muscle didn't have to do anything to scare me by now. He just had to be there. Punch
held me down in the easy chair as the Joker produced a
little black bag. It could have belonged to a doctor, but for
the clasp: a cloisonné representation of the Joker's face.
The Jolly Roger. The label on the poison bottle.

Out came rubber tubing, a Pyrex bottle, a long, long
hypodermic. I nearly fainted. "You wanted something to
draw with, yes? Let's see how dedicated you are to your
craft," the grinning man said as he tore my sleeve and
swabbed my arm with alcohol. I couldn't watch as the
needle pierced my skin. The glass bottle slowly filled
with a syrupy liquid. "You have to put more of *yourself*
into the work. Try drawing with your own blood for a
while. I figure about a pint will be enough for a week's
worth of strips."

The level of liquid in the bottle rose. "Red shows up as
black under the photostat cameras, doesn't it?" The
Joker laughed. He laughed until I passed out. In the
nightmare I had, he was laughing still.

I speak with millions of people every day, without having to meet them, touch them, talk to them. You might
think that garnering such an audience is a consolation
to someone who finds it hard to make friends, but it's
not. It only reinforces my loneliness. I think I learned
how to draw as a way to communicate with people I
couldn't befriend. My drawings were a way of shining a
beacon, a flashlight out into the mist, searching for kin-
dred spirits. Yet even the closest of soulmates can disap-
point one another. Cartoon characters, like imaginary
playmates, are always there when you need them. They
never let you down the way real people do.

But I'd have given anything for real company. I
needed a real friend.

The Joker let me in on a joke of the "good news-bad
news" sort. The good news was, he was running out of
jurors. He intended to leave my duplex soon. The bad
news was, he would kill me before he departs, maybe

having me draw a rebus of my own name into the strip beforehand as a final irony.

"Look on the bright side," said the Joker. "Think how much your artwork will be worth . . . after you're dead."

"I can't work tonight," I told the grinning man as he inspected the next week's strips.

"Awwwwwww, come on," he said, feigning disappointment. "Don't get depressed just because your days are numbered. America's depending on you for a chuckle over its collective morning coffee. It's your responsibility, your *job* to give it to 'em! Make 'em laugh, pal, make 'em laugh!"

"I didn't say I *won't* work. I said I *can't*. The lights in the atelier have blown. I won't be able to work on the next week's strips in the dark. My eyes burn in the daytime as it is."

"Well, well. Glad to see you burning the midnight oil. Your dedication is touching. Punch will reconnect the phone and get you lamps. Lots of 'em. Fluorescent lights. Hundred-watt bulbs. Even spotlights, if you want 'em. Your garret will look like a Hollywood premiere, I promise."

"And I need ink," I said. "Real ink this time."

This made the Joker slap his knees. "The genuine article, black India ink. My friend, you'll have yourself a bucketful."

It finally happened in the night. There were stealthy footsteps, but not so stealthy that they didn't awaken me.

I didn't dare exhale. Was this the Joker, about to carry out his threat?

I thought I saw a moving shadow. It seemed to be a silhouette of a tall man, but there was barely no telling where the silhouette ended and the shadows began. All the lamps the Joker had brought in were blazing above me in the atelier, but not all the light in the world could have illuminated the hooded figure that crept by me in the dark.

Slowly, so as not to creak a single bedspring, I craned my head and shoulders up to look at this patch of blackness, this living inkblot, carefully wending its way through the gloom.

The shadow rose higher and grew against the farthest wall. I could see it for what it was. A mythical creature. Half man. Half bat.

It was there . . . and it was gone.

I couldn't see anything after that. The night became a radio play, an *Inner Sanctum* story told in sound effects. The man-mountain woke with a grunt. He must have been having a pleasant dream about killing small animals. He made a disappointed moan over being shaken out of his reverie. He made no other sound. There was a noise like the cracking of knuckles, and I heard his unconscious body hit the floor.

This thud woke up the Joker. The shadow creature saved his wrath for the grinning man. The Joker's voice caught in his throat as though he was surprised to encounter the Batman . . . but then, not so surprised at all.

The Joker forced a laugh. "You could at least tell me . . . how did you know where to find me?"

But there was not a word of reply, save groans of pain from the Joker, until he collapsed.

Night air wafted the sound of sirens closer and closer till I realized they were just outside the building.

I looked at my studio with new pride. Stacked atop my drawing table were all the lamps and lighting fixtures ordered from the art supply store by the Joker. Every single one in the pile was turned on, arranged to force their light out the skylight window, on whose glass I had painted the silhouette of a bat in black India ink.

It was a makeshift distress call, but it was one everybody in Gotham knew. The Bat-Signal. It had summoned a real friend for me. It had done its job, so I started to switch the lights off.

But I decided to let the light burn, bright as a victory bonfire.

Bone

Will Murray

"Oh, I'm collecting kitties and puttin' 'em in bags," sang the gangling green-haired man.

Few in Gotham City paid attention to the author of that singsong ditty. His pinched bone-white face, shining under a full moon, brought few comments from passersby. His full red lips were curled into a threatening sneer, but those who passed him smiled back through greasepaint and brittle plastic masks of their own and complimented him on his mask.

Only, the green-haired man wore no mask.

It was Halloween, and the Joker was stalking the streets of Gotham City, blending in with flocks of street-crossing trick or treaters.

Like them, the Clown Prince of Crime carried a bag. It was no mass-produced black-and-orange candy bag, but was a simple white laundry sack. And instead of candy, the contents of the Joker's sack *squirmed*.

"Nice costume," a man dressed in astronaut-white called in passing.

"Thanks," said the Joker in a voice like powdered chalk, not breaking his stride. He wore a purple zoot suit over a Day-Glo orange shirt. His tie was a new affectation, a bola. The silver-mounted clasp stone was turquoise. His black hat belonged on an oatmeal box.

The Joker's Cuban heels clicked on the pavement like a joke-shop skull with chattering teeth. The left heel spat a spark as he skidded to a sudden stop at the dark maw of an alley.

Looking both ways with bloodshot eyes, the Joker slipped into the alley, whispering, "Here kitty, kitty, kitty."

The bulging sack mewed. The Joker smacked it with long fingers and the sack fell silent. But the mewing sounds continued.

The Clown Prince of Crime worried a haphazard stack of garbage can lids with a pointed purple shoe.

"Here, kitty," he hissed.

A solitary mew emerged from a cardboard box.

The sack dropped to the ground. The Joker stepped on its mouth to keep it shut and bent over the box. He lifted it free. A triangle of moonlight brought an innocent gleam from three sets of baby-blue eyes.

"Meow?" a gray kitten asked forlornly. The others joined in.

"Ah," the Joker cooed, harvesting him with a hand under its stomach. "You *are* a tempting morsel, aren't you?" And he stuffed him into the sack. The others followed.

When he was done, the sack mouth had to be held shut by both hands. The Joker started out of the alley, his ghoul's grin wider than before.

A fat tabby scooted around the corner, paused, and hearing the mewing from the bulging sack, gave out an anguished cry.

The Joker swept it from his path with a vicious kick.

"No room for you, you mother!" he snarled, and melted into the night, resuming his lunatic ditty under his breath.

"I'm collecting kitties and puttin' 'em in bags. Tum-te-tum-tum."

No trick or treaters approached the mansion of Archie Bittner. Bittner's palatial redbrick home was set back from an elm-guarded dirt road on forty acres of land in a southwestern suburb of Gotham City. A fieldstone fence ringed its grounds, broken only by a Spanish-style

wrought-iron gate marred by a big metal sign. The paint
was fresh. The sign read: POSITIVELY NO TRICK OR
TREATERS.

The custom sign had cost millionaire Bittner ten
times the money it would have to supply the gate guard
a box of treats. But that was Archie Bittner.

The pit bulls that roamed his grounds were also Archie Bittner. Even the guard was frightened of them.

They were the reason the guard—whose name was
Donovan—kept to his guard station, well outside the
gate, where the pit bulls could not go. They were an
added incentive for him to uphold Bittner's standing
prohibition against letting visitors in.

Tonight, Donovan was doubly grateful for his station,
as he huddled in the warmth of the electric heater he
carted to and from work during the winter months.
Winter had come early this year.

So when the purple TV repair van came down the
road, its headlights throwing the benighted elms into
stark relief, Donovan made no move to leave his shelter,
not even when the van coasted to a stop and the driver's
window cranked down.

The driver called out to Donovan, his face in shadow.

"What's that?" Donovan called back.

The shadow-faced driver repeated his question. It
sounded like "Mumble muff muff" to Donovan's old ears.
Grumbling, he slid back the glass door and trudged over
to the van.

"What's that you say?" he asked querulously, his
lined face smarting in the crisp night air.

"I said," the driver repeated, shoving his lean chalk
visage into the moonlight, "Trick—or *treat?*"

He displayed his teeth. It was more a creepy baring of
teeth than a smile and it made Donovan think of those
dreaded pit bulls.

"You startled me for a second there," Donovan said,
his heartbeat slowly returning to normal. "You look like
that there Joker fella."

"Sorry," the white-faced man said contritely.

"Me, too. I got no treats. Boss's orders."

"Then how about a trick!" the other said, tossing a

dark object in Donovan's startled face. He fumbled, catching it with both hands before it could strike the ground.

Curiously, Donovan looked it over. It was a hand-sized jack-o'-lantern. It was heavy, as if made of lead. But the pumpkin skin felt plasticky. There was a metallic ring through the stem.

"Should I open it?" Donovan asked.

"Oh, I don't know, *should* he?"

The white-faced man called the question over to the seat beside him. It was empty. But he received an answer—a kind of mewing chorus. The sharp profile snapped around.

"I think that was a unanimous yes," he hissed. His lips peeled back in a toothsome grimace.

Donovan looked from that leer to the identical one on the jack-o'-lantern's face and shrugged. He plucked the ring. It came up. The lid stayed in place.

"I think I broke it," Donovan called out, holding out the dangling ring.

"Awww, poor baby," said the driver. And something in his voice made Donovan take a second look at the metal ring. It seemed vaguely familiar on second inspection. When he recognized what it was, he hastily dropped the ring.

That was a mistake. He should have dropped the pumpkin and found the nearest deep hole.

The hand grenade concealed inside the jack-o'-lantern obliterated Donovan's right hand and most of his face in a smoky flash.

The Joker stepped out of the van and walked past the dead guard, the sack of mewing kittens slung over his back.

"Nice bridgework," he remarked to the fleshless grin that dominated what little remained of Donovan's face.

Coming to the gate, the Joker transferred the sack mouth to his eternally grinning teeth and started to climb. At the top, he straddled the wrought-iron scroll-work and opened the sack.

"Meoow!" he told the clustered plaintive faces staring

up at him. Kittens climbed over one another blindly. "Hungry? Good. I'm going to feed you now."

The Joker plucked out a calico kitten, looked it over, and dropped it to the gravel below, adding, "I'm going to feed you to the dogs!"

The kitten landed on its feet and stepped around dazedly. Another followed. And another. After some difficult labial contortions, the Joker pursed his lips and vented a long, piercing whistle.

And out of the manicured shrubbery charged a blunt furious engine of snapping snarling teeth.

"Bon appétit!" the Joker called as one of Archie Bittner's guardian pit bulls tore into the first chunk of feline bait.

Gathering up the wriggling sack, the Joker stepped from the gate to the top of the fieldstone fence. He walked gingerly and on tiptoe, for the fencetop was set with jagged fangs of broken glass.

Halfway along the south wall, his right-heel tap caught on a short chunk of glass. The Joker's grin widened—in fear. His right hand clutched the sack in desperation. His other arm windmilled and he threw out his free foot in a reflexive attempt to keep his balance.

He failed. On the way down, he whistled.

The Joker landed like a stack of cordwood.

The sack burst open at the mouth and spilled dizzy kittens.

And twin pit bulls came charging in their direction.

The Joker saw them coming. He scooped up a kitten in each hand and leaped to his feet. Legs apart, he stood his ground as they bore in on him. When he could count their teeth, he began throwing kittens. Jaws snapped like beartraps. And kept chomping.

"Here's dessert," the Joker said, tossing a few more. The last kitten landed in front of the bone-worrying dogs and its ears went back.

The Joker tiptoed around the dogs, throwing a limp-wristed wave after him. "Tah-tah," he squeaked. "Don't forget to clean your plates, children."

*   *   *

Archibald Bittner mistook the sound for a tree branch scraping an upstairs windowpane when the brass knocker clanked the first time. He made a mental note to have the gardener prune the pear trees.

The knocker sound repeated, this time more insistent. Then impatiently. And then frantically as if a lunatic had gotten hold of it.

Archie Bittner wasn't sure what to do. He was not used to callers. He employed a gate guard to turn away the unwelcome—which to Archie Bittner meant everybody. Too stingy to hire a butler, Bittner was forced out of his easy chair to answer the door himself.

So secure was Archie Bittner in his castlelike home that he neglected to ascertain the identity of his visitor by peeking through a window. He simply opened the door.

The face framed in the doorway was so much a caricature of a human being that, at first, Bittner took it for a grotesque statue placed on his doorstep by pranksters. That illusion was dispelled by a nervous stretching of the rictuslike grin on the visitor's jester visage.

"Trick or treat!" it chortled.

"I beg your pardon?" Bittner replied.

"It's Halloween," the clown scolded. "Don't you read the funnies?"

"Yes, yes, of course. Aren't you rather *old* for this?"

The wide grin thinned. The long face sucked in at the cheeks, and his eyes grew clown-sad.

"Awwww, do you really think so?" he asked.

Taken aback, Bittner demanded, "State your business."

"Monkey business." He held up his white sack and fingered the drawstring open. "Give or take?" he said.

"Again?"

"If you have no treat, I will share with you."

Archie Bittner blinked. "If it will end this quickly, very well," he growled. But the gleam in his eyes said that Archibald Bittner was not a man to turn down something for nothing.

"Uh-uh. Naughty, naughty," the trick or treater told him. "You don't just put your hands in. Look before you leap."

Bittner cleared his throat. "As you say." He bent over to look into the fat hollow of the sack. "I can't see anything. Bring it up to the light."

"Up to the light? Surely." And suddenly the sack was in his face and an insistent steel-strong hand was at the back of his neck, pushing him in.

The sack went over Archie Bittner's balding head and the Joker looped his bola tie around Bittner's neck. He pressed the clasp stone and tiny motors whirred. The slide raced along its cord track to squeeze Bittner's throat. It kept on squeezing.

It was so dark inside the sack that Bittner never registered the transition into unconsciousness.

Police Commissioner James W. Gordon looked up from his desk and the quarterly budget reports that seemed to land there six times a year to the smart rapping on his office door.

His aide McCulley poked his blank face in the half-open door.

"Yes, what is it?" Gordon demanded gruffly.

"The switchboard is lighting up. TV reception all over the city has gone haywire."

"Then why don't they call the stations?"

"It's not one station, Commissioner, it's all of them. And you know what *that* means."

"Oh, God," said Commissioner Gordon, who did know what it meant. He turned to the portable TV set he kept in his office to watch himself during his frequent evening news appearances. The ruddiness of his cheeks drained to near-white—almost the color of the chilling face he saw in his mind's eye.

The picture tube took a seeming eternity to warm up. In his many years in office, Gordon had contended with serial killers, terrorists, and other vicious criminal elements. But none of them froze his blood as did the thought that the Joker was again on one of his wild tears.

Terrorists had agendas. Serial killers fit psychological profiles. And criminals, even the deranged ones, operated to *modus operandi*. Not the Joker. He was outside
the pale—beyond insanity. Psychosis personified.

The commissioner watched the picture jump and
twitch over a familiar macabre melody. *Funeral March
of the Marionettes,* Gordon recalled.

The picture resolved into a flat whiteness. For a moment, he wondered if he had turned into an *Alfred
Hitchcock Presents* rerun by accident. Then a gray outline appeared on screen. The figure of a man seen in profile. Not the rotund profile the music had come to
suggest, but the reed-thin, Ichabod Crane silhouette of
the Joker.

Then the Joker glided into view. He lined up with the
silhouette and turned to face the camera. He smiled. But
then, he always smiled.

"Good eeeevening," he said in an unctuous Alfred
Hitchcock imitation. "Our story for tonight is about a
man who had no treats, and therefore had a trick played
upon *him.*"

Gordon groaned. He fingered his eyeglasses nervously.

The camera tracked the Joker as he stepped up to an
overweight man who sat, bound by purple ropes, to a
highchair. The man's balding forehead shone in the TV
lights as if waxed. His mouth was gagged with a baby's
bib.

"Meet Archibald Bittner, captain of industry, Scrooge
extraordinaire, and dishonorer of Halloween," said the
Joker in his normal reedy voice. He went on: "You may
be asking yourself, you out there in TV land, what has
Mr. Bittner *done* to deserve my attention. The answer is
simple: Nothing! Nothing at all. Mwee-hee-hee-hee!"

Gordon clutched his armrests at the familiar laugh. It
never failed to make his blood run cold.

The Joker went on.

"I am after bigger game," he said. "Batman. You all
know Batman. I know Batman. Yet, who really, really
knows Batman? Who is this . . . this masked rodent? No
one knows. He comes, he goes. I stick my finger up my
nose. That's a joke. Laugh if you've got the moxie."

The Joker snapped his fingers in the air. Two men stepped on camera to take their places on either side of the bound figure of Archie Bittner. One wore a black jumpsuit with an orange pumpkin over his head. The other wore orange with a black pumpkin.

"Before I go on, and believe me, I will go on," the Joker said, "meet my costars. Jack-O'-Lantern and Punkin Head. Which is which, you wonder? Dear me, I can hardly tell myself. They're twins, you know. That's why they dress that way. That, plus I pay their salaries."

The two henchmen stood with their jack-o'-Lantern faces impassive. They looked like Halloweeny smile buttons. Except their fixed pumpkin grins exactly copied the Joker's own.

The Joker leaned into the camera and said conspiritorially, "Nonspeaking roles. That way I don't have to pay 'em so much." And he winked like a demented owl.

Pulling back from the camera, the Joker straightened his trademark purple zoot suit and said, "As I was saying: Batman! Who is he? Why does he vex me so? These are tonight's questions. And answers? Answers I have none. But I'm gonna get 'em. For tonight begins the Joker production of the miniseries, *The Unmasking of Batman*. Sorry it wasn't in your local listings. Lack of advertisers. They *hated* the script."

McCulley poked his head in Gordon's office.

"The TV people say it's a microwave transmission," he reported. "Remote. Probably mobile, or on a mobile relay. No trace possible."

Gordon waved him away impatiently. The Joker was speaking again.

"In tonight's stunning opening episode, and in honor of Halloween night, we're going to begin with the unmasking of Archie Bittner. What do you say to that, Arch, me lad?"

Bittner made inarticulate noises through his gag.

The Joker yanked the gag away. "Speak up, man. Don't be camera shy."

"I—I-I'm not wearing a mask," he sputtered, his eyes shifting nervously from the camera to the Joker's rigor-mortis face.

"I'm not wearing a mask!" the Joker shrieked in delight. "Let's all write that down. It's destined to become a classic in the annals of television, right up there with 'To the moon, Alice' and 'Just the facts, ma'am.'"

"But I'm not," Bittner repeated.

"Isn't he a scream, ladies and germs? Isn't he a find? Oooh, I am *such* a casting genius. Now, the unmasking of Archie Bittner. Shall we begin? Get a good grip now, boys."

Punkin Head and Jack-O'-Lantern laid their hands on Bittner's shoulders to quiet his squirming, as the Joker presented his back to the camera, revealing his hitherto-concealed left hand curled around the bone shaft of a wicked knife.

Gordon gasped. And all over the city, that gasp rose from a million throats.

The Joker lifted the knife in a quick upward stroke.

"But I'm not wearing a mas—mummph." Archie Bittner's voice choked off as an unseen hand clamped his mouth. He began to jump in his seat. His agitated shoulders were visible around the Joker's narrow purple back. On either side of him, Jack-O'-Lantern and Punkin Head strained to hold him steady.

The knife fell. Only the Joker's elbows moved after that. There was no sound at first. Then came the gritty grating sound of metal scoring bone blended with the drumming of feet. Archie Bittner's feet, Gordon realized, as horror crept over his craggy features. He knew men only made such sounds in their death throes. Mewling noises, muffled and frantic, added to the horrible symphony.

Commissioner Gordon turned away, moaning, "That fiend!"

"Here it comes, the grand unmasking!" The Joker's voice chortled. "Did he do it? Or . . . ?"

Irresistibly, Gordon's sick eyes were drawn back to the screen. He knew that he'd have to see how far the Joker had gone for himself. Just as the rest of the Gotham City audience would. For a lunatic, the Joker manipulated like a master psychologist.

As Gordon watched, the Joker's back slowly straightened.

He spun like a dervish, venting a maniacal tittering laugh.

"Unmasked!" he shrieked. "Unmasked for all the world to see!" And then he stepped aside to reveal the seated figure of Archie Bittner, his naked skull, like a meat bone that had been rendered, staring with uncomprehending eyes—staring because his eyelids had been peeled from the raw bone along with the rest of his face.

His eyes, however, were dead.

The Joker held something limp and pale in front of the camera.

"Under it all, lies the ultimate mask," he said gleefully. "And its name is bone, bone, bone!"

He stuffed the face of Archibald Bittner into his breast pocket and leaned drunkenly into the camera.

"Tune in tomorrow at this same time for chapter two and the unmasking of—but that would be telling. It may be a lucky member of our audience. It may be *you!* And if my dear, dear friend Batman is watching, if you'd like to spare the people of Gotham further installments, meet me at the place where it all began. I propose a temporary truce. Unmask for me, on camera, and my collection of faces will grow no larger." He pointed to the camera like a bizarre parody of Uncle Sam. "You see, it's *you* I really want to make a star."

The screen went black. Within seconds, local affiliate transmissions resumed. A TV anchorwoman cut in with a hasty recap of the Joker's latest outrage. Gordon switched channels. All around the dial, anchorpeople were recapping the Joker's pirate transmission.

A phone outside Gordon's office started ringing. Others took up the clamor.

"Who is it?" Gordon asked when McCulley put his head in.

"Everybody," McCulley said. "The mayor. The governor. But mostly it's the press."

"Tell them all I'll get back to them. And then meet me on the roof."

"Yessir."

Up on the roof of Gotham City Police Headquarters, Commissioner Gordon hugged himself against the biting air as his aide turned on the modified spotlight. The big tungsten lamp came on instantly. It sent a brilliant yellow beam into the sky. Fortunately, there was low cloud cover. Against the steely banks, a familiar symbol showed mistily—a stylized bat in a disk of gold.

Hours later, the clouds had thinned and the Bat Signal ghosted in and out of view. Gordon's teeth chattered and his thick hands were stuffed deep into his pants pockets to warm them.

McCulley came up the roof hatch.

"Nothing, Commissioner," he said morosely. "No calls. No visitors."

"Go home, McCulley. It's going to be a long night."

"Yes sir. Shall I—"

"Leave it on," Gordon said curtly.

"Yes sir." He turned to go. "Sir?"

"What is it?"

"Do you think he sees it, or—"

"Or what?"

"Maybe he's afraid."

"We're all afraid, McCulley. Now good night."

McCulley disappeared down the hatch and Gordon shoved his hands deeper into his pockets, seeking warmth.

By midnight, he accepted the truth. Batman was not going to appear. Commissioner Gordon walked up to the humming spotlight, whose heat beat against his face, and shut it down.

He went down the roof hatch a saddened man.

The next night it was Dawson Clade. Unlike the late Archibald Bittner, Dawson Clade was neither rich nor prominent. Clade was a down-and-out private detective.

His last minutes of life were broadcast to Gotham City to the strains of *The Twilight Zone* theme while the Joker expressed his profound disappointment over Batman's lack of response in a doleful Rod Serling voice.

This time the Joker faced the camera while he "unmasked" his victim. Clade sat with his back to the audience. After the Joker finished outlining Clade's face with the point of his knife, he peeled it away so the audience could glimpse bits of cartilage snap as flesh parted from bone.

The Joker proudly displayed his trophy, turning it around like a stage magician proving that, yes indeedy, the handkerchief was empty. The audience had a good look at both sides—the pink outer mask and the raw inner flesh that looked like the inside of an eyelid.

McCulley entered the commissioner's office, white-faced.

"Shall I turn it on, Commissioner?"

Gordon sighed. "Yes. For one hour. Then shut it off and go home."

"You'll be here?"

"I'll be here," Gordon said leadenly. He picked up the phone and dialed the mayor directly. It would be their sixth conversation of the day—each one more strained than the one before.

"I'm telling you, Gordon," the mayor said without preamble, "if you have any idea who your Batman really is, it's your duty to divulge it."

"We can't hand him up to this madman, even if I did know."

"He's a damned vigilante!"

"But he's not a criminal. It's the Joker who's cutting off faces."

"The citizenry is panicked. No one wants to end up—excuse the expression—facedown in an alley over a feud between a circus fugitive and a human bat. The people don't see Batman as a hero in this one."

"Cooler heads will prevail."

"And where is Batman? Hiding?"

"I don't know," Gordon said slowly.

McCulley entered without knocking. "Another body, sir."

"Have to go, Mr. Mayor. I think Clade just turned up."

Gordon grabbed his hat and shoved out the door.

Outside, he looked up and down the street, half expecting to see the Batmobile slither around the corner.

When it didn't materialize, he got into his car and drove off, his moustache points bristling.

Gordon ducked under the yellow police-barrier tape and spoke to a detective at the entrance to an open basement on Crime Alley. A pair of M.E.s were inside working over a corpse lying on its stomach. They appeared reluctant to turn the body over.

"Anything unusual?" he asked bluntly.

"Other than the fact that the deceased has no face, no. But we're still processing the crime scene."

"Keep at it," Gordon said, turning to go. The first TV newsvans came around the corner causing Gordon to curse under his breath.

They came at him, camcorders held high. Microphones were thrust at him like inquisitive antennae. And the questions began.

"Commissioner Gordon, who's next?"

"No comment." He tried to shove through the knot of reporters. They followed him like steel filings attracted to a moving magnet.

"Commissioner Gordon, where is Batman?"

"No comment."

"Commissioner Gordon, is Batman a coward?"

"I don't know!" Gordon said hotly. Then red-faced, he added, "I wish I knew." And it hurt to say it. He ducked into his car and roared off.

Bruce Wayne's head started to throb as soon as the cab entered city traffic. He had had the identical headache only ten minutes into the ride from the airport when he'd arrived in Mexico City five days before. It was a pollution headache—one of the problems of being a North American vacationing in the most populous—polluted—city on earth.

Out among the ruins of Teotihuacán, the air had been cleaner. But now, in the heart of the city—choked with pollution-spewing cars—his head began throbbing again. He sighed.

"Driver."

"Sí, señor?"

"Hotel Nikko."

"No Zona Rosa?"

"The Zona Rosa will be there in the morning. I'm suddenly not up for any nightlife tonight."

"Muy triste."

The taxi turned off Viaducto beneath the big electric Coca-Cola sign and skirted Chapultepec Park on the Paseo de la Reforma side.

Bruce Wayne overtipped the driver and entered the spacious neo-Aztec hotel lobby. At the desk, he checked for messages. He was told there were none. It reminded him that he had told no one where he was vacationing.

Wayne rode the elevator to his room, entered with his magnetic keycard, and took a bottle of purified water from the mini-bar. Kicking off his shoes, he sat on the edge of the bed, feeling the tightness in his head lessen now that he was out of open air. Only in Mexico. Beyond the window, lightning flashes illuminated the congested Mexico City skyline. It was going to be another elemental Mexican night.

Sighing, Wayne turned on the TV. He had avoided television during his stay. But tonight, it was either that or boredom. He cruised the Spanish-language stations until he heard an American voice. It was a network news program. Wayne gave thanks for the miracle of cable and lay back to watch.

"In Gotham City," the newscaster said melodramatically, "the question tonight is—where is Batman? After two nights of unspeakable televised mutilations of Gotham citizens by the maniac who calls himself the Joker, that refrain haunts the nation. How much longer will these depradations go on? Will Batman, now widely believed to be in hiding, branded a coward by some, accept the Joker's bizarre ransom demand to unmask on camera? Or is the long nightmare for Gotham City only beginning?"

Wayne sat up abruptly, nearly upsetting his drink.

"Here with the latest is Gotham City correspondent Lesley—"

Bruce Wayne's eyes hardened as video clips of the mu-

tilation murders of Archie Bittner and Dawson Clade
were replayed.

He watched enough to get the gist of the situation and
shut off the TV. He called down to the front desk.

"I'm checking out. Immediately. Please have a cab
waiting to take me to the airport."

As Bruce Wayne packed, the lightning storm outside
his window intensified. But he had no eyes for its elemental fury. His mind was thousands of miles away, in
Gotham City. His city. The city he had sworn to protect.

Alfred Pennyworth started from sleep. The sound of a
car on the circular gravel driveway outside Wayne
Manor was an unfamiliar one, but it promised hope. He
struggled into a flannel bathrobe and hurried downstairs.

A cab driver was putting two suitcases on the hall
floor. Looking tired, Bruce Wayne peeled a twenty-dollar
bill from his billfold.

"Keep the change," he told the driver. The door shut
behind him.

"Master Bruce!" Alfred cried. "You should have
called. I would have come for you."

"No time," Bruce Wayne said in a flinty voice.

"I tried to reach you, sir."

"A vacation, Alfred, is no vacation if everyone has
your phone number."

"Of course, sir. I hadn't realized Wayne Foundation
matters pressed so heavily on your shoulders."

"Not that," Wayne said, shucking off a Chesterfield
coat. "It's the other work."

"I understand, sir. I assume you've heard the terrible
news. Do you require anything?"

"Coffee," Wayne said, striding for the grandfather
clock in one corner. He pushed it aside, revealing a secret door. "And I'll take it below."

Bruce Wayne was poring over the last two days' newspapers at an ornate ebony desk when Alfred came down
the Batcave steps carrying a sterling silver tea service.

Wayne regarded the pot of tea as it was laid before
him and remarked, "Tea?"

"Better for the nerves, sir. There *is* coffee, as well."

Frowning, Wayne accepted the tea. His eyes returned to the latest edition of the *Gotham Gazette*.

"The place where it all began . . ." he mused. "Only he and I know where that is."

Alfred gasped. "Surely you do not contemplate—!"

"I don't have a choice, Alfred," Bruce Wayne said coldly.

"But if you give in to this . . . this terrorist's demands, what is to stop him from—"

"The Batman."

"Sir?"

Bruce Wayne stood up in the crepuscular atmosphere of the Batcave. The gold shield on his gray chest caught the light, making the nonreflective bat emblem seem like a bottomless black hole.

"The Batman will stop him," Wayne repeated. "This is between the Joker and him."

Dutifully, Alfred lifted the black ribbed cloak and cowl of the Batman to his master's shoulders.

"Not yet, Alfred," Wayne said crisply. "There's something you must do first."

"As you wish, sir."

Commissioner James Gordon braved the new November winds on the roof of police headquarters impatiently. The stars were out tonight. He always dreaded cloudless nights like this, but somehow the clear night sky no longer mattered. It was the third night. And the body of the third victim—investment banker H.P. Quincy—had been found floating skull-down in the Gotham River. His face would arrive wrapped in a plastic sandwich bag with the morning mail, just as the others had.

Gordon switched on the Bat-Signal. Its ghostly finger stabbed at the stars. But without cloud cover, the bat emblem was lost in the stars.

Gordon sighed. He wondered why he kept faith with the masked man whose name he never knew.

He didn't hear the roof hatch ease up and a tall inky figure emerge. The figure padded forward, wrapped in a

ribbed black cloak against the bitter night. Burning
eyes looked out from a cowl whose erect ears resembled
Gothic church steeples.

"Gordon." The voice was sibilant and breathy.

Commissioner Gordon turned just as the silhouette of
the Batman spread its cloak to display a lean gray-clad
body.

"Batman! Where have you been?"

"Never mind. Long story. What counts is that I'm
here now."

"I had given up on you."

"Had you?" the other said, nodding to the Bat-Signal's
attenuated beam. His upraised cloak kept his face in
shadow.

"Almost," James Gordon admitted.

"I'm going to meet him."

"I can't stop you."

"Would you if you could?"

"The city's in an uproar. The mayor wants your head.
Politically, I'm between hammer and anvil."

"The mayor wants my head and the Joker wants my
face. I much prefer the Joker's alternative. I'm going to
have to unmask. I thought you'd want to be the first to
behold my true face."

Gordon started. "I-I'd be honored," he said solemnly.

The inky black figure drew closer. His boots were
eerily silent on the tarpaper roof. It was as if he glided
instead of walked.

As he entered the Bat Signal's backglow, his pale
pointed chin became visible. And the thin-lipped scarlet
leer it framed.

"Mwee hee heee!" the Joker cried, throwing back his
cowl.

"Joker!"

"Did you think that *you* were immune, Gordon?"

Gordon took an involuntary step backwards. "Stay
back!"

"The Batman doesn't care about the ordinary folk of
Gotham," the Joker growled. "So I thought I might lure
him from his belfry with a dear, dear, friend. *You!*"

Commissioner Gordon retreated to the roof edge.

There was no escape. The bat cloak followed him, enveloping like a shroud. He never felt the hypodermic bite into his forearm.

In the network of alleys near police headquarters, Batman parked the Batmobile in a deserted loading dock. He kept his cloak tight about him to stifle the betraying yellow-gold of his utility belt and chest emblem as he flitted from shadow to shadow.

Outside police headquarters, twin green globes shed a welcoming glow, but the Dark Knight ignored them. His shadowed eyes went to the rooftop where moths danced in a tunnel of light like paper bats.

Batman tested the old brick building facade with gloved fingers and began to scale in utter soundlessness.

He slid over the roof edge like something out of a Bram Stoker nightmare. The roof was deserted, the Bat Signal unattended. He reached over to shut it off when the backglow reflecting on glass stopped him. He strode over to the reflection and knelt.

He touched a familiar pair of eyeglasses resting on a pasteboard playing card. The leering face of the Joker stared back at him through the lenses.

The visible part of his face hardened into a grimace of hatred. Batman straightened up, crushing the card in one hand.

In a swirl of cloak fabric, he turned and disappeared over the parapet.

High above, the moths swirled around the Bat Signal as if feeding on a ghostly rag.

"Get those cameras set up!" The Joker called the order down from the gloomy catwalks of a vast industrial storage building.

Dutifully, Punkin Head and Jack-O'-Lantern hefted video cameras onto their Halloween shoulders.

"I don't get it, Boss," Jack grumbled. "Why are we bothering with all this junk? He won't show. And even if he does—"

"Leave the thinking to me, piefilling-for-brains," the Joker snarled. He turned to Commissioner Gordon, who sat with his wrists and ankles bound to the armrest and legs of a wooden chair perched precariously close to the catwalk's lip.

"You're mad!" he said gratingly.

"Thanks for the reminder," the Joker said acidly. "I had almost forgotten. And I'm getting fed up with your whining." He looked around the box-strewn catwalk, saying, "What to do, what to do? Ah!" His maniac eyes alighted on a carved jack-o'-lantern. Grinning, he upended it over Gordon's furious head.

"If you get hungry," the Joker told the upside-down jack-o'-lantern face as he descended the catwalk steps, "feel free to *gnaw*."

"Cameras all set up, boss," Punkin Head said, throwing the Joker an A-OK sign.

"Take your positions," the Joker snapped. "And let the charade begin. If he's going to come, he won't wait for tomorrow night."

Batman piloted the Batmobile through the industrial side of Gotham City. Through the knife-nosed steel bat's head mounted on the grille, he watched the headlights sweep the road. He had taken the old Batmobile out of storage. It was like driving an aircraft carrier on wheels. But the sporty open-cockpit version would not do for tonight's showdown.

The smokestacks of the Monarch Playing Card Factory came into view. He could almost smell the nostril-stinging vapors from an adjoining chemical plant even through the Batmobile's bulletproof Plexiglas dome.

It was there it had all begun. It was there that Batman had first accosted a red-hooded thief in the act of a crime. And it was there that the nameless man, fleeing the dreaded Batman, had fallen into the industrial waste sluice to emerge, white-faced and crack-grinned, as the Joker.

The gate came into view. Batman threw the wheel sharply to the right. The massive bat head rammed the padlocked fence apart. He accelerated. A corrugated loading door appeared in his bouncing headlight beams. The throaty roar of the Batmobile's engine became a song.

The door crumpled, and lifted, to bounce off the cockpit bubble. The Batmobile slewed right, sending a stacked pyramid of industrial drums rumbling and rolling in all directions. It skidded to a stop in the middle of the open concrete floor.

Batman waited.

"Did someone knock?" It was the Joker's mad voice. His narrow face peered up from a stack of drums.

Batman picked up a dashboard microphone and spoke into it. His steely amplified voice reverberated off the walls.

"I'm here, Joker."

"Noooo!" the Joker mocked. "And I thought you were the lead float of the Macy's Parade." He snapped his fingers. Punkin Head and Jack-O'-Lantern scooted down from the catwalks, lugging video cameras on their shoulders like a lunatic TV newscrew. They clambered atop the Batmobile, pressing their lenses to the dome.

"Any time you're ready," the Joker prompted.

Batman shook his head. "Commissioner Gordon, first," he said. "I have to know that he's alive."

"Alive?" the Joker squealed. "He's positively *jumping* with enthusiasm." The Clown Prince of Crime retreated into the shadows and pressed a wall switch. Overhead machinery started to grind. And down from the catwalk shadows came Commissioner Gordon, bound to a wooden chair, his head encased in an upside-down jack-o'-lantern. Gordon struggled in his suspended seat, making the chain hoist rattle like a skeleton. The chair legs clicked as they touched down beside the Clown Prince of Crime.

"You offered truce conditions," Batman said evenly.

"I give you my word you'll be allowed to leave unmolested," the Joker said. "If your performance is up to par. Ratings, you know."

"Throw in Gordon," Batman added. "Or no deal."

"That wasn't part of our bargain," the Joker sniffed.

"It is now," Batman said, his voice brittle. "Take it or leave it."

The Joker's eyes gleamed avidly. "And if I leave it?"

Batman gunned the Batmobile. It surged ahead, throwing the Joker's henchman onto the oil-stained concrete. The Joker cowered behind Commissioner Gordon, his eyes for once wider than his ear-threatening grin.

The Batmobile screeched to a stop with mere inches to spare. Its knifelike ram nose severed Gordon's leg bonds.

"You know this Batmobile is impregnable," Batman said. "I don't need your guarantee of safety. On the other hand, I *could* impale you to the wall."

The Joker smacked Gordon's pumpkin head. "Not without hurting the finest of Gotham's finest, your friend."

"You dare not harm him while I'm here—and you can't hide behind him forever."

"Hmmm," the Joker mused, fingering his needlelike chin. "Tell you what. I'm a taxpayer, too. Why don't I let our beloved commissioner walk away, and then we'll roll tape?"

Batman nodded. The Joker removed Gordon's pumpkin helmet and began untying his hands. Gordon stood up, rubbing his chafed wrists. He faced his antagonist.

"You—you vermin," he sputtered.

"Moi?" the Joker said archly.

"Gordon. Go. Now." Batman ordered in a no-nonsense voice.

Fixing the Joker with a final hate-filled glare, Commissioner Gordon walked away. He didn't look in Batman's direction.

"And don't even *think* of calling in your blue minions," the Joker called after him. "Or the whole thing's off."

After Gordon had left, Jack and Punkin Head climbed back onto the Batmobile. Their video camera zoomed in like a glassy-eyed cyclops.

"Are you ready, you annoying rodent?" the Joker called.

Without a word, Batman unfastened his cowl. As the Joker, fascinated, crept closer, he lifted it slowly.

The cowl fell to his lap. The face that looked out from the Batmobile's bulletproof dome was rough, the cheeks marred by tiny pockmarks, the nose bent from some ancient punishing blow. Batman patted unruly red locks back into place.

The Joker pressed his nose to the Plexiglas.

"No *wonder* you wear a mask," he squeaked. "You have a face even *my* mother couldn't love."

Batman said nothing. His green eyes were unreadable.

"Get him from every angle, boys," the Joker urged. "Don't scrimp on his best side. You *do* have a best side, don't you?"

"Yes. My dark side."

"Good quote. I'll use that. How do you feel, knowing that by this time tomorrow night, the entire population of Gotham City will be gaping at your naked puss on their TVs?"

"No comment."

"Awww. I was hoping for something more . . . pungent."

"All set, Joker," Jack said.

"Okay, let's get off the man's car. He's probably got a fortune sunk into the wax job."

The Joker's henchmen climbed off backwards, their cameras fixed on the Bat's impassive rough-featured face.

"How about a shot of you defiantly driving off into the sunset?" the Joker taunted.

"This isn't over yet," Batman said, replacing his cowl. He threw the Batmobile into reverse and backed out into the road. The wheels squealed as it shifted into drive and fled into the night.

"Did you get it?" the Joker said frantically. "Did you get it?"

"I'm checking," Punkin Head said, pulling a cassette from his camcorder. The Joker slapped it out of his hand. "Not that, you cretin! The overhead cameras."

Dropping their equipment, the Joker's henchmen

went up into the catwalk maze. They opened concealed panels and pulled out heavy metal photographic plates. Down below, the Joker was going through stacks of drums, doing the same.

They made a pile of plates on the floor.

Regarding his booty, the Joker's smile was like sick sunshine.

"Bring the van around," he snapped suddenly. "I don't trust that Gordon."

The lights of the Batcave came on automatically, actuated when the Batmobile intercepted a photoelectric beam at the cave entrance. They illuminated a giant penny, a full-sized Tyrannosaurus Rex, and other strange trophies of past cases.

Batman parked the old-model Batmobile beside the compact version and popped the dome.

He climbed out, shrugging off his long cloak and draping it over a computer. The cowl came off next. Batman looked inside. Flesh-colored gunk stuck to the lining.

Seating himself before a black vanity table, he began peeling latex appliances from his face. Wire inserts were plucked from his distended nostrils. Then came the bushy red eyebrows and green contact lenses.

The rock-jawed face of Bruce Wayne began to emerge as Alfred descended from Wayne Manor.

"It went well, I trust?" he inquired.

"Yes, thank you, Alfred. Your makeup job was excellent."

"I had a good foundation to work with," Alfred said modestly.

"Find out for me Commissioner Gordon's whereabouts. And be discreet, Alfred. I just want to know that he's safe."

"Of course, sir."

Bruce Wayne reached into his hairline and lifted the red wig affixed to his slicked-back hair with spirit gum.

"The joke is on you, Joker," he told his reflection. But he wasn't smiling.

* * *

"There is nothing wrong with your television set," the Joker's solemn voice intoned. As the Joker slipped into the familiar opening monologue to *The Outer Limits*, Bruce Wayne sipped tea in the warmth of the fireplace that had been transported, stone by stone, from a Zurich chalet, and watched the big-screen television. A VCR quietly toiled on a shelf, its record light angry and red.

The scrambled TV picture blipped and the Joker's lean figure appeared, seated at a pepper-green desk before a jet-black background. He held up a grainy blowup of Bruce Wayne's made-up face, obviously copied off a videotape.

"Have you seen this man?" the Joker asked seriously. "No?" He tore the photo in half and tossed it over his shoulder. "I'm not surprised. He's not Batman, any more than I am."

Bruce Wayne sat up tensely.

"Nice try, Bats. But next time get a better makeup artist. I recommend Dick Smith."

"I'm sorry, Master Bruce," Alfred called from the next room.

"It couldn't be helped, Alfred," Wayne said unhappily. His jaw muscles were hardening with tension.

The Joker reached out of camera range and brought forth a gleaming plastic skull. He held it up beside his face, as if for comparison purposes.

"Have you seen this man?" he asked. "This is the true face of Batman, after *all* the masks have been peeled away."

Behind him, the black background lit up. It was a mosaic of countless X-ray negatives, shot from every angle. Bruce Wayne recognized the subject. It was his own head, taken as he was in the act of removing his cowl. The X rays showed his skull from every conceivable angle—sides, back, and top.

"You are looking at the skull of the Batman," the Joker went on, "painstakingly recreated from the slides you see behind me."

The Joker set the skull down and brought a wet cone

pyramid of grayish clay impaled by a shaping tool into camera range. He used the tool to slap a dab of clay on the skull's cheek.

"Those of you of the *forensic* persuasion may have an inkling of what I'm doing," the Joker said, as he smoothed the clay onto the plastic bone with a white thumb. "Every skull is unique. Ask your neighborhood anthropologist. If you can find him. The one who constructed this little number for me, I fear, *expired* from overwork. Then you build up the features with clay, and presto—you have a recreation of the poor deceased's face."

Another blob of clay landed on the forehead. The Joker used his thumbs to smooth it into a smear. As he talked, the skull-white face slowly acquired a slick gray skin.

"You thought the joke was on the Joker, *didn't* you—Batman?" he mocked. "But the joke is on you. I have your skull. And soon I will have your face. And you can't stop me. As for the rest of you, tune in tomorrow night for the *real* unmasking of the Batman. I now return control of your television set to you—until *next* time. Toodles."

The screen went blank. The local newscasters came on, shuffling hastily prepared copy and trying not to stumble over their words. Bruce Wayne hit the remote off-switch.

"Can he really do it, Master Bruce?" Alfred asked timorously.

"I don't honestly know, Alfred," Bruce Wayne said distantly. "But the Joker is right about one thing—every skull *is* unique. And the technique he's using has put a face on more than one skeletal murder victim."

Commissioner James Gordon rubbed his tired eyes in the dark-wood sanctity of his office. He had just heard the bad news—the body of noted anthropologist Richard Parris had been discovered in Old Gotham Cemetery. The good news was he still had his face.

"Perhaps *these* will relieve your eyestrain," a cool voice said from the shadows.

Gordon started. He blinked at the long batlike silhouette standing framed by the window. A gauntleted hand opened to display Gordon's folded eyeglasses.

"How did you get in here?" Gordon demanded. "I posted men at the door."

Batman approached, his cloak rippling in a sudden draft. Gordon noted the open window behind him.

"My God, we're twelve stories up!" he blurted.

"But only three down." Batman's smile was tight and grim. "From the roof."

Gordon accepted the glasses and put them on.

"I looked for you when I left the factory," Batman said casually. "Thought you might appreciate a ride."

"I flagged down a black-and-white unit. Didn't tell them what had happened. Not for me, you understand. But the panic that would ensue if my abduction got out would—"

"I understand."

"Where were you?"

"Out of the country. I came as soon as I heard."

The tension in Gordon's face visibly lessened. "What are you going to do?" he asked.

"Steal back my skull," Batman said evenly. "But I'll need your help."

"What can I do?"

"I checked the card factory on my way over. Deserted. It's not the broadcast studio. But if I find it, I've got him."

"Do you think he can pull it off?"

"You know how reliable Facial Imaging Reconstructive Morphology is. He'll come close. Too close. I want to see videotapes of the first transmissions."

"No, you don't," Gordon said quickly. Then, relenting, "We have them upstairs. Come on."

Waving the surprised police guards aside, Commissioner Gordon led Batman to a conference room where a television and video hookup occupied a corner shelf.

Gordon loaded the first tape, saying, "We've been over these. There are no sound clues or signal signatures, no leads."

"We'll see," Batman said. He watched both tapes in

silence, without flinching. Only the stress of the black fabric over his gauntlet knuckles signified the ordeal he stoically endured.

"You can't blame yourself," Gordon said, noticing the telltale tightening of fabric.

"I don't," Batman clipped. "I blame the Joker. Let's go through them again," he added, cupping his chin in one hand.

Gordon shuddered. "I'm not sure I'm up for another rerun."

"Just one scene, Jim," Batman said, reinserting the first cassette. "Look at this." Batman fast-forwarded to the spot where Punkin Head and Jack-O'-Lantern first appeared on the Bittner murder tape, and let it run.

"Which is which, you wonder?" the Joker was saying. "Dear me, I can hardly tell myself. They're twins, you know."

Batman turned to Gordon. "What do you think?"

"A joke?"

"Know any career criminal twin brothers?"

Gordon snapped his fingers. "The Melopopone twins! Carlo and Remo."

"Never heard of them."

"Small-timers. Punks. Losers. And not very bright."

"Exactly the kind the Joker likes to surround himself with," Batman pointed out. "No self-respecting criminals would wear pumpkins over their heads. Any known associates? Or a recent address?"

"Let's find out."

Moments later, the sullen, unintelligent faces of the Melopopone twins stared up at Batman from a thick mug book.

Commissioner Gordon read from a file. "They live in Crime Alley. Or did." He looked up. "That's where the second body turned up."

"I'll be in touch," Batman said, exchanging the mug book for their address. He slipped out the window. Gordon shut it behind him, feeling as if a crushing weight had lifted from his shoulders.

*   *   *

The Gotham skyline was turning pink when the Melo-popone twins' flashy convertible finally pulled up to their Basin Street tenement, just off the notorious Crime Alley section of town. Their complaining voices rose as they stumped up the delapidated stoop. It reached the hooded ears of Batman, up on the roof. He went over the parapet to an open third-floor window he'd jimmied hours before.

"Thought this night would never end," Carlo was say-ing as they clumped up the hall stairs.

"Did you see the way he was flinging clay on that thing?" Remo shot back. "Like a crazy guy."

"He *is* a crazy guy, stoopid."

"Oh, right."

Carlo unlocked the apartment door and pushed. "It's stuck," he complained. Remo pushed him aside and hit the door with his shoulder. Momentum carried him in. A crunching black boot to his flat face propelled him out again.

Carlo watched stupefied as his brother tumbled down the winding steps like a human accordion. He looked back at the apartment door.

A terrible black and gray figure stood in the doorway. It lifted batlike wings and advanced on him.

"He's in the Stigman Building," Carlo blurted out.

Batman stopped. "What?"

"The Stigman Building. That's what you want, isn't it? That's where he broadcasts from. Top floor. Company name is Wildcard Video."

The frightening cloak lowered slowly, almost disap-pointedly.

"What else can you tell me?" Batman hissed.

"That's all of it. Honest."

"Thanks," Batman said, driving a right hook into Carlo's undershot jaw. Carlo went down the stairs to land on top of his insensate brother. Batman stepped over the pile of human wreckage on his way to the wait-ing Batmobile.

The Batmobile careened through the early morning

light. Batman hated to prowl by daylight, even this
early, before most decent citizens were up. Night was his
wine. But it was a race against time. In his mind's eye,
he could see the Joker hunched over that mocking plastic skull—his skull—maniacally applying clay and
molding features up from the bone, recreating the well-
known face of millionaire Bruce Wayne.

The Joker worried the corner of his red lips with a pink
tongue. He squinted one eye as he carefully held the
clay-covered skull up to the flourescent light.

"Too much jaw," he decided, and pulled a pinch from
the point of the chin. He smoothed the indentation, nodded and added a tiny cleft with a wooden tool.

"Perfect! I don't know who you belong to," he said,
addressing the mute skull, "but tonight I make you a
star. Remember, I get ten percent of the rest of your
life."

He returned the skull to a pottery wheel, sprinkled it
with water to keep the clay malleable, and covered it
with plastic. Carefully, he placed the skull in a white
cardboard hatbox, sealing the lid with Scotch tape.

"I'll fire you after the show," he muttered. "Can't risk
that million-dollar face cracking in the kiln."

Clutching the box, the Joker rose up. Just as quickly,
he sat down again. His eye had caught sight of the Emmett Kelly clown plaque by the door. Its red nose glowed
like a radioactive cherry.

"Uh-oh, company," he said. "Now who would come
calling at *this* hour?" He set the box before him and
reached under the table with one hand. It came up holding a black plastic Uzi. He shook it. It sloshed reassuringly. His grin stretched taut like a rubber band.

The Joker fixed his beady eyes on the bank of windows that lined the north wall and waited. He was surprised when he heard footsteps behind him.

The Joker spun around, coming to his feet.

"Clever. Very clever," he told the batlike figure in the
now-open doorway. It stood like a bat at rest, its capelike

wings drooping as if in sorrow. "I expected you to come in through the window," he added.

The figure said nothing. It simply stood there, the head an indistinguishable blur.

"And I heard you coming a mile away. You're slipping, Bats."

The figure stood resolute. "I suppose you want this," the Joker said, hefting the hatbox high. The other hand kept the plastic Uzi trained on the figure. He tried to sight on the bat symbol, but it was lost in the shadow of the enfolding cloak.

"Well, don't just hang there, say something banal." Silence. "No? Then show me some *bone!*" The Joker squeezed the trigger and a jet of yellow liquid squirted the length of the room. It struck the figure of Batman square in the chest, sending up hissing billows as the acid ate away at the cloak fabric.

The Joker squinted through the stinky vapor, looking for the welcome expression of pain under the cowl. Through the rags of smoke, he saw the cloak shrivel like burning paper . . . revealing an old-fashioned wooden coatrack. His eyes went wide.

Then he screamed.

The crash of glass came from the north wall. The Joker whirled. Too late. Flying boot soles propelled him the length of the room. The Uzi went flying. But the Clown Prince of Crime held onto his precious box. On his stomach, he crawled for the acid pistol. He reached out. A black boot stamped on it.

The Joker scuttled back. He came up on his feet, laughing softly, warily, his eyes darting crazily, as if inflicted by nystagmus.

"I guess you *know* what's in the box?" he taunted.

"I know what's in the box," Batman said. His face under the cowl was grim. He wore no cloak.

"Trade you?" the Joker suggested. "The box for your cowl?"

"No deal," said Batman, striding toward him.

"Just as well. I won't be satisfied until I unmask you right down to the bone. That's where the truth really lies, you know. In the bone. It's the *ultimate* nitty-gritty."

The Joker backed into the wall. The Emmett Kelly plaque was directly behind him. When he felt the nose against his spine, he leaned back. He heard a welcome click. A ladder-equipped trapdoor dropped from the ceiling. The Joker slid up it like an eel.

Batman leaped for it, snaring the lowest rung. He rolled onto the ladder as the trap lifted flush with the roof.

The Joker was waiting for him, knife in hand. He slashed down, the box held clumsily in the other hand.

Batman rolled to one side, evading the awkward blow. He leaped to his feet.

"You'll need more than a knife to protect yourself from me," Batman warned. He feinted with one hand. The Joker ducked. Batman kicked out, clipping the Joker's ankle. The Clown Prince of Crime stumbled back, brandishing the knife before him.

"No, you don't. It may be your skull, but it's my handiwork," the Joker taunted. "Behave and I'll cut you in on the royalties."

Batman reached into his utility belt for a Batarang and clipped a length of nylon line to it. He started swinging it overhead like a bola. It made a dull warning sound like an old-fashioned roar devil.

Batman came on. To his surprise, the Joker pocketed the knife and undid his bola tie. Holding it loosely by the cords, he mimicked Batman's stance, copying the whirling action.

"Duel of the bolas, Batman? Or is yours a bolo? I'm so bad with names. If only the cameras were running. This is priceless." He looked behind him, toward a solitary toolshed, and began walking backwards.

Batman let fly. Simultaneously, the Joker released his bola tie. The Batarang tangled the Joker's legs. He went down. But the tie snared Batman's neck like a noose. The turquoise slide raced for his neck like a spider after a web-caught fly. Batman grabbed his throat and doubled over.

"Did I say *bola?*" the Joker chortled. "Well, excuuuse me. I mean *boa*—as in constrictor!"

And while the Dark Knight Detective struggled with the mechanical garrote, the Joker calmly severed the

Batarang cord with his knife and stumbled toward the
toolshed, the box in hand.

He undid the hasp and pulled out a hang glider with a
death's-head moth painted on the wing. Assembling it
quickly, he climbed into the harness. The hatbox
clutched tightly, he set himself for the run off the roof.

Back by the ladder trap, Batman had sunk to his
knees, pulling on the constricting bola tie with both
hands. The lower part of his face was turning a sullen
lavender. His nostrils flared, straining for air.

"Don't you just *hate* these choked-up good-byes," the
Joker squealed and began running. He vaulted into the
air. The hang glider dipped unsteadily, then rose again
as an updraft caught it. The Joker leaned into the wind
and sent it circling back, his eyes gloating.

Down below, Batman was struggling on. One hand
groped for his utility belt and brought forth a plastic
capsule. He broke it against the tie clasp. There was a
spurt of white smoke and the tie snapped away like a
broken spring.

Batman came to his feet unsteadily, shaking off an
acid-burned glove. He looked up, his cowled countenance
an Art-Deco abstraction.

"Sorry I can't stick around," the Joker called down.
"But the show must go on." He lifted the cardboard box
mockingly. "Write if you get work."

The hang glider began to rise.

Calmly, resolutely, Batman retrieved his Batarang
and pitched it.

It rose, looped, and came around in a wild impossible
curve. It missed the hang glider by twenty yards on the
way up.

"Nah, nah, you missed," the Joker taunted.

His smug expression broke apart as the Batarang
flashed by his purple shoulder on the way down. The
hang glider listed. The Joker fought to get it level. He
saw the tear the Batarang had made in the fabric above
his head. His eyes went stark.

Down below, Batman caught the returning Batarang
with practiced ease.

He called up. "Care to go again?"

The Joker saw that he was losing altitude. He kicked off his purple shoes. The glider rose slightly, but its downward spiral resumed immediately. Resting his chin on the control bar, he began emptying his pockets in a desperate attempt to lighten the wing's burden. A long-barreled pistol came out, followed by a deck of razor-edged playing cards, an acid-squirting flower, and finally his knife. The roof slid out from under his woolly purple stockings and he was looking down the sickening drop to midtown Gotham City.

"Toss me the box," Batman called. "Or I clip your wings."

The Joker hesitated. If he could reach the roof, Batman had him. If he didn't, Batman would send him to a hard, hard landing. Either way, the box was lost.

"Curses," he muttered in a Snidely Whiplash voice. "Foiled again." He pitched the box, and fought to regain equilibrium.

Batman ran to intercept it. The heavy box fell into his hands as if meant for them.

Like a limping goonybird, the Joker glided off into the sunrise. He was already out of Batarang range.

Batman stood on the parapet edge, oblivious to the fifty-story drop, and watched him go with cold empty eyes. Long after the Joker had dwindled to nothingness, he kept his eyes on the horizon.

Then, wordlessly, he walked away, the box safe under one arm.

Hours later, the box lay, still unopened, on the ebony table in the Batcave. Bruce Wayne was in costume, his cowl resting on a fresh cape next to the box.

He was talking into an untraceable phone.

"No sign of him, Commissioner?" he was saying. "I see. Yes, I agree. We'll hear from him again. But not soon. He likes to lick his wounds awhile. At least we got the Melopopone twins."

Wayne's eyes went to the hatbox.

"The box? No, I haven't opened it yet. I'm afraid I'll

have to keep what I find inside a secret. You understand.
Yes. Good-bye, Jim."

Batman hung up. His eyes went to the box again.

Alfred came down the stairs and cleared his throat.
"Don't you think you should rest, Master Bruce? It's
noon. And you've not slept in nearly twenty-four hours."

"One last item and I'm done for the night," he said,
lifting the lid.

Alfred drew closer as Batman reached into the box
and withdrew the plastic-covered object.

He lifted the plastic. His jaw tightened. Alfred
gasped.

The face that stared up at him was a face only in that
it had eye sockets, a nose, and a mouth. The features
were twisted, bloated and gouged like an elephantiasis
sufferer. There was nothing recognizably human in its
slick gray contours.

The gash of a mouth clamped a folded notecard. Batman pulled it free. He opened it and read the green ink
message:

IF YOU HAPPEN TO READ THIS, BATS, YOU
NOW KNOW MY DEEPEST, DARKEST SECRET: IN
KINDERGARTEN, I FLUNKED MODELING WITH
CLAY!

The note was signed "The Joker."

Dying Is Easy, *Comedy* Is Hard

Edward Bryant and Dan Simmons

Seeing Johnny Carson rip off his own face, just like one of those effects in an early David Cronenberg movie, was bad enough. But what came next was *truly* grotesque.

I gotta admit, I stared. But then we all had to be an appreciative audience—the goons with Uzis and MAC-10s, and H&K miniguns made sure of that. If you're wondering how I know so much about all that cool ordnance, it's not 'cause I spend a lot of time on the street—it's because I see a lot of B-movies. . . .

I really hope I live to go to a lot more. . . .

The Aladdin Theater is named after the dude that rubbed a lamp and got a genie. Right now I wish I had the three wishes that guy received. All of us here on the stage do. No genie coming out tonight. Nope, just pain, blood, and a whole lot of grief.

Frankly, it's enough to make me rethink my career. . . .

I admit it, I come alive—*truly alive*—only at night. Then I descend on the concrete canyons and brick catacombs of Gotham City, take the train into its decaying downtown between Art Deco skyscrapers from some earlier age, walk its rainswept streets and ratty back alleys smelling of garbage and the homeless, seek out its base-

ment improv clubs and East Side nightclubs sandwiched
in between the porno palaces and hotsheet hotels—the
clubs smelling of cigars and cheap perfume and urine
and something much worse: *flop sweat*—and then, only
then, in the dark belly of this dying city, performing for
the drunks and adulterers and lost souls and lonely in-
somniacs, *then* I come alive. Then—in the dark, with the
bile of fear burning at my insides and the stench of
failure and humiliation just a short arc of silence
away—then my *true* life begins.

I know now that I'm not alone. There are others who
come alive at night, in the back alleys of Gotham City.
Others who wait through the mundane turning of days
for the violent whirl of night's greatest realities. Others
who shed their daylight skins and become *other people*. I
know that now.

The creature that calls himself the Joker is one. The
Batman—that human puzzle wrapped in a cowl and
enigma—is another. I know that now.

And I almost understand.

This isn't going well. Where to start?

My name is Pete Tulley. I'm twenty-nine years old,
black—or African-American as the self-appointed
spokespersons of our race now say, not married, not living with anyone right now, and during the day I'm a
manager of the Burger Biggie franchise on the corner of
Sprang and Robinson. It's not really that bad of a job.
The hardest part is keeping a steady flow of kids trained
and working behind the counter, getting them to understand that Burger Biggie is a *job*, a responsibility, and
not just a place to hang out and laugh with their friends
while the customer stands and waits for his Biggie and
fries. I'm a graduate of Burger Biggie Hamburger College—the franchise's four-week training school in
Peoria, Illinois—and as stupid as that sounds, as easy as
it is to sneer at the idea of a Hamburger College, the
chain actually stands for something (even if that "some-

thing" is only good fast food, prepared promptly to na-
tionwide standards of taste and quality of ingredients, in
clean surroundings), and I try to communicate those
standards to the people I train and manage. I must be at
least partially successful at that since my Biggie at
Sprang and Robinson has won the Gotham City metro-
area B.B. Excellence and Cleanliness Award two years
running.

And despite the obvious temptation—since stand-ups
are like fiction writers in that they *use* everything
around them—I've never done hamburger franchise
jokes in my routines. It seems like too cheap a shot. Plus,
I owe *something* to the people who keep me employed in
the daytime so I can come alive at night.

But I'll use the gags someday. In the long run, nothing is sacred.

I've been a stand-up comic for three years. Three
years this March. Like most would-be comics, I started
by getting a laugh from my family when I was a little
kid. (I remember the first time—it was unintentional—I
was six and watching a Dolly Parton special on TV and
said, "I bet she can swim real good with those inflated
things on her chest." If we'd been alone that evening, my
mother probably would have frowned and my dad would
have swatted me on the side of the head, but we had
Uncle Louis and Aunt Nell and Cousin Sook and a
bunch of other folks over—they'd been drinking beer
since the picnic that afternoon—and the room just
howled with laughter. It became a sort of family joke—
Uncle Louis used to mention it about everytime we got
together—and it was really the first time I'd been noticed by everyone. Or at least the first time they'd all
noticed me and *liked* me.)

Anyway, it taught me that sex gets laughs, and if you
can throw in some popular culture or a public figure, so
much the better.

I went to Charity Hills High School—although there
were no hills in our old Southside suburb of Gotham and
by the midseventies there was damned little charity either—and I became a comic there just to survive.
Charity Hills had inherited most of the Gotham City

gangs by then, sort of gang franchises, I guess you might say, and to stay an independent you had to be incredibly smart or damn tough. I was neither. So I made myself funny.

The caption under my high school yearbook photo says "Always good for a laugh" and that was my armor and chameleon cloak. I figured that the jocks and street goons and dopeheads and musclebound dipshits who ordinarily showed their superiority by beating up wimpy types like me would think twice if I had a reputation as a clown. I figured that it might be easier for them to laugh at me—make me perform for their peers in the hallways and gyms and cloakrooms of dear old CHHS rather than stomp the crap out of me. And it worked. Most of the time.

Anyway, I started taking comedy seriously a couple of years ago, after I realized that nothing else in my life was going to give me a life worth living. I started out in the suburban improv clubs, getting in on amateur nights where people came to laugh *at* us rather than *with* us. That was okay. I was used to it. I always threw up before a performance, but I soon began to judge audience response by whether I threw up *after* the show.

I spent a long, hungry summer out in the Los Angeles area, getting booked for very few performances of my own, but getting to see a lot of the greats in the field at their old comedy club stomping grounds. The field of amateurs was too rich for me to compete out there, so I came back to Gotham City—where at least I knew a few of the club owners, had done them favors and could get a few in return. And besides, Burger Biggie doesn't have any franchises west of the Mississippi.

And so I came alive at night for two years and then some, taking the 10:38 P.M. train in from Finger Park to Gotham Center, performing for money when I could— usually at one of the East Side back-alley basement clubs, a place for the slum dwellers to come in out of the cold and for the yuppies and dinner-jacket types to go slumming—but usually I had to settle for another amateur night, another contest, or another free-drinks and dinner-if-you-get-here-early-enough performance.

I got to know most of the other comedy club circuit people. A few went on to the ranks of the serious professional. One got rich and famous and died snorting bad coke in Las Vegas last fall. Most got discouraged, dropped out, and have been replaced by younger would-be somebodies. A few, like me, have hung in there and taken what they could get—honing their material, slowly improving their performances and on-stage personalities, trying to make up in experience and sheer persistence what they lack in talent. A few of these other survivors of the Long March have become friends. Some of the rest are real assholes. All of them, friends and assholes alike, are competitors.

But in a strange way we are like some medieval guild: aging apprentices hoping to become journeymen and praying to be elevated to Master. We're sort of a family of misfit hopefuls, sharing nothing but our common dream and the fact that we come alive only at night, in front of the audience.

And then the Joker started killing us.

It was last November in that gray, dead-branch period between the childlike nonsense of Halloween and the all-too-adult loneliness of Thanksgiving. The Carob Comedy Club on Alameda and Franklin had been staging a three-week Comedy Countdown—shows every Tuesday and Saturday—with a bunch of us eliminating each other via applause-o-meter showdown for a five-hundred-dollar first prize. That sounds like a decent amount until you realize that Al Jacobs, manager of the Carob, had over a dozen amateur comics firing off their best material twice a night, two times a week for three weeks, and only the winner would end up getting anything.

Anyway, it was the final Saturday night and the original mob of stand-ups had been winnowed down to seven—me, my cracker friend Boonie Sandhill, a tired old ex-borscht-belt comic named Dandy John Diamond, a Roseanne Barr imitation called Tiffany Strbynsky, a gifted black teenager named Fast Eddie Teck, a beau-

tiful but not very funny medical student named Diana
Mulhollen, and George Marlin. I'd drawn the first slot
for the late show and the audience wasn't just cold, it
was frigid. I gave it my best shot—using my Cola Wars
stuff where every major world event of the past three
decades was explained as an incidental by-product of the
global sales war between Coke and Pepsi—but either
the material was too cerebral for this crowd or it just
wasn't my night. I knew I was out of the running even
before I took my bows, reset the mike on the stand, and
backed out of the spotlight. At least Tiffany waddled
onstage to a warmer crowd.

Al Jacobs lets us early casualties sit at the bar and
down a few comped drinks while we watch the others
work. Tiffany was hot this night, but she still was only a
good imitation of the real thing and even though the applause-o-meter swung almost half again as far to the
right as it had for me, I knew that the race would be
between Fast Eddie and George Marlin.

Marlin was next and he hit the audience hard and
fast. New Jersey was overweight but he never did fat
jokes; his dialect was so Brooklynesque that it made
Boone Sandhill's drawl sound normal, but Marlin didn't
rely on dialect or borough in-jokes. He rarely did the off-
color stuff that makes up ninety percent of club routines
these days. George was just *funny* and he generally just
schmoozed along with tales from his childhood and early
adolescence that had the sense of *this-really-happened*,
which every comedy bit needs and so few have.

So George was telling about his days as a lonely teenager and how he was convinced he was a superhero—the
Dung Beetle, armored nemesis of evil-doers everywhere—and the audience was roaring and I was on my
third vodka rocks and the applause-o-meter was pinning
itself and I was wondering idly whether Fast Eddie's
street-smart vulgar strut'n'jive routine could top this
stuff, when suddenly George stopped in midroutine and
stared at the microphone in his hand.

The head of the mike was growing, inflating like a
balloon. George stepped back, still holding the thing and
watching it expand, and because Al Jacobs was too

cheap to install cordless traveling mikes, George got
tangled in the wire and glanced back to see what was
stopping him. Meanwhile, the audience was still roaring, thinking—as I did for a second—that the expanding
mike was part of the routine, some phallic gag.

In those final seconds, George knew it wasn't part of
the night's entertainment; the head of the mike was a
metal sphere and it had grown to the size of a soccer ball.
Still tangled in the cord, George started to drop the microphone as if it were the business end of a snake.

The audience roared. The mike exploded in some sort
of shaped charge, taking off most of George's head and
smearing the maroon curtains behind him with hair,
blood, and brain matter.

Laughter is like an avalanche—slow to get started,
but once its moving it has an inertia of its own. Even
with the gasps and screams of shock, it took ten or fifteen seconds for the last waves of laughter to die out.
Then, for a moment, there was silence except for a few
sobs from a woman near the front.

George's pear-shaped body had stood there for a second or two, headless, his fingers still curved around the
mike he was in the process of dropping. Then the corpse
fell forward and hit the boards with a sound I will never
forget, arterial blood sprayed the closest tables, and the
room was filled with chaos as everyone—myself included—stood, shouted, cried for help, or merely
screamed. I remember that Diane Mulholland rushed
from backstage and knelt next to George—the knees of
her pantyhose wicked red from the blood. She looked offstage as if seeking help. Al Jacobs rushed onstage, froze
as if he were physically incapable of coming closer to the
corpse, and stood there, wringing his hands and grimacing.

I set down my drink and stood on the lowest rung of
the barstool, just trying to see over the heads of the
mindlessly surging crowd.

And then, a moment after the laughter ended and the
shouts and sobs and cries of confusion began to ebb toward a more sinister silence, then the *laughter* began.

It was not quite laughter. It was more like the

frenzied barking of a jackal or the amplified cough of a
hyena than any sound of mirth I'd ever heard come from
a human throat. And then the face appeared.

Ten feet tall, white-skinned and green-haired, teeth
yellowed within the terrible rictus that passed for a grin,
the giant head materialized and floated in midair above
George's body. If George's corpse had remained standing, this bloated visage would have replaced his missing
head like someone poking his face through a cardboard
cutout at a boardwalk photo booth.

It took me a second to realize that I was looking at the
Joker. Living in Gotham City most of my life, I'd seen
news photographs and the rare snippets of videotape,
but they had seemed unreal, cartoonlike, and this nightmare face floating above George's corpse was all too real.

Diane screamed and flinched away from the appari-
tion. Al Jacobs backed to the edge of the stage, teetered,
and crouched, holding one arm above his bald head as if
ready to ward off a blow.

The Joker laughed. The image seemed solid. I saw the
pores in the white flesh, noticed the pink gums above
yellow teeth, and watched as the wide eyes blinked in
merriment and pure insanity. The laughter echoed off
walls and curtains as patrons fled, shoving over tables in
their haste to reach the fire exits. Diane Mulholland
slumped unconscious in a pool of George's blood.

The image of the Joker glanced down at her as if the
projection could actually *see,* smiled, and lifted its long
chin. It . . . *he* . . . was looking across the heads of the
crowd directly at me.

"TUT, TUT, TUT," came the amplified voice. I re-
member seeing Charles Manson interviewed once on
Sixty Minutes. Manson's voice sounded like Dan
Rather's compared to the black-ice tones I heard now. "I
GUESS THIS FELLOW HAS NO HEAD FOR COM-
EDY!"

The crazy laughter rose in volume. Behind me I heard
shouts at the front entrance, knew the cops had arrived,
but I wasn't able to turn away from that wild-eyed gaze.

"WELL, HE WON'T BE THE LAST TO GIVE HIS
ALL TO LADY COMEDY," echoed the mad voice. The

image giggled, and then a strange transformation came
over the face. It was as if rats were scurrying under the
white cheesecloth of the Joker's flesh. At first, I though'
it might be a malfunction of the projector or whatever i:
was, but then I realized that it was the Joker's actua
features that were shifting, sliding into different pat
terns, jerking like the expression of a doll in a clumsily
made claymation cartoon.

The Joker was no longer smiling. His green hai:
seemed to wave like seaweed in a strong current as h(
glared down at the last fleeing patrons, flicked a glanc(
at the corpse, and then returned his gaze to me. "THERF
IS ONLY ONE JOKER IN GOTHAM CITY."

He was gone. The cops burst in, ran around, swung
their revolvers in that self-conscious two-armed pose w(
see on TV every night, and shouted at each other ove
the din. Some stood around George's corpse and looke(
as helpless as Al Jacobs had, while others rushed back
stage, guns still drawn.

I knew they wouldn't find the Joker. I lifted my glas:
and finished my drink. My hands were shaking so har(
that I had to use both of them to get the glass to m:
mouth without spilling the last of my vodka.

They kept us until almost four in the morning. I'd neve:
been interrogated before and it wasn't much like th(
movies. They didn't grill me, they didn't use the good
cop, bad-cop routine, and nobody shone a bright light ir
my face. In fact, they interviewed us one at a time in th(
long, narrow storeroom in the back of Al's club, and
there was hardly enough light to *see* the two homicid(
detectives asking the questions. They sounded more
tired than I was. One of them had a serious smoker':
cough and sucked on lozenges between cigarettes.

Mostly, it was boring. They went over everything
twice, then a third time. Then they started again.

"Are you sure Mr. Marlin said nothing to you in the
green room?" the cop with the cough asked.

I sighed and began to give the same answer I'd giver
them thrice before. Then a shadow in the corner behind

them moved, detached itself from the darkness there, and glided toward us.

"Holy shit," I whispered.

It was the Batman. I heard his cape rustle, caught a glimpse of the peaked points on the dark cowl, but mostly he blended into the darkness in that little room. Only his face and that weird emblem on his chest seemed to reflect light.

He glided forward until he loomed over me, wrinkles in that cape glinting like black silk where they glinted at all. The cops made room for him but said nothing. I *couldn't* say anything at that moment.

I know, you live in Gotham City most of your life, you're supposed to see the Batman all the time. Well, you don't, any more than you chat with Dustin Hoffman a lot if you live in L.A. or lunch with Donald Trump if you hang around New York. Oh, you see photos in the paper every once in a while and I *almost* saw Batman at a dedication of a new community center in Charity Hills once when I was twelve . . . but my dad and I got stuck in traffic and when we got there he was gone. You live in Gotham, you take a sort of pride in being identified with the Bat Guy . . . sort of like San Francisco residents are proud of the Golden Gate Bridge . . . but you don't *see* him. To tell the truth, it'd been so long since I'd even read about him, that I'd sort of forgotten he was real.

He was real enough now.

I sat back, tried to look cool, tried not to gulp visibly as this cowled face leaned forward, neck muscles all corded under black silk, tried to listen coolly rather than scream when that gloved hand touched my shoulder. I'm thin, average height, but no wimp. Still, I had the definite impression that his hand could pulverize my collarbone and shoulder just by giving a squeeze.

He didn't squeeze.

"Mr. Tulley," he said. His voice sounded soft, almost preoccupied. But I sure as hell wouldn't want to get the owner of that voice angry. "Mr. Tulley, do you know any reason why someone . . . even the Joker . . . would want to kill George Marlin?"

"Uh-uh," I said, always a snappy one with repartee.

I could see his eyes through slits in that midnight cowl. I'm pretty observant—stand-up comics have to be—but I have no idea what color they were.

"Mr. Tulley, is there *anything* that you haven't mentioned which you think might help us with this investigation?"

"Uh-uh." This time I managed to punctuate it by shaking my head.

The Batman nodded—more toward the two cops than at me—and then he took a step back and seemed to blend back into the shadows like black ink spilled on a dark velvet cloth.

The cop with the smoker's cough led me to the door while I strained to keep from peering over my shoulder at the corner.

"Thanks, Mr. Tulley," said the detective. I could smell the lozenge he was chewing on. "Go home and get some rest. We'll call you if we need you, but I think this'll be all."

"Uh-huh," I said, grateful to be leaving, grateful to be getting out of that little room.

But it wasn't all. Not by a long shot.

Bruce appeared one day after the second murder.

It was three nights later, some of us were working the old Aladdin Dinner Theater, figuring that whoever was taking notes on comics for the joke-off would probably hit Aladdin's traditional Tuesday Night Laugh Riot.

Somebody hit it all right.

The Aladdin is one of the great old movie palaces built during the early days of the Depression. It's part Taj Mahal, part Pharaoh's tomb, a bit of Baghdad, and a whole lot of old-movie fantasy. The place is gigantic, with two levels of balconies, box seats, red carpets, murals, and corridors like caverns out of an Indiana Jones movie: rococo ornamentation everywhere, bronze hands holding torches for lighting fixtures, dusty chandeliers—the whole bit. Aladdin's had decayed to the point of being a downtown porno theater in the sixties, was converted to a disco during the seventies, was aban-

doned for a while, and then became a dinner theater cum
nightclub during the mid-eighties.

The place was too big for comedy: the night Tiffany
was murdered, there were almost as many of us waiting
to go onstage as there were people in the audience. The
rows of theater seats behind the tables were empty, the
balconies were dark, and the private boxes were sealed
off. The small lamps on the dozen tables near the stage
shed little light. The place smelled of mildewed carpets,
old cigars, and rot.

And *flop sweat.*

There was a plainclothes detective in the audience.
Max Weber, Aladdin's manager, had pointed him out.
He didn't need to. Anybody could have spotted the shiny
black suit, paunch, clip-on holster, and white socks and
made the old guy as a cop.

People weren't laughing when Tiffany died. She was
having a bad night; the Roseanne Barr material wasn't
working, there was a heckler down front whom she
couldn't out-nasty, and she was sweating heavily . . . obviously just trying to get through to the end of the routine. I was on last, still at least forty-five minutes to go
after Fast Eddie and a couple of others, so I was having a
drink at an empty table and feeling sorry for Tiffany.

Suddenly, in midpunchline, a glass box came sliding
down on wires from the dark catwalks above and
slammed onto the stage, enclosing Tiffany as surely as
an entymologist's plastic jar would trap a bug.

There was a click, the mike cord was severed, and
Tiffany stumbled as some sort of bottom slid under her,
sealing the glass box. It couldn't be glass of course—I
realized even then that it had to be some sort of plastic
or Plexiglas—but it *looked* like a glass phone booth.

Tiffany screamed, but her shouts were made almost
inaudible by the cage. The plainclothes cop stared a moment and then jumped to his feet, groping for the gun on
his belt.

The Joker walked onstage, aimed his cane, and shot
the cop. Actually, the head of the cane flew through the
air, trailing a thin wire, and slammed into the cop's
chest. The fat detective spasmed and collapsed. We

learned later that the cane had fired something called a taser . . . a sort of high-voltage stun weapon. It wasn't designed to kill. The Joker couldn't have known that the detective had been fitted for a pacemaker . . . or maybe he did.

Anyway, the cop spasmed and died, Tiffany's mouth moved as she pounded the Plexiglas, and the Joker bowed. He was wearing an old-style tuxedo, the formal effect spoiled only slightly by a bright green cravat he wore in lieu of a bow tie, purple spats, and purple gloves. He completed his bow and looked at Tiffany in her box as if he had just noticed her. "*God*, how sad!" He pouted almost effeminately. "*Poor* girl . . . trying *so* hard, and your only reward is *flop sweat!*"

The Joker snapped his fingers. Water began pouring from invisible ducts in the box, pooling around Tiffany's ankles. She screamed more loudly; it was just audible through the plastic. Fast Eddie Teck charged onstage, a switchblade knife in his hand. The Joker tasered him unconscious with a flick of his cane.

"For those of you who don't *know* theater talk," lisped the Joker, showing us flashes of his yellow teeth all the way back to the molars, "*flop sweat* is the ultimate pan notice . . . the sheen of ultimate failure, the glow of abject panic . . . the *perspiration* of *expiration!*"

The liquid rose to Tiffany's shoulders, then to her chins. Her orange silk caftan floated around her. She jumped, pounded at the walls, clawed at plastic. The fluid rose until only her mouth and nose were clear of it as she strained against the roof of the box.

I rushed toward the stage and stopped as the Joker tasered two would-be rescuers in front of me. He snapped his fingers and a second cane appeared in his other hand.

"Tut, tut." The Joker grinned. "Never interrupt an *artist* at work." He glanced over his shoulder at Tiffany. The box had filled with clear liquid; she was no longer struggling. A few final bubbles of air rose from her nose and open mouth and tangled in her swaying hair.

The Joker walked over to the box and patted the side

of it almost affectionately. "You don't sweat much," he said to Tiffany's corpse. "For a *fat* lady."

A dozen of us had come out of the shock and horror sufficiently to prepare to rush the Joker *en masse*. He twirled his cane. "Oh, I wouldn't recommend giving fatso mouth-to-mouth," he said, showing an expression of revulsion. "You see, this *flop sweat* isn't *water*, it's hydrochloric *acid!*" He grinned at us, waggled gloved fingers, and said, "Ta ta! See you all—or at least the survivors—at the joke-off!"

He laughed insanely. A bunch of us climbed onstage, rushed him. The Joker calmly bowed, caught one of the wires above the box, and rose out of sight into the darkness.

It took us almost five minutes to find a fire ax to crack the plastic box.

It *was* acid.

The guy named Bruce appeared and performed the next night at the Carob Club. He was awful. He did a routine that wouldn't have gotten a laugh in 1952, much less during the beginning of the hip, raunchy nineties. The jokes were flat, his timing was nonexistent, he didn't seem to care whether the audience was there or not, and his body language was *bad*. I mean, I saw the guy move before and after the show, and although he dressed like a cartoon of a pimp—zoot-suit-shouldered polyester gold jacket, baggy green pants, a matching monkey-puke-green open-collar shirt with layers of gold chains showing, even a greasy little Wayne Newton moustache that looked like an anemic caterpillar had crawled onto his upper lip to die—despite all that, this guy *moved* like an athlete. No, better than that, he was as unself-consciously graceful as a big cat on the veldt.

But on stage . . . klutzville. He moved like Pee Wee Herman doing an imitation of Richard Nixon.

The audience didn't boo him, they just sat and stared as if a traffic accident was occurring on stage. There was even a splattering of applause when he got off—probably from pure relief. I mean, the man was *bad*.

That's why it was all the more confusing that night when I was hiking the six blocks to catch the subway up to Gotham Center where I'd catch the el out to Finger Park station, and who do I see down an alley but Bruce. I mean, I wouldn't have been surprised to see this guy heading down an alley in search of a flophouse . . . he wore one weird suit and had that handsome but driven look, sort of like some out-of-work actors I've known . . . but there he is, 2:00 A.M. in an alley, in the rain, and he's getting into a *limousine.* The chauffeur is some old guy, and it's some stretched European *übermenschen* limousine! It's hard for most of us to take the tension and abuse and *we're* all hoping for a break, the big time, money we can't make any other way . . . or at least any other *legal* way. So why the hell would this poor schmuck take all the abuse and embarrassment if he didn't have to? A guy who could afford a European limousine like that could *buy* an audience.

The next night at the Pit Stop, a strip joint that does comedy every Wednesday, Bruce was there again. Same routine. Same floppo, although this crowd was boozed up enough to start booing early. They were on the verge of throwing things when Bruce wrapped it up, bowed into that wall of boos, and walked calmly offstage.

Fast Eddie was ready to go on after him. Eddie leaned over to me and whispered, "*Anybody'd* look good after this jerk."

Later, Boonie Sandhill and I went up to this Bruce guy in the green room.

"Howdy, y'all," said Boonie, showing off the prognathous underbite that passed for a grin with him. "Caught your monologue, man. It's . . . uh . . . original. Real different. Makes the rest of us look the same as stripes on a coon's tail."

Bruce raised an eyebrow and nodded, obviously not sure if Boonie was pulling his chain or not. I wasn't either. We made introductions, shook hands. The guy's handshake was easygoing enough, but I had the idea he could crush my fingers like breadsticks if he wanted to.

"Bruce," said Boonie. "Is that your first name or last?"

The guy twitched a smile. "It's my stage name. My . . . stand-up-comic pseudonym."

Boonie rolled his eyes at the vocabulary. I said, "Any reason you chose the name Bruce?"

Bruce hesitated. "Homage to Lenny Bruce, I guess. He was sort of my hero."

Boonie and I glanced at each other. This guy's style and content bore about as much resemblance to Lenny Bruce's stuff as did Mr. Rogers.

"Hero, huh?" said Boonie. "Too bad Lenny O.D.'d on speed."

"Yes," said Bruce. He was watching the closed-circuit monitor the Pit Stop had to let the green-room folks watch the action on stage. It was a crude picture—stationary camera, black-and-white fuzzy picture with poor sound—but Bruce seemed rapt. "It is too bad," he said. "Lenny Bruce would have had a great future."

Boonie and I looked at each other again. This guy was as miserable a liar as he was a comic; anybody who knew anything about Lenny Bruce knew that he died of an overdose of heroin.

"How come you joined the cavalcade of stars?" asked Boonie.

Bruce rubbed his chin. The guy was older than I was, but I have no idea how much older. He had the sort of rugged but understated good looks that lets a man ignore birthdays between his early thirties and late fifties. "I wanted a crack at the Gotham City Laughs of Tomorrow competition," he said.

"You mean the big jerk-off?" said Boonie.

"Joke-off," I said. "We call it the joke-off."

Bruce nodded, eyes roving back to the closed-circuit TV. I had the idea that nothing made this man laugh; the idea of him making others laugh seemed . . . well . . . laughable.

"Don't you worry about getting killed?" asked Boonie. There was no banter in his voice now and very little southern accent.

Bruce raised an eyebrow. "Oh, you mean that Joker fellow. . . ."

"Yeah, that *Joker fellow*," mimicked Boonie. "He sorta caught some of our attention."

Bruce nodded as if mulling this over. "Sure, it worries me. But I figure it's a chance I have to take to get a shot at the bigtime for the Gotham Comedy ... ah ... the joke-off. The odds seem decent."

Boonie started to make some smart-ass reply, but I surprised him and myself by elbowing him to shut up and saying, "Right, man. That's the way most of us feel. Say, Boonie and I are going out for coffee after the last show. Want to come?"

Bruce seemed to weigh the invitation with the same seriousness as he did everything else. "Yes," he said. "I would."

For the next week or so, Boonie and I spent a lot of time with Bruce after the show—in those thin, cold hours between the closing of the nightclubs and the rising of the sun through Gotham's smog banks. Usually we hit an all-night café, mainlined strong coffee, and talked about comedy. *Boonie and I* talked about comedy. Bruce listened a lot. To tell the truth, he was a nice-enough guy. Just way too serious to be funny. He was even serious about comedy. Actually, he seemed to want to talk about the Joker most of the time: What did we think made the Joker do what he did? Why would the Joker be killing stand-up comics? What did we think of the Joker's sense of humor?

"That ain't a sense of humor, man," Boonie answered more than once. "This Joker pissant is *nuts*. His idea of a punchline is pain." And then Boonie would say, "Y'all want to analyze everything, Bruce. Petey and me, we just want to get *laughs*."

"But just what, precisely, makes people laugh?" Bruce asked late one night, early one morning. Outside the diner, cold rain was turning to snow in front of the street-sweeping machines.

Boonie snorted. "Shit-fire, boy. If we knew that, old Pete and me'd be livin' in Bel Aire an' sittin' on Johnny Carson's couch twice a week."

"But there must be *some* formula," persisted Bruce. "Some secret."

Boonie shook his head. "If there is, nobody knows it. Good comedy's like . . . like good sex. . . ."

"Good sex?" repeated Bruce. Any other comic would have snapped back, "Is there such a thing as *bad sex*, lint brain?" but Bruce was listening again. Seriously.

"Uh-uh," I interrupted. "Not sex. Surfing."

Both of them looked at me.

"I mean it," I said. I'd had a good night. The laughs had been strong and constant and sincere. "When I was out in California last summer, watching them surf at Malibu, I realized that a good stand-up routine's like that. You gotta catch the wave just right . . . it's like judging the audience . . . then get a good start, stay right on the break or curl or pipeline or whatever they call that sweet point just under the crest . . . and then ride it for all its worth, but still know when to end it." I stopped, embarrassed, and slurped cold coffee.

Boonie stared at me. Bruce said, "And what's the secret of riding the wave?"

For once my gaze was just as serious as Bruce's. "The secret is using material that *means* something," I said, surprised to hear me talking this way. "To go at the thing that's most serious to you, most . . . well, most sacred . . . and to *make it funny.*"

Bruce pondered his own coffee cup.

I pushed ahead. "I mean, look at your material, man. It's stuff you bought from a street-corner gag writer. Am I right?"

He nodded. I *think* he nodded.

"It's not *you*, man," I said. "It has nothing to do with you. It's not what scares you, what hurts you, what bugs you . . . you got to go for the stuff that's hiding in the deepest closets, then get it out. Share it with others who're hiding the same thing. Make it *funny*. Take some of the sting out of it."

I had Bruce's attention. "Do you do that, Pete?"

"Yeah," I said and sipped coffee. I was lying. I never dealt with the core of *me*—the guilt and fear and pride and terror I'd felt since I was four years old and realized that I was black: middle-class, reasonably well-educated, not street smart, not cool, but *black*. I realized why and who I'd really been lecturing there: I'd never had the guts to do a routine about my childhood in Charity Hills, or what it means to be the only kid on your block who didn't belong to a gang. "Yeah," I lied again, looking at my watch. "Hell, it's almost four-thirty. I don't have to be at Burger Biggie until ten, but it's a little late." I threw some change on the table. "See you losers tomorrow."

Boonie gave me his hillbilly grin. "Yeah, y'all can see me hang out my dirty linen then. *I* ain't got no hangups about talkin' about my miserable upbringin' and poor but honest family."

"Yeah," I said, pausing at the door. "Tell us again about how you slept on bare mattresses with burlap for a cover . . . too poor to buy sheets or blankets."

Boonie grinned more broadly. "Shee-it. We had sheets. But they was cut full a holes 'cause of all the Klan meetin's we had to go to."

I shook my head. "See you tomorrow, Bruce. I'll watch *you* bomb, my cracker friend."

Instead, I watched Boonie die.

We were uptown, at the ritzy *Chez* Harpo, and the place was crawling with cops. We were only a day away from the selection deadline for the joke-off, and there must have been forty comics competing for mike time that night. Bruce didn't survive the auditions for *Chez*, but he was there that night. So were about fifty cops: on the roof, backstage, in the audience, in uniform out front, and monitoring things from a trailer command center out back.

The mayor and the commissioner of police . . . what's-his-name . . . Gordon, had decided that the Joker comedy killings were making Gotham look bad. Whatever the reason for the security, I didn't see any way the Joker could get through it.

He did.

Boonie had them laughing. He was riding the wave real well, letting the laughter build and then punching it up higher, pausing at just the right spots, using the silences, when suddenly one of the silences stretched too far. The audience paused to breathe, waiting for the next funny bit.

Boonie started smiling as if he had just thought of something funnier than the story he'd planned to tell. The audience tittered in anticipation. Boonie's smile grew wider. His lips stretched back over his rear teeth. Some of the audience's laughter fell away, turned to gasps.

Boonie's color drained until his sunburned Georgia look gave way to a deathly pallor, grew paler still—by the time people started screaming, Boonie's complexion was the kind of white a corpse might show after a week in the water. His lips were stretched from ear to ear as if someone had pulled his cheeks back with meat hooks.

Boonie dropped the mike, gurgled something, and collapsed.

The cops went nuts. Bruce was the first one to Boonie, but I was there a second later. My friend was dead, already cooling to the touch.

Bruce pounded his fist on his knee. "Damn, damn, damn . . ."

"What?" I said. "How?"

Bruce touched Boonie's neck where the tiniest dart was visible, barely larger than a mosquito. "Joker Venom. He's used it for years. Keeps altering the formula so no antidote works. Hardly elegant, but very effective. A message."

The cops were sealing all exits, searching the premises, frisking patrons, shouting orders.

Bruce shook his head. "The Joker's gone by now. Probably disguised as a police officer."

I was crying. I couldn't help it. "But why Boonie? Why him?" I spread my jacket over my friend's face to hide the terrible rictus. "I mean, he wasn't the best comic tonight. Certainly not the worst. Why'd that bastard choose *him?*"

Bruce seemed elsewhere—not in shock like the rest of us, merely—elsewhere. "I thought the Joker might be eliminating competitors," he said, almost speaking to himself, "but now I know it's something else."

I wiped away tears with the back of my hand. "What, dammit? Is he trying to sabotage the joke-off?"

"No. Definitely not."

Paramedics and cops had shoved through and pushed Bruce and me away from Boonie. They worked fast, tossing IVs, syringe cases, and technical terms around . . . but Boonie stayed dead.

I stood up and looked out over the heads of the crowd. "It doesn't matter," I said. "I'm going to enter that damn contest and win. Win for Boonie and for me. No way that this homicidal asshole is going to scare us away."

"You're right," said Bruce. "We do have to be in it. Both of us. And we will."

The word came just like a summons from the Almighty. Uncle Louis would have loved it. He always wanted me to be someone genuinely significant—like an African Methodist preacher-man. Becoming a fast-track management clone at Burger Biggie was sort of okay—but a no-account stand-up comic didn't cut it.

Anyhow, the message from God arrived via Gotham Bonded Messenger. No bicycle delivery here—nosirree. I was just heading out of my apartment to cover the night shift for an asshole buddy whose plane had gotten stranded in Cleveland when he'd gone home to see his father. Dad had started that long day's journey into kidney cancer. . . . Anyhow, I saw the sparkling silver BMW pull up to the curb. I figured it had to be a crack dealer, so I ignored it.

Naturally I was surprised when a hunched-over guy in a blue uniform got out and said directly to me, "You would be Mr. Tulley?"

I resisted the impulse to say something like, "Why yes, Mr. Stanley?" and just nodded my head.

The old guy crabbed up to me and handed over an envelope. Then he produced a smoky-gray Lucite clipboard and said, "Sign here." No "please."

What the heck. I signed. Could be there was an inheritance, though far as I knew, nobody in the family had died. Maybe it was a desperate creditor. I checked the return address. Just a box number in Clovertide, up on the north side.

I shrugged and ran my right index fingernail under the flap. The folded letter felt like vellum. I straightened it, smoothed the creases, and read the calligraphy. Classy stuff. At first I didn't register what it was I was seeing on that page. Then I let out a whoop that probably triggered all the car alarms on the block and raised at least a half-dozen of my more gris-gris–conscious dead kinfolk.

I was in. Damn. How about that. But I was supposed to report to some address up on the north side for an orientation. Tonight.

Faulkner said that when it came to sacrifice for writers, a good novel was worth any number of little old ladies. I figured I could extend that to artists of all kinds, so I kept it in mind when I called my understaffed B.B. and told the woman who answered that I was going to be a no-show tonight.

"What's wrong?" she said. "You sick?"

"Nope," I said. "I just got a formal notice saying I'm going to be competing in the big joke-off, the Gotham City Laughs of Tomorrow contest, the golden path to the Johnny Carson Show. There's a heavy-duty meeting tonight."

"Right," she said, clearly sounding as if she didn't believe the tone of my voice, much less a word I was saying. "Get in when you can, Pete. We really need you. Listen, take something, get better fast." She clicked off the line.

Yeah, right. I'd *better* get better fast. The joke-off was only three days away. And me, I was going to be there. Son of a bitch. I started humming along with the tune on the oldies station I'd left on as a burglar deterrent: "Laugh, laugh, I thought I'd die . . ."

I took the train north and got off at a station just a little different than my usual stop. This one had spotless tile—and no graffiti—with tasteful turquoise accent stripes. Maybe the stations downtown did, too, but you would never notice for the krylon street art. When I got on the T-local at the Sprang Street station, I'd seen a jagged scream painted on the wall in Day-Glo purple: JOKER LIVES. Someone else had sprayed an *X* over the second word and added LAUGHS in bright scarlet.

The address on the invite was two blocks west. This was a business neighborhood, lots of low office blocks in brick and glass. It was getting dark now. I hardly saw anybody who looked like me—hell, there was hardly anybody at all on the street. They'd probably all headed home at five to the 'burbs.

My destination was a nondescript office tower that disappeared somewhere up there in the darkness. There weren't any lit windows. When I walked past the alley that bordered one side, I caught a glimpse of a familiar vehicle—A European stretch limo parked in the back.

Bruce was here, too? I realized I was phrasing it in my head as a question. I hadn't seen him perform since Boonie bought the farm, but I couldn't imagine his improving sufficiently to make any kind of final cut for *any*thing. I mean, he was a nice guy and he had heart, but Jesus what a stiff.

"I think I owe this to you, Pete." The deep baritone came from the darkness behind my left shoulder. I jumped. A reassuring hand came down, the steel fingers wrapping around my scapula. I wasn't reassured. "You taught me some first-rate lessons."

"Holy shit!" I said. I knew who was there. "You scared the crap out of me."

"I don't recall you being so scatological in your delivery," said Bruce. I could hear the trace of a smile in his voice. I turned and looked at him. He was dressed somberly in dark wool trousers and a black turtleneck. More like his namesake, it suddenly occurred to me. Good for him. Anything beat that Bozo zoot-suit he'd boasted the first time I'd seen him bomb. "Congratulations on jumping the final hurdle to the joke-off."

"You, too," I said. He put out his hand and I took it. Again, I felt like I was sticking my fingers in a walnut crusher. "Do you know what we're getting tonight?"

Bruce shook his head and motioned toward the dark

building with the folded letter in his left hand. "I know only as much as you do."

Both of us started walking toward the front door. I realized there was a light inside, the dim glow from a gang of security monitors behind a lobby desk. The glass door opened as we approached. There were two big guys in rent-a-cop uniforms waiting for us. Both had mean eyes, though they each smiled. "Mr. Tulley? Mr., ah, Bruce?" said the bigger of the pair. At our nods, the other guy checked his clipboard and made marks. Obviously they'd been well-briefed. "Please take the elevator on the left and go up to the thirtieth floor. You both want room one-oh-one."

Bruce cocked his head. "Why is room one-oh-one on the thirtieth floor?"

The first guard shrugged. "I didn't set up the numbering system. I just know which place you're supposed to go."

"I was just wondering."

"You two are the last," said the second guard. "You better hurry. Mr. Carson's waiting."

We got in the elevator and punched thirty. As the doors slid shut, I said to Bruce, "Something significant about room one-oh-one?"

"Aside from the fact one wouldn't expect it to be on the thirtieth floor, it's also the designation of the room in *1984* where prisoners encounter the thing they fear most."

"Swell," I said. The elevator car suddenly seemed smaller, more claustrophobic.

Actually, room 101 turned out to be a respectably sized suite that didn't seem sinister at all. Nearly a dozen and a half comics were there, all ones I knew and a few I was friends with. Then there was Johnny. It was kind of weird seeing him without Ed or Doc. He was surrounded with four or five harried-looking aides. He was taller than I expected, but what can you expect when you've only seen someone on a nineteen-inch tube? I guess maybe I was expecting him to be nattily dressed in an Armani. Nope. He was wearing a perfectly tailored suit that I was pretty sure was from his own line. I couldn't be positive because I wasn't in that shopping bracket, but I figured Johnny wouldn't be disloyal to his own label.

One of his assistants raised his voice and said, "If you'll all find a seat, Mr. Carson would like to have a few words with you."

I sat on a leather-upholstered couch with Bruce on one side of me, Diana Mulhollen on the other. She's such a sweet kid. I was glad she'd made the final cut. As long as I still won.

Johnny got up in front of us and said, "Ladies and Gentlemen, I'll keep this short. You're all here because you've been selected from among all of Gotham City's considerable ranks of the comically gifted." He grinned. "You're all among that select group of folks who end up going to parties that have been primed by some friend who told everybody else there, 'Hey, you've got to talk to so-and-so, he's the funniest guy you'll ever meet.' So what happens? You get there and everyone's looking at you expectantly, waiting for you to knock 'em dead." We smiled. Some of us snickered. Johnny smiled back and continued, "It's a tough life, being funny. It's our hope that the Gotham City Laughs of Tomorrow competition will make that life easier for some of you."

He went on to talk about the charities that would benefit, and about the live national TV hookup that would carry the proceedings across all America. Then he got to what I suspected most of us really wanted to hear about.

"The winner will be on the show the following week. We'll fly you out to Burbank and put you up like a king—or queen. And if that works out . . ." Johnny grinned and spread his hands beneficently. "There's no telling where you'll go. This will be the break of a lifetime."

I sensed eighteen indrawn breaths being held. Well, maybe seventeen, including mine. I'd glanced aside at Bruce. He didn't seem quite as mesmerized as the rest of us.

"My associates," said Johnny, "will give you full details about your time leading up to the competition. There will be," he added, "no formal rehearsals as such.

The director will want to block out times with you, but you won't deliver your material." Diane and I exchanged glances. "The idea is to keep your humor as fresh as you can, as topical as you wish. Besides, most of you are already familiar with your fellow comics' routines."

Someone laughed appreciatively. There were smiles.

The rest was pretty much pro forma, with the exception of a revelation that stirred some enthusiasm. Robin Williams would make a special appearance at the beginning of the show. Very brief, but very funny, Johnny said. That was great. I couldn't think of anyone living I would rather have as a comedy role model.

Johnny asked for questions. There weren't many. Then he excused himself and turned us over to his aides, who passed out laminated photo passes and rehearsal schedules. It turned out the telecast was originating from the Aladdin Theater, the very same place where Tiffany was drowned in *flop sweat*.

That didn't make anybody happy. Fast Eddie Teck brought it up. Johnny suggested we all just consider the competition a dedicatory memorial to Tiffany, George Marlin, Boonie, and the others in our little community who had died as the butts of the Joker's sadistic jokes.

Then the meeting was over. With a smile—I realized that Johnny had never displayed a straight face for the entirety of the evening—our host thanked us for our time and wished us well on Saturday night. People started to shuffle, shrugging on jackets and coats.

"Come on, Pete," said Bruce. "I need to be down at street level before the crowd."

I had no reason to stick around, so I beat him to the elevator and punched the button. There was something about Johnny's smile that weirded me out.

"One to a customer, gents and gentlettes," I said, "get'em while they're cold." Within five minutes I'd found myself in a situation that reminded me of doing volunteer labor (or not-so-volunteer if a guy were directed by the court to do a community service gig) in a downtown mission bread line.

When Bruce and I had exited the office building and walked to the head of the alley where his car had been parked, I found that the old codger who drove for him had turned that great gleaming barge around and popped the trunk lid. The luggage compartment was full of wrapped packages.

I looked down at them. "Bond market down, Bruce? You selling tailgate bargains now? Watches and Walkmen that fell off a truck, maybe?"

"I'm afraid not," said Bruce. "But I would appreciate it if you would walk over by the door and steer everyone here to me. *Every*one." The tone in his voice was all business. I wasn't about to say no.

Getting sixteen comics to congregate in the dark by an alley mouth where one of their colleagues was handing out butcher-paper-wrapped parcels was not the easiest job I've ever done.

"Listen," I said to them. "Humor him. Maybe he's the Joker. Just take a package."

"What *is* this shit, man?" said Fast Eddie, bouncing his packet on his palm a couple times. He tugged at the twine wrapping it, ripped some of the paper loose. "Old *clothes?*"

He was the last one to accept a package.

"All right," said Bruce. "Please, just a minute of your time. Then you can go."

They quieted. They crowded around the rear of the limo. They were still pumped up with the afterglow of having rubbed shoulders with the guy who could make the rest of their lives work like Swiss clockwork.

Bruce looked seriously at us all. "This might well save all our lives." His tone was convincing as all hell. "And if you think it's too weird, please, just trust me. It might save you from ending up like poor Tiffany or the rest."

Any grumbling or snickers ended at that.

"And if it is not something that's needed," Bruce continued, "then perhaps we still can provide a finale for the joke-off that no one in the audience will *ever* forget."

That was the hook. Having sunk it, Bruce went on. What he suggested to us was a hell of a lot funnier than any of his onstage jokes had been.

*   *   *

I like to think I own a healthy amount of self-confidence, but let me tell you—for three days I woke up soaked in, wore under my sodden clothes, and tried to wash off at night, more anticipatory *flop sweat* than had devoured poor Tiffany's whole body. I must have lost twenty percent of my bodyweight from evaporation, and didn't even have any spare pounds to lose.

I kept thinking about what I was going to spring on Johnny and Robin and sixty million viewers Saturday night. None of my usual material seemed funny anymore. Maybe it was time for fast-food jokes. Probably not.

Damn.

Maybe I could find a way to use the package Bruce had handed me out of the cavernous trunk of his limo as a prop. Maybe not. I wondered whether I was going to get ulcers out of this. Herpes lesions. Colitis. Pellagra. Pellagra?

I kept on sweating.

Saturday came and with it, the sort of feeling I hadn't had since I was five years old. I can remember wondering whether my folks would remember my fifth birthday. I wondered whether my dad would come back from a business trip down south. His trips on the road had been getting longer and longer. The feeling was anticipatory and scary, and a little sick with apprehension. When Dad showed and the cake started to smoke in the kitchen and the party started, it was almost an anticlimax.

I woke up at six, then dozed and rocked and tossed until about noon, when I finally rolled out of bed. My dad called ten minutes later to wish me luck and to inform me that the whole family would be home watching the show on TV. I'd gotten eight comp tickets for good seats at the Aladdin, but there were just too many in the family who wanted to go. So no one was. Dad had given the tickets to our church pastor and he was going to find worthy recipients. Shoot. I didn't say anything, but I was willing to bet I could have scalped those suckers for enough to keep me at least a month if I didn't win the joke-off.

Then Mom came on, and then Cousin Sook, and everybody else who was over at the house, and they all said they loved me and hoped I'd do 'em proud. I promised I would.

Then I went into the bathroom and threw up.

The Aladdin seemed a lot different than it had the evening of the fatal Tuesday Night Laugh Riot. The few handfuls of human beings, both performers and audience, who had been in attendance then had been dwarfed by this old Arabian nights deco barn. Tonight the two thousand seats were full. It was obvious that there had been a quick sprucing up. The sheets of paint, which had threatened to peel all the way off the ceiling and skate down into the crowd, had all been scraped and replaced. The gigantic stage curtains had been dusted— the maintenance crew must have beat them with telephone poles. But the place still smelled of mildew and outright rot.

The plan was simple. All us contestants were to be seated right at the front in the orchestra section. No hiding back in the green room. We would be in plain sight so the cameras could zoom in and catch our sick expressions as other performers outclassed us. Johnny was slated for the opening monologue; then he'd introduce Robin Williams, and Robin would hand the show back to Johnny. Then it would be *our* turn. Five minutes max. Not even the fifteen Warhol had promised us all.

I amused myself for a while looking back for friendly faces in the rapidly filling auditorium. I didn't see any, at least no one who was familiar.

"Hello, Pete," I stopped craning my neck. Bruce settled himself in the theater seat beside mine. No mutant zoot tonight. He wore a perfectly cut tux. Very formal-looking. Class act. I started to rethink my policy of wearing exactly the sort of bright street clothes I had worn to

the comedy clubs. At least my shirt was clean. I'd remembered to select one off a hanger in the clean end of
the closet just as I was ready to go out and treat myself
to a cab over to the theater.

"Hey, Bruce." I wished I felt as light as my voice.
"How's it going?"

"I'm hoping for the best—and wishing you well."
Those dark eyes stabbed toward mine. "You remembered
to bring the package?"

I nodded. Yeah, I'd remembered after almost spacing
it out. I'd been out the door with the key in the deadbolt
before I remembered the parcel. Almost didn't go back.
Then said the hell with it and unlocked the door again.

"Actually," said Bruce, surveying out colleagues, our
friends, our competition, "I wish us *all* a great amount of
good fortune tonight."

There was an undertone I couldn't quite interpret.
"What's that supposed to mean?"

He smiled slightly—"Nothing important."—and hesitated even more slightly, but I still caught it. "Perhaps
I'm a bit concerned about *flop-sweat*."

I laughed. "Don't worry. I've cornered the market
right here in my armpits."

He touched my wrist reassuringly and sat back in his
seat. The floor director signaled that it was one minute
until airtime. The lights were already uncomfortably
warm. Then the manic theme music—sort of a strange
mixture of "March of the Marionettes" and the main
theme from *Bubo the Clown's Afterschool Fun Club*—
swelled up from the house PA system, and we were off.

God, the Gotham City Laughs of the Future competition
started. The joke-off was on the air. I was simultaneously terrified and ecstatic.

And then, thirty seconds later, I was only terrified.

It happened almost as soon as the offstage announcer
introduced Johnny and he virtually skipped onto the
stage. The follow-spot found him and he waited patiently for the wild applause to die down.

"Good evening, ladies and germs," he said, grinning

with all those sparkling teeth. "Or maybe just good evening, germs."

At that, I don't know what we all expected. Asian flu jokes, maybe.

That's not what we got. From the contestants' section, I had an especially good view of what happened next. Johnny cupped his hands into claws and reached up toward his own face. He sank his nails into his rosy cheeks and started moving his fingers as though kneading dough.

Then he ripped off his own face. He pulled away what seemed to be strips of pink flesh as the audience stared. As my little sister would say, it was totally gross. Another set of features emerged. I admit it—I was expecting Freddy Kruger.

It wasn't. It was Robin Williams.

Ripples of applause started with us in the front, then spread back into the loge and the balconies. On the stage, Robin Williams grinned and it seemed like he was looking straight down at me. He held up his palms, acknowledging the delighted cheers.

I hadn't realized he was so tall.

Then Robin Williams ripped off his face, too. Just like Johnny. What the hell was this going to be, an endless series of Chinese boxes in the form of latex full-face masks?

I stared at the new persona of the man on stage. He yanked off his toupee and fluffed out his scraggly hair. Green hair.

Oh shit, I thought, along with, I'm sure, most of the rest of the audience all at the same time. It's the Joker.

The guy on the stage grinned from ear to ear, but he didn't look like a happy camper. "Ladies and gentlemen," he said, "a funny thing happened on the way to the theater." There was a great deal of consternation behind me in the audience. The Joker held up his hands for silence. There was a rapid-fire crackle of automatic weapons' fire and a few screams. The audience quieted down.

"That's better," said our lanky host. He slipped off his tux jacket and slipped the sleeves inside out. When he donned the garment again, I saw it was a tasteful metallic purple. This guy was for real, I thought. This wasn't another gag. I suddenly flashed on George Marlin and Tiffany and Boonie, all their faces, twisted and pained and dying.

I'll cop to panicking. I started to bolt out of my seat, but I felt a hand firm as wrought iron holding me down. "Hang in there," said Bruce. "You'll never get past his men."

That brought me back. I looked around. All the rent-a-cop security types were clustered around the auditorium doors. Funny, I'd never seen rent-a-cops carrying assault scatterguns and automatic weapons before.

The Joker cleared his throat with a sound like scraping snot off sandpaper with a putty knife. "As I was saying, a funny thing occurred. I happened by a nearby warehouse where your favorites, Mr. Carson and Mr. Williams, are presently safe but confined." He paused. "They said to say they were sorry they couldn't make it here in person tonight, but that they were tied up." The Joker laughed. He was the only one.

He stalked across the stage to the right, then back to the left. The spot followed. I noticed that the lighting tech had slipped in a purple gel. I had a feeling the Joker had covered every detail.

"If you're thinking that the outside world will see all this on television and collectively alert the National Guard and the Marines, be advised I've addressed that possibility. Even as I speak, some sixty million of your fellows are watching an advisory crawl across their screens apologizing for technical difficulties. By way of substitution, a rerun of *Wild Kingdom* is playing." The Joker giggled.

"Now." The Joker stopped centerstage and leered down at us in the first few rows. "Let us cut right to the heart of the matter, figuratively now, later perhaps literally. I have reason to believe that among you is my old nemesis, the Batman." I could hear murmurs in the audience. "Do I speak plainly enough?"

I think the question was rhetorical. I leaned closer to Bruce. "The comics he killed . . ."

"Bait." Bruce's voice was quiet. I looked sidewise at him. He stared at the Joker like a tomcat stares at another tom who's invaded his territory. That fixedness frightened me.

"Don't worry," said the Joker. "You'll still get to see the show you bought expensive tickets for, but you'll get a real bonus in addition. The comics who competed for the Laughs of Tomorrow finals are hoping for a new life. Now they can expect an additional treat—the possibility of death as well."

"He's gonna kill us all?" I said.

Bruce answered, "I don't think so. His plan will be mad, but it will still be a plan."

"Anyone who pays close attention to that caped clod who hounds me," said the Joker, "knows he possesses all the granite-jawed wit of Mount Rushmore. We are about to discover just how minuscule a sense of humor the man owns." He gestured toward us in the orchestra. "All of you up here. All eighteen. *Now!*"

I guess none of us saw any room for argument. Not with the Joker. Not with the two guys with Uzis who escorted us onto the stage.

When we were assembled like a herd—a gaggle—a flock—I don't know what they say out in the sticks—of sheep guarded by gun-toting goons, the Joker surveyed us cheerily. "You're all going to do your routines," he said. "I'm the judge for this. But guess what? I'm not looking for the funniest one anymore. I am searching for the worst, dumbest, least-funny among you. *That* one, I'm guessing, will be the Batman." He chortled. "*Then* we'll see just how a bad comedian dies on stage."

We all looked at each other. At least Diana Mulhollen and a woman named Winnie Morales had nothing to worry about. The thought must have occurred simultaneously to Winnie. She held up her hand like a schoolgirl.

"A question?" said the Joker, "or do you have to go to the little girls' room?"

"Do I gotta go through my routine, too?" said Winnie.

"Everyone does," came the answer. "My dark foe is a

devilishly clever master of disguise, even as I am. Each one of you is suspect."

"But—" said Winnie. I halfway expected her to drop her trousers and give the Joker some physiological proof of her not being Batman.

"No exceptions, unless you'd like to forfeit your participation in the competition. . . ." The Joker's tone was ominous. Winnie seemed to pick that up. She said nothing and lowered her gaze to the stage at her feet.

"All right, then," said the Joker, his tone lightening. "Let's get to it. Time for our first contestant. Remember, friends, you get points for delivery and timing. For being funny, you get your life."

This was absolutely crazy, I thought. Batman working incognito as an aspiring stand-up comic? Bat guano. I remembered the man I'd met in the police interrogation after George Marlin's death. That aura of brooding power wasn't anywhere among my colleagues.

I glanced over at Bruce as we both got up from our seats. That poor sucker might as well have a signed death warrant. He was as funny as— I tried to stop the thought. Too late. —a grave.

"Don't worry, Pete," he said. "We'll all do our best. We'll all pull through this together."

Sure, I thought. Together—in a mass grave. One big pine box. Piano crate. God, was I getting hysterical? I took a deep breath. I figured I'd better start thinking about how to buff up my material to a higher sheen.

But as the Joker consulted his list, picking the first contestant, in my head I kept seeing a field of bleached skulls. Eighteen of them.

". . . so the chief says, 'Fine, then. I decree death *by* mongo . . .'" And that wrapped up five minutes of pretty decent material by Goombah Dozois, the Cajun comic. The audience exploded into deafening applause. Goombah wasn't *that* good, but I'd gotten the feeling as we'd gone down the list of contestants that the crowd both needed a catharsis and wanted to do whatever they could to help us all survive. So they cheered everyone, good, bad, or indifferent. And even under the circumstances of being forced to be funny at gunpoint, or maybe *because* of it, some of us weren't even as hilarious as we would have been at, say, the Carob Club Comedy Countdown.

Goombah staggered out of the spotlight and rejoined us. The Joker scanned the list and said, "All right, my friends, we only have a few contestants to go." That included me. "So keep your pants on." Everytime he used one of those damned catch-phrases, we all cringed, not knowing if he was about to tie it to some crude wordplay-made-flesh. This time, he didn't.

"Our next competitor is . . . Mr. Bruce!" The crowd clapped. Bruce and I exchanged looks. His was enigmatic. He touched my arm with those iron fingers and then stepped into the spotlight. He blinked a couple times, I guess adjusting to the glare. He glanced at the Joker, then turned fully to the crowd.

"If any of you have heard me in the clubs, you know what kind of material I use. 'Hey, being a filthy rich kid isn't all it's cracked up to be . . . I remember how other kids brought their lunch boxes to school. *I* had caterers from Maxim's come to the cafeteria every day.' Not too funny, right?"

Right, I thought. Not too funny. Not then and not now.

Bruce paused a moment. A long moment. "I've been thinking a lot," he said, "about something my friend, Pete Tulley, told me." He shrugged. "I started thinking about some things I'd vowed never to think of again." I heard something in his voice. As little as I knew Bruce, I could still hear the keen of pain. "Let me tell you about someone I used to know."

I sneaked a look at the Joker. He was frowning, angular chin propped on one startlingly white palm, fingers curled up around his mouth like spider legs.

"This was when I was a student in the fourth grade," said Bruce. Huh? I thought. Richie Rich's childhood anecdotes? "A new school-year had just started and I was in my homeroom class for the first time. It was right after lunch and I was logy. You know, feeling about like an anaconda that's just eaten a goat. I could tell the teacher was, too."

Good delivery, I thought. He's picking up steam. The crowd could sense it. I saw some of the folks in the front starting to sit back in their seats instead of leaning forward anxiously.

"We looked like a perfectly good class, maybe thirty kids, all pink and scrubbed and full of enthusiasm. But as I said, we were all ready for an afternoon nap, and I think the new teacher was, too. Here he was, facing us all, and I think that for a moment, all he could do was to stare at us." Bruce shook his head and smiled. "I think he decided to try something new. He figured he'd stall us for a bit, make conversation while he was picking which way he wanted to take the class."

Hey, I tried to warn him telepathically, you're starting to wander, just a little. Get back on track.

"Finally—it was only a few seconds, but it seemed like an hour in my mind—he started with the first student at the near end of the far left row, a boy. 'Son,' he said, 'I'd like to find out a little bit about each of you. I want to ask about your families. Tell me something now, tell me what your father does.'

"So then the first boy said, 'My dad's a fire fighter.' And he told him about what his father did. I guess that worked out so well, the teacher went on to the next student, a girl. 'And what's your father do?' he asked. 'He's in the Army,' came the answer. 'He fights people.' And so it went," said Bruce. "On down the ranks of students, row by row, until he got to a young boy sitting right in back, in the very center."

I was trying to think, did *I* know this joke? It was new to me. I wondered where Bruce had dug up some new material. Or maybe he was spinning the truth, maybe this really was something that had happened to him back—I still couldn't quite believe it—when he was a fourth-grader.

"This little boy was short and dark—dark hair, dark eyes. He was quiet and very, very serious," said Bruce. "You could tell just by looking at him that he was lonely." There was the touch of something I couldn't immediately identify in Bruce's voice. Then it came to me—it was the sound of someone who wanted to cry, but couldn't. Just that tiniest of cracks.

"I was that little boy."

There was an odd tone in the way Bruce said it. I felt like I should hold my breath and stay very, very still.

"So then the teacher looked at the little boy and asked, 'Son, what does *your* father do?' I didn't answer, but just stared back at him. I think he suddenly knew that he ought to drop it then and there, but he didn't."

Bruce coughed and offered the crowd an apologetic half-smile. "But then it was for him about like it is for me now. He just kept on going, bulled right on ahead. He tried to get through what he thought was my shyness and said, 'It's okay, son, you can talk to me. Tell me what your dad does.'

"I finally looked him straight in the eye and said in a low voice, 'Sorry, sir, he doesn't do anything. My father's dead.'"

Somebody in the audience gasped. I swallowed. This was weird. There was *something* about Bruce's delivery.

"He knew right then," said Bruce, "that he ought to get out of this any way he could. He should go on to the next student. He was entering some kind of Vietnam of primary education." He shook his head sadly. "He couldn't. God knows why, but he looked back at the little dark-haired boy—me—and said, 'It's all right, son, go ahead and tell me . . . what did your daddy do before he died?'"

Bruce paused so momentarily that I thought I was maybe the only person catching him swallowing.

"I looked back at him, still straight in the eye, and said, 'Well, he went *cckcckccckkkccckkk!*'" Bruce grabbed his own throat and mugged the visual image to go with the strangling sounds.

The crowd was stone silent.

It was like they didn't know what to do, didn't know how to react.

Then it began. A laugh somewhere in the balcony. A titter to stage-left in the loge. People giggled, groaned, started to guffaw. The laughter spread like the Philippine flu. So far as I could see, about the only people not absolutely breaking up were the thugs with machine guns.

Then the applause began to overwhelm the laughter. As best I could see Bruce's features from the side, he looked overwhelmed, too. He bowed slightly.

Above the roar of the audience rose a cackling from the stage. I turned my head and saw the Joker on the floor. Literally. He was holding his sides and roaring with laughter, that terrible hyena bray I first heard at the Carob the night George Marlin blew his top.

I looked back at Bruce as he stared out over that ocean of reacting human beings. In his eyes I saw the shine of tears. What did this mean? I wondered. What had it cost?

The next one up was Winnie Morales. It was pretty obvious she didn't relish having a turn in the barrel right after Bruce's bravura performance. She stared out over the crowd, obviously swallowed, then said, "Okay, so there were these three clergy-guys walking down the street. There was a Jewish rabbi, a Baptist preacher-fella, and an Irish bishop. They were on their way to play golf, when suddenly Saint Peter . . ."

And the next one up was me.

Well, I figured I could beat Winnie Morales. Maybe. I knew I couldn't beat Bruce, but hey, I didn't want to. I just wanted to save my own hide. At least that's what I thought until I actually stood out there, bathed in a bloody red gel-light from the follow spots. I know it's a cliché, but time slowed for me.

Bruce's routine replayed in my head. Something came to me with all the subtlety of getting whupped up along-side the head with a flying mallet. I felt the shock of the brilliant white light, you know?

That tired old poor-little-rich-kid routine of Bruce's had somehow evolved to what he'd performed tonight. I was pretty sure it hadn't come easily. I still couldn't

quite see all the cross-connections—it really was hard to
see Bruce as a little boy in the fourth grade. But somehow he knew something about parents and death and
had formed it into an awful-yet-effective story that had
destroyed an entire theater.

It came to me. Yeah, he'd learned from me, all right.
He'd listened to what I'd said back when he and Boonie
and I'd been talking. Then he did the things I'd never
done. He'd faced up. He'd gone *real*.

Just like I claimed to do, but didn't.

Hey, nothing like making myself feel like shit just
when I was supposed to spend the most important five
minutes of my life making people laugh.

The voice grated into my consciousness. "Oh, Mr.
Tulley, are you going to perform or not? Has the cat got
your tongue?"

Shit. I focused and saw the Joker smiling easily just a
few yards away. Things snapped together inside. I
hoped.

I nodded and took a deep breath. "Hey, how many of
you out there realize I'm not really black?" That got a
few titters. "Nope, truly I'm not. I'm black Irish."

"Oh, yeah?" That was maybe the first heckler of the
night. Good, I thought. Then I squinted and realized I'd
been needled by one of the Joker's goon squad.

So "Yeah," I said. "The name on my driver's license is
O'Rio." The thug looked bewildered. Nobody out beyond
the lights laughed, so I used exaggerated cheerleading
gestures to spell out the name I said. This time there
was a ripple of laughter.

"Good, you got it. Am I going too fast for you? Hey,
let's go. You think it's *easy* being an Oreo in the inner
city, man? I mean, you should have heard me playing
the dozens with tough dudes on the corner. I mean, they
got to serve first—

"'Hey, man, yo mama wears combat boots when she
gives it away in the alley.'

"So I snap back with, 'She ain't givin' it away, man.
She's in the alley pickin' aluminum cans outta the
Dumpster to pay for my Harvard education, man.'"

More laughter. Thank God.

"No, I mean it—the other dudes from the block were like Fast Eddie Teck, you know? Carried switchblades. Me . . ." I slipped my hand into my hip pocket and pretended to snap something out. "One time this homeboy from the Night Vultures jumps me, and so I go for my calculator . . ."

A little more laughter. And so it goes.

When all of us were done, the Joker had the house lights brought up. The eighteen of us pretty much looked like the condemned, about to be shot as examples by some military junta in a soccer stadium.

"Well—" said the Joker. "That was quite a round of performances. I'm impressed that many of you, if you should survive this evening, might actually have a future in comedy—especially now that you'll have a great new experience to draw upon. Think of me as your agent of change; but remember, if you use any material pertaining to yours truly, to give me due acknowledgment. Otherwise I'll have to track you down and extract my fifteen percent." He giggled. "And I'll wager that, for most of you, fifteen percent is a great deal more than a mere pound of flesh." He looked contemplative, as though imagining harvesting his fee.

Then his voice changed mercurially. "Ah, yes, the matter of the incognito Bat-comic. I rather unwisely predicted I would have to make final disposition of the least funny of you." He ambled toward us. "Unfortunately that reflects badly on *you*." The Joker raised his cane and lightly touched it to Winnie Morales's chest. "Don't worry, my dear, you seem too much the mammal to be mistaken for my nemesis in a clever plastic disguise. Still—" he mused. There was fear in Winnie's expression. "—I really ought to be consistent in my declarations." Then he shook his head. "No, Ms. Morales, I won't slaughter you where you stand. The memory of your performance is punishment enough."

He stalked away, spun on his heel, walked back. "I have an idea. It had occurred to me that if the least funny of you *weren't* the Batman, what I might do is to

follow the maxim of my old mercenary friends and simply kill you all and let God sort you out." I knew I was
looking death in the distorted, grinning face.

"No," said the Joker. "One more chance. I must be
mellowing." He chuckled, a horrible sound like a gerbil
being pulled under the water and gargling as it
drowned. "Yes, a chance. I'm going to extinguish the
lights. When I bring them up again, I expect to see a
clear sign that one of you is the Batman. I realize there
is no phone booth—" He smirked. "Oh, yes, that's our
other good friend. But you get the point." The Joker
raised his hand. "All right, are you ready?" All of us sort
of looked at each other. "If anyone tries anything funny,
so to speak, my men will rake both the stage and the
theater auditorium with automatic fire." I wondered if
we'd all remembered our twine-bound, butcher paper-
wrapped parcels.

"Now," said the Joker.

The lights went out.

Did you ever see *Spartacus?* There's that great scene
where the Romans order the rebellious slave army to
give up their leader and then first one, then another, and
eventually every slave there proclaims, "*I* am Spartacus."

I thought of that when the lights came up.

You see, we were all—all eighteen of us—the Batman.

I'd worn the costume from the package Bruce had
given us under my clothing, as I guessed the rest had,
too. In the sudden darkness, I'd struggled out of my
street clothes, unfurled the thin cape from under my collar, and pulled the cowl over my head. I had donned the
rest of the gear.

So here we were in the glare of the house lights. Eighteen Batpersons: white, black, brown, yellow, male,
female, fit, paunchy, young, middle-aged. We were a
sight.

The Joker stared at us. With some satisfaction, I saw

there was genuine surprise on his face. Then he began to laugh.

I don't think it was wholly because we were all dressed in Bat-attire. It may have had something to do with the fact that all of us wore Groucho glasses, the heavy black-rimmed kind with the attached big rubber noses and bushy moustaches.

While we stood there waiting for summary execution, the Joker giggled, then chortled, finally whooped with merriment. Tears, or at least something viscous, dripped from his eyes. I thought the ends of his grin would meet around the back of his head.

When he finally could speak, he said, "Perfect. Absolutely perfect. Better than I'd ever hoped." He burst into laughter again.

And then he let us go.

It was that abrupt. The Joker made some hand motions. Smoke rolled across the stage. Blinding lights flashed. Choking, we fell to our knees. But then the fumes cleared. They weren't toxic.

The Joker was gone, along with his men.

I felt a strong arm help me to my feet. Bruce. He set his hand on my shoulder and steadied me.

It had been one hell of a show. You might say we'd knocked the audience dead.

Just kidding.

I've had a lot of time to think about that night. I'm in law school now—no more Burger Biggie, and no more suggestions of seminary from Uncle Louis.

I still do some stand-up comedy, but there isn't a hell of a lot of time. In such clubs as I still play, I've never again seen Bruce.

About that night . . . I remember how I always used to think I only came truly alive at night, when I could change into somebody different from who I was in the sunlight, somebody more powerful, someone who could move people to react.

I mean, I'm no dummy. I can put two and two together. After what I've been through, there ain't nothing that seems unlikely now.

The newspapers really did a number on what happened at the Aladdin Theater and the joke-off. The writers speculated about why the Joker hadn't simply triggered a massacre. The consensus seemed to be that the big *J* must be entering some new phase of his "humor," something seriously weird, maybe absurdist or the surreal.

Me, I've got a different idea. Maybe somebody just got a little bored. No, check that. *Seriously* bored. And maybe somebody decided that the lack in his life was his opponent.

He decided his antagonist had one crucial shortcoming—no sense of humor. Or at least one so rudimentary it needed a little jarring loose to set it in gear.

A worthy villain *needs* an equally worthy antagonist.

Just speculation, folks.

I keep my theories to myself. See, I figure that one day I'll return to the night—and when I do, I might just need a friend.

Double Dribble

George Alec Effinger

Police Commissioner Gordon and wealthy philanthropist Bruce Wayne certainly had better things to do on that drizzly afternoon in March. The former was absent from a luncheon with Gotham City's mayor and several influential civic leaders, and the latter had postponed an important consultation with the Wayne Foundation's legal advisors. Instead, the two men had gathered with members of the news media in a small, overheated meeting room in Gotham Garden, the historic sports and concert arena. They'd all been invited to attend an important press conference called by Joculator, Inc.

"Were you able to learn anything about this corporation?" asked Wayne.

Commissioner Gordon shook his head. "Nothing at all. Joculator, Inc. seems to consist of just five names, none of them listed in the police records."

Wayne, in his alter ego as the Batman, had made his own investigation, using the extensive crime files stored in the Bat-Computer. He had turned up much the same results—which is to say, none at all. "I would have ignored the invitation completely," he said, frowning, "except it reminded me too much of certain other invitations I've seen in the past." He didn't feel it necessary to point out to his old friend that *joculator* was the Latin word for "joker."

"I had the same reaction," said Gordon grimly.

Before they could compare notes any further, a short, heavyset man with a perspiring red face appeared from behind the velvet curtains that draped the front of the meeting room. He glanced nervously at the assembled newspaper, radio, and television crews, then went to a wooden podium decorated with the emblem of the Gotham City Knights, the city's National Basketball Association franchise that played its home games in the Garden.

The man took out a large pocket handkerchief and mopped his face. "My name is Robert Branford," he said in a soft, hoarse voice. "I'm the president and CEO of Joculator, Inc. I'd like to thank you all for coming here today. We have an exciting announcement to make, and rather than draw it out any longer, I'd like to get right to it. As of today, Joculator, Inc. is the new corporate owner of the Gotham City Knights."

A loud murmur rose up among the newspeople. Camera shutters began to click all over the room, and video equipment captured Branford's every word and nervous gesture. Gordon leaned over and spoke softly into Wayne's ear. "I'm surprised that old Bob Jennings sold the club. I didn't think he needed the money and I know that owning the basketball team was his favorite hobby."

"Maybe Joculator, Inc. made Jennings an offer he couldn't refuse," whispered Wayne.

Branford passed the handkerchief across his forehead again. "I'm sorry that Robert L. Jennings, the longtime owner of the Gotham City Knights, couldn't be with us today, but I'd like to introduce my silent partner, who will show you the team's newly redesigned uniform. He'll also tell you about a promising new addition to the Knights' roster."

Branford stepped away from the podium and held out his hand toward the velvet drapes. There was a hushed moment of anticipation, and then a sudden collective exclamation as out stepped—the Joker himself! Someone in the audience shrieked, and two people got up and fled the room through a side exit. The photographers all rushed forward to get better positions. The Joker stood at the podium, displaying his maniac grin and enjoying immensely the confusion and consternation he'd caused.

Commissioner Gordon leaped to his feet. "Arrest that man!" he cried to the Gotham Garden security officers on duty.

Bruce Wayne put a hand on Gordon's arm and pulled him back down. "He hasn't done anything to be arrested for, Commissioner," he said. "Let's find out what this is all about. After all, there isn't anything valuable enough here for the Joker to risk his own safety."

Gordon resumed his seat grumpily. "I guess you're right, Wayne," he said. "It just makes my blood boil to see that lunatic gloating up there like that, with who-knows-what insane plot up his sleeve."

The Joker waited until the uproar had settled down. Then he swept his gaze from one side of the room to the other. He seemed satisfied that he had everyone's full attention. "You know, my friends," he said in a loud voice that was pitched near hysteria, "I sometimes get the urge to try to fit into your decent, honest society."

Gordon grunted disgustedly. "I don't believe that for a second," he muttered.

"Let him have his say," said Wayne.

"Really, I do," the Joker continued. "A few weeks ago, I thought, Wouldn't it be fun to be the owner of an athletic team? How I envied George Steinbrenner and the other team owners I saw on the news. Sports sums up the essential human drama, don't you agree? The joy of victory and the agony of defeat!" He spread his hands and let loose with the mad laughter that was his trademark.

"Somebody must have written this speech for him," said Gordon.

"I'm sure he's fooling no one, Commissioner," said Wayne.

The Joker's laughter ended, and his expression became mournful. "Over the years, I've put together a modest nest egg through my ventures, and I definitely had the purchase price of the team of my dreams—our very own Gotham City Knights. Imagine my disappointment when the lords of the NBA told me that I couldn't buy a team, merely because I'm as crazy as a squid on skis! A thin technicality! When has lunacy ever stopped anyone from owning a basketball team, or a baseball, football, or hockey team for that matter?" Again the meeting room was filled with the Joker's echoing cackles.

"That's when I had the wonderful idea of urging Mr. Robert Branford and some of his associates to form Joculator, Inc., a corporation duly registered with our state government. I have no official connection with Joculator, Inc., but I do have a certain amount of influence with Mr. Branford and the four other board members. Don't I, Bob?" He flashed his blood-chilling grin at Branford, who gasped and fell back a step.

"Don't worry, Bob," said the Joker, returning his attention to the cameras and tape recorders, "you've done a splendid job. There'll be a couple of free passes to the next Knights' home game for you at the box office."

"That explains it!" cried Gordon. "The company is just a cheap front for the Joker's nefarious schemes!"

Wayne regarded the Joker thoughtfully. "Yes, of course, but what does he hope to achieve by buying the Gotham City Knights?"

The Joker went on smoothly. "Let me say that my first suggestion to the new owners was to redesign the team's horrid old uniforms. Remember those depressing, dark, Batmanish tunics and trunks? Remember the awful yellow oval and the sword symbol? Well, we've gotten rid of all that!"

He held up the Knights' new uniform shirt. "We favor purple and green and gold now. A green tunic—green, like my hair, you know—with gold lettering, and purple trunks." The oval was gold instead of yellow, and it now enclosed a grinning playing-card joker in cap and bells.

"Why," exclaimed the Joker, "I've just noticed how much this uniform resembles my own favorite outfit! What a coincidence!" He stood at the podium for a moment, then began to glare at his audience. "That's, I say, that's a *joke,* friends. You may all giggle merrily now." A few strained, frightened laughs came from the crowd.

"That's better," said the Joker, putting the basketball uniform down. "Oh, as Bob hinted, I do have one final announcement concerning the team roster. At our next home game, which will be on Friday night against the Boston Celtics, this particular jersey will be worn by the Gotham City Knights' new starting point guard—none other than I, myself!"

The reaction to the Joker's bombshell was instantaneous, dwarfing any of the crowd's previous outbursts. The Joker stood at the podium, enjoying his moment of glory to the fullest. "Yes, yes," he shouted happily over the clamor, "you heard me correctly! This is my number, fifty-three, because the Joker is the fifty-third card in the deck. I'll answer no questions now, but I invite you all to come back on Friday, to cheer us on against our worthy opponents from Boston!"

He began to laugh hysterically, until no one in the meeting room could doubt the full extent of the Joker's dementia. Finally, ignoring the shouted questions from the reporters, he hurried from the stage, disappearing with Robert Branford through the part in the velvet curtains. His psychotic shrieks of joy faded away, and the Joker did not reappear.

Commissioner Gordon and Bruce Wayne stared at each other in amazement. "Can he do it?" said Gordon at last.

Wayne shrugged. "You and I have both heard Batman speak of the Joker's surprising strength and agility."

"The Joker may be strong and agile," Gordon objected, "but he's not a trained professional athlete. If he has strength, it's the strength of a madman."

"We'll see," said Wayne, oddly curious in spite of himself. "Maybe he's a madman with a good fadeaway jumpshot."

"Well, Chuck, we should extend a warm welcome to all our affiliate stations along the Gotham City Knights' radio network. This looks like the largest crowd of the season here in Gotham Garden, and with good reason. Tonight is the first game of the Knights' four-game home series, and it's also the one in which the Joker, the Clown Prince of Crime, claimed he'd appear in a Knights' uniform. I imagine a lot of these people are here to witness that, to see if it's more than just another of the Joker's loony pranks."

"Right you are, Tom, although if the Joker does go out on the court tonight, he may have more in mind than shooting a few baskets. In the past, when the Joker shot something, he usually used bullets."

"Well, on the legal front, he evidently has some very clever attorneys. They've managed to outmaneuver the NBA commissioner's office, getting a court order preventing the commissioner from banning the Joker from playing. A hearing has been set for next Tuesday, however. In the meantime, the Joker will be permitted to suit up and appear on the court, if that's what he really has in mind."

"And who can ever say *what* the Joker has on his mind, Tom? I'm sure Police Commissioner Gordon and the Batman are nearby, to prevent him from pulling some truly insane and dangerous stunt in this jam-packed arena. In any event, a lot of people will be following this game closely. Now let's go down to courtside for the introduction of the teams."

"Ladies and gentlemen," came the voice of Gotham Garden's announcer, "welcome to tonight's game between the Boston Celtics and *your* Gotham City Knights!"

The announcer paused while the more than twenty thousand fans cheered. First he introduced the starting lineup for the Celtics: Larry Bird, Kevin McHale, Robert Parish, Dennis Johnson, and Reggie Lewis. As their names were called, they got up from their team bench and ran onto the court. There was mild applause from the Gotham City partisans. The Celtic players shook hands with each other and waited until they'd all been introduced, then went back to their bench and stood staring across the hardwood floor at the Knights. The Joker was nowhere in evidence.

"Now, ladies and gentlemen, *your* Gotham City Knights!" The crowd jumped up and shouted its approval. "At forward, number six, from Ivy University, Hilton Foster!" Foster ran onto the court, grinning at the ovation he got from the fans. "At the other forward position, number fourteen, from Saint Didier College, Kennedy Turner." Another long, loud cheer, and Turner joined Foster at the midcourt stripe. "At center, number four, from Hanson Tech, Monroe Parks. At guard, number sixteen, from Wray College, Bobby O. 'Dogtrot' Brown. And at the other guard position, number fifty-three—" the announcer paused for a moment "—from . . . Arkham Asylum . . . *the Joker!*"

The crowd went wild. There were thundering waves of boos, but there were also a few shrill cheers mixed in. The familiar white-skinned, green-haired figure emerged from the runway to the Knights' locker room, laughing insanely and blowing kisses to the angry, howling fans. He joined his teammates at midcourt. The others hesitated to greet him, fearing some deadly Jokerish trick, but at last Turner shook his hand. Then Foster, Brown, and Parks welcomed him, and the Knights retired to their team bench.

"Well, Chuck," said one of the radio announcers, "we're witnessing history of a sort being made here tonight."

"I suppose so, Tom, although I never would've believed I'd see anything like this. They're getting ready for the opening tip-off down there. The officials for tonight's game are Tony Mangiani and Cliffort Dupree. Mangiani's taking the ball out to midcourt, between Robert Parish and Monroe Parks. Mangiani puts the ball up . . . and it's batted by Parks into the hands of the Joker."

"Okay, now we'll see if the Ace of Knaves, as the papers in town like to call him, knows one end of a basketball from the other. The Joker dribbles the ball a couple of times, then starts bringing it up slowly on the left side. He's calling a play down there, although Coach Jim Westfahl no doubt set one up in the locker room. The Joker's got that bizarre, evil grin on his face, and the

Celtics can't seem to take their eyes off him. The Joker passes the ball in to Parks, the Knights' center. Parks holds the ball out of Parish's reach. Now the Joker and Dogtrot Brown cross each other just in front of the foul line. Parks fakes a shot, Parish goes up, Parks feeds the ball into the Joker—*yes!* The Joker made a nice move around Reggie Lewis and drove to the basket for a clean lay-up. The Knights draw first blood and lead, two to nothing."

"Have you noticed that the booing hasn't stopped, even though the Joker canned those two points? He doesn't have a lot of fans in this crowd. I'm impressed now by how he's hustling back on defense. The Joker's keeping close to Dennis Johnson, not letting the Celtics' point guard have an easy time moving the ball up. Johnson clears it out to Reggie Lewis, who feeds it in to Larry Bird. Bird's open for a second, goes up with that beautiful, soft shot of his, and the score is tied."

The game stayed close all the way to the end, with the Gotham City Knights coming out of it with an exciting win, 114 to 109. The Joker finished with impressive statistics: He was in the game forty-one minutes, had twenty-one points, eight assists, two steals, and was two out of three from beyond the three-point line.

Immediately after the game, reporters and sportswriters from all around the country rushed down to the Knights' locker room, but the Joker was nowhere to be found.

That same night, many blocks away in the new Seaside Coliseum, a few furtive figures made their way down a broad, carpeted corridor. It was after hours and the Coliseum was closed to visitors, but these six men hoped to arrange a private tour of one of the exhibit halls. The night watchman heard their steps and lifted his feet from his desk. "I'm sorry," he said, looking up, "but—ulp!"

"Forgive me, my good man," said the Joker. "I hope we didn't startle you. I understand there is a rare treasure on display here, the fabulous Corsican Condor."

"Why . . . yes, it is, but—" the night watchman stammered.

The Joker gave his insane laugh and gazed down at the watchman affectionately. "Don't tell me any more, I know *exactly* what you're going to say. Believe me, I've heard it all before, countless times! Something about the exhibit hall being closed now, and no one's allowed in until morning, and that if I don't leave, you'll have to call the police, and all that sort of thing. Am I right? *Hmmm?*"

The night watchman looked terrified. He'd heard about the horrible things the Joker had done to scores of other men and women in exactly his position. "Yes," he said in a fearful voice, "I'll have to. It's my job."

The Joker looked around at his five henchmen. "Isn't he wonderful?" he cried, spreading his hands. "Isn't he just the perfect night watchman?" The Clown Prince of Crime turned back to the cowering man. "Ah, if only I had a dollar for every time someone has said that to me in my long, illustrious career. But I wouldn't be the Joker if I took you at your word, now, would I? I mean, if I did just turn around and leave, what would be the point of all my elaborate preparations? I have my reputation to think about, too, you know!"

The night watchman tried to speak, but his throat was too constricted. Finally he managed to get out, "I . . . I don't know."

"You're afraid," said the Joker solicitously. "You've heard about my acid-squirting flower, haven't you?" The night watchman nodded, his eyes wide. "Well, I don't need my acid-squirting flower. You've heard about my deadly joy buzzer, too?" Again the watchman nodded. "Well, I won't use that toy, either. In fact, Mr. Night Watchman, I don't need any of my wonderfully amusing gimmicks, because I have official permission to be here tonight for a private showing of the Corsican Condor. Here's the engraved invitation, signed by the executive secretary to the director of the Seaside Coliseum herself." The Joker laid the card on the watchman's desk and waited.

The night watchman glanced down at the invitation,

then back up at the Joker. Then he removed his eyeglasses from his shirt pocket and put them on and picked
up the invitation to study it more closely. "I'll admit,
this does seem to be in order," he said thoughtfully. "It
sure looks like Miss Brant's signature, too. Maybe I
should just give her a call and—"

The night watchman gave a sudden, startled gasp,
then rose halfway out of his chair. He dropped the invitation to the desk and began clawing at his shirt collar.
His facial muscles began to tremble, and then his mouth
pulled back in a ghastly grin, the hideous, telltale mark
of the Joker. The corpse of the night watchman fell
heavily forward across the desk.

"I couldn't very well allow him to disturb Miss Brant
at this late hour, could I?" said the Joker, looking innocently from one henchman to another. Then he threw his
head back and laughed his cold, grim laugh.

One of his accomplices began to reach forward to take
the invitation from the desk. The Joker slapped his hand
away. "Careful, you fool," he said. "Contact poison. Absorbed through the skin. I'm wearing gloves, but you're
not."

"Ah, brilliant, Boss!" said the henchman.

The Joker merely shrugged. "It's a gift," he said modestly. "Now, if I were a five-hundred-year-old gold and
jeweled statue of a bird, where would I be?" He led his
gang down the corridor toward the exhibit halls.

The Batman stood in one corner of Exhibit Hall B,
watching Commissioner Gordon's expert investigators
gather what little evidence the Joker and his men had
left behind. The commissioner himself stood with the
Caped Crusader, shaking his head in bewilderment. "I
don't know what to think, Batman," he said. "The dead
night watchman shows all the marks of one of the
Joker's victims, but that damn villain has a perfect al-
ibi."

The Batman rubbed his jaw thoughtfully. "You mean
that between eight o'clock and eight-thirty, when the
watchman was killed, the Joker was in plain sight be-

fore twenty thousand spectators, in the uniform of the
Gotham City Knights."

Gordon turned and looked at the smashed display
case, where only a short time before someone had removed the priceless artifact known as the Corsican Condor. "I don't know what to think. It could be that the
medical examiner is mistaken in his estimate of the
time of death. Or else there are *two* Jokers in town
tonight!"

"That's a terrible thought, Jim. I've seen the videotape of the Joker's news conference, when he announced that Joculator, Inc. had purchased the basketball team. I'd stake my life and reputation on the fact
that *he* was the real Joker. Who the other Joker is—if
there is, in fact, a second one—is the mystery."

Commissioner Gordon slammed a fist into the palm of
his other hand. "It's more than that, Batman. At the
press conference, the real Joker merely made fools of us
and the legal system. I suppose I can live with that, although it makes my stomach burn. But whoever came in
here tonight committed murder, as well as a variety of
lesser crimes up to and including grand larceny. That I
can't live with. If it's the Joker or an impostor, we have
to catch him and put him where he's no longer a threat
to society. It's our duty, Batman."

The dark, cowled figure nodded. "I don't think your
men will learn anything more of value," he said. "I'm
going to begin my own investigation, using my own
methods. I'll keep you informed of my progress."

Commissioner Gordon threw up his hands in frustration. "The Joker!" he cried, and then he kicked some
shards of broken glass across the room.

The Batman had much to think about as he made his
way through the cold March rain from the Seaside Coliseum to the Batmobile. The theft of the Corsican Condor
was an audacious crime, the sort of thing in which the
Joker had specialized in years past. Now, of course, the
Clown of Crime had graduated from mere smash-and-
grab antics to become the insane killer all Gotham City
had come to dread.

Perhaps a decade ago, the Corsican Condor would

have been enough of a temptation for the Joker. No
longer, though. Now his motivation was a single-minded
determination to prove his cleverness and superiority
over Batman, to humiliate his foe where all could see—
and if one or ten or a hundred innocent victims died in
the process, the Joker only shrugged and took no further
notice.

So the Batman felt sure that the disappearance of the
Corsican Condor was only a small part of the Joker's
grand scheme, whatever it was. Wars had been started,
tens of thousands of soldiers had perished in battle, and
towns and cities reduced to rubble—all to gain posses-
sion of the legendary Corsican Condor, which the Joker
may well have unceremoniously tossed into a corner. It
was possible that the dazzling golden sculpture meant
nothing to him now. It was merely a prop he no longer
needed in his urgency to get on to the next part of his
mad plan.

The Batman stood staring back at the Seaside Coliseum, at the flashing blue lights of the police squad cars
parked haphazardly around the main entrance. He
rested his arm on the roof of the Batmobile and pondered
his helplessness. The worst part was that he'd learned
nothing at all tonight. He knew only that the Joker was
introducing another of his crazy puzzles, and he would
have the upper hand until he revealed enough clues for
the Batman to figure out the Crime Clown's theme. Until that time, the ball was very definitely in the Joker's
court—and the Batman hated having to wait on the
Joker's pleasure.

"Thirty-four seconds left in the fourth quarter, the
Knights up by a single point over the fiercely determined Lakers. The lead in this game has been seesawing
back and forth since early in the first period, and neither
team has been able to build a lead better than six
points."

"It's going to go right down to the wire, Chuck, a typ-
ical Knights–Lakers matchup. All right, Dogtrot Brown
inbounds the ball for the Knights. He passes it to the

Joker, who brings it up slowly, using as much of the clock as he can. He dishes it back to Brown, who throws it in to Foster. Back out to Brown, who puts it on the floor and thinks about trying the lane. No, he passes it across to the Joker. Now in to Turner—the game clock is down to fourteen seconds—back out to the Joker, who drives on Byron Scott, stops, goes up—the shot is good! The Knights increase their lead, one hundred and seven to one hundred and four. The Lakers immediately call a time-out. Down on the court, all the players are moving toward their respective benches except the Joker, who is still treating the crowd to that awful laughter of his. It's enough to make your flesh crawl."

"Well, while we've got a minute, I just want to say that I think one of the high points of this game came in the middle of the third quarter, when the Joker stole that offensive rebound from Magic Johnson."

"You're definitely right about that, Chuck. It was a smart play. The Joker definitely showed that he knew what he was doing out there. At six feet five inches, he's giving away a good four inches to Johnson, but the Joker never tried to outmuscle Magic for the ball. Instead, he used the kind of instinctive positioning and timing that mark the superior NBA guard."

"He had Johnson completely blocked out of the play. When the ball hit the rim, the Joker slipped in front of him. Johnson would have had to climb the Joker's back to get that rebound, and he would've been called for the foul. The Joker grabbed the ball, faked once, and put it in for the Knights' go-ahead basket. That seemed to take the steam out of the Lakers at a time when they looked as if they might be taking over the game."

"The NBA commissioner's office is still trying to find a way to rule the Joker ineligible to play, but the Joker's attorneys have so far blocked every attempt. I have to say that, forgetting for the moment the Joker's previous history, and judging solely by what he's shown us down there on the hardwood, he's certainly qualified to play with the big boys."

"Well, Tom, that pretty much sums it up, except that a lot of people—myself included—find it pretty hard to forget the Joker's history, even for a moment."

"And now the referees are signaling to both benches. We're down to six seconds remaining in the final period, with the Knights ahead one hundred and seven to one hundred and four. I wonder if the Lakers will hope to score a basket and draw the foul, or get the ball to Magic Johnson or Byron Scott at the three-point stripe."

"I'm sure that none of the Knights will get in the Lakers' way if they want to put it in the paint, Tom. Two points won't do the Lakers any good at all. All right. We've got Johnson, Scott, Worthy, Divac, and Thompson on the floor for Los Angeles, and the Joker, Foster, Parks, and Turner for the Knights, with Willie Watkins in for Dogtrot Brown.

"Scott flips the ball in to Johnson, who fires it down to Divac. Over to Worthy, back out to Johnson—the clock is down to three—and over to Scott. Scott takes it up, lets go a rainbow shot, and the buzzer sounds! Scott's jumper hits the back of the rim. No good! The Knights win!"

"They win their second in a row under their new ownership, Chuck, and the Joker again made a major contribution to this victory. If it weren't so near the end of the season, I'd say he's playing like a candidate for rookie-of-the-year honors. Tonight he had nineteen points, ten assists, three steals, and pulled down eight rebounds, including that big one in the third quarter."

"I had my doubts about him at first, Tom, I have to admit that. Now I wonder where the Joker learned to handle a basketball this well. He must have played competitively as a younger man, in high school or college. I guess we won't learn the answer to that until the Joker decides to reveal the truth. All right, we'll be back with a recap of tonight's game after these important messages."

Once again, after the game, the Joker was unavailable for comment or interviews. None of his teammates could even guess where he'd gone after they all went to the locker room.

For the second night in a row, Commissioner Gordon and the Batman stood in one of the exhibit halls in the Seaside Coliseum. Tonight they were joined by Eileen

Brant, the executive secretary to the director of the Coliseum. Once again, they had been called there because of a break-in, a murder, and the theft of a one-of-a-kind item. And once again, the prime suspect was the Joker.

"Damn him!" growled Gordon. "I wish I could wipe that evil grin off his hideous face. I wish I could pay him back for the way he taunts me and the whole law enforcement profession."

"It's a mistake to get so emotionally involved with these crimes," said the Batman.

"I suppose you're right, Batman. We can't afford to let our reasoning be affected by our personal reactions. But don't you ever feel the same way? Doesn't the Joker get under your skin, too?"

The Batman turned his cowled head away for a moment. "More than you know, Jim," he said in a flat voice. Then he shook his head as if to clear it, and returned his attention to the matter at hand. "Let's go over what we know about tonight's burglary."

Eileen Brant shrugged. She wore a peach-colored silk blouse and a severe blue suit. She seemed personally insulted by the crimes that had been committed in the Coliseum. "There are two functions sharing the facility this week," she said. "The first is a traveling exhibit of Renaissance-era relics, of which the Corsican Condor was the main attraction. That show is using Exhibit Halls A through E. Exhibit Halls F through J are occupied by the Three Eyes, the International Illusionists Institute. They're having their annual convention in Gotham City this year. On display here in Exhibit Hall G are historical memorabilia of famous illusionists such as Blackstone and Houdini."

"The item that was stolen—Houdini's Spanish Maiden—had no actual intrinsic value?" said Commissioner Gordon.

"No, that's the puzzling thing," said Brant. "Houdini wrote up descriptions of a number of illusions and escapes that he did not live to build. In his papers were notes that indicated he wanted to display on stage several familiar torture devices from history. He planned to allow himself to be confined in them, and then make a spectacular escape from each one. The only two he described in detail were his plans for a rack and the Spanish Maiden.

"The Maiden is a wooden box shaped roughly like a human figure, with spikes on the inside that would prevent his movement. The Maiden could be padlocked shut from the outside, but Houdini had thought up a brilliant way of disassembling the box's hinges from the inside. The maiden would be hidden behind a screen, and the audience would never see him slip out through the hinged side and then reassemble the hinges. He never actually built a working model of it."

The Batman stooped to examine the place where the Spanish Maiden had stood. There was nothing there now but a shallow depression in the thick carpeting. "So the item on exhibit here—"

"Was constructed by students and admirers of Houdini, who followed his notes. The Spanish Maiden didn't even have much value to a collector, because it had no direct connection to Houdini at all. Anyone with a moderate amount of mechanical ability could have built a duplicate from Houdini's diagrams."

The Caped Crusader stood up and looked around the exhibit hall at the other items on display—elaborate stage props made of wood and steel and glass, all carefully constructed to disguise the ingenious placement of mirrors, trap doors, and spring-loaded mechanisms. Some were objects that had great value to their owners and other specialized collectors; but the Spanish Maiden had not been made from rare, expensive materials and didn't have any true historical worth. It was certainly not valuable enough to motivate the Joker to commit murder and risk capture.

"I don't understand why the Joker would bother with the Spanish Maiden," said Commissioner Gordon. "There are other props here in this room that are worth much more. And he bypassed the other exhibits in the Renaissance show to get here."

The Batman spread his hands. "No use trying to apply logic to the Joker's motives. I think it may be one of his puzzles, the kind of thing he used to do. He liked to tease us with hints suggested by the items he stole. If that's what he's doing now, perhaps we could get a clue to the next crime in this series. And there *will* be a next crime."

"We can be sure of it," said the commissioner grimly. "C for Condor, S for Spanish Maiden? Does that mean anything to you? C for Corsican, H for Houdini? Is he spelling something out for us?"

The Batman let out a deep breath. "It's still too early to tell. Well, he's broken into this building twice, and murdered two watchmen. Miss Brant, I suggest that you hire extra guards for the exhibits after hours. The Joker may be deranged enough to strike this same place again tomorrow."

"Yes, I'll do that, Batman," said Brant. "Commissioner Gordon, may I expect some uniformed reinforcements from your department?"

"Of course, I'll see to that immediately. And, Batman, I suppose I don't need to mention that the medical examiner determined that the night watchman who was killed here tonight died about nine o'clock?"

"While the Joker was in full view, playing basketball at Gotham Garden."

Commissioner Gordon nodded. "Exactly."

"Well," said the Batman in an ominous voice, "it's been a long time since I've watched an NBA game in person. Maybe it's time for me to see how the Knights are playing this season."

"Chuck, I'm down here at courtside with Robert Branford of Joculator, Inc. As the fans in the radio audience know, he's the president and chief executive officer of the corporation that recently purchased the Gotham City Knights. Bob, thank you for agreeing to answer some questions before this afternoon's game with the Chicago Bulls."

"It's a pleasure to be here, Tom," said Branford. "I think—"

He was interrupted by the voice of the Gotham

Garden's announcer. "Here's today's starting lineup for the visiting Chicago Bulls." There was a mild smattering of applause and a few catcalls. "At guard, number twenty-three, from the University of North Carolina, Michael 'Air' Jordan!" There was appreciative applause from the Knights' fans, who were eager to see this NBA star in action.

"We're going to have to talk in-between these introductions, I guess, Bob. Now, do you have anything to say about the statement issued earlier today by the NBA commissioner's office?"

"At guard," said the announcer, "number fourteen, from Long Beach State, Craig Hodges!"

"Well," said Branford, "I don't know any more than you do. We were informed that the commissioner will hold a news conference on Tuesday, and he's said that he will announce at that time his decision concerning the status of the Joker. Tuesday's an off-day for us, so—"

"At forward, number thirty-three, from Central Arkansas, Scottie Pippen!"

"Let's move along, then," said the radio announcer. "Speculation has it that the commissioner will rule that the Joker does not meet the moral standards of the NBA."

"Let me address that issue, Tom," said Branford. "The Joker has been accused of many things over the years, but he has not been found guilty in a court of law. The basketball commissioner is resorting to innuendo and—"

"At forward, number fifty-four, from Clemson, Horace Grant!"

"Bob, you may be technically correct about the Joker's lack of convictions, but that's only because he's always been judged mentally unfit to stand trial. And if he's avoided prosecution because of his mental instability, then isn't the commissioner acting correctly in barring him from playing?"

"And at center, number twenty-four, from San Francisco, Bill Cartwright!"

"I think, Tom, that we're getting into a gray area

here. In any event, the Joker is perfectly willing to let the courts decide whether or not the commissioner has the right to make such a ruling. If the court sides with the NBA, then the Joker has said he will not appeal, but abide by the commissioner's pronouncement."

"I think basketball fans everywhere will be glad to hear that, Bob. The last thing the sport needs is to have such a wrangle drag on through long, tedious, and expensive legal proceedings. Now what about—"

The Gotham Garden announcer took a deep breath and cried, "Now, ladies and gentlemen, *your* Gotham City Knights!"

Neither the radio announcer nor Robert Branford tried to speak while the Knights were introduced and the hometown fans shouted their approval. Finally, when the Gotham City team had returned to its bench and there were a few moments before the opening tip-off, there was time for one last question.

"Bob," said the radio announcer, "how do you feel about so many of Gotham City's concerned citizens picketing the Garden, protesting the fact that the Joker is playing for the Knights? How about the fact that almost twenty-five percent of the Knights' season-ticket holders have returned their tickets for the remainder of the season and demanded refunds? And despite the fact that the Joker's been playing remarkably well, virtually no one in the crowd is on his side. The Joker seems to be so universally hated that these fans wouldn't cheer for him if he scored a hundred points a game."

"Well," said Branford uncomfortably, "as to that—"

"Excuse me, Bob," the radio announcer interrupted, "let's join now with Gotham Garden organist Millie Vollenweider in singing our national anthem."

Later, the statements of all the witnesses to the third crime were collected and compared. Oddly, though, the more one tried to sort out the robbery, the more it became an enigma. It was difficult to understand, not because it was elaborate and complicated, but for precisely the opposite reason—whoever had stolen the book had been quick, clever, and had attracted very little attention.

This was how Commissioner Gordon's detectives put together the facts: Shortly before half past two in the afternoon, almost exactly on schedule, a 747 jumbo jet landed at Gotham City International Airport. The flight had originated in Amman, the capital city of the Hashemite Kingdom of Jordan, and the plane bore the markings of ALIA, the official airline of that country. It carried only a skeleton flight crew and two passengers.

Those two passengers were escorting the plane's single, small item of cargo—an eight-hundred-year-old copy of the Qur'an, the holy book of the Muslim religion. The classical Arabic text of the book had been copied by one or more skilled calligraphers, but the pages were now much too fragile to be read. The original binding had long since been replaced with covers of pure gold worked in exquisite detail and decorated with perfectly cut precious gems.

The materials of the book's binding could have been sold for a few thousand dollars. What made this particular copy of the holy Qur'an priceless, however, was its history. It had once belonged to the sister of Yūsuf ibn-Ayyūb Salah ad-Din, or Saladin, as he is known to Western scholars.

In 1174 A.D. Saladin rallied other warriors from all over the Muslim world to join him in a *jihad*, or holy war, to throw the invading Crusaders out of the Near East in general and Jerusalem in particular. The French king of Jerusalem decided that this was an appropriate time to make a peace treaty with Saladin, thus neutralizing the overwhelming numbers of Muslim warriors. Under the terms of the truce, Christian pilgrims were given unhindered access to the holy sites in Jerusalem, and Muslim pilgrims were allowed free passage to Mecca.

All of this would have led to an era of peace and mutual tolerance, except that one of the French military leaders was a greedy old man named Reynald de Châtillon. In 1181 he broke the truce by plundering a caravan on its way to the holy city of Mecca. One of the pilgrims in that caravan just happened to be Saladin's own sister. Reynald's deceitful and ill-timed act required some response from the Muslims, and Saladin began attacking Christian strongholds throughout the region.

Four years later, Saladin soundly defeated the Crusaders and recaptured the city of Jerusalem. A few of the highest-ranking Christian officers were brought before Saladin for questioning. One of them, as it turned out, was the treacherous Reynald de Châtillon himself.

Saladin took the opportunity to chastise Reynald for breaking the negotiated peace in the first place. Reynald, in an act of supreme stupidity, could come up with nothing better to say in his defense than a vile, coarse insult. Saladin, reaching the end of his patience, drew his own sword and separated Reynald from his thoughtless head on the spot.

The city of Jerusalem had been liberated from the marauding Christians, and the robbery of Saladin's sister had been avenged, but what *hadn't* turned up was her personal copy of the Qur'an. That wasn't located again until much later. In the centuries that followed, the book was celebrated as a symbol of Muslim moral superiority over the Crusaders.

Under heavy guard, this copy of the Qur'an was carried out of the ALIA 747 and loaded into an armored car, which sped toward the Seaside Coliseum with a police motorcycle escort. When the armored car arrived at its destination, it was discovered that the guard in the back of the vehicle had somehow been murdered, his face contorted in the hideous death-grin of the Joker. The Qur'an, bound in gold and jewels, was missing.

When King Hussein loaned the holy book to the exhibition of Renaissance-era relics in Gotham City, it was the first time it had left the Hashemite Kingdom in more than five hundred years. Now it had fallen into the hands of Gotham City's most nefarious criminal. Reading the account of the theft the following day, knowledgeable experts on the Middle East wondered if this incident might cause a deeper rift between America and the Muslim world. There was no way to know if the Joker had even considered that possibility.

A large figure of a condor made of gold and jewels. A stage prop made of painted wood. A centuries-old book bound in gold and jewels. All three were connected to exhibitions in Gotham City's Seaside Coliseum. Did they have anything more in common?

The Batman began to see a connection. As he studied the schedule of the Gotham City Knights' next few home games, he told himself that it was time to test his theory. He would bet his own life—and possibly the lives of many others—during the Knights' Monday night game against the Houston Rockets.

The next evening at eight o'clock, Exhibit Hall J of the Seaside Coliseum was filled with more than two hundred members of the Three Eyes. They had all come to see Diane Cristall perform her feats of mind reading and hypnotism. Diane Cristall was one of the world's most successful mental telepathists, and although she attributed her abilities to years of arcane studies, there were many skeptical observers in the audience who were glad of the chance to see how she actually executed her tricks.

The lights in the room slowly went down until there was only a single, tight spotlight on the tall, raven-haired woman. "Ladies and gentlemen," said Diane Cristall, "thank you for coming here tonight, despite the unpleasant events that have occurred in this building recently. I can assure you that the management of the Coliseum has added extra security guards, and that we're all perfectly safe. At least, we're safe from human villains. I can't guarantee the behavior of the spirit world!" She flashed a dazzling smile, and her audience laughed appreciatively.

"First of all, as a kind of warm-up, I require the services of a volunteer from the audience. Anyone at all. Do I have a volunteer?"

There was a brief pause, as the professional magicians and illusionists glanced around to see who would offer himself up as Diane Cristall's experimental subject. Finally, a shrill voice spoke up. It came from the far side of the raised platform that served the room as a stage. "Well now, Miss Cristall," said the Joker, suddenly illuminated by a second spotlight, "as much as I've enjoyed your act over the years, I think it's time that you took a seat in the audience and let me show you how a *real* hypnotist works!" He rubbed his gloved hands together and filled the room with his unnerving laughter.

There was immediate consternation in the room. The Joker raised his hands for quiet. "Please, please, ladies and gentlemen! You above all should know that this sort of thing requires the utmost concentration! I'm going to try something never before attempted on such a scale. I'm not going to hypnotize a member of the audience. No, that's for beginners and mediocre mind readers such as Miss Cristall. No, I'm going to put you *all* to sleep! Isn't that a fascinating gimmick? Don't you wish you'd thought of it first?" The Joker's whole body seemed to rock spasmodically with his laughter.

Before the audience could react, the Joker's five henchmen stood up in the darkness. Each man had a rebreathing device fitted tightly between his teeth, and each held a green cylinder of some kind of gas. At a signal from the Joker, they opened the valves. The hissing sound of the escaping gas was drowned out by cries of panic, as the audience members began to fight their way through the gloom toward the two rear exits.

The Batman entered the exhibit hall with a squad of uniformed Gotham City police. "All right, Joker," he said in a cold voice, "your show's over." The police officers pushed their way through the crowd and took the Joker's henchmen into custody. They shut off the poison gas cylinders before enough of the unknown vapor was released to do anyone harm.

"Ah, very good, Batman!" said the Joker, clapping his hands. "I see you finally deciphered the clues! It certainly took you long enough! The three dead guards will probably want to discuss that with you, when I send you to join them in the afterlife! You've ruined my wonderful finale this time, Batfool, but let me ask you one final question."

The Batman pushed his way toward the stage. "No more questions, Joker," he said. "It's time for me to put you back in your box." As he stepped up on the platform, someone turned up the lights in the exhibit hall. Where the Joker had been, there was now only a gossamer screen. His presence in the room had been only an illusion, a projection.

"You *are* a Batfool, you know!" crowed the Joker's voice from beyond the folding partition that separated Exhibit Hall J from its neighbor. "Now, here's something for you to ponder: How well can you hit a screwball?" And then there was only the raucous, crazy sound of his laughter, fading away as the Joker made his escape.

Commissioner Gordon joined the Batman at the front of the hall. "He won't get away," he said. "My men have completely surrounded the Coliseum. They're watching every exit."

The Caped Crusader took a deep breath and let it out. "Do you really believe they'll catch him, Jim?" he asked.

Gordon started to say something, then thought better of it. "No," he replied. "The Joker's beaten us again. At least, this time we stopped him from achieving his ultimate goal, murdering this entire crowd of two hundred innocent people. If you hadn't realized that his crimes were linked to the names of the visiting basketball players, we would have had a horrible, senseless massacre on our hands tonight."

"First, Larry Bird and a 'bird' crime," said the Batman. "Then Earvin Johnson and a 'magic' crime. Next, Michael Jordan and an 'Air Jordan' crime. And tonight the Knights played the Houston Rockets."

"With Akeem 'The Dream' Olajuwon and Eric 'Sleepy'

Floyd," said the police commissioner. "If all the crimes hadn't centered around the two exhibits here at the Coliseum, we might never have been able to stop that madman. We've spent so much time here in the last few days, though, that we both knew about Diane Cristall's hypnotism demonstration tonight."

The Batman watched as the shaken Three Eyes convention members filed out of the hall. "Have you taken the other Joker into custody?" he asked.

"The young man who was playing for the Knights? Yes, although we'll probably have nothing to charge him with. I personally think he was an innocent dupe. His name is Bo Staefler, and he was a promising college player who'd been overlooked in the NBA draft. Joculator, Inc. offered him a lucrative contract to play for the Knights under the conditions that he wear that grotesque Joker outfit, and that he neither ask any questions nor answer them."

"Staefler played so well for the Knights," said the Batman, "I wouldn't be surprised if they signed him to a valid contract under his own name."

"Incidentally, now I see how the Joker disappeared so quickly after each game. Staefler went into the locker room, removed the makeup where no one could see him, and then slipped out again."

"Well, Jim," said the Batman, "what matters is that we stopped the Joker again. I'm sure we'll even recover the stolen times from the offices of Joculator, Inc."

"The Joker couldn't have kept this string of crimes up much longer," Gordon said. "He knew that tomorrow the NBA commissioner was going to ban him from the game. The league will no doubt void the sale of the team, as well."

"The crimes themselves weren't important to him. I think our own sense of morality tends to blind us to just how insane the Joker is. He was willing to murder two hundred innocent people just to make me look bad. We have a hard time believing that such a monster can exist in our society."

"Well, old friend, it's true," said Gordon. "And he's out

there still, somewhere. What do you think he meant by those last words to you?"

"He wanted to know if I could hit a screwball. Well, he's certainly screwball enough. I just hope . . ." The Batman's voice trailed off.

"What is it? What do you think he meant?"

The troubled man in the midnight-blue costume turned away and gazed into space. "I just hope he doesn't start this whole thing all over again at the beginning of baseball season!"

—Thanks to Martin Harry Greenberg, who gave me the idea.

The Joker's War

Robert Sheckley

There was a flash of white light, brief, brilliant, blinding. The man sitting at the writing table blinked and looked up irritably. "What was that?" But there was no one in the room to answer him. He frowned, the lines on his long white face turning down. Whatever it was, it had passed. Outside his cabin, he could hear the ship's horns and sirens hooting. He was aboard the German ship *Deutschland*. It was March 13, 1940. The steamship had just finished docking at Hamburg.

There was a discreet tap at the door. The man turned. "Who is it?"

"Ship's steward, Mr. Simmons. We are ready to disembark. Please have your passport ready."

"Thanks. I'll be there soon. Oh, Steward. Did anything go wrong with the lighting?"

"No, sir. Is something the matter?"

"No, everything's fine. Send some porters to take my bags."

"Yes, sir!"

The man stood up and took off his dressing gown. He dressed in his usual outfit—purple formal jacket, trousers with black pinstripes, green shirt with purple string tie. He added an orange vest. Black shoes with white spats came next. Finally, since it was a chilly day outside, he put on his lavender overcoat. Pausing, he looked at himself critically in the mirror.

Although he traveled under the name of Alfred Simmons, his clothing and appearance proclaimed him none other than the Joker. He studied his green hair, red lips, and long face. His face split into an impossibly wide smile. The Joker was happy. He had waited a long time for this. Now one of his old dreams was going to come true. He was going to get extremely rich, and he was going to have a lot of fun doing it.

The Joker was the focus of all eyes as he sauntered down the gangplank. Hamburg was gray and cold that March morning, and recent raindrops glistened on the old gray walls of the big old buildings. There was a platoon of S.S. troops just behind the immigration booth. Police in their distinctive red-collared uniforms and small peaked slate-blue caps stood around looking sullen and violent. Enormous signs in gothic black letters proclaimed many things *Verboten*. The sky was gray and storm-tossed. Vehicles were crowded into the landing area, and there were tanks and armored cars there, too.

The Joker breathed it all in, expanding his chest as he stood on the soil of Nazi Germany. Yes, it was just as he had thought it would be.

He walked up to the immigration booth. The official examined his passport and peered at him suspiciously. "Herr Simmons? You come to Germany at a strange time. We are at war, you know."

"Yes, I know," the Joker said. "Against France and England. Nothing to do with us Americans. Anyhow, there's not much happening yet, though, is there?"

"We conquered Poland last month!" the official said.

"Big deal." The Joker smirked.

The official stiffened. His eyes narrowed. "I could have you arrested for a remark like that. I have a good mind not to let you into Germany."

"Read the note in back," the Joker said, flicking his finger toward his passport.

The official opened the passport and took out a piece of paper. He unfolded it and read it, once, then twice. He looked at the Joker and his jaw fell open.

"But that signature—"

"Yes," the Joker said. "Are you satisfied? I'll be off,

then." The Joker retrieved his passport with a quick movement of his purple-gloved hand, and walked through the barrier to the waiting cars outside.

One of those cars was an enormous Mercedes-Benz, gunmetal gray, imposing. The chauffeur came over, clicked his heels, bowed. "Herr Simmons? I will attend to your luggage. Please get in."

The Joker settled down in back. His trip was starting well.

Soon the limousine had left the gray city of Hamburg under its haze of smoke, mist, and rain. They were on the *Autobahn* now, moving at high speed to the south. There were thin dead woods on either side. Nothing was in bloom yet. The trees looked unreal in the thin shimmering mists that clung to them.

After a while they were in the Black Forest. Here the limo turned off onto a side road, and then another side road. At last it went through an open gate onto the wooded estate of the Bad Fleishstein Spa.

The proprieter, Herr Gerstner, a small, balding, worried-looking man in a tuxedo, hurried out to open the limo door and greet the Joker personally. "Herr Simmons! So very happy am I to greet you and welcome you to our spa. We had received Herr Obermeier's phone call alerting us to the imminence of your arrival. We have prepared our finest chalet for your occupancy. It is called 'The Kaiser' and your driver can proceed to it and unload your luggage."

"Great," the Joker said. He turned to the chauffeur. "Go do that, Hans, and I'll accompany Herr Gertie here to the spa."

"You must have a glass of cherry liqueur with me," Herr Gerstner said. "It is the finest in all Germany. *Heil Hitler!*"

The Joker smirked but did not reply. The two men strolled up the curving path that led to the main building. There was only a scattering of people around, since it was still early for the spa season. But those the Joker saw were well-dressed and had a prosperous, self-contented look. The Joker decided at once that this was one of the nice things about dealing with cultured and wealthy people. They looked good and they had money.

After drinking a glass of cherry brandy with Herr Gerstner, the Joker strolled through the woods to his chalet. Hans had hung up his clothing, but, following orders, hadn't touched several suitcases with special locks on them.

"OK," the Joker said, "you go find yourself a place to stay in the village we passed. Telephone your number to Gertie when you're settled. Be prepared to move at any time."

Hans saluted and left. The Joker made several telephone calls from the chalet, one of them long-distance to Rome. Then he went outside and strolled around the chalet, knocking off the heads of early spring flowers with his walking stick. Going back inside, he unlocked a small pigskin case and took out several sheets of paper. He studied them carefully, then locked them away again. By then it was time for dinner. He checked his appearance critically in a tall mirror, and substituted a floppy silver and mauve cravat for his black shoestring tie, and strolled back to the main building.

Herr Gerstner had given him a table to himself beside one of the long French windows. The Joker ate the soup and salad without comment. But when the waiter brought him a plate of greenish brown things curled into circles and swimming in a suspicious-looking sauce, he bent over it apprehensively, smelled it, and tapped with his knife on a wineglass to get the waiter's attention.

"What is this?" he asked.

The waiter, a tall blond boy with a bad foot, which had kept him out of the military service so far, blushed and said, *"Rollmops,* sir."

"And what exactly," the Joker asked, "is *rollmops?"*

"It is herring, Meinherr," the waiter said. "It is a special delicacy here in our great country. The sauce is light and contains vinegar—"

"*You* eat it," the Joker said. "What else have you got?"

"The main course is roast pork with prunes, sir."

"I don't eat prunes. Haven't you got any real food?"

By then Herr Gerstner had seen that something was wrong and came hurrying over.

"What is the trouble, Herr Simmons? How may I serve you?"

"That's easy," the Joker said. "Have somebody clear away this slop and bring me some real food. I was assured when I made my booking in this joint that you could cook food of any nation."

"I assure you, we can. Our chefs are world-famous! What would you like?"

"A hamburger steak, medium-well done with plenty of fried onions, french fries, coleslaw, and the trimmings."

"Trimmings?" Gerstner asked, struggling with the idiom.

"Excuse me, gentlemen, perhaps I could help." A woman dining alone at a nearby table had overheard the conversation with considerable amusement. Now she swiftly told Gerstner what to bring, breaking off to enquire of the Joker, "Would you like to finish with apple pie and vanilla ice cream?" The Joker nodded, staring at her. The woman completed the order. Herr Gerstner bowed and went away.

"Where'd you learn about American food?" The Joker asked. "You've got a good accent but you're not American, are you?"

"No, I am not," the woman said. "But I have relatives in America. I visited them on their estate outside of Philadelphia a few years ago, before the war. I am the Baroness Petra von Sidow."

"And I am Alfred Simmons," the Joker said, smiling his smile that split his face laterally from ear to ear. The Joker's smile was a sight that, under other circumstances, had made strong men flinch and had given women nightmares. But the Baroness Petra seemed not to be disconcerted by it.

The Joker looked at her and saw a young woman dressed in the latest Parisian fashion. She was not exactly pretty; her features were too severe for that. But she was as handsome as a young lioness, and looked about as dangerous. Her ash blonde hair was pulled tightly back. Her thin lips were outlined in a dark red lipstick. Her blue eyes were highlighted by dark makeup. Her off-the-shoulder dress displayed her magnificent shoulders and bosom.

"Perhaps you would care to join me for dinner, Herr Simmons?" she said.

"Only if you permit me to buy a bottle of the finest champagne," the Joker said gallantly.

The dinner went well. The Joker was amazed, because he had never been much of a ladies' man, certainly not since the death of Jeanne and his bath in the chemical vat while making his escape from Batman. The immersion in the hellish mix of chemicals had resulted in permanently dying his face dead white, his lips red, and his hair green. But Petra didn't seem to mind. After dinner there was a dance in the spa's grand ballroom. The Joker hadn't planned on attending. But Petra wanted him to go. He accompanied her to her room so she could get a light stole.

Her room was a suite on the spa's top floor. Petra let them in with her key. The first sight that greeted their eyes was a little chambermaid in black costume and frilly white cap asleep in one of the big armchairs.

The Joker found this amusing. Not so Petra.

"Asleep?" she cried. "How dare she sleep when she should be tidying up my things!"

Petra looked around furiously as the maid stumbled to her feet babbling apologies. Petra's gaze fell on a riding crop hanging from the wall. She seized it and flailed furiously at the maid, once, twice, three times, reducing her to tears.

"Now, little fool," Petra said, "find me my stole and don't let me ever find you sleeping in here again!"

The maid hurried off and returned a moment later, wiping her tears with the stole. It was at that moment that the Joker fell in love with Petra.

*   *   *

That evening, dancing with Petra under the stars, on the balcony of the hotel, was the most romantic evening the Joker had ever spent. Petra seemed to be taken with him, too.

"I hope to see you again," the Joker said, when the evening was at an end.

"But of course! We are staying in the same hotel, after all."

"Unfortunately," the Joker said, "I must leave tomorrow on business. But I'll be back in a day or so."

"You have not told me what is your business, bad boy," Petra said.

"I'm a businessman," the Joker said, "I get things and sell things. You know how it is with business."

"I have always thought business was very dull," Petra said. "But perhaps that is because my family has not had to engage in it. We have lived from the income of our family estates in East Prussia for hundreds of years."

"You got a good thing going," the Joker said.

She shrugged. "East Prussia is home, of course, but I have always wanted to travel. I enjoyed my stay in America, but there is another place I want to go to."

"Where's that?"

"Rio de Janeiro!" Her eyes gleamed. "I have relatives there. They tell me it is the most fabulous life. And I simply love to samba!"

"I've got some contacts there, too," the Joker said. "Look, Petra, we must talk more about this."

"I would be delighted," Petra said. "Good night, Herr Simmons. Or should I say—Herr Joker!"

The Joker returned to his chalet. He was walking on air. It took an effort to remind himself that he had come to Europe for a purpose, and that the time for action was almost at hand.

Early the next morning his chauffeur arrived punctually at the chalet. The Joker had him put two suitcases into the trunk, and then told him to drive to

Flugelhoff Airport, the nearest international airport to the spa. Arriving, he saw that most of the field was taken up with military activities. There were two squadrons of Heinkel bombers parked wing to wing at one end of the field. Security was tight. But the Joker's passport and the letter in it from Obermeier were more than sufficient to get him through. Soon they were in the air. The Joker watched through the window as they crossed the Alps and began the journey down the Italian peninsula.

Despite the air of ingenuousness that he put on, the Joker was very well aware that there was a war on. It was inescapable, even far away in America. He had followed Hitler's progress, taking the Rhineland, the Sudetenland, then launching the blitzkrieg against Poland. The Poles had resisted gallantly but couldn't stand up to the German army of more than a million men and the great panzer divisions that raced on ahead of the troops. Norway and Denmark had fallen. Britain and France were in a state of war with Germany, but so far little had happened. Both sides, Allies and Axis, mobilized, but the French stayed behind the Maginot Line, the Germans behind the Seigfried Line. And the world waited to see what would happen next.

The Joker was a master criminal. He knew that war brought great opportunities for those who could move fast, fearlessly, and with imagination. Those were his qualities. A scheme had lain in the back of his mind for a long time. The present state of upset in Europe made it the perfect opportunity. Now he was doing it.

The German plane flew down the Po Valley and at last began the descent at Rome's Leonardo da Vinci Airport. Customs and immigration were simple. The Joker had several letters of introduction. And he had a well-filled wallet and spread money around liberally among the delighted customs and immigration people.

He went through the formalities quickly and there was a chauffeur to meet him just outside the customs area.

"Signore Simmons?"

"You got it," the Joker said.

"Giuseppe sent me," the chauffeur said. "I am Pietro.

I am to take you to where the others are awaiting your arrival."

"Sounds good to me," the Joker said. He let Pietro open the door for him. The vehicle was an old but immaculate Hispano-Suiza, the deluxe model with gold fittings.

"Nice bus," the Joker commented.

"Nothing but the best for you, Signore," Pietro said. "That is what Signore Giuseppe said."

They drove off into the streets of downtown Rome. It was late afternoon. The brilliance was just going out of the sky. By the time Pietro had fought the traffic and brought them to Trastevere, it was early evening.

Evening in Trastevere. The skies of Italy were as brilliant as those of Germany were gloomy. The streets were filled with banners from a recent Fascist rally. Huge portraits of Il Duce hung from the sides of the tall terracotta buildings. The limo pulled up in front of a large restaurant. There were potted palms in front. Several men in business suits lounged in front of the entrance. From the sag in their pinstriped suits, the Joker could tell they were armed. He had no doubt they were the guards for Giuseppe Scuzzi, his contact in Rome for the coming operation.

The Joker emerged, and his bizarre and colorful appearance gave pause for the moment even to these hardened criminals. They didn't let their awe show for long. One of them said, in broken English, "You are the Signore Joker, eh? They are inside, waiting for you."

The Joker swept inside past the guards. The restaurant was large, but it was nearly empty. All the tables were neatly stacked, with chairs on top of them. Only one table was filled, and that was at the rear. There, a group of about a dozen men sat over straw-covered bottles of Chianti and little plates of *calamari,* deep fried to a golden brown. They were arguing together in low ominous voices, but looked up when the Joker pranced in.

One of them, a short rotund man sitting at the head of the table, stood up. This was Scuzzi himself, mastermind of mafia operations in the Rome area.

"Eh," Scuzzi said, "that's-a da Signore Joker!" He stood up, the white-and-black check suit emphasizing his girth. He swept the broad-brimmed Panama hat off his head and made a mock bow. "Long have I heard of your fame, Joker, since it stretches to the four corners of the Earth, and beyond! It is a privilege for me and my associates, poor hoodlums though we are, to be permitted to assist you in what our associates assured us would be the caper of the century!"

The Joker smiled his ghastly smile. He had no difficulty detecting the note of irony in Scuzzi's gallant speech. The other mafia men at the table were grinning and nudging each other.

"And how is our mutual friend?" Scuzzi said. "I refer, of course, to Antonio Patina, the famous *padrino* of Gotham City?"

"Patina is well," the Joker said. "As you know, he is presently behind bars in Gotham Penitentiary on a trifling charge of income tax evasion. We are working night and day to get him off, and expect to succeed in the near future. Patina sends you his great love and asserts again that you are to obey me in all things during the course of this job."

"Of course!" Scuzzi said, his grin too broad to be convincing. "You are a world-famous figure, Signore Joker. It brings great honor upon us to serve you in this. There also is the matter of the division of the booty."

"That has already been arranged," the Joker said. "Half for you and your men, half for me."

"That is correct," Scuzzi said. "We are only poor mafiosi, we are of course content with half to be divided among us. The rest goes to you, eh, Joker?"

"I need a full half," the Joker said. "I would remind you that I have been setting up this scheme for a long time. I have had high expenses, traveling to Europe, bribing people, either buying or making special equipment. Are you dissatisfied, then?"

"Not at all!" Scuzzi said, with too great heartiness. "It

is only fair, as you point out. And now, perhaps you will favor us with the knowledge of what this job is. We have noted that you did not entrust us with the secret of your destination before now. Are you going to tell us, or do we go into the job blind?"

"There has been a need for secrecy," the Joker said. "As long as only I knew, there was no chance of anyone else finding out. I do not talk in my sleep, gentlemen! But yes, now is the time and now you shall know." The Joker opened his briefcase and took out a large folded sheet of paper.

Next day, early in the morning, the crowds came across the Vittorio Emanuele Bridge and onto the broad Via della Conciliazione. There were no French or British tourists in that war year, but they were more than made up for by the crowds of German and Austrian tourists, plus the Italians, of course, and a large group of Spaniards and Portuguese. They were like sightseers at any time and any palace; they stopped to peer at the Swiss guards in their traditional uniforms of red, yellow, and blue stripes, carrying their ceremonial halberds. They stood for a while in Saint Peter's Square, each group gathered around his docent. Lectures in many languages were carried on near the big ranks of tourist buses. There were many independent tourists as well; they flocked up the stairs, leaving the Arco delle Campane on the left, with the Vatican Palace and museums and the Sistine Chapel on the right. There were many native Italians among the sightseers, some seeking audience with the pope, others merely passing a mild day in mid-March.

Within Saint Peter's Basilica they went, clustering around the great statues, especially the great bronze Saint Peter by Cambio, where many stopped to kiss its foot.

Inside they scattered in many directions, some exploring the transept and apse, others examining the tombs of Pius VII and the monument of Leo XI.

All of this was under the watchful eye of guards.

Those within were armed with pistols. There were many guards, because within these walls were some of the costliest as well as holiest treasures in Europe.

All day the tourists came and went. By five in the afternoon the last of them had left, ushered out by the guards. A careful double check was made to be sure that no one had been left behind. Despite its holiness, it was considered unlucky to be locked into Saint Peter's at night. Some said that the ghosts of early martyrs still walked these marble halls.

By nine in the evening everything had been carefully locked up. The alarm system was tested. A last examination of the galleries was made. And at last Saint Peter's was ready to settle down for the night.

Dark and mysterious, night came again to Rome. Lights were burning late in nearby Castel Sant'Angelo, where the pope worked late with his assistants, trying to bring some sense and order to a Europe gone mad with war.

Guard dogs prowled the grassy walks and the colonnaded aisles. A special patrol of *carabinieri* made their rounds and declared that all was well. The Vatican was safe again for the night. Or so it seemed.

Dim lights glowed in the great art galleries. Saint Peter's chair glowed with the color of soft gold. Michelangelo's *Pietà* seemed like old ivory in that subdued lighting.

In the picture galleries, bearded popes and antique saints looked down from their golden frames. In the Vatican Picture Gallery there were row upon row of them.

Not all the paintings were of religious subjects, however. Here and there was a portrait of a shepherd. And at the far end of one gallery, life-size, was a portrait of a Venetian reveler. He wore clown's costume, a white satin outfit with dark blue polka dots. A domino half mask covered his eyes, and his lower face showed a smile that stretched from ear to ear and seemed to mock the somber religious paintings on all sides of him. He was perfectly immobile, a strange figure in his finery.

The Lateran clock struck midnight. The figure of the

Venetian clown moved, stretched, and stepped out of its frame.

The Joker stretched luxuriously, then walked quickly toward Leo the Great's monument. He moved behind it and located the little door set in the stone, sealed many years before. He had a knapsack under his white gown. Taking from it a small amount of plastic, he patted it quickly into place. Then he looked up. He could hear footsteps approaching.

Two *carabinieri* came, walking their rounds. The Joker made no attempt to conceal himself. He had been expecting these men.

"Hi, fellows," he said.

The guards looked up unbelievingly.

The Joker grinned even wider, advanced toward them, saying, "Look, guys. I can explain everything. It was a bet, you understand what I mean? Look, I got something for both of you. . . ."

He reached them and opened his hands. A cloud of dust flew out. The guards coughed, sneezed, and then slumped to the floor.

"You'll be OK," the Joker said to their recumbent bodies. "Just a slightly altered formula of my Joker venom, in handy powder form. Sweet dreams, fellows."

The Joker moved swiftly through the basilica. He had memorized its layout, back when he first conceived this idea. He remembered the time well. He had been reading about the Huns and how they had marched down the Italian peninsula and sacked Rome. The Joker had always admired Atilla. There was a man for you! And the Joker had thought to himself, anything Atilla can do, I can do, too. And I don't need a million Huns to help me.

Just a few mafiosi, who, according to the plan, ought to be outside waiting to be let in.

The Joker went out into the soft Roman night. He went past the tall poplars to the gate on the left side. This was a small gate, solidly barred. The Joker met two more guards on his way there. Swiftly he put them to sleep with his patented gas. A plastic explosive was enough to blow open the lock. He swung the gate open, hearing it make a soft screeching noise.

"Come on out, fellows," the Joker said.

A group of shadows detached themselves from the dense shadows along the Vatican wall. It was Giuseppe and a dozen of his men. They looked in awe at the open gate, hesitated before going in.

"Well, whatsa matter?" the Joker asked. "This is what we agreed on, isn't it?"

"I just never thought you could bring it off," Giuseppe Scuzzi said. "Come on, boys!"

They hurried into the Vatican.

Spreading out, they went about their tasks like a well-oiled machine. The Joker had shown them on a map of the Vatican which were the paintings to take, the ones which were small enough to be portable but worth a lot of money. They hurried around to the rooms while the Joker himself went to the crypt.

The door did not hold him up long. He went down, following the strong yellow beam of a flashlight he'd had under his clothing.

There was deep dust on the steps. They had been a long time unused. The flashlight threw great shadows over suits of armor, great chests, more paintings. The Joker went to one side of the room and searched more carefully. Yes, here it was, just as his researches in America had shown him. The never-used doorway into the secret underground crypt.

Working more quickly now, the Joker found the ring-bolt in the floor. With the aid of a miniature fulcrum of his own invention he hoisted it up. The trapdoor, which was a slab of marble half a foot thick, yielded grudgingly. The Joker finally had it levered up and pushed aside. He went down into the subcellar.

He was in a sort of underground dungeon. Skeletons hung in chains from the wall. A scurry of movement proved to be rats, scrambling back to their holes. The sight of them amused the Joker.

"I won't disturb you for long, fellows," he said. The Joker had always felt a kinship with rats.

In a far end of the dungeon he found what he was looking for: a small coffer, about two feet long by one foot wide and a foot deep, made of rare enameled wood, now dusty and with no shine. He pried it open. Yes, just as he had been told, here was a box full of the rarest treasure—great pearls, some lustrous white, others dusky. There were diamonds and rubies, too, some of them set in red-gold, others loose. There were ornaments—brooches and pins, all made of pure gold and crusted with precious stones. This take alone was worth millions.

The Joker glanced at his watch and saw that it was almost time to go. He hurried back to the inhabited levels, closing the vault behind him. He lugged the casket outside. The mafiosi had been busy and efficient. They had rolled out the great sheet of reinforced canvas he had had them bring, and in the middle of it dumped the paintings and statuary he'd told them to take. Everything was inside the great square of canvas. And now Giuseppe Scuzzi came up to him.

"But tell me this, Joker," he said, "how are you going to get this stuff outside? You didn't tell me that part of your plan."

"One part at a time, that's my motto," the Joker said. "Never fear, I have my methods. Now, tell your boys to fold over the edges so we can make one nice pile of it."

"You must have hired a truck," Scuzzi said, giving the orders to his men. "But I didn't see it around. Come on, Joker, what did you set up?"

"Don't worry about it," the Joker said. "You'll see when it's time."

"I think we have to see now," Scuzzi said. The Joker looked at him and was not entirely surprised to find a gun leveled at his chest.

"Scuzzi," the Joker said sadly, "I thought we were friends?"

"Of course we are," Scuzzi said, "But you're the sort of friend I don't really trust. I don't think you have anything worked out beyond this, Joker. I think you mean for us to carry it out through the gate. That's not a bad idea. Then we can load it into our cars."

"That's not what I had in mind, at all," the Joker said. "And I will thank you to point that gun in a different direction."

Scuzzi laughed. The rest of his men had gathered around now. They all had their guns drawn. They were all pointing at the Joker.

"Don't try any funny stuff," Scuzzi said. "I saw what you did with the guards. Nice work, Joker, but you're not going to get us that way."

"What do you intend?" the Joker asked.

"I'm afraid this is the end," Scuzzi said. "The end for you, Joker. Thanks for leading us to this haul. But I really don't think I can afford to have you take half. Ready boys?"

The Joker stepped into the middle of the treasure. He had the two ends of the rope that bound the ends of the bundle together. He began to laugh.

"What in hell are you laughing at?" Scuzzi snarled.

"You, my friend! I'm thinking what a nice headline this is going to make in the morning newspaper!"

"What're you talking about?" Scuzzi asked.

"Look on the wall," the Joker suggested.

Scuzzi and his men did so. There, lined up five feet apart, were at least fifty *carabinieri*. Their guns were at the ready.

"Where'd they come from?" Scuzzi cried.

"I thought the police might like to take care of this," the Joker said. "It saves me the trouble." He whirled and raised his arms. A gas bomb concealed on his person exploded, emitting a thick cloud of yellow smoke. It billowed up around him, hiding the Joker from their view. The mafiosi began firing, but the police were ready and started firing back. Men started to curse and fall. Above it all could be heard the Joker's high uncanny laughter.

"Maybe they'll get us," Scuzzi said, "but they'll get you, too!"

"Oh, I think not," the Joker said.

Scuzzi tried to take aim at him, but the Joker was invisible in the clouds of yellow smoke. Then Scuzzi saw a sight he wouldn't have believed possible.

The great square of canvas, with the Joker in the middle of it, had suddenly drawn together. As he watched, incredulously, he saw the entire mass, the canvas, the treasure, the Joker within, drawn straight up in the air.

For a moment he thought his eyes were failing him. Then, looking straight up, he saw, almost invisible in the gloom, a small dirigible. It had come down low over the Vatican, a free-swinging hook catching the ropes that bound the treasure, and now it was being drawn straight up into the air.

"I'll get you!" Scuzzi screamed. "I'll get you! Boys! Shoot down that blimp!"

But the mafiosi were having their own troubles. Shots from the *carabinieri* had already decimated their ranks. Scuzzi saw that he was going to have a lot of trouble saving himself. He rushed toward the exit, straight into the arms of a waiting group of policemen.

"What about him?" he asked the lieutenant of police who put the cuffs on him.

"Him? Who do you mean?"

"The Joker, you idiot! He's making off with the treasure!"

The lieutenant looked up in the direction Scuzzi was pointing, saw the great canvas bag swing into the air. Before he could call his men's attention to it, it was gone.

The pilot of the dirigible let the lighter-than-air craft steer itself while he guided the canvas load onto a platform beneath the operator's cupola. The Joker stepped out and made the load secure, then joined the pilot in his compartment.

"Thanks, Chang," the Joker said.

The pilot removed his goggles, showing his Mongolian features and thin moustache. He grinned at the Joker.

"Went good, didn't it?"

The dirigible continued north to Germany, piloted by Chang, personal pilot to one of the Joker's friends, Fu Yu, the Mongolian warlord with whom he had made a deal earlier. So careful had the Joker been of this operation that he hadn't wanted to use a European. Fu Yu had been amenable to a deal, and had had one of his air units stationed in Albania, part of a complex deal he had been putting together.

Assisted by the dirigible's powerful pusher engines, they were back over Germany before daylight.

As the dirigible hovered, the Joker said, "I've already put aside the art treasures I promised your master. You can look them over and see that everything is correct."

The Mongolian pilot shrugged. "If you say OK, is OK. You'd have to be crazier than I think you are to double-cross my master. He isn't soft like those mafiosi."

"I didn't double-cross them, Chang," the Joker said. "They double-crossed me. I just happened to have an ace up my sleeve."

"You called the cops on them."

"Precisely. Because I knew they were going to double-cross me."

"But what would you have done if they hadn't double-crossed you?"

"I would have figured out some way to get them out," the Joker said. "I'm an honest criminal, at least that's what everyone says. You can put me down here. My chalet is right down there."

"You've got it," Chang said.

"My regards to General Fu Yu," the Joker said.

"Thank you, Joker," Chang said. "I will tell him."

Before dawn brought curiosity-seekers, the Joker was able to put the treasure away in the spare bedroom of his rented chalet. He stacked the paintings carefully. Some of those Michelangelos and Raphaels were priceless; or so the wealthy South American collectors who had contracted with him had told him. This done, he showered and changed, and looked over the casket of treasures. He selected one particularly nice piece—a genuine Cellini, to judge by the long wavy lines on the side the brooch. It was a magnificent piece, a sculpture of a sea horse done in amber and covered in precious stones. Smiling to himself he slipped it into his pocket. Next he needed a few hours' sleep. But the excitement was too high in him to permit him to rest for long. Instead he took a drug that had been specially developed for him by a black-market genius. It gave great clarity and intellectual acumen

and wiped away the effects of sleeplessness. The only
trouble with it was that repeated use tended to rot the
brain stem and send a person into delirium tremors. The
Joker thought it was a small price to pay for feeling
good.

Now that he had the treasure safely stored away in his
chalet, the Joker had but to complete his arrangements
to get it out of Europe, to the wealthy and unscrupulous
men who had contracted with him for it. He could still
remember the oily smile of old Soao Goncales, in his
planter's white drill uniform, with the bullwhip in the
pant loops instead of a belt. "These paintings will serve
me well," he had told the Joker. You have seen my house
here in the outback. It is very fine, no? With paintings
on the wall, my new bride Miriam Da Silva, whom I im-
ported from Portugal, will have something to look at
during the day when I am away sweating the rubber
planters to keep up their pace." And the other planters
had felt the same way, too. They were a long way from
civilization, far even from the dubious thrills of Manaus
on the Amazon. With these treasures they could at least
play at being European grandees. And since they had
the price, the Joker was willing to oblige.

The Joker was well content with himself. As evening
approached he telephoned the hotel and made a reserva-
tion for two. He had been unable to get Petra out of his
mind. Few women had ever affected him so deeply.
Looking at her, he could conjure for himself a life beyond
crime, a life lived with a beautiful blonde wife whose
tastes seemed so clearly to coincide with his.

But what did she think of him? That was still unan-
swered. He would learn that this evening.

He put the Cellini brooch in his pocket, first wrapping
it in a piece of Kleenex to keep from scratching it. He
then dressed carefully in his green tuxedo, brushed back
his dark green hair, grinned at himself in the mirror,
and walked over to the hotel.

*   *   *

Petra was glorious in an off-the-shoulder silver lamé evening gown. The waiters did not have to be told to bring the strange American his favorite hamburger steak. And this time, wonder of wonders, Herr Gerstner had managed to find a bottle of genuine American ketchup! And, remembering what he had read of American dietary habits, he had caused to be cooked a quantity of onions with the hamburger steak. Petra looked on fondly as the Joker gorged, murmuring, "Eat, eat, my green-haired wolf." It was about as domestic a scene as the Joker had known in quite some time.

Later, the orchestra played Viennese waltzes.

Though the Joker was not much of a dancer, he managed to galumph around the floor in credible fashion. When they sat down again, over chilled champagne, he thought the time was right to give her the present.

"I have something for you, Petra," he said. He took the brooch out of his pocket and handed it to her. She peeled back the Kleenex and exclaimed when she saw what lay within it.

"But my dear Joker!" she exclaimed. "It is perfectly splendid. The workmanship is very fine."

"It's a genuine Cellini," the Joker said. "You can tell by those wavy lines on the side. Do you like it?"

"*Ach*, but I adore it! And what shall I give you in return? She leaned toward him, bosom heaving against the silver material of her dress. "Perhaps a kiss, yes?"

"That's always good for openers," the Joker said.

She made an expression of mock dismay and tapped him on the arm with a forefinger. "Oh, but you are naughty! We have punishments for naughty boys! Would you like me to punish you?"

"We'll get to who does what to whom a little later," the Joker said. "Listen, Petra, all fooling aside, I'm crazy about you. You've got class and breeding. You're sophisticated, beautiful. And I am the master criminal of this age, and perhaps any age. Don't you think we would make a nice couple?"

"Herr Joker, what are you suggesting?" There was a

hint of amusement in her corn-blue eyes, and a hint of intrigue as well.

"I want you to go away with me," the Joker said. "Come with me to America. Or maybe South America would be better. I'm rich now." He gestured at her brooch. "There's plenty more where that came from. We could start a new life together in Rio."

"Rio!" she murmured, and there was the scent of hibiscus in her voice.

"Sure, Rio, why not?" the Joker said. "A new place for us both. What do you think?"

She looked at him, then at the brooch. Her eyes fondled the ornament while her fingers stroked his arm. "You tempt me very much! But it is impossible."

"Why?" the Joker asked. "It's my green hair, isn't it?"

"Not at all! I love your appearance! I would love to run away with you, and to live with you in a tropical paradise far from the concerns of old Europe. But it cannot be."

"So why?"

"Because there is a war on. Much as I care for you, I care yet more, greater, for the Fatherland."

"The Fatherland," the Joker mused. "I suppose you are referring to Germany?"

"I am speaking," she said, "of our glorious Third Reich and its great leader, Adolf Hitler!"

She raised her voice when she said this, and several diners at nearby tables automatically said, *"Seig Heil!"*

She let the Joker accompany her to the door of her suite. But no further.

"It is not because I don't want to, dear Joker," she said at the door, her voice husky. "But I could not trust myself with a man such as you. And it must not be. It is written in the stars that I am to belong to one who does a great deed for the Fatherland."

"You're sure of that, huh?" the Joker said.

"Yes, I am. Hitler's own astrologer, Herr Otto Obermeier, read the cards and told me so."

That gave the Joker quite a lot to think about. In the morning, he telephoned Obermeier in his Munich apartment and got an appointment for that afternoon.

* * *

Munich was adazzle with Nazi flags. Armored columns filled the streets. Hitler Youth marched on the broad boulevards. The famous beer halls were filled with soldiers. The Joker went to Obermeier's address and instructed his chauffeur to pick him up soon after. He rang the bell and climbed the three flights of stairs of Obermeier's atelier.

Obermeier answered the door himself. Despite being Hitler's astrologer, he lived modestly, ploughing back all his earnings into a great project. He was convinced that Frederick Barbarossa and his knights still lived somewhere in a deep ice cavern under a river in Germany. When not prognosticating the future, Obermeier went off on expeditions to find the lost cave of Barbarossa. This used up a lot of his earnings. More went to maintain his daily diet of pâté de foie gras and champagne, which his physician, Dr. Faustus, had prescribed for him as the only diet for visionaries. Obermeier was short and round and pink, with albino-white hair and thin reddish eyebrows. He was overjoyed at the Joker's visit.

"I am your greatest fan!" he declared, ushering the Joker into his living room. "I follow all of your exploits, Herr Joker, and I have told the Führer more than once that if Germany had a regiment of men such as yourself the war would soon be over."

"Even a platoon would help," the Joker said. "But it's tough; there's only me and none like me."

They talked idle talk for a while. The Joker expressed his gratitude for the letter Obermeier had sent him. It had opened many doors for him in Germany. Their talk turned inevitably to the war. Obermeier was vehement in his objection to the slow course it was taking.

"Look at our lightning victories in Norway, Denmark, Poland! We have the mightiest war machine the world has ever known. All Europe stands ready to fall at our feet. Our thousand-year Reich is ready to take over. But what are the generals doing? They sit timidly behind the defenses of the Siegfried Line, waiting. Hitler has the

right instinct. He wants to attack through the Ardennes,
throw his troops through Belgium. It is the Schiefflin
Plan, which almost won the First World War for us. It
would be bound to win the Second."

"And why is this plan not put into action?" the Joker
asked.

Obermeier shrugged and made a comical-sad face. "It
is the conservatism of the generals. Although the Führer
has supreme power, yet he still listens to those
bemedaled idiots. I try to advise him, but although he
listens to me, he still waits and hangs fire."

"You're pretty sure this plan would succeed?" the
Joker asked, studying the map which Obermeier had
opened in front of him.

"Certain of it! And the man who convinced Hitler of it
would be a hero of the Reich."

"Is that a fact?" the Joker said. "Let's just go over the
whole plan once more. . . ."

The Brownshirt rally had been a great success. Adolf
Hitler had stood on the little balcony on the third floor of
the Chancellery in Berlin and harangued the crowd for
the better part of four hours, often repeating himself for
greater emphasis. Now, as the applause died down and
then rose again, he came in from the balcony, wiping his
brow with a large handkerchief. Although it was a cool
day, he was perspiring. These speeches took it out of a
man.

He threw himself into an armchair, moodily pushing
back the fold of dark hair that had become his trademark. Then he looked up abruptly. He suddenly knew,
with a sixth sense that rarely failed him, that he was not
alone in the room.

"Who iss dass?" he asked, his voice harsh.

There was a movement to one side of him. A tall figure in clown's costume stepped out from behind a drap-
ery. The man had green hair, red lips, a dead-white face.
He was grinning—a horrible rictus of a smile that
stretched his face from ear to ear.

"Hi, there," the Joker said brightly, stepping out into
the middle of the room.

"It iss dass Joker!" Hitler exclaimed. "Herr Obermeier told me that you were in Germany and wanted to see me. I agreed. But this is not the usual channels. . . ."

"No, it's not," the Joker said. "You've heard of me, right?"

"Of course!" Hitler said. "I love the way you constantly confound that beefy Batman and his catamite boyfriend Robin! I follow all your exploits! It is a pleasure to meet you, even if the circumstances are unorthodox."

"Unorthodoxy is what is needed to fight a war," the Joker said.

"Exactly what I have told my generals," Hitler said. "But they just snicker and say, 'Leave the fighting to us, mein Führer; war is for professional men.'"

"But you know better than that, don't you?"

"Of course I do!"

"And I know it, too," the Joker said. "Listen, Adolf, I've been studying this Shuffling Plan—"

"You mean the Schiefflin Plan," Hitler said.

Hitler seemed almost mesmerized by the tall grinning figure. He followed as the Joker led him to the desk. Taking a large map out from his cape, the Joker unfurled it.

"Now look here. This shows present positions. Don't worry about how I got this! Your secrets are safe with me! Now then, look, you've got Manfred's divisions here and here, and Von Rundstedt is sitting on his ass over here near the Swiss border, and Keitel is larking around in front of the Maginot Line. Well, why not pull them all out, except for Keitel near the Swiss border. He can make a diversion, make them think you're going to hit elsewhere. But you take all these guys, and the motorized panzers, and push them straight through here." The Joker's gloved hand came down hard on Belgium and Holland.

"It is what I want to do," Hitler said, almost in a whisper. "But if it goes wrong . . ."

"Adolf," the Joker said, "I've been doing stuff like this for quite a while. I've got something to tell you."

"I'm listening," Hitler said. "But can I get you a drink?"

"Later. For now, pay attention. You have to put your mind into an outrageous scheme and then do it without looking back. You got me?"

"Yes, yes, it is what I want to do. But the generals—"

"Who rules Germany? You or the generals?"

Hitler looked up. His eyes were on fire. His hands trembled as he seized the Joker's hands in both of his and shook them fervently. "Joker, I'll do it! This is too big for generals to sit back advising caution. I would probably have done it anyhow. But you have convinced me that now is the time. Joker, how may I reward you?"

"Just scratch a few words on a piece of paper telling what I've done for you and for Germany," the Joker said. "I want to show it to my girlfriend."

On May 9, the Joker visited Hitler again to make sure that the Führer had everything straight. Hitler was glad to see him. He had been haranguing his generals and setting up the new plan. There were a few details he was unsure of, however. The Joker was able to clear these up for him. On the Joker's advice, Bock's army group B was combined into two armies rather than its former unwieldy three. The detached army, the 18th under General George van Kuchler, was detailed to attack the Netherlands. Runstedt's army advanced on May 10. They were on a broad front between the middle Meuse and the Moselle. They drove forward with forty-six divisions, seven of which were armored. On the Joker's insistence, they were backed by twenty-seven divisions. While they were preparing for the attack, Von Leeb's army group C, composed of two armies, threatened an attack on the Maginot Line, thus pinning down large numbers of French troops.

Von Runstedt's forces rumbled forward in the blitzkrieg. It brushed aside the weak Belgian resistance in the Ardennes and fought through two understrength French armies still equipped with horse cavalry.

Hitler didn't like to have the Joker around his headquarters because the man's crazy smile unnerved his staff, and there was always the fear that the generals would think their leader too much under the influence of an American crazy. The Joker grinned when Hitler told him this, saying, "Hey, I know when I'm not wanted," and took up residence at the Princeknacht, the best hotel in Berlin at that time. There he had a direct line to Hitler, who also picked up all his bills.

By mid-May the die was cast. The Allied armies were retreating in confusion, German tanks were completing a huge envelopment, and the British Expeditionary Army was retreating to the dead end of Dunkirk. It looked like the war was over not long after it had properly begun.

The Joker returned in triumph to the spa in Bad Fleishstein; back to his stolen art treasures, and Petra. In his pocket was a letter signed by Hitler, praising the part he had played in the glorious victory and declaring him a Friend of the Third Reich, First Class.

Back at the spa, the Joker went straight to his chalet. He saw the first sign of trouble as he approached. There were several armored cars packed in the grass around his house. When he came in, he found Germans in air force uniforms taking out his treasures. They had found it without difficulty. There aren't a lot of places to hide a huge assortment of paintings, statuary, and jewelry in a small rented chalet.

"What do you guys think you're doing?" he asked.

A young lieutenant came up to him and snapped his heels as he saluted.

"Lieutenant Karl von Krausner, at your service," he said. "How may I serve you?"

"Easy," the Joker said. "You can tell your goons to put all of my stuff back where they found it."

"You claim this as your treasure?"

"Of course I do! It's been in the family for years!"

"And do you always travel to Europe with uncountable millions of dollars' worth of Italian art treasures?"

"You're damned right I do," the Joker said. "I like to have good art around me, not these tacky magazine repros." He gestured at the artwork on the chalet's walls.

"There is nothing I can do," Lieutenant von Krausner said. "These objects are confiscated under the direct orders of Field Marshal Goering himself."

The Joker cooled off immediately. He recognized the name of the second in command in Germany, and head of the Luftwaffe, Germany's air force.

"There must have been some mistake," the Joker said. "I have permission from the highest authorities."

"I know nothing of this," the lieutenant said. "You will have to take it up with the Reichs Marschall himself."

"Where'll I find him?"

"He is presently a guest at the spa."

The Joker hurried back to the hotel and asked the manager where Goering was.

"He is in his suite," Gerstner said. "But he left orders not to be disturbed."

"Big deal," the Joker sneered, and hurried off despite Gerstner's protests.

The Joker bounded up the stairs, pushing people aside as he hurried down the hall. He reached the door of the special suite. There was something familiar about it. Yes, of course, this was Petra's suite! The Joker was getting really angry now. What were these people trying to put over on him? There was a German soldier with a Schmeisser machine pistol on guard at the door. The Joker pushed past him, ready to knock.

"Nein!" the soldier shouted. He fumbled for his gun.

"Cool off, baby," the Joker said to him, and, reaching into his pocket, took out a handful of a white substance and threw it into the soldier's face. The guard sneezed violently, three times, then sagged to the floor unconscious.

"The new Joker sleeping venom always works," the Joker mused. "He'll wake up in a couple hours with a hangover and a memory of snowflakes." He tried the door. It was not locked. He opened it and barged in.

*   *   *

Inside the room he heard the sounds of laughter from the bedroom. One of the voices had a high-pitched, slightly hysterical voice. Petra. The other was deep and gruff and weird. That had to be the Field Marshal. The Joker walked into the bedroom.

There he saw Goering sitting in an easy chair. He was a huge fat man with a particularly obnoxious expression. His sleeves were rolled up revealing forearms like hamhocks. His military jacket with the many rows of medals had been hung neatly over a chair. The Field Marshal was just leaning forward to pour champagne into two tall glasses when the Joker entered. Petra was also in the room. She was wearing her negligee, her blonde hair unbound and falling loosely around her shoulders. On the bedside table next to the champagne there were various drugs and little bottles with syringes. A phonograph was playing a German army march. The midday sun, streaming in through the venetian blinds, showed the craters and pits in Goering's face. It was said that he suffered from many different diseases, all of them brought upon by drugs and unhealthy living.

Petra was the first to react. "Why, Joker, I thought you were still away. I would like you to meet my very good friend, Field Marshal Hermann Goering."

"I have heard of you," Goering said. "You are the crazy American who has been advising the Führer. Though, of course, the Führer needs no advice."

"He needed some when I saw him last," the Joker said.

"The Führer never needs advice," Goering said. "To say otherwise is treason."

"I've got a signed letter from him thanking me for my help and declaring me a hero of the Third Reich. And now you go stealing my treasures. How did you find out about it in the first place."

"Word gets around," Goering said, giving Petra a sidewise glance.

"I can see that it does," the Joker said. "I want it back."

"Oh, I'm afraid that would be quite impossible," Goering said. "These art treasures that you stole from the Italians are actually German property. We've had a claim on them for over two hundred years."

"Then you should have picked them up yourself," the Joker said.

"Why do that when we had your services to do it for us so much better? No, my dear Joker, they will stay in the army depository at the camp here in Bad Fleishstein. You will be recompensed for your services. Shall we say a thousand marks?"

The Joker sneered. "I've stolen treasure worth millions of dollars and you're offering me a lousy thousand marks?"

"Well," the Reichs Marschall said, "I suppose I could make it two thousand. That's the absolute top."

The Joker paced up and down the room. He was getting agitated. Then he managed to calm himself. He looked at Goering, who had now put on his jacket, buttoned it, straightened the collar, and stood, trying to look every inch a warrior and commander. The Joker remembered what he had heard about Goering; how much the man wanted to excel in martial deeds.

"Listen, Goering," he said, "I want that stuff back. I stole it and it's mine."

Goering shrugged, a gesture that made his belly ripple. "Well, so, what is that to me?"

"Only this," the Joker said. "Maybe we can do a deal. Maybe I can do something for you, and you can give me back my stuff in return."

The fat Reichs Marschall laughed. "What can you do for me? I am the second most powerful man in Germany."

"I'm aware of that," the Joker said. "But your influence at this point isn't quite what it might be. There's something you want, isn't there? Something you want badly, and Hitler won't give it to you."

"Damn you!" Goering said. "How do you know these things? You are a devil!"

"No, I'm a joker," the Joker said. "People like me know all sorts of things. It helps being crazy. You know more that way. I happen to know that you've begged Hitler to let you and your Luftwaffe kill off the British army at Dunkirk, entirely on your own."

"Yes, well, that is so," Goering said. "I've told the Führer over and over again to call off the troops. It's risky to use them against a cornered enemy. We need them for the big onslaught against Russia. And I have the English swine trapped on the Dunkirk beaches. My planes can easily finish them off with no help from anyone."

"Suppose I could set that up for you?" the Joker asked.

"You could do this? But it is quite impossible!"

"But suppose I could?" the Joker asked. "Would you make a deal?"

"Yes, of course I would make a deal. You could have it all, all, and more, if I could just get this opportunity to prove what my air fleet can do. But it's impossible."

"Listen," Petra said. "Listen to him. He knows what he is talking about."

"Do you think so?" Goering asked.

"The man is a genius," Petra said. "He is probably the outstanding criminal genius of our age. He has influence over the Führer. He can do this for you, Hermann. And then yours will be the undying glory."

Goering's little pig eyes lit up. His mind was filled with the wonderful picture of his Stuka dive bombers crashing down their bombs upon the helpless British standing around on the beaches.

He said, "If you can do this, you have my promise. I will give you back your fleet, and I will even put an aircraft at your disposal so that you can transport it anywhere in the world."

"Will you sign a paper saying that?"

Goering looked at Petra. She said, "Do it, Hermann! You have nothing to lose!"

"Very well, then. I do it. Bring me pen and paper. Quick!"

Hastily he scribbled a note, then looked up. "But you understand, this paper is no good until you get me the

command to do the sole attack on the British at Dunkirk."

"I know," the Joker said. "Just give it to me and don't
worry about a thing. Stand by for further messages."

When the Joker went to see Hitler the next day, he
found the Führer in a state of high excitement. He was
in his private offices, making marks on his big wall map
and moving little markers on the position plot on his
desk to show the advance of German forces and the increasing compression of the Allied forces.

"Ah, Herr Joker!" he said. "I'm glad to see you. Your
advice, as it turned out, was good. Not that I needed it, of
course. I was coming to that conclusion anyway. But it
was good that you were here at the time I made it."

Hitler took the Joker by the arm and led him up to
the position map. "Look, see for yourself. Is it not good?"

"Oh yeah, it's great," the Joker said. "I'm really very
happy for you. But I've got another hot flash for you
now."

"Ah?" said Hitler. "And what is that?"

"Dunkirk!" the Joker said.

"Dunkirk? Yes, I have them all trapped there! What
about Dunkirk?"

"Let Hermann do it," the Joker said.

Hitler stared at him. His face worked. His moustache
twitched. He said, "Are you sure?"

"Trust me," the Joker said. "Have I ever led you
wrong?"

On May 24, Hitler ordered German troops to cease their
advance toward Dunkirk and await further orders. The
Luftwaffe was sent in. The great attack by Goering, designed to wipe out the British armies and secure Europe
for the Nazis for the next thousand years at least, maybe
longer, had begun.

When Herr Obermeier heard what the Joker had
done, he was horrified. He said, "But it's not possible! All
of my astrological readings show that Goering, in spite

of being in command of the air force, has an unlucky air sign. Alone he will not succeed."

The Joker said, "I sort of figured that."

"Then why did you do it?"

"Well, he wanted it so badly. And he's got something of mine. Something that I need back. Obermeier, thank you for all of your help. I think I will be leaving Germany shortly."

"It has been a very great pleasure," Obermeier said. "I have enjoyed dealing with you."

As the Joker reached the door he turned and said, "Tell me, what do your stars show for Hitler's outlook in this war?"

"He will be fine," Obermeier said. "As long as two conditions are met. The first is, America must not enter the war. The second is, Germany must not attack Russia."

That evening the Joker went to his room. Using his special equipment he did a job of forgery on the paper the Reichs Marschall had given him. All he needed to change was the date, making the order effective immediately for release of the treasure and for an airplane. Then he packed. He was preparing to leave that evening, when there was a knock at the door.

It was Petra, "Joker," she said. "I'm sorry. I know you were hurt when you came into my suite and saw me with Hermann."

"Oh, think nothing of it," the Joker said bitterly. "There was only one woman in this world who was ever really for me. That was Jeanne, my wife, and she's dead."

"But I am for you, too," Petra said. "It is not my fault what came before you. The Reichs Marschall saw me several years ago and insisted that I become his mistress. I had no choice in the matter."

"Well, it's not a bad choice you made," the Joker said. "Hermann's doing well. Even if he falls on his face over this Dunkirk thing, he'll probably still be fine, and you'll be fine with him."

"But I do not want him!" she said. "Do you still remember our dream of going to Rio?"

"Sure, I remember it," the Joker said. "It was a pipe dream."

"Not so! It can come true! Listen, I will meet you there. Instead of returning to America, why don't you fly to Rio?"

The Joker lowered his long hideous face. She looked back at him without flinching. "Joker, I love you."

It was well before dawn when the Joker set out on what he expected would be the final part of his European treasure hunt. Hans, his chauffeur, showed up about 4:30 A.M., when the sky was still dark and one could still see the thin yellow searchlight beams probing the sky far to the north in Hamburg. He had brought six men with him in the stretch limo. Each man carried a duffle bag. They filed into the chalet at the Joker's invitation. The Joker told the men to wait in the living room. He took Hans outside so they could have a brief private conference.

"These men you brought me, Hans, are they good?"

"Oh, yes, sir, they are very good indeed. They are first-rate criminals from the slums of Hamburg, Berlin, Stuttgart, and other places. I recruited them with great care."

"And they have no love for the Third Reich or Hitler?"

Hans laughed—a short, ugly sound. "None whatsoever, Joker! These men are criminals. If the Third Reich could find them, they would execute them. They are desperate men and very willing to do anything to get out of Germany, out of Europe."

"And they all have their costumes?" the Joker asked.

"Yes, sir. I know a certain tailor who was able to run them up for me. The cloth is genuine field gray. At a pawnshop I was able to buy them a suitable bunch of decorations. I did not know if I should get a uniform for you, sir."

"No need. I brought mine along," the Joker said. "Made in the good old U.S.A., but with German cloth

and labels. Wait until you see it. You'll be falling all over
yourself saluting me."

The Joker and Hans went back into the chalet. The
Joker swiftly changed into an officer's uniform. He said
to Hans, "Are you sure you don't want to come along? It's
going to be a whole new life for us in Brazil."

"No, Herr Joker," Hans said. "There's good work for
me here, and you have rewarded me so well I will be able
to buy a piece of land where Greta and I and the children
will be able to farm. Perhaps in Sweden with our false
papers. Then it's an end of the life of crime for me."

"Well, you've probably chosen well," the Joker said.
"Now, let's inspect these men. Once we pick up the treasure and reach the airfield, your duties are over, and I
will have a little extra reward for you at that time."

The Joker inspected his men. It was amazing what a
few uniforms could do. These men no longer looked like
riffraff from the lowest slums. Instead they looked just
like any Nazi officers. As for the Joker, he had come prepared to disguise his face also. A tight-fitting rubber-
and-plastic mask went over his face. It gave him the look
of a hardened combat veteran. With it he had a wig of
close-cropped blond hair. Hans looked him over critically and declared that he was perfect.

They piled into the limo. Hans attached the flag to the
front fender showing that he had a general officer
aboard. They set out for the Luftwaffe camp at Bad
Fleishstein.

The roads were almost deserted at that early hour.
They did come upon one army convoy. Flashing their
lights, they went past it.

Half an hour's rapid driving brought them to the air
force depot at Bad Fleishstein. They pulled up to the sentry gate. The guard stiffened to attention when he saw it
was an official German air-force staff car. When he
peered inside and saw the tall austere shape of the general wrapped in his gray coat, Hans handed over the papers. The sentry glanced at them and snapped to a
salute. The Joker touched a negligent forefinger to his
cap as the car sped into the camp. So far, so good.

They drove past row upon row of barracks. Hans

drove with calm sureness, for he had memorized this
route a long time ago. The depot, where the treasure was
stored, was at the far end of the field not far from the
perimeter fence. Hans pulled up in front of it. The two
guards, who came out to check their papers, were of a
sterner make than those at the front gate. They read the
papers carefully, conferred with each other in low tones,
and said, "This is most unusual, General. We usually
receive advance warning when objects of value are to be
transported out of here."

"In wartime," the Joker said, in a harsh, grating
voice, "only the unusual is usual. The Reichs Marschall
did not want to alert anyone to the transfer of this treasure. Its destination is a top secret."

The guards were still unsure. One said to the other,
"Perhaps we should call up the captain of the guard."

"Do so, by all means," the Joker said. "And give me
your names and serial numbers also, so I can remember
the men who delayed an order from the second in command of the Third Reich."

Another conference. Then both guards saluted. The
senior of them, a corporal, said, "Please proceed, Herr
General. We do not wish to delay you. But it is not good
for us to be remiss in our duties, either."

"Good," the Joker said, "You have done well."

Hans stayed in the car as they had arranged. The
Joker, at the head of his seven men, marched into the
depot. It was an enormous wooden structure. As far as
the Joker could see, it was heaped to the ceiling with loot
captured from all over Europe. There was furniture from
Denmark and Sweden—chairs, lounges, all sorts of
things, enameled sideboards, an endless array of paintings. The German army was making a good profit out of
the loot of Europe. In the distance before they entered,
the Joker had seen other large buildings under construction. These would be to hold the art treasures of other
countries as they fell.

"Well," the Joker demanded of one of the guards,
"where is the Italian art treasure?"

"Which Italian art treasure, General?" one of the
guards asked.

"The one that that crazy fellow brought in for that Joker."

"Ah, *jawohl, mein generell,* it is right over here." The guard led him to a pallet on one side. There, still wrapped in the original canvas that the Joker had put around it, was the entire mound of the Vatican art treasure. The Joker turned back a fold and looked inside to make sure: there was no sense getting the wrong stuff now. But sure enough, it was exactly what he wanted. He saw the stacked Raphaels, the Leonardos, the Titians, and the Reubenses, plus the statuary and all the rest of the good stuff.

"*Jah, jah,*" the Joker said, "*Dis is dass.* Bring me a cart here, quick. We have no time to waste."

The guards hurried away and came back with a motorized hand truck. The Joker sent them back for a second one: There was so much good stuff lying around he saw no sense in leaving it. In fact, he thought, if he'd been aware of this, he could have saved himself all the trouble of raiding the Vatican and come straight here. But of course he had always wanted to raid the Vatican. It was one of the accomplishments he was most proud of. Outside, he had his men load the bags onto the roof rack of the limo. Everyone saluted everyone else and the Joker and his men got back into the vehicle. They sped off. But as they approached the gate they saw a sudden flurry of activity.

"Oh-oh," Hans said. "I don't know what this is."

"Just stay cool," the Joker said. "Don't shoot until you see me do it first."

They stopped. One of the guards came running up. He was waving a piece of paper. "General!" he said. "One final thing. You forgot to sign for this!"

"*Ach,*" the Joker said, "how silly of me." He hastily scrawled a signature and thrust it back to the guard. The guard saluted. The gates opened and they sped out.

"OK," the Joker said, "so far, so good. Now, Hans, to the airfield, and don't spare the horses."

Dawn was fully up by the time they reached the airfield. They piled out of the car. There was a captain on duty and he was suitably overawed by the Joker's rank and

medals, and general air of hauteur. The Joker was at his
swaggering best, commandeering a good-sized military
transport, an old but very sound Dornier with camou-
flage paint. At the Joker's orders, extra tanks of gas
were fitted to the wingtips. The gasoline was topped off.
The propellers were spun and clearance was given. The
Joker's hired men scrambled aboard. Hans and the
Joker shook hands.

"Good luck, Herr Joker," Hans said. "It has been a
pleasure working with you."

"Thank you, Hans," the Joker said. "The pleasure has
been all mine. And here is a little parting gift for you."
He handed Hans a small chamois bag. Opening it, Hans
found five perfect pearls.

"Ah Joker, you are more than generous. It is too
much! It is far greater than the price we agreed upon."

"That's all right," the Joker said. "It didn't cost me
anything. Good luck, Hans."

Hans got back into the command car and sped off.
Aboard the plane, the soldiers had strapped themselves
into the seats, all except one, Dietrich, who was an ac-
complished pilot. He was up in the nose of the plane, in
the copilot's seat. The Joker sat down in the pilot's seat,
tested the controls, revved up the engines. The four big
props spun, coughed, spit blue exhaust, and then spun
firmly. The Joker ran the engines up and signaled the
tower for final clearance.

"Yes, General, you are clear. But you have neglected
to file a flight plan."

"Do that for me, old boy, all right?" the Joker said.

"But where are you going?"

"Eagle's Lair!" The Joker said, naming the Führer's
mountain retreat in Bavaria. "The Führer is throwing
the party of the century there."

"Jawohl!" the tower replied.

The Joker pushed the throttles forward and the plane
began to creep out onto the takeoff area. Then there was
a crackle of static. The tower was calling.

"Just a moment, General! There is something which
is not in order."

"Oh? What's that?" the Joker asked.

"The guards from the depot have come. It seems that when you signed for the treasure, you signed yourself Herr General Joker."

"Just my little joke," the Joker said, keeping the plane going toward the takeoff area.

"We would like you to sign again," the voice on the other end insisted.

"Fool! You know I cannot keep the Führer waiting!" The Joker ran the engines up, released the brakes, and started to rumble down the field. There was a noise of confusion mixed with static. Then a voice said, "Ah well, good luck, General!"

Then he was in the air.

The Joker peeled off his mask. Grinning now, he came back to see how his troops were doing. "Everybody all right?" he asked.

"Yes, Herr Joker!" They chorused.

"I hope you packed plenty of sandwiches," the Joker said.

The men grinned. "Yes, we have packed sandwiches and beer, much beer!"

"Good," the Joker said. "Enjoy yourselves. The hard part of this is over."

But in that, he was very mistaken.

The Joker's flight plan called for him to fly due south. He wanted to get out of the war zone as soon as he could. It would be ridiculous to be shot down now. He flew over Switzerland, not bothering to respond to questions radioed to him from stations along the way. He continued south along the Tyrrhennian Sea, with the mass of Italy on his left. When Sicily came into view, he made a right turn to fly west across the Mediterranean and then out into the Atlantic.

It was at this point that a single-seater fighter appeared out of the clouds and quickly closed in on them.

"Who the hell is that?" the Joker said. "Dietrich, can you make out any markings on his wings?"

Dietrich looked long and steadily through binoculars at the pursuing craft. "Well, Herr Joker, it seems to have some sort of symbol on the wing but I can't make it out."

"Italian Air Force?" the Joker asked.

"No, I don't think so," Dietrich said. "It has none of their characteristic markings."

There was another crackle of static. Then a loud voice enquired in Italian, "What plane is that?"

"German military transport," the Joker replied, "on a special mission."

"Is that so?" said the fighter pilot. He came closer still and at last the Joker could make out the markings on the wing. The symbol was like nothing he had ever seen before. The insignia on the wingtips and side of the plane showed a heart with a dagger through it, lying atop a coiled noose.

"What the hell is that?" the Joker asked Dietrich. "Must be some country I've never heard of before."

Dietrich cursed. "Ah! Herr Joker, it is the marking of the mafia!"

"Since when have they got their own airforce?" the Joker asked.

"The mafia always has what they need," Dietrich said. "Especially in Sicily."

The Joker got back on the radio. "Stay out of my way! I'm on special orders from the Führer himself!"

The fighter plane spun in and circled around them at close range. They could see a dark unshaven face staring at them. The Italian pilot said, "Aha! It is the Joker! Land your ship, Joker! You have what belongs to Italy and to us."

The Joker said to Dietrich, "Tell the men to man the machine guns."

The fighter plane circled them again, staying out of range. They could hear radio conversation in a Sicilian dialect, which none of them understood. Two more planes appeared out of the clouds and came toward them. When they were within range, the Joker said, "Open fire."

The three planes wove a pattern of death around the slow-flying transport. Machine guns chattered and were met by answering fire from the nose and tail gunners aboard the transport. Machine gun slugs ripped through the transport's light covering.

"Shoot them down!" the Joker screamed at his gunners.

"But we can't see them, sir! They're diving out of the sun!"

"Then shoot down the sun!" the Joker shouted.

Meanwhile he was turning acrobatics in the plane, dodging and twisting, taking advantage of every vestige of cloud cover. One of the men scored a hit. One of the three fighters spun into the ocean in a plume of black smoke, crashing at last into the bright sea. The remaining two redoubled their efforts. Smoke began to pour from one of the transport's port outboard engine. The Joker feathered the prop and shut down the engine. The Dornier flew on steadily. They gained more cloud cover. The fighters found them and bored in again. Then the Joker performed an unorthodox maneuver. He turned the plane on one wing, sweeping around like a scythe. He caught one of the mafia planes off-guard and shot it down, watched it explode in a trail of smoke and sparks. That left one airplane. It came at them this time head on. From the radio the Joker could hear Scuzzi's voice, "I will catch you, Joker; I will kill you!" And then the plane dissolved into a fireball and plunged into the sea. The Joker resumed his course, west and south. "Hang on, boys," he said, "We're going to Rio!"

Two of his own men had been killed. The Joker told the others to throw their bodies out through the hatchway. "It'll be just that much more treasure for the rest of us to divide," he told them. Soon they were eating smoked bratwurst sausages and drinking beer as if nothing had happened.

The plane flew on through the rest of the day. Night saw them well out into the Atlantic. They left the Azores behind them and finally made their turn to go due west across the shortest part of the South Atlantic. Rio lay dead ahead and about a thousand miles away.

Morning found them still making good time. But a second engine was beginning to miss. More seriously, the plane had begun gradually to lose altitude. Checking, they found that the machine bullets had cut through one of the gas tanks. Hasty calculations showed they were not going to have enough fuel to make it all the way in.

The Joker fought with the big plane, taking advantage of stray bits of wind and thermal updrafts, edging for altitude. But he could see it was not going to be enough.

"Dietrich," he said, "we're going to have to throw out the statuary. Order the men to do it. Then tear out the seats, anything extra you can find. We must lighten the ship. There's no way to turn back. Between here and the landing field at Rio there's nothing but water."

Priceless Michelangelo marbles went tumbling out of the aircraft and into the sea. Equipment followed. It was helping, but it was still not enough. The Joker put the ship on autopilot and went back into the main cabin. He said to his men, "Well, you've all been really good and you've been a great help. I hate to do this but I'm really afraid that I have to. You, you, and you. Throw out life rafts and continue after them."

They protested. "Surely you are not serious, Herr Joker? We would stand little chance of survival, even with the life rafts."

"You will stand no chance at all," the Joker said, "if you stay here. All there is for you here is a bullet in the head."

With submachine gun at the ready he herded them toward the open hatchway. One of them tried to jump him. The Joker shot him. Then at gunpoint he made the others jump out one by one. He watched as their parachutes opened.

He was left now only with the lightest of the treasures. He was prepared to die before throwing anymore of it overboard. Only he and the remaining treasures were left in the plane. And Dietrich.

He became aware of Dietrich as the man opened fire on him from the cockpit. The Joker, with his special sixth sense for danger, had been waiting for this and clung to the open hatch high over the steel-gray sea moving below to escape the barrage of bullets from Dietrich's gun. In fact it helped him solve a problem. He was fond of Dietrich, who had done well by him. But the man weighed at least two hundred pounds. That would be weight well saved.

Bullets crashed around him. The Joker fired once, and caught Dietrich square in the forehead. The man went down and stayed down. The Joker pulled his body to the hatch and threw it overboard. And then he was alone on the plane, just him and the treasure, on a wounded German transport that was still losing altitude, though slower than before.

But even though it was slower, it was enough. He was no more than fifty feet above the wavetops now, and the plane was bucking hard. It had taken so many hits, both from the attack by the mafia planes and the combat that had gone on inside, that the plane was threatening to come apart.

At last the Joker could see, far ahead, a dim dark line on the horizon. Brazil! He was almost there!

The plane rushed on, its engines misfiring. He was skimming the wavetops, but the land was coming up strongly. He saw a stretch of beach and, behind it, green jungle. Quickly he checked his position. Yes, there it was! There was the landing field built out to the water's edge, just to his left. But he didn't know if he was going to make it. He was almost in the water now; water was splashing up through the bullet holes. If he'd had his landing gear down he would have been dragging his wheels in the water. Now the landing field was dead ahead. He could see people standing in a little crowd, waving at him. One of them was a blonde. He looked more closely. Yes, it was Petra! She had come! She was waiting for him! How sad it would be, the Joker thought, to have come this far and die just before reaching Rio.

By sheer strength of will he forced the nose up. The plane's tail was already starting to touch down in the water as he swept across the beach and finally brought the plane down belly first on the edge of the tarmac.

He stood up, unbuckled himself from the seat. He had made it! It was all his! He'd done it! The greatest caper of the century, maybe of all time! And he was safe. And Petra was down there waiting for him.

He ran down the bullet-pocked aisle, pushed open the door. As he began to step out there was a blinding flash of light. White light bathed him and suddenly, for a moment, he lost his orientation and had to close his eyes to keep from being blinded.

When he opened his eyes again, he was lying on a cot that was being wheeled by men in white clothes. "Is this Rio?" he asked. And then remembered that he didn't speak Portuguese. But he needn't have worried because the man grinned at him and said, "Rio? I guess you've had a pretty nice dream, huh, Joker?"

"Dream?" the Joker said. "Where am I?"

"This is the Arkham Asylum for the Criminally Insane," the man said. "You just had your shock treatment."

"I'm in Arkham Asylum? How did I get here?"

"This is where Batman put you, Joker," the attendant said. "After your last caper."

"What about the war?"

"Which war?"

"The war with the Germans."

"You must have had a really good dream," the attendant said. "That war was over decades ago."

The Joker understood. And he began to laugh. It was a horrifying laugh, an insane laugh, and it echoed through the darkened corridors of the asylum. He was still laughing when they locked him up again in his cell.

The Joker Is Mild

Edward D. Hoch

There was a time when the Joker went away from Gotham City and all was at peace. It began quite unexpectedly on a summer's evening while Police Commissioner Gordon and the other good citizens of the city were watching the local newscasts. It was a quiet news day with nothing more exciting than a new baby lion at the zoo, when suddenly the picture faded into a field of static and snow. That was replaced almost immediately by an image of the grinning Joker, the mad genius with the white face and red lips, who had thrown the city into a panic so many times before.

"Good evening, ladies and gentlemen of Gotham City," he began, leaning forward toward the camera. "Tonight I have a most important message for you all, a message that I believe will please you. I have decided that my life of crime should come to an end. I have to leave Gotham City forever and begin a new life far away. I want to live like other men, enjoying a life of travel and art. This is my last farewell to you, and I say it with a heavy heart." As if on cue, a tear appeared at the corner of one eye and ran slowly down his face. "Good-bye, Gotham City. You have been good to me. I will never forget you."

The picture faded and suddenly the news returned. It had been so brief a message, and so startling, that some viewers rubbed their eyes, wondering if they had really seen it at all. One of those was Commissioner Gordon himself, who sat and stared at the television set for a full minute before getting to his feet to phone Headquarters.

"Did I see correctly?" he asked the captain of detectives. "Did the Joker just announce his retirement from a life of crime?"

"That's what it looked like to me."

"Are we supposed to believe that?"

"I'll get some men on it right away."

Across town, on the outskirts of Gotham City, there was another interested viewer of the evening news. Bruce Wayne sat in his easy chair staring at the screen, and like the Commissioner he could hardly believe what he had seen. The door behind him opened softly and Alfred the butler entered. "Did you ring, sir?"

"Were you watching television just now, Alfred?"

"Yes, I was, sir. I saw that Joker person."

"Do you believe what he said, about leaving Gotham City and starting a new life?"

"One never knows, sir, but it seems highly doubtful."

But in the weeks that followed there was no new message from the Joker. He seemed to have disappeared from the Gotham City scene. There had been periods before this when the Joker had been inactive, generally when he was plotting some new outrage, but this time it seemed different. The city seemed different, as if a great weight had been lifted from it.

Late one night at the Commissioner's office, a most unusual meeting took place. It was not the first time that Commissioner Gordon and Batman had stood face-to-face in that room, but their previous meetings had always been necessitated by some new crime. Never before had they met because of the absence of crime.

"What do you think, Commissioner? Is the Joker really gone?" Batman asked, his midnight-blue bat-winged cape hanging down behind him.

"Our informers tell us the word in underworld circles is that he disbanded his gang and left town after that television announcement. No one knows where he is."

Batman simply shook his head. "I'm certain we

haven't heard the last of him, Commissioner. Do you remember the things he's done to the people of this city? To you personally? There's no reason to believe he's changed after all these years."

"All right, suppose he's simply moved on to another city. We're rid of him, and I've alerted every other major police department in the country to be on guard. Maybe we should be satisfied with that."

Batman whirled around and walked to the window overlooking Gotham City. He liked to think of it as his city, his to preserve and protect. There were other enemies besides the Joker, and if he was the most heinous of them, he was also the most irrational. Perhaps there was no time to worry about the twistings of an irrational mind. If the Joker was gone, let him be gone. Commissioner Gordon had a point.

"All right," Batman reluctantly agreed. "But if we're wrong, if this is all some devious scheme on the Joker's part, we may both be sorry we didn't spot it in time."

"At the first indication of his return, I'll call on you," the Commissioner assured him.

"The first indication may be too late," Batman replied glumly.

As summer blended into fall, the good citizens of Gotham City began to talk of other things. The Joker was truly gone, and the most important event in town proved to be the opening of a traveling exhibition of priceless French paintings at the City Museum of Art. The exhibition would be on display for only four weeks before moving on to the next city on the tour, and from the beginning there were long lines of art lovers and the just plain curious waiting to get in.

Security was tight all during those four weeks, but there was little cause for alarm. One afternoon an obviously unhinged young man tried to slash a Renoir painting, but he was seized by security guards before he got near enough to do any damage. Otherwise all was peaceful.

Still, when time came for the exhibition to be crated and moved to the next city, the job was not entrusted to

the staff of the City Museum of Art. Three art experts
from different parts of the country had been commis-
sioned to supervise the work and offer their guarantees
that the priceless paintings would not be damaged in
transit.

Megan Farley had never met any of the three men sent
to pass on the arrangements she was making for disman-
tling the exhibit. As assistant director of the City Museum she'd naturally come upon their photographs and
articles in *Art World* and other trade publications, but
none had ever visited Gotham City before. Apparently
the French owners of the paintings had thought it better
to have impartial observers who would not be influenced
by past associations with the individual museums.

What surprised Megan was the realization that the
three were strangers to each other as well as to Gotham
City. The first to arrive that Friday afternoon was Eric
Wollcott, a slim middle-aged man with black hair and a
pencil-thin moustache. He was very pale and Megan had
the impression of someone who spent much of his time
indoors.

"So you've never met Mr. Clarkson or Professor Melrose," she said, leading him up to her second-floor office.

"No, indeed, though of course I know their work. Both
are highly respected in the art world."

"They should both be here within the hour. Then I'll
show the exhibition to all of you at once."

The next arrival proved to be Professor Melrose, a
hairy man whose whiskers covered much of his face, and
whose bulky body gave the impression of a stuffed Santa
Claus. He shook hands briskly with Eric Wollcott. "This
won't take long, will it? I hope to get a plane back to
California once the paintings are safely delivered to
Washington."

"How long can it take?" Wollcott turned an inquiring
gaze toward Megan. "There are forty-four paintings in
all?"

"That is correct."

"And each has its own wooden crate. I would guess
the task could begin this afternoon and be completed
tomorrow morning."

"The truck is due at noon tomorrow," Megan con-

firmed. "Believe me, the sooner they're out of here the
happier we'll be. The security costs of this exhibition
have been staggering."

"Exactly what are we supposed to do?" Professor
Melrose asked.

"Didn't you read your letter?" Eric Wollcott asked in
his high-pitched voice. "We have to certify the packing of
each piece, and then the unpacking when the shipment
reaches Washington, the next stop on the tour. We're
being well paid to make certain no forgeries are substituted for the real paintings."

The telephone on Megan's desk buzzed to announce
the arrival of the third art expert. Tom Clarkson was the
art editor of a popular weekly newsmagazine, a man in
his midforties with a ready smile and a pleasant manner. He was the most normal one of the three, Megan
decided, taking an instant liking to him.

"Sorry I'm late," he said, greeting the others. "It's a
pleasure to meet you both after all these years of reading
about you."

"The pleasure is mutual," Professor Melrose declared.
"Now let us get down to business." He turned to Megan.
"Is your crew ready to dismantle the exhibition?"

"I have them standing by," she confirmed.

The paintings, mainly by the French Impressionists of
the late nineteenth century, had been removed from their
wall hangings and were by their crates, which were unmarked except for an identifying number. The experts
inspected each in turn, and when they were satisfied of its
authenticity, the painting was sealed into its crate for
shipment. The work went fairly fast, and by the end of the
afternoon twenty-five of the paintings had been crated.

"We'll finish the rest in the morning," Professor
Melrose assured the others.

Tom Clarkson, the art editor, wasn't completely satisfied. "How do we know someone won't switch these
crates during the night?"

"We'll have a guard on duty," Megan assured him.
"And you can inspect the seals in the morning to be sure
they weren't tampered with."

That seemed to satisfy everyone, and Wollcott and
Professor Melrose decided to go off to dinner together.

Tom Clarkson begged off joining them and hung back until they'd departed. "Do you have any dinner plans?" he asked Megan.

The invitation startled her. He'd noticed her bare left hand, of course, and assumed she was available. For the first time she considered him as a man as well as an art expert. He was at least ten years older than her thirty-two years, but she'd taken a liking to him at once. The smile came readily to his lips, and she imagined he would be a good conversationalist over the dinner table. "Well—" She hesitated and then plunged in. "No, I don't."

"Then please join me. I'd love to hear more about Gotham City and your museum."

He left the choice of the restaurant up to her, and she suggested a little Italian place within walking distance of the museum. Over wine she talked about the museum, and what it meant to her. "I'm lucky the director is in Europe this week. It gives me an opportunity to meet you all and show you around myself."

"I'm quite impressed from what I've seen so far. You certainly have tight security."

"We need it in Gotham City. We've had a high crime rate in the past, especially involving jewelry and art treasures. There used to be a criminal called the Joker—"

"I've read about him. Whatever happened to him?"

"He claims to have retired and gone away, but no one is quite certain yet. A mild-mannered Joker doesn't fit with his usual image."

"Do you think there's a possibility he might try to steal the paintings?"

Megan shook her head. "I've no idea, but I do know that Police Commissioner Gordon will be at the museum tomorrow to make certain they get out of Gotham City safely."

"Probably a good precaution," Clarkson agreed, turning his attention to the menu.

She was at the museum early the following morning, ready to greet the experts and finish up the packing job. Eric Wollcott arrived with the professor and she marveled at what an odd couple they made, walking together down the long marble corridor toward her office. Tom Clarkson arrived a moment later.

As they headed for the gallery she found an opportunity for a private word with Tom. "Thank you again for last night. It was a most pleasant evening."

"I'm happy you enjoyed it. A night like that can make the entire trip worthwhile."

"I hope Gotham City has other charms to entice you."

They made quick work of the remaining nineteen paintings, and by eleven o'clock the last of them was being sealed into its crate. Shortly after that, Commissioner Gordon and two of his men arrived. "Everything under control?" he asked Megan.

"So far." She introduced him to the three art experts.

It was Wollcott who gave the Commissioner a wide smile and asked, "Haven't we met before?"

"I doubt it, Mr. Wollcott. Are you an art expert?"

"An appraiser. This is my first trip to Gotham City."

Commissioner Gordon looked him up and down, a bit distastefully. "I hope you enjoy it. Miss Farley, how's the timing?"

"We're right on schedule, Commissioner. The truck is due at noon."

He glanced over at the stout one, Professor Melrose. "Will you men be accompanying the shipment to its destination?"

The professor nodded, his beard bobbing up and down. "Oh, certainly. We'll be following behind in a car. One of us might even ride with the truck driver."

Promptly at noon, a bony man wearing a baseball cap and a Gotham Gorillas T-shirt appeared at the door of Megan's office. "Interstate Transport. I'm here for the shipment to the Washington Museum."

"Is your truck at the loading dock?"

"That's right, ma'am. You have forty-four crates for me?"

"Correct. Do you have a loading crew?"

"Just me and one helper. We could use a few more hands."

"All right. I'll have them bring the crates down and help get them in your truck."

Megan followed the others and watched while the

crates were being loaded. The driver seemed to know
what he was doing and was careful with the procedure.
"Let's put this big Monet against the left side, and then
we can load the medium-sized crates," he told his helper,
a short, stocky man with a bald head.

It took less than an hour to load the crates. Tom
Clarkson gave them a final check and nodded his approval. "We'll follow along in my car."

Professor Melrose shifted his large frame uncomfortably. "I think I should ride in the cab of the truck, if
there's room for me."

The driver squinted at him uncertainly, then replied,
"Sure, if you want to. We can fit three in there."

The professor climbed into the cab with them while
Clarkson and Wollcott prepared to follow in Clarkson's
rented car. Just before he slid behind the driver's seat,
Tom walked over to where Megan stood watching. "It's
been a pleasure. I hope we'll meet again."

She returned his smile. "I hope so, too."

As the truck pulled away from the dock with the car
close behind, one of the Commissioner's men ran up to
him. In his hand he held a piece of foam-rubber padding
with an elastic belt attached.

"Commissioner, I just found this in the men's room
upstairs, near Miss Farley's office."

"What?" Commissioner Gordon held it up. "This is
stomach padding, like you might wear with a Santa
Claus suit. One of those people is wearing a disguise."

"The Joker?" the detective asked.

"Who else? And only one of the three could have been
wearing padding. The other two are fairly thin."

"Professor Melrose!"

The Commissioner was already hurrying toward his
car. "And he's in the cab of that truck. Come on!"

Megan sprinted after them. "I'm going, too! Those
paintings are still my responsibility."

Commissioner Gordon muttered something about it
being dangerous for a woman, but he didn't argue when
she slid into the backseat of his car. Gordon rode in front
with his driver, and as they drove off in pursuit he un-
snapped the riot gun from the brackets beneath the
dashboard.

The truck had reached the nearby expressway and was traveling at a good rate of speed. Megan could see Tom Clarkson's car behind it, keeping up the pace. The Commissioner turned to his driver. "Give 'em the siren."

But if he thought that would bring the truck to a halt he was mistaken. Its speed seemed to increase, and suddenly a stream of thick black smoke emerged from beneath it. Megan was forced to hang on as the car swerved to avoid the worst of it. She saw that Clarkson's car had already pulled up just off the road.

"What is it?" Commissioner Gordon asked. "A smoke screen?"

"Looks like it." They kept driving through it at a reduced speed with the windows rolled up. Most of the other traffic had come to a halt as the dense smoke covered the expressway lanes in both directions.

Then suddenly they were out of it and the big truck was dead ahead, crashed into the center guardrail. And there, climbing from the cab with his chalk-white face a study in fury, was the Joker.

"He's got a gun!" the Commissioner yelled as the car screeched to a stop. He opened the door on his side, using it as a shield, and tried to aim the riot gun.

Then another figure emerged from the cab, launching himself through the air at the Joker. "Who—?" Megan gasped.

"It's Batman!"

It was indeed Batman, and he flattened the Joker with a single solid blow. Commissioner Gordon and his driver ran up to cover the man on the ground, as Gordon turned to the caped figure. "What are you doing here, Batman?"

"When I tumbled to his scheme, Commissioner, I thought you might be able to use some help."

"We found his padding in the men's room and realized he was disguised as Professor Melrose."

Batman smiled. "You have it a bit wrong, Commissioner. The Joker was the truck driver. I was Professor Melrose. Hello again, Miss Farley."

*   *   *

By that time, Clarkson and Wollcott had caught up with them, and the police had pulled the Joker's bald accomplice from the cab of the truck. Commissioner Gordon surveyed the activity and admitted, "I don't fully understand."

"I think you and I had the same idea about the Joker's plans," Batman explained. "On his farewell television address he mentioned wanting to enjoy the world of travel and art. This exhibition seemed like the sort of art he'd most enjoy. When I discovered the three men hired to certify the artworks didn't know each other, it seemed like a perfect opportunity for one of the Joker's disguises. I arranged with the real Professor Melrose to take his place, expecting that one of the others might be the Joker. I was wrong. In fact, I'd just about given up when the truck arrived with its driver. I thought I saw through the Joker's disguise but I wasn't certain until during the loading operation when he told his helper where to put the Monet. The crates had been sealed when he arrived, and they were unmarked except for a number. Only someone very familiar with the paintings would know that the largest was the Monet. When I realized what was happening, I arranged to ride in the truck, shedding some of my padding so I'd be ready for action. When he released his smoke screen, I knocked out his assistant and grabbed the steering wheel. You saw the rest."

"The museum owes you its thanks, Batman," Megan told him.

"And so does Gotham City, once more," the Commissioner agreed. "We'll try to keep the Joker behind bars this time."

Tom Clarkson was waiting by his car. "Do you need a ride back to the museum, Megan? It looks as if Wollcott and I will be staying until they can send another truck for these paintings."

"Thanks," she told him with a smile. "I'd like that."

Happy Birthday

Mark L. Van Name and Jack McDevitt

Inever wanted him dead, you know."

"Sure, Boss." Harry's grin was only a shadow of my own, naturally, but he tried. I liked that. Liked his sense of humor. His ability to see the little incongruities that are the only real pleasures life offers. I liked *him*. I almost touched my boutonniere, tempted to freeze his face forever in that appealing smile. But no: not just then. One day, perhaps, I would do it for him.

"I am not vindictive, Harry."

"No, Boss. They could never accuse you of *that*."

"Truth is, I feel sorry for him."

"Sorry for *him*?"

"Yes." Harry nodded. I could almost see the bat-shape flickering in his irises, huge behind the thick lenses of his glasses. "You know how single-minded he is. How humorless. He never smiles. Never seems to enjoy himself except when he's inflicting pain."

"You can say that again, Boss."

"I wonder if he has a life away from the rooftops?" Harry's gaze went past my shoulder. I knew he was looking out the window, across the top of the city. "Can you see him, Harry?"

He shuddered.

I got up and walked toward the fireplace. It glowed cheerfully. "We never really know, do we? He could come charging in here at any moment."

"It's a hard world, Boss."

"Yes, it is. And harder than it need be. You know, it's always bothered me that I, I of all people, could not provide him with a sense of balance, of perspective. Of what counts in this life. I would like to do that for him. He needs to understand. Life is not to be taken seriously: not mine, not yours, not his. It's the great lesson."

"He's never learned that."

"And I've tried to show him, Harry. I have explained it to him with my boutonniere, I have demonstrated it with venom, I have laughed at him out of the mouth of a .38." The Gotham skyline was cold and hard in the moonlight. "He lives out there. And he calls *me* mad."

A log broke in the fireplace, scattering the carpet with sparks. I watched them disappear.

"It's the world that's nuts."

"That's right, Harry. It's an evil old world. But that's not my fault. I stand for laughter, which, in the end, is all we can hope to come away with. And Batman just cannot see that." In that moment, I was moved. Was there anyone on the planet more in need of my help than that unfortunate maniac? "Perhaps if he could see himself as we see him. If we could show him his true nature."

"And what is his true nature, Boss?"

I whirled around to face him. "He's a predator, Harry. A sadist. Vicious. He enjoys watching people suffer. It's the only time he really comes alive. Have you noticed how his eyes blaze when he's committing an assault? He's a lot like us, really, when you think about it."

"Yeah. But he's not as good at it as you are."

"True. But who is?" I threw myself back into the armchair. "Harry, when's his birthday?"

"Birthday?"

"Yes. His birthday. Even a bat has a birthday, right?"

"Sure. I guess. But I have no idea how we could find out when it is."

"Well, since we don't know—" I glanced at the calendar over my desk. "—the sixteenth would be a good date. Yes: let's call it the sixteenth. That gives us time."

"For what?"

"To get him a present, Harry. To show him our hearts are in the right place."

"Oh. You've got to be kidding, Boss."

"I never kid. We're going to give him truth."

The wind had begun to pick up. I listened to it rattle the windows, and then allowed myself a good hard laugh. It built until it rocked my body and brought tears. After a moment of hesitation, Harry joined in, not knowing yet why he was laughing, but laughing nonetheless. I like that in a man.

I told Harry what I wanted and left him to handle the arrangements. He was good at that sort of thing.

We hired a lot of people, equipped many of them with portable phones. We assembled a logistics team and alerted our bail bondsmen. If Batman was paying attention, he noticed that there were, during the next few days, an unusually high number of car thefts in and around Gotham. Since we didn't know where he'd first appear, we needed a sophisticated transport system.

I chose the date partly because it was a Saturday. Plenty of people on the streets. On the fifteenth, as darkness crawled over the city, I set up my command post on the top floor of a decaying hotel off the VanDamm Expressway. Then I had dinner sent up and, since I expected to be awake all night, napped for a few hours. At eleven, one of the three phones on my communication console rang. It was the purple one, the one I'd reserved for Harry.

"We're ready," he said.

The stars were remote behind the thick veil of pollution that hung over the city. A three-quarter moon rode among thick clouds. The air smelled vaguely of rain. *His* kind of night. Exciting. I could almost see him, perched on a roof high over the city. Waiting.

"How many?"

"Fifty teams, spaced out every couple blocks, all set to move. They'll assault anybody in the area. If he's anywhere in center city, we'll draw him in."

"Good." I love my work. But never more than moments like that. I could feel the electricity. "The back-ups?"

"Standing by."

"Okay. Harry, I like the way you're handling this."

"Thanks, Boss."

"Start them."

Twenty minutes later, the purple phone rang: "We got him. He just jumped Big Eddie at 132nd and Governor. We never saw where he came from."

I pushed a pin into the location on my city map. "Where are *you*?"

"About five minutes away. I'm on my way over there now. Cass and Wocket are watching from McGuire's Bar. Everybody else is moving to Phase Two."

"Excellent. How's Big Eddie doing?"

"Not so good. Cass says he's just lying on the pave-ment."

Nice to know there are things in this world you can count on. Big Eddie had been saying for years that he wanted a chance at Batman. I wished I'd been there to see it.

Harry was still talking. "The boys are going to start a fight, like you said. I can't see Batman bothering with a bar brawl though."

"Trust me, Harry. Trust me. You don't know him like I do. The man can't leave trouble alone. Just do what I told you. Keep him occupied."

"You got it. The next unit is moving in."

"You'd like this, Joker. You'd really like this."

Yes: I was sure I would. "It's turned into a riot, no doubt?"

"Damn near. There's half a dozen fights out in the street. Sounds like more in the bar. Both plate-glass windows are broken. Lotta blood."

"Where's Batman?"

"Still across the street. He's at a call box. Getting the police. It doesn't look like anybody in this mob has no-ticed him."

"Can you see either of our people?"

"Cass is standing off to one side, watching the Batman. I *think* it's Cass. Hard to be sure from here. I'm a half-block away, and the bar's gone dark. No streetlights nearby."

"Any women out there?"

"Yeah. A couple. They're keeping out of the way."

"I don't know what to think, Harry. Women in cheap bars. McGuire's *is* a cheap bar, isn't it?"

"Oh, yes, Boss. Very cheap."

"No place for a lady."

"No."

"A woman could get attacked in a place like that."

"I read you, Boss."

Harry left the car phone on. I heard him relay my wishes to Cass. "No way, Harry," Cass said. "Not with the Batman standing there."

"The Boss says *do it.*"

I heard Cass grunt. "Yeah, right," he said. I dislike subordinates who don't take direction cheerfully. Cass was dead.

Harry got back on the line. "Looks like you were right, Boss: he's starting across. My God, he's big. I'd forgotten. Eddie's cuffed to the call box, but it doesn't look like he'd be going anywhere anyhow. Wait: one of the broads just went down. Cass is trying to get away from her. The Batman's stopped. He's looking at Cass. Now the crowd sees him. Everything's getting quiet. I can't hear nothing but somebody crying. They're getting out of his way. Cass is trying to get back inside, but he's not going to make it. Boss, he keeps staring at the Batman like he can't take his eyes off him. And the Batman just keeps coming. Boss, this is happening too quick. We're not set up yet."

"You could throw yourself into the fray, Harry. Buy us some time."

"This is not time for jokes, Boss."

"There's always time for jokes, Harry. That's the difference between us and *him.* Where's Juliana?"

I was asking about a shotgun-wielding thug who was to be the centerpiece of the evening's festivities. Though he didn't know it.

"On his way. But we still need a few minutes."

"Anybody hurt yet?"

Harry laughed. "Cass is about to be."

"That's not enough. Tell Wocket to fire a few rounds into the crowd. Create a panic. That'll keep him there awhile."

"Boss, that's going to make him awful mad."

"Do it, Harry—"

We got three before Batman got Wocket. Eight or ten more got trampled. No sense of humor, those people. I could hear most of it over the open link. Screams. Cries for help. Profanity. How much better off we'd all be if we could just loosen up.

Harry cut back in: "Ready at Emory's."

Emory's was an electronics outlet at the other end of the block, next to a vacant lot. Discount electronics. We were about to discount them a bit more. "What's Batman doing now?"

"He's kneeling over somebody, Boss. Hard to see, but she's not moving much. One of the broads, I think."

"Okay: Go."

I could hear Harry whispering instructions into his other phone. Then: "I should be able to see them in a minute. Wait: Yeah, here they come now. They're in a pickup. Coming around the corner, stopping at Emory's."

"Tell them to take their time."

"They know that, Boss, but it's hard for 'em. Goes against their grain. Lennie the Lift is running this team, and Lennie tends to be a safety-first kind of guy."

"That's not my problem. If Lennie can't handle it, you should have got somebody else." I knew he wanted to explain, but he was smart enough not to say any more. "Don't let me down, Harry."

"No way. Don't worry. They're out of the truck now. Two of them. They've left a driver. Batman sees them."

I could hear him breathing.

"He just turned back to the broad. I think he's too busy to worry about Lennie." Harry's other phone crackled. "Juliana just checked in. He'll be ready to go in a minute." I heard a siren over the link. "No problem," said Harry. "It's an ambulance. Couple of blocks away."

"Block it off."

"We can hold it a few minutes. No more."

"That's plenty. What about *him?* Is he still with the woman?"

"Yeah, he's still there. New problem: police are coming. We've overturned a truck on Bensonhurst, so they'll have to come around on the Extension. That'll take time."

"Where's Cass?"

"He cleared out."

"Get him on the phone. I want him standing by in my car during the final phase. Tell him—" The moment lifted my spirits. "—tell him there'll be a little extra something in it for him."

"Okay, Boss. Things are still cooking here: Shotgun's in position. Lennie's picked up something from the vacant lot next to Emory's. It looks like a brick. Maybe a bottle. He's showing it to the Batman."

"—who's wondering why he hears all those sirens and sees no police." A delicious moment. It warmed my heart just to think of it.

"They've turned the pickup around, faced it away from the Batman." I heard glass shatter. A burglar alarm erupted. "Lennie's going inside."

"Batman?"

"Staying put."

"I suspect he's a trifle upset. Let's help him out. Can we let the ambulance through, but not the cops?"

"Yeah, Boss. They're coming from different directions."

"Okay. Let's give the medical resources of this great city a chance to come to the rescue of these sorry barflies."

Armand (Shotgun) Juliana was a psychotic punk. A young man with considerable natural talent, afraid of nothing. Not even me.

He was unsubtle, harsh, as direct as a blast from a double-ought six. He had a passion for shotguns, especially the side-by-side two-barrel. But he loved them all. I can't ever remember seeing him that he wasn't cradling one of the things in his arms, polishing its barrel, caressing the trigger housing. It's a brutal weapon. Mindless. The weapon of a six-pack personality.

Still, he wasn't stupid. He'd never been caught. Had no record. Man like that has his uses.

"Here comes the ambulance."

"And Batman?"

"He's still with the woman, but he's watching Lennie and the boys. They've been carrying stuff out of that store and loading up the truck. Wait a minute." I could just hear the noise from Harry's other phone.

"What?"

"It's Lennie. He wants to get out now. He's nervous."

"Tell him to calm down and finish loading the truck. We might as well make a little money tonight. No reason for Batman to be the only one who gets a present. Tell Lennie Batman won't touch him."

"The ambulance is pulling up. Medics getting out."

"Okay. Start Juliana. Make sure Batman's vision isn't blocked. And Harry: Tell him to wish Batman a happy birthday."

"We're moving it to this side of the street to make sure. Batman can't miss it. Listen: there's nobody available just now to mug, so we'll supply one. Al English. He's just in from Charlotte. Batman doesn't know him. And Al doesn't know Shotgun."

"Okay."

"Shotgun swears he won't hurt him."

"Doesn't matter. As long as it's not fatal. We don't want the judge denying bond."

"He knows, Boss. Whoa. Lennie's getting into his truck. They haven't taken off yet, but he's taking no chances. Batman's starting for him."

I heard the cry for help. It was a good, healthy scream.

"Shotgun has Al against a wall. My God, that looked real."

"What happened?"

"I think Al's really hurt."

"Well, we'll try to be philosophical about Al. You can't celebrate a birthday without having a bash."

"Batman turned in full stride. Shotgun's taking off with Batman right behind him."

"I'm glad we arranged to have an ambulance on the scene, Harry. Just in case things don't go well."

"Shotgun's headed for the alley that connects with Lincoln. Boss, he's just barely going to make it in there. Which means he won't get through before Batman catches up with him. Things could come apart here."

"Don't worry. Batman won't follow Juliana in. He's not that dumb. It'll go slower than that. He'll be waiting for Juliana on Lincoln. Did you warn him against using the shotgun?"

"Yeah. But you know how he is. He might have stashed one in the alley. And he might just blow Batman away."

"That would be a great disappointment to me, Harry. But I'm more inclined to suspect that, under those circumstances, Juliana would get to eat the gun. Head for Lincoln."

"He's gone. The Batman. He was in the shadows at the mouth of the alley. Now he's gone. But I'm sure he didn't go in there."

"Boss, I'm on Lincoln. He's got Shotgun."

"You change cars?"

"Yes. How does he do it? Damn, he gives me the creeps."

How indeed? Dark, savage creature: he seems barely human. I understood in that moment that I had embarked on the right course: force him to see himself through *my* eyes. Lift the mask behind which he hides. The ultimate gift. I did not expect that he would ever be grateful. But one could hope. It would be an eminently satisfactory conclusion to our long association.

"The cops are coming."

I could hear the approaching siren. I could also hear loud, muffled voices. "This is our marital problem?"

"Yeah. We're using Carroll House. It overlooks the alley."

Glass exploded, and the voices became clearer. A man

and woman were screaming at one another. "Wonderful," I said. "Batman called in to settle a domestic dispute."

"He's handing Shotgun over to the cops. He's under a streetlight. I can see him pretty good and I can tell you he doesn't like Shotgun much." Pause. Then: "Damn."

"What's wrong?"

"He's turning away. Paying no attention to the fight."

I was on my yellow phone. To Manny DeSailles, my lead bail bondsman. "They're bringing in Juliana," I told him. "I want him out in two hours."

"What're the charges?"

"Probably attempted robbery, assault, nothing serious."

"How about the victim?"

"Maybe a little under the weather."

"I can't do it in two hours."

"You said you could."

"I said I could if he didn't hurt anybody."

"We can't have everything, Manny. I want him out by three."

"Did he shoot anybody?"

"No."

"Thank God for that. Joker, you guarantee all this?"

"You know you can trust me, Manny. You won't lose a dime." I'd invested in a judge, too. Spared no expense for Batman. "Just get him out, Manny. Fast."

I switched back to Harry. "—in the street. She damn near got hit by a car. Nice timing, Joker: she's good. One of the cops is trying to help her. Uh-oh, here comes Hawk. He's got an AK–47, and he's waving it around. Everybody's ducking for cover." Harry's voice changed, and I realized he was doing some ducking himself.

There were a couple of quick bursts, followed by sustained firing. I wonder whether there is any sound on the planet quite so restful as the rhythm of automatic fire, punctuated by screams, brakes, squealing tires, and colliding cars.

"We got trouble," Harry said. "One of the cops is down. Shotgun is making a run for it."

I picked up a pen. "He's not supposed to do that, Harry."

"Reflexes, Boss. Hawk's blazing away at traffic, and Shotgun just couldn't let his chance go."

"Stop Shotgun. Tell him to get back to the police car. If he doesn't, the whole idea goes down the drain."

"I've got no way to reach him."

"Then chase him down. Just do it, Harry."

"All right. By the way, Batman's back. He's beating on Hawk. I'll get back to you in a couple minutes."

When Harry called again, the air was filled with sirens. "It's okay," he said. "I turned Shotgun over to the cops. He gave me an argument, but I told him we'd make it worth his while."

"Oh, yes, we will, Harry. We will certainly do that."

"They talked about giving me a medal for bringing him back."

"I hope you told them you were just another concerned citizen doing his duty."

"Yeah. Something like that. Listen: a lot's happened here since I got off. We're running the slasher bit."

"Max Domingo?"

"Yeah."

"Good. He makes a marvelous slasher."

"Yeah. Everything's right on schedule. Hawk clubbed Batman a pretty good shot, too, so maybe he's not moving quite as fast as he was. But it's really funny: he no sooner finished off Hawk than Louise came running around the corner covered with blood. She's screaming and carrying on about a slasher, so he's off again. Another squad car's just pulling up, but they won't be able to help him. They've got their hands full here.

"Did you get Louise away?"

"Yeah. She's with me. I'm going to switch to the bike, and leave her with the car. I'm heading over to Calvin Street now. Max'll lead him to Universal Pump over there. Uh-oh—"

"What's wrong?"

"An old couple just came out of Carroll House. They don't look happy."

"Is there a reason we should care, Harry?"

"Uh—"

"Are they talking to the police, Harry?"

"Yes."

"Are they pointing up at the apartment that we used to stage this little performance?" The long silence answered the question. "Are they by any chance the people who live in that apartment?"

"I don't know, Boss. They might be."

"Why, Harry, are they alive?"

If Batman thought he was chasing a demented slasher, he could hardly have been more wrong. Max Domingo's weapon of choice is not the knife. He was an acrobat and a black belt. I'd promised him a bonus if he could take out Batman. I knew it wouldn't happen, but he might inflict some damage.

The quickest route from Carroll House to Universal Pump was through back alleys and across decaying corporate lots. We had a cycle waiting for Harry, to ensure that he could get there before the combatants.

I had chosen the headquarters of Universal Pump because I could see its grounds from my command post. I wanted a good seat for the fight. The building was gray, run-down, one of those ugly converted factories built during the '20s. About four stories high. A low iron fence enclosed the grounds. Delivery docks lined the building's north side. The security lights have always been bad, and we'd shot out a few more to enhance the atmosphere. The roof, which sloped just enough to provide drainage, was accessible only by a ladder at the northeast corner. For ordinary people, that is. I listened to the police radio, waited for Harry's call, and watched. At the west end of the building, a flashlight drifted through the gloom. A guard.

The purple phone rang and I hit the speaker button. "Go ahead, Harry."

"I'm here, Boss. Behind a dumpster out back."

"Okay. Wait and watch."

I scanned the roof and the approaches with binoculars. Nothing yet.

"Maybe we should have given Max a phone," said Harry.

"No. Not with people who are going to wind up in jail. It wouldn't take *him* long to see a pattern. And by the way—"

"Yeah?"

"You might be interested in knowing that the old people from Carroll House have talked extensively to the police. Judging from the radio traffic, they're a little confused now, but even those dummies will eventually figure out that the fight was a setup."

"Boss, I'm sorry. Even if we'd killed them, the truth would have come out."

"Sure. In a few days, maybe. But not tonight." As we talked, I used a red marker to make a circle on the wall, and printed Harry's name inside it. "Well, don't worry. It doesn't really matter."

"You figure Batman knows?"

"It would be wise to assume it." I drew a stroke across the circle. Rim to rim.

"Boss, Max is on the ladder."

"Is he alone?"

"I can't see anyone else." Nor could I. I was able to make out Max: long, scarecrow figure, dark, moving against the deeper black of the old factory.

I turned out the lights, opened the window, and dragged an armchair over. The air was cold and thick with the smell of brick and decaying wood and weeds. A river of automobile lights—the VanDamm—passed behind Universal Pump, casting flickering shadows across the roof, the docks, the grounds. The traffic was curiously silent, a magic lantern show.

Max reached the top of the ladder, paused, stepped off onto the roof, and crouched near an exhaust vent. If someone came up the ladder, Max would be waiting.

But no one would come up the ladder. *I* knew that. And I'd warned Max. Doesn't anybody listen anymore?

I sighed and settled back in my chair.

A bat-shape materialized at the ridgeline, atop the roof. It paused, almost thoughtful. And then glided down toward Max.

"Nothing yet, Boss," said Harry.

Batman might have kicked the damned fool over the edge without Max's ever knowing he was there. But he

stopped, and must have said something, because Max
got up and turned slowly around. They faced each other
for long moments, caught against the moon. Max assumed the fighter's stance, while the wind played with
Batman's cape. He looked surreal, ghastly. I knew he
was solid, vulnerable. Human. Of all men living, none
knows that better than I. Still, I shivered.

Max did what he could: a few jabs, a couple of kicks.
They might have merely passed through the phantom,
or it might have been that he floated just outside their
reach.

Suddenly it was over: a dark swirl of movement, and
Max was staggering. Batman seized him, took him
down, and whatever happened then was blocked off by
the cape. When he stood again, Max hung limp over one
shoulder. Batman strode to the edge of the roof, paused
(and in that moment I had the eerie sensation he was
staring directly at me), and started down the ladder.

"It's over," I told Harry.

"I see them," he said. "I wouldn't have thought anybody could take Max."

"What's next?"

"The shootout. It'll look like drugs."

"Get it started. He's almost down."

By 3:00 A.M., Batman must have established an all-time
personal best: we gave him a string of seven consecutive
muggings along Fourth Avenue, knocked over the Red
Spot Liquor Emporium, blew up a church belonging to
one of those splinter religious groups that nobody likes,
and blasted the door off the vault at the Wheat Exchange. We got away with enough cash to fund the entire operation. But Batman nailed two of the boys.

About the same time that the comptroller's unit was
at the Wheat Exchange, Manny DeSailles was bailing
out Juliana. Twenty minutes later, Batman collared him
again trying to stick up a cab.

The driver was one of my people, and afterward he
called me on the white phone. "You wouldn't believe it,
Boss," he said. "He lifted Shotgun off his feet and I
thought for a minute he was going to throttle him on the
spot. He was still waiting when the cops came and he

told them to see if they could hold onto him this time. They looked kind of scared of him themselves."

"Beautiful," I said, and called DeSailles. "Manny, I got another job for you."

We kept Batman going. We robbed all-night markets, broke into private homes, knifed winos, blocked off downtown streets and attacked drivers who couldn't get through. I even took advantage of the situation to bomb the Penguin's headquarters down on Eighth.

Gradually, we led him across town to Carlay Park, to the old John Elk tractor plant abandoned years ago during the war. As fast as the police carted them away, Manny and his associates bailed them out. We threw as many back at him as we could.

At four-thirty, I called for my car. It rolled up in front of the hotel, and one of my associates opened the door for me. I climbed in. "Hello, Cass," I said.

He swiveled around and nodded. "Hello, Joker. Where to?"

Not a likable man under the best of circumstances. Thin, with narrow eyes that you could never trust, a permanent scowl. Not young, either. Old enough that I could see there was no hope for improvement. "*I'm* going over to Carlay Park, Cass. But I suspect you have another destination."

I watched his hand slide inside his jacket. "What do you mean, Joker?"

I was fingering my boutonniere, casually, like a man without any serious concerns. "It's all right, Cass. You'll enjoy the trip." I pressed the stud imbedded at the top of the stem. It was too dark in the car to see, but I felt the pressure release, heard the faint hiss, and listened to the sudden strangled cry. "Bought and paid for, Cass. Compliments of management."

Thirty minutes later, Harry parked across the street and just down the block from a three-story tenement that the city had promised to renovate a year earlier. In the end, it would be up to me.

It was mostly vacant, but enough poor families had homesteaded there that it would do. On Harry's signal, a

car raced past Batman (who was wearily putting the
wraps on two muggers whom he'd already seen once before that evening), and screeched to a stop in front of the
tenement. Three men jumped out and lobbed Molotov
cocktails through the windows. Then they roared away
while the building burned and the screaming began.

I had taken a rifle onto a rooftop across the street.
From there, I watched him pound across the pavement
and, wrapped in his cape, charge into the building. The
grace and power I'd seen earlier had dissipated. He was
tired now, uncertain, almost clumsy.

A crowd gathered quickly. One or two tried to follow
him in, but were driven back by the heat. People were
pouring out of the building. Batman came out with two
children and went back in.

A wall collapsed. People screamed on the upper floors.
I watched him bring out several more. A roof collapsed
and fire belched out, driving them all back. He turned
and looked over at the building where *I* was waiting.

Sirens sounded. Far away.

He bolted across the street and disappeared into the
doorway immediately below me. I heard him coming up
the stairs.

It was a bad moment.

He would come through the trapdoor. The same one
I'd used. And which I'd left open. But there was no time
to close it.

And no place to hide.

I got as far from the light cast by the flames as I could,
and stretched out on the roof. I sighted the rifle on the
trapdoor.

In the third-floor windows of the burning building,
people were getting ready to jump.

I thought of Max atop Universal Pump and glanced
nervously behind me. When I looked back, he was already out and on the roof. But he wasn't interested in
me, had no idea I was there.

Our building was a few feet higher than the tenement. He secured a line to the trapdoor, heaved it across
the street, and stepped off the rooftop. Then he disappeared into the smoke and flame.

I went back out to the edge and tried to spot him. He

was anchored to the side of the building, taking people out of burning rooms.

I set the rifle into its black tripod and locked the sight on his back. The weapon was a night-sight, CIA-issue assassin rifle, state-of-the-art.

A woman clung to his neck while he tried to coax an old man out a window. As I watched, the glass exploded, and the man literally *fell* out. Batman caught him, but the force of the blast spun them around. But they all held on.

How easy it would have been then. I zeroed in on the yellow spotlight and the bat symbol, held them, played with the moment. And then, as they dangled, as he began to drop toward the street, the woman swung through the sight.

She was young, black, perhaps a mother. I shrugged, tried to change my angle so the round wouldn't go through both of them. When I was satisfied, I squeezed off a round.

It was enough. She fell into the street. And I saw the agony and the rage in his face. The mask could not conceal it.

"Boss, somebody else is playing this game."

"What do you mean?" Batman was almost to the pavement.

"A woman he was bringing down. I think somebody *shot* her. Hard to be sure. There's a lot of noise here."

Yes: sirens and a raging fire. Who can hear a rifle in all that? "Harry, help him."

"Help who?"

"Batman. I want you to help him. Play the public-spirited citizen again. Do what you can."

"Boss, the firemen are forming up. I don't think they'll let me through."

"Do the best you can, Harry. Try to help. We owe it to a suffering humanity."

"Okay, Boss. Whatever you say."

Batman was on the street now. But it was still chaotic down there. Harry hurried toward him, holding his arms over his face to shield himself from the blaze. He was the first to reach the woman.

I broke the phone link with him. "This will just kill Batman, Harry. And you—"

And you, Harry. I watched him kneeling beside her. I watched Batman hand the old man off to a rescue worker, and then join Harry, who was feeling for her pulse. They were kneeling beside her, very quiet.

A good moment to die. Not happy, Harry, the way I would have wanted it for you. But fate doesn't always give us what we want. Life is so arbitrary.

I sighted on Harry, squeezed the trigger, and sent him to a better existence.

The first stars were fading in the east. We were running a little late. I waited in a stolen squad car just off Carlay Park, across the street from the John Elk tractor plant. I checked my makeup in the mirror, straightened my tie, and rubbed my sleeve briskly across my badge. A plume of black smoke from the tenement hung across the far side of the park.

I waited for the blast of a shotgun.

It came, finally, shattering the early morning tranquility. Juliana had arrived.

At that hour, there were few abroad other than derelicts. Easy targets. Both barrels fired again. And again. A wino stumbled out of the bushes that lined the street, fell across a bench, rolled to his feet, and kept going.

Batman, on the edge of the park, but a block away, was dealing with yet another mugger. He turned him loose and disappeared into the shrubbery. I hit the siren.

Juliana caught the cue: there was no fourth round. Moments later he hurried out of the park, still carrying his weapon. It was a sawed-off. He crossed Carlay Street directly in front of me, climbed the wooden security fence around the tractor plant, and ran inside.

I started the car and, siren wailing and lights flashing, pursued. In the highest tradition. As Batman entered the scene, I was scrambling out of the front seat, reaching for my .38. "In there," I said needlessly. "I've called for an ambulance and a backup." He nodded and kept running, took the fence at a leap. He'd managed to keep a utility shack between himself and the factory. I climbed over at the same point. Truth is, I didn't entirely trust Juliana. Man with a shotgun has no discretion.

I knelt beside him, enjoying his presence. Enjoying the heft of the police special.

I knew where Juliana would be: the foreman's office on the second level, at the rear of the assembly area. I had told him the room would be safe. There was a loaded over-and-under waiting for him. And he believed we would trap Batman there.

The side door had been left unlocked. I glanced around as though I were estimating my chances, felt Batman's hand tighten on my sleeve, restraining me. But I shook it off and bolted for the door. The ground was hard underfoot, frozen, full of half-buried bricks. Hard to see in the half light. Gutsy move. I could sense his admiration.

He was beside me, and we went through the door together. He scrambled for a rusted tractor frame, not moving quickly at all, and I hit the dirt floor. Juliana almost got him. He fired both barrels, and buckshot ripped through his cape.

I ran for a sidewall staircase and put a couple of rounds over his head. Still functioning on the script, Juliana ducked back into the supervisor's office.

But Batman was ahead of me. There were hoists and guy wires strung throughout the building. He hauled himself aloft. And even though he was visibly straining, fighting exhaustion, he arrived on the landing while I was still running up the stairs. He disappeared into an adjoining office.

Damn. I was moving too slow.

No sound came from either of the offices, which I knew had a connecting door. "Juliana," I said, to try to head off the possibility of a mistake before stepping through the door. Then Juliana was out on the landing, and he had the over-and-under, and it was pointed at *me*. I signaled, gave him the sign. But he only smiled.

"Batman," he said. "Show yourself. Or I'll blow this cop away." Harsh voice. No polish.

The moment stretched out.

"Batman?"

I said nothing. It was a situation filled with ironic possibility.

And then, behind him, a shadow detached itself from the supervisor's office. The over-and-under went sailing far out into the dark. And Juliana very nearly with it. He went down and Batman stood over him, glanced at him, lifted his eyes to me, and looked again at Juliana.

"You can put away your gun," he said to me.

The moment of truth.

I pointed it at Juliana. His eyes widened and locked on the muzzle. "How many times, Batman?"

I could hear everybody breathing.

"How many dead out there?" I asked. "If I take this punk back, they'll just turn him loose again. How many more will die?"

Batman nodded. The gesture was barely perceptible. But it was there.

"Maybe not tonight. Maybe not for a couple years. But it'll happen. Won't it, punk?"

Juliana knew I wouldn't let him speak. So he only stared. Sometimes at me. Sometimes at the .38.

"Next person you kill," I said, "would be my responsibility." I looked steadily at Batman. "And yours." I motioned him to stand clear.

And then I saw it: the flicker of agreement in his eyes. The subtle shifting of lines around his mouth that said yes. Yes. Do it. The long hesitation that somehow transmitted itself to me.

Maybe I was enjoying the situation too much. Maybe I wanted something more tangible. I don't know.

But I let the moment pass. And, before I realized what he was going to do, he stepped between us. His hand brushed the weapon away.

I struggled then. Tried to turn the gun on him. Saw his eyes widen as he looked into my face. And when he recognized me, he *still* couldn't bring himself to smile.

"It doesn't matter," I said. "You wanted Juliana dead."

He looked from me to Juliana. And the mask came down.

So I won that one. And sometimes at night, when the moon is high, and I know he's out there, I feel a little better. The distance between us isn't as great as it used to be.

Masks

Garfield Reeves-Stevens

s if in a dream only one man can know, he tastes the dirt of the alley he crawls through, the filth of it mixing with the hot taste of his own blood and the cold taste of his own defeat. Laughter, mad and maniacal, peals from the dark brick walls, diminishing even the heaven's thunder and the white-noise hiss of the nightstorm's downpour. In this place, at this time, the Batman's reign is ending.

And the Joker laughs.

Like a dying animal, propelled by instinct unknowing of reality, Batman drags himself across the rain-slicked paving stones of the nameless Park Row alley. His trembling fingers search for gaps between the stones. His breath coalesces in small pale clouds, smeared by rain. His failing muscles contract, and he pulls himself forward another few inches. Another few useless inches. For in this place, at this time, he has nowhere left to hide.

The laughter is like bullets.

Batman hears footsteps behind him, splashing, spritely, like a dancer in the rain. He recognizes their childlike rhythm.

The Joker skips toward their final confrontation.

Batman rolls against the soaking ground. There is a dull metallic clink as his bullet-pocked emblem slips from his chestplate to fall into a puddle of mud and garbage, lost forever, the bat eclipsed.

The Joker howls.

Batman heaves himself against a formless mass of rain-decayed debris. The Joker stands before him, long face curtained by the sheet of rain that falls from the wide brim of his hat. But clearly through that curtain, blood-red lips curl in glee and wild eyes glow with madness fueled by genius beyond measure.

"Caped Crusader," the Joker sings. His laughter is hysterical.

Batman wills his battered arm to obey him, sends it to the belt, fifth compartment, second layer, feels for a familiar shape. But the Batarangs are gone, expended uselessly an hour ago as the rain began to pour. His hand fumbles to the third compartment, first layer. But the ampules are exhausted. All the compartments, all the layers, all are empty. Everything used up except for the binary chemicals in his hollowed heels. But his broken legs lie unmoving, and his last remaining weapons are forever out of reach.

The Joker steps closer, kicking playfully at a puddle. "World's greatest detective," he sniggers as if it were the punchline to God's greatest joke. He raises his arm.

Batman narrows his eyes against the rain that streams across his cowl, forcing himself to focus on the Joker's hand. But he sees nothing with eyes still blurred by the beating he has endured.

"Dark Knight," the Joker screams as his hand lifts higher, a maestro's command for the final crescendo. A volley of lightning streaks down in answer to the night's new ruler and the monstrous arcs strobe over the alley.

In the flashes Batman sees others standing where shadows had hidden them. But his technology is spent, his body has betrayed him, and he is helpless.

The Joker leans forward, chortling with delight. "Stupid little boy!" It is the final insult. The ultimate joke. The Batman revealed as he always feared he would be.

Batman's lips tremble with the cold, with shock, with loss beyond anything he has felt before. He cannot form the words he needs to say, the apology he must make for the failure his life has been.

The others in the shadows point at him and stare.

The Joker laughs again and brings his other hand up

to clap against the raised one, purple gloves meeting with a thunder of their own. "Hit it, boys," he merrily commands and the lightning fades before the onslaught of the searchlights that burst into life atop the surrounding buildings. The tableau is fixed, the mask of night removed from the Batman's defeat.

The sudden brilliance brings physical pain. Batman hears the whirr of motor-driven cameras and sees the light-fogged outlines of television camera crews moving forward in the rain.

"Ladies and gentlemen of the press," the Joker intones, then breaks into mindless giggles. "You may wonder why I've asked you here today."

Batman senses the madman moving to stand at his side but can do nothing. Then suddenly he knows what the Joker plans to do. Everything else was nothing compared to the final defeat that faces him.

"What the Joker promises . . ." the Joker announces. He bends down beside the fallen man in black.

Batman feels cold cloth-covered fingers on his face. At first they are gentle, almost a parting caress, and then they are an unrelenting pressure, pushing hard against his bloodied cheek and deep beneath his cowl.

". . . the Joker delivers!"

The cowl separates from the Batman's face, pulling, cutting, ripping skin, lifting away, crushed in a purple fist.

Batman's cry of rage, of pain, of loss, is incomprehensible.

The cameras whirr.

"Look on my works, ye mighty," the Joker shrieks as the dark cowl bursts asunder in the light, "and *despair!*" And the reporters gasp as they peer beneath the Batman's mask and at last see that Batman is revealed as . . .

Batman's waking scream of anguish echoes in the dark shadows of his lair. He is drenched in sweat. His body trembles. No sleep for ten days. Because of the nightmares.

Because of the Joker.

Further sleep is impossible this night and he knows
he approaches the threshold where even his superbly
trained body will exhibit sleep-deprivation deficiencies.
He arises and cloaks himself in cowl and costume.

This time, the Joker's science is beyond him and he
has only one chance to free himself from the effects of
the Joker's latest weapon. He must return to where it
began. He must return to where the answer may yet lie.
He imagines the Joker's laughter in his lair, and it chills
him.

The Batman must return to Arkham.

Sunlight filters in through the wind-tossed leaves of ivy
crowded too closely around the leaded glass window of
the chief psychiatrist's office. Dr. Bartholomew seems
not to notice. The grounds of Arkham Asylum are always rich and dense and overgrown, never in control.
The grounds of Arkham Asylum are like its inmates.

The psychiatrist studies the charts spread over his
desk. A man cloaked in black waits in the corner of the
office, beyond the window's shaft of sunlight, wrapped in
his webbed cape, protected by his mask. There is impa-
tience in his stillness.

Bartholomew looks up, adjusting his glasses, twin
round circles of glass turning white in the glare from the
window. He is bald, pink, featureless, with pursed lips
like a cupid's. His finger taps a gas chromatograph print-
out. "I've seen a compound something like this before."

The Batman steps into the sunlight. His costume
stays as dark as always, swallowing the light. "The
Joker's venom."

"Ah, yes," Bartholomew says. He smiles himself, nodding his head nervously. "I've conducted autopsies on
victims of that. Extraordinary chemical. Brilliant man."

The Batman's silence encompasses the room.

"All things considered, of course," Bartholomew adds
quickly. He looks back to his charts.

"You know how the Joker venom works?" Batman
asks.

"The textbook explanation," Bartholomew says without looking up. "Absorbed through the lungs, carried by

the bloodstream into the brain. Direct stimulation to the portions of the amygdala controlling emotional responses. In the case of Joker venom, the stimulation leads to an unrestrained feeling of . . . good spirits. Well-being. Uncontrolled laughter as a sequela. Incredible knowledge of neurochemistry. Quite impressive."

"Victims die of cardiac arrhythmia and suffocation." The Batman's voice is as dark as his cape.

Bartholomew stares up at him for a long time. "We all die, Mr. Batman. At least the Joker's victims die happy."

There is the sound of creaking leather as Batman closes his fists, considering his reply. "How is this compound similar to the Joker venom?" he asks at last, fists opening back into hands for the moment.

"By 'this,' you mean the compound to which you were exposed when you last fought the Joker?"

"Yes."

Bartholomew leans back in his red-leather-covered chair. The old wood complains. He takes off his glasses and rubs the bridge of his nose, gazing up at the age-darkened patterned plaster of the ceiling. "According to my analysis, this new compound has the same general molecular structure as Joker venom so I would assume it, too, would be absorbed into the bloodstream through the lungs and then be able to cross the blood-brain barrier."

"To stimulate portions of the amygdala."

"Exactly." Bartholomew studies what little he can see of Batman's expression beneath the mask. "Have you had bouts of extreme and . . . inappropriate emotional responses since your exposure to the compound?"

"Yes."

"Care to provide details?"

"No."

Bartholomew smiles, a nervous tic. "General parameters, perhaps?"

"Disruptive dreams."

"Nightmares?"

"They could be called that."

Bartholomew leans forward, hunching over his desk, hands clasped together. "That a mind like his should be locked away here, and not turned loose at MIT or DARPA or . . ."

The Batman looms over the desk. The shadow of his cowl falls across the little man.

"The compound is stimulating other areas of the amygdala than those affected by Joker venom, Mr. Batman—the portions that control your reaction to senseless fear, to danger, to personal threat."

"The things I fear, Dr. Bartholomew, are not senseless. They are precise and specific. How could any compound trigger such exact stimuli?"

Bartholomew waves his hand, the fluttering of a frightened bird. "You don't understand, Mr. Batman. The Joker has gone far beyond your understanding of biochemistry and psychology. It is *your* brain that provides the details of your nightmares. What the Joker's compound does while you're asleep is trigger the release of enormous amounts of chemicals and hormones just as if you had been badly frightened. Your sleeping mind, having to deal with this terrible feeling unleashed as the fear chemicals spread through your system, creates an extremely detailed dream of the thing you fear most in order to 'explain,' if you will, the feeling and its intensity." Bartholomew smiles and holds it. His teeth are small, pearl-like, perfect. "You see, the genius of the Joker has made it possible for one compound to affect each person differently. Each individual exposed to it will experience his or her own worst nightmare." He claps his hands in delight. "Oh, I must ask him if we might write a paper on it together. Has he written other papers before, do you know?"

"Will it wear off?"

Bartholomew grudgingly looks back at his charts. After a moment, he sighs. "Technically, yes. But practically, no."

"Explain."

The nervous smile appears again. "The compound should take about six months to be fully metabolized by your body."

"So in six months the nightmares will stop?"

"Oh, dear me, they'll stop sooner than that, Mr. Batman." He holds his smile. "If you don't develop an antagonist for this compound within another two to three weeks, you'll die. Of exhaustion, insanity . . . whatever."

Bartholomew shakes his head as he folds up his charts. "Bloody genius," he whispers to himself. "Incredible."

The Batman's outspread hand descends on the doctor's desk, covering over the papers there. "I want to see him."

Bartholomew at last looks shocked. He answers in outrage. "Mr. Batman! You of all people should know that's impossible. Here at Arkham our goal is to help our patients over their past troubles. To point them toward the future as fully functioning, well-adjusted citizens able to—"

The black glove becomes a fist. "Now."

Bartholomew stands, all five feet four of him. He glares back at the eyes burning within the black mask. "As his psychiatrist, I cannot permit it. A confrontation with you could destroy everything Arkham has achieved with him in his long years of therapy."

"Between his escapes. His crimes. His murders."

"One must have hope, Mr. Batman."

"I *will* see him."

"No, you will *not*. I forbid it. And I can have an injunction drawn up to keep you away from him. And away from Arkham." Bartholomew straightens the charts on his desk, tapping them into perfect order. "Besides, he specifically asked that you not be allowed to bother him."

"Because he knows," Batman says.

"Knows what?"

"That he's the only one who can help me."

Bartholomew takes a clipboard from the side of his desk. "Perhaps you should have thought of that last week before you beat the poor man senseless and dragged him in here again. No wonder he's afraid of you." The little man marches to an ornate wooden door. "Now, if you'll excuse me, Mr. Batman, I have my rounds."

Batman stands helplessly by the window, staring out at the setting sun, seeing darkness grow among the thick bushes and gardens and high stone walls. Arkham's darkness. Like its grounds, like its inmates, rich and dense and uncontrolled.

Night is falling. The time of dreams. He makes the only decision he can.

"You know, Harv," the Joker says, "you're not *half* the man you used to be." Deep in the ancient cellars of Arkham, the Joker's laughter echoes down the long, dark corridors. From one of the other high-security cells, something wails in answer.

The other patient in the recreation lounge turns slowly away from the ceiling-mounted television. The half of the patient's face not corroded by acid smiles calmly. The other half, what little remains within it that is recognizably human, drools. The two-faced man reaches down the side of his leg and pulls out the slim shining needle of a commissary spoon, filed to a deadly point.

In one hand, he holds the weapon ready to strike. With his other hand, he expertly flips a silver dollar into the air and snatches it in flight. Then he studies the coin in his open palm and the half smile goes away. The man with two faces slips the weapon back into his sock, gets up, and leaves the lounge.

The Joker cackles. "Hey, Harv!" he calls out to the departing patient. "I think you've *flipped!*" He chokes with laughter, pounding his hand against the side of his chair.

Then he realizes that he is alone.

And not alone.

"Who's there?" the Joker asks the shadows in the hall outside the lounge.

One shadow answers.

"You're not supposed to be here," the Joker says happily. "Yet."

Silently, the Batman closes the door to the corridor behind him.

"I need your help." Batman says the words as if he were spitting out poison. "I want the antidote."

The Joker slaps his hands to the balls of his cheeks. "What? No buttering me up? No asking me about the wife and kids? Just, 'Gimme the antidote,' as if . . . as if . . . I mean nothing to you?" He wipes a single heartfelt tear from his eye. "And here I thought we had something special between us, a certain *je ne sais quoi?* A, how you say, give-and-take relationship."

The Batman waits.

The Joker holds two fingers to his lips to cover a giggle. "You know. I *give* you the antidote. And you . . . *take* me away from all of this."

"There is no negotiation."

The Joker shrugs and sits back down to watch the television. "Then there is no anti—"

The Joker's feet dangle above the floor as Batman jerks him into the air by the collar of his Arkham-issued white shirt. But the white-faced man rolls his eyeballs back, sticks out his tongue, and hangs limply, offering no resistance. Batman heaves the man across the room.

The Joker stretches out on the floor where he has landed and rests his head on his hand. Then he thrusts out his bottom lip. "Whatsa matter, Batikins? In the old days you could have held me up like that a good three or four minutes without breaking into a sweat." He narrows his eyes in concern. "Say, are you getting enough sleep?"

"Get up," Batman says.

"You're not thinking too clearly, Batpal. If you beat me silly—well, sillier—what are you going to do with me then? Take me away to . . . Arkham? Naa, a tad redundant. You going to kill me? Naa, what would the ACLU say? You going to torture me to reveal the secret of the antidote? Maybe slip toothpicks under my nails until I—"

A black hypodermic needle glints as Batman fills it with a clear ampule from his belt.

The Joker stands, grinning. "Would it make a difference if I just said no?"

Batman snaps the hypo into the barrel of his gas pistol.

The Joker carefully undoes the buttons of his institutional shirt, offering his pale chest as an easy target. "If I have an antidote to the nightmare compound, don't you think I also have an antidote to your truth compound? And don't you think I loaded myself with it because I knew you might try something like this?"

Batman takes aim.

"Go ahead, Batchump. All it'll do is put me to sleep for a day or two. A day or two during which you *won't* sleep. And by the time I wake up, you can bet that pink toad, Bartholomew, will have an injunction against you *and* have transferred me someplace you'll never find me. Not in the time you'll have left."

Batman hesitates.

The Joker smiles. He lowers his voice, twitches his lips. "So what you got to ask yourself, punk, is, 'do I feel lucky?'"

Batman lowers his pistol.

"Oh, wipe that silly frown off your face," the Joker says as he slowly buttons his shirt again. "You get me out of here tonight and the antidote's all yours."

Batman holds his pistol uselessly at his side. He looks away, shakes his head to clear it. "I . . . I can't help you escape."

The Joker waves his hand. "Of course you can. It's easy. I do it all the time myself."

"No," Batman says.

The Joker checks his reflection in the television screen and rubs his hands through his hair until it all stands on end like a green cloud. He smiles at his perfection and turns away from the television. "Think of it this way: If you don't help me, inside two weeks you'll have your own cell here and inside a month you'll be dead. Then I'll escape anyway but there won't be anyone who'll be able to bring me back."

He holds up a finger. "*But,* if you get me out of here tonight, I'll give you the antidote, and things will be back to normal, or abnormal in your case. I'll be free, like I'm going to be anyway, but you'll still be around to hunt me down and give my poor life some meaning in these dark and dangerous days." He holds out his hand. "Whaddaya say, B.M.? Is that a deal or is that a deal?"

Batman stares at the Joker's mad eyes. He breaks down his pistol and replaces it in his belt.

The Joker waves his hand toward Batman. "C'mon, shake on it?"

Batman's hands stay at his side. The Joker reaches out to his own hand, rips it off from his wrist, and holds the stump up to Batman's face. "See? Nothing up my sleeve . . ." He cackles.

Batman snatches the fake hand from the Joker and hefts it in his own. "Gas or explosive?" he asks.

The Joker smiles as he stretches his arm and pushes his real hand through the cuff of his shirt. "Remember who you're dealing with here, B.M. Of course it's explosive. It's a *hand* grenade." When his laughter subsides, he adds, "Pull out the thumb, count to five—or is it two?—then toss and run. That's the only way to smuggle things into Arkham, you know. By making them look like things that already belong here."

Batman disables the explosive hand, turns his back on the Joker, and goes to the door. He opens it silently and checks the hall beyond with a narrow sliver of mirror from his belt. "Come here," he says and the Joker goes to him. "We do it my way, understand? No one gets killed. No one gets hurt."

"Didn't anyone ever tell you that a thing worth doing is worth doing well?" the Joker protests. "I've got a reputation to maintain and an Arkham breakout without a few gratuitous deaths will never make the eleven o'clock—"

Batman's hand goes around and tightens on the Joker's throat. "Or we could both end it here and now. Together."

The Joker pats Batman's cheek and for once he doesn't laugh. "You forget, Batman. Nothing ends in Arkham. Nothing."

Batman's cape moves with the beat of an immense batwing as it flows through the air and envelopes the Joker in blackness.

"My way," Batman says again, and then the two of them, the Batman and the Joker, move out into the tunnels of Arkham, into the shadows where nothing ends.

Together.

The moonlight and sudden night air on his face remind the Joker of birth. The swift flutter of Batman's cape as it withdraws fades to nothing, and the Joker stretches out his hands and arms to steady himself and finds he is on Arkham's south wall, fifteen feet up, tottering on the rough-edged stones.

"Jump," says Batman but the Joker cannot see him.

Behind the Joker, the dark mass of Arkham is silhouetted against a night sky of low clouds faintly underlit
by the distant glow of Gotham City's lights.

"A perfect escape," the Joker says wistfully. "Without
a single death. How amazing. How disappointing."

"Now!"

With a snicker, the Joker throws himself from the
wall without knowing where or how he will land, or even
if. But Batman catches him, saves him, lowers him
gently to the ground.

"That's it," Batman says.

The Joker turns away and brushes his hand against
the ancient stones of Arkham's walls. He has never
touched them from the outside. "So quickly?" he asks.

"My way," Batman says.

"I wish you had let me see more of it." The power of
Arkham resonates beneath the Joker's fingertips, calling him back.

"I wish you had seen less as it is."

The Joker nods and takes his hand away from the
wall. His smile widens. "Perhaps that's our secret," he
says and turns back to Batman, a living shadow against
the dark surrounding forest.

"Our secret?" Batman asks.

"If we saw less, if we knew less, then we would not
need to be what we are, don't you think?"

"If we saw less, if we knew less, then we would *be*
less."

"Of course," the Joker says. "Of course, you're right."
And he laughs and he screams and he swings his fist at
Batman's face.

A fraction of a second too late, Batman blocks and the
Joker's blow connects with the top of his cowl. He flips
backward, landing in a crouch, balancing on both feet
and one hand. The other hand holds a Batarang. Dried
leaves crackle beneath him as he shifts his weight. Behind him, the forest is dark and silent.

"Have you guessed?" the Joker asks, turning his body
to provide the smallest target. "Has it taken you this
long?"

The subtle crunching of the leaves is silenced.

"You haven't?" The Joker's laughter stops in amazement.

"There is no antidote?" Batman asks.

"Right again, B.M." The Joker chuckles. "For getting me out of Arkham, your reward is a few more weeks of sleepless nights, and an end to dreaming. You know what happens when you're prevented from dreaming?"

The Batarang sings through the air. The Joker arches back and the weapon sparks against the stones of Arkham and buries itself in the ground.

"The dreams build up inside you—" the Joker laughs, "—until they burst out while you're awake." He dives and rolls away as a second Batarang slices the air above his head, dying against the stones.

"Only then," the Joker says as he comes back to his feet and clasps his hands together, "they're called hallucinations. And because of my nightmare compound, they'll be hallucinations of the things you fear most as well." He pulls his arms apart. Two hands move grotesquely with one wrist. "Just like your dreams." He pulls a thumb from his second false hand.

Batman's arm snaps down and a billow of smoke erupts at his feet just as the Joker's second hand-grenade flies at him. The Joker twists and dives away. The explosive hand detonates. The Joker hears the grunt of a man who has lost his breath.

"Just like your *dreams*," the Joker cries into the night. He pulls a button from his shirt, scrapes a nail across it, counts to three then tosses it into the air. The button flares with four seconds of magnesium light. Long enough to see the stark outline of a man crawling away on the ground, seeking shelter beneath the trees.

The Joker pounces. He feels the explosive huff of breath burst from Batman's lungs. Batman's arm comes back to drive an elbow into the Joker's side but the countermove is slow and the Joker is on his feet again without being touched. Slowly, the Batman rolls over.

"It's only been ten days without sleep, B.M., but already your reflexes are off. You let me jump on your back! You couldn't block my punch. You're decaying in front of me."

The Joker laughs.

Batman sits up, hands at his belt. The Joker flicks another flare button and the unstable chemical bursts into metal flame and adheres to Batman's emblem. Batman's hands leave his belt and swirl his cape around him as he rolls on the forest floor to extinguish the flame. But by the time the flare is spent, the Joker's foot has found the Batman's head, again and again.

A final kick goes into the side of Batman's chest, just beneath the lip of his body armor. The Joker falls back, laughing with the memory of the satisfying give he had felt as a rib collapsed.

Batman moans, face down in the dead leaves and dirt.

The Joker sniggers as he catches his breath. "Whaddaya say, B.M.? You want to spend the last days of your life fighting hallucinations till you drop and die? Or would you rather end it? Here and now?" The Joker pulls the rest of the buttons from his smuggled shirt. Ignited in the proper positions, in the mouth, on the eyes, there are enough buttons to kill.

Batman rolls over. Blood glistens at his mouth, bubbling at the corner of his lips as he wheezes with each breath. The Joker drops to his knees at the Batman's side. He holds the fistful of flare buttons in his hands. "Tell the truth. Haven't you always wanted to go out in a blaze of glory?"

"Here and now?" Batman asks. His voice is weak, confused.

"That's the idea," the Joker says. He holds the buttons in the open palm of his hand.

"No," Batman says.

The Joker picks out the first button. He shrugs. "All good things . . ."

"Not here," Batman coughs. He tries to get up, can't make it, falls on his side with a sigh, hand going to his side. "Not now."

The Joker scratches the surface of the button and begins his count. "Count of two," he says. "Or is that five?"

The Batman's arm snaps up toward the overhanging trees. The Joker hears the hiss of a Batarang, the twang of a silken rope, the creak of a tree branch.

The button flares. The rope tightens on the suddenly

stretched branch and the stretched branch straightens. Batman lifts up into the air, roaring in pain and defiance, until he is upright, holding himself on his rope above the ground.

His feet snap closed on the Joker's hands. The Joker's real hands.

Wrapped by white skin, pressed in against the others resting there, the button flares.

The Joker howls.

Batman shouts in triumph as his protective boots push in on the Joker's flaming hands. The blinding white glow of the raging magnesium shoots out from between charred fingers like a captured sun. Thin strands of glowing white smoke stream into the Joker's red-rimmed mouth as he takes in another desperate gasp of air to scream and scream and . . .

. . . there is nothing to wake to.

The chemical ignition is spent. The Joker twitches spasmodically. Batman releases his feet and drops to the ground, stumbling as the pain of his shattered rib burns through him.

The Joker babbles deliriously on the floor of the forest. The ruined flesh and bones of his hands are fused together. The skin of his hands is no longer white.

Batman limps over to stand above the Joker. He coughs out blood but the injury is still not enough to stop him. Never.

"You're wrong," Batman says hoarsely. "It *does* end in Arkham. For you."

With one arm clenched against his side, Batman snaps his rope from the tree branch and ties the Joker's legs together. Then he drags the writhing man around the great stone walls of Arkham to the thick twisted iron bars of the main gate. The Joker screams as he is pulled across the hard ground, but not in pain.

The gates swing open before the man from the shadows and the gibbering burden he pulls. All the lights of Arkham blaze through its windows like eyes searching for something that has been missed.

The Joker lies on the cold stones of Arkham's front plaza. Batman leans beside him. A black blade slices through the rope that binds the Joker's legs, but he cannot move. His hands are locked before him, beyond any sensation.

"*Nothing* ends in Arkham," the Joker gasps. His throat burns with the aftertaste of the smoke from his own charred flesh. "*Nothing!*"

Batman's cowl becomes a sudden black shadow over the Joker as a searchlight hums into life on Arkham's roof. Then another, and another, until the mask of night is removed from the Joker's defeat.

Batman steps back and lifts his head. The Joker squints through the blinding light and sees the outlines of others who have been waiting. One of them is the man with two faces. But they wait no longer.

"It's time it ended," Batman calls out to the watchers of Arkham. He looks down at the Joker and suddenly the Joker knows what Batman plans to do. Everything else was nothing compared to the final defeat that faces him.

"Time to see you as you really are," Batman says. He bends down and his black gloves are like claws as he digs into the soft white folds of the Joker's flesh. He grabs at the outthrust cheeks, slips long fingers into the grimacing mouth, squeezes them like talons to get a good grip, a sure grip.

The Joker isn't laughing.

And the Batman pulls against the flesh. And pulls against the blood. Until the watchers of Arkham gasp as they peer beneath the Joker's mask and at last see that the Joker is revealed as . . .

The Joker's waking scream of anguish echoed down the dark corridors of Arkham. The viewing panel on the door to his cell slipped open.

"Ten days," Bartholomew said. "Been like this for ten days." The chief psychiatrist slipped off his black-framed glasses and pushed his hand through his graying hair. "Ever since you brought him in."

Beside the doctor, Batman stepped up to the viewing panel. In the cell, the Joker flopped on the padded floor, arms firmly held against him by the straitjacket he wore. He cackled softly to himself. The words he said were unintelligible. A thin trickle of drool at the side of his grinning mouth fed a growing dark stain beneath him.

"I finished my analysis of the chemical compound he had packaged in that shipment of sandbox sand," Batman said.

Bartholomew whistled softly and turned to look at the costumed man beside him. They were almost the same height. "Johns Hopkins told us they'd need two more weeks to even finish the preliminary spectroscopy on it."

Batman didn't acknowledge the awe in the psychiatrist's voice. "It's molecularly similar to his Joker venom."

Bartholomew shuddered. "Hideous stuff."

"Absorbed by the lungs," Batman continued. "Crosses the blood-brain barrier. Direct stimulation to the amygdala."

Bartholomew nodded. "Causing the victim's sleeping mind to create its worst nightmare."

The Joker sat up slowly in his cell, becoming aware of his audience at last.

"Exactly," Batman said. "The children of Gotham wouldn't have had a chance if that sand had made it into the toy-store distribution network."

"Neither would you," Bartholomew said, "if the Joker hadn't inhaled the dose he tried to use on you."

The Joker pulled himself up on his cot, then stood. He seemed to make an effort to adjust his straitjacket. He wiped his spittle-covered chin on his shoulder. He was making himself look presentable.

"Do you know what the prognosis is?" Bartholomew asked Batman. He held his pen ready to make a note on the Joker's chart.

"His system should metabolize the compound within six months," Batman said.

Bartholomew snorted with surprise and slipped his glasses back on. "How unfortunate," he said. "Because if the effects of that compound prevent him from dreaming much longer, I'm afraid he's going to be driven quite mad."

In his cell, the Joker began to laugh. Batman said nothing.

Then the Joker shivered once, and turned to stare at those who stared at him.

"I wonder what it is?" Bartholomew asked Batman. "I wonder what a man like the Joker would fear most?" He shook his head. "I wonder what he dreams?"

The Joker lurched toward the door of his cell and Bartholomew stepped back. "Don't ask me you baby-faced moron!" the Joker cried. He bashed his head against the padded door. "Ask him! The lunatic in the cape!" He clenched his eyes shut. "C'mon, Bats! You know, don't you? You know what I dream!" He howled in a staccato burst of laughter. It wasn't funny.

Bartholomew blinked at the Joker's outburst, then scribbled on the chart he held. Beside him, Batman's gloved hand reached up to the side of his cowl and pulled it down imperceptibly. It was an almost unconscious habit he had developed over the years. Something he did just before he was to go into action, making sure his mask was firmly in place. Protective. Concealing.

Bartholomew stared into the Joker's blazing eyes. "Is that true, Batman? Do you know what the Joker's nightmare is?"

Batman didn't answer so the psychiatrist turned to him. "Do you?"

But Batman was gone. Swallowed by the shadows. Cloaked by the darkness. Protected by the concealing mask of night.

Bartholomew shook his head again as he peered down the dimly lit basement corridor. He turned back to the man in the cell.

"How can he know what you dream?" the psychiatrist asked.

The Joker leaned up against the viewing window and dropped his voice to a whisper.

"Because, he dreams it, too," the Joker hissed. "He dreams it, too."

The laughter that followed almost burst Bartholomew's eardrum.

Outside, within the beckoning shadows of Arkham's stone walls, Batman returned to the night, haunted by the sound of that mad laughter, driven by a dream only two men know.

Best of All

Marco Palmieri

For once, he wasn't laughing.

Something was very wrong, Wally realized as they walked down the darkened streets. In all the weeks he'd worked for him, he could remember no time when the Boss wasn't at least on the verge of giggling hysterically. But that manic joviality, which had always seemed so inseparable from him, was gone now. As they strode through the gutted neighborhood, footsteps smacking sharply on the broken pavement, Wally looked up into the Joker's face and was suddenly terrified, for not even a smile adorned those blood-red lips.

Then up ahead he saw the house.

It was an old, dilapidated brownstone, its sole distinction from the others being that it was completely bricked up. They went up the crumbled steps, frightening a skinny cat that fled silently into the shadows. The front door looked like a solid oak slab, sealed by bolts and several heavy padlocks. The Joker stopped and stared at the door.

"Open it."

Wally took out the keys and was surprised at how easily the old locks responded. He grew almost excited as he drew back the last bolt and yanked on the door handle, but the Boss's hand slammed it shut before Wally could open it more than two inches. The Joker glared at him dangerously.

"Wait here."

Wally blinked uncertainly and stepped back. The Joker pulled open the door, revealing a cold womb of blackness, and disappeared into it, pulling the portal closed behind him.

Wally stuck his hands into his jacket and glanced around, hating every moment that he was forced to guard the door. He hated this town, and though he didn't think himself superstitious, the whole neighborhood spooked him. It was rotted and decayed, like a corpse crawling with maggots. Whatever the Joker wanted here, Wally hoped he'd get it over with fast. He just couldn't understand what any of this was about. Nothing the Joker did ever made any sense to him, but this trip was the worst. And that, Wally realized, was precisely what scared him. The Joker was getting *weirder*.

He lit a cigarette to calm himself. Easy, man, easy. Whatever's going on can't last all night. Boss said he wanted to get back to Gotham by morning. Just be cool.

Thirty minutes later, there was a glow down the street, and Wally saw a police cruiser making slow progress in his direction. "Aw, crud," he muttered, and flattened himself against the door. The car kept coming, ignoring the junkies huddling in the doorways and alleys, and getting closer to the house. His fingers clawed at the door. The glow from the headlights grew brighter. He found the handle and got it open, slipping inside as the cruiser went by.

"Damn," he whispered in the darkness. If the cops were looking for them, they had to get out, fast. But where the hell was the Joker? "Boss? Hey, Boss, where are you?" No answer. His eyes were adjusting to the darkness, but not enough. All the windows were bricked, and not even moonlight was getting in. Wally fumbled for his penlight, which cast a weak yellow beam ahead of him. A large black rat scurried away in fright, disappearing through a crack in the dusty wooden floor.

In that dust he found a trail of narrow footprints.

Wally went forward hesitantly, putting his hand out to feel his way. Too often he encountered cobwebs so thick he had to pull hard to part them. A wide archway in the lefthand wall opened into the living room, littered with broken lamps and overturned furniture that looked as if they had lain that way for decades. Across the room was another doorway, and down a short hall he found a staircase. The footprints went up.

He almost fell into a wide hole that had rotted through the middle of the stairs. Steadying himself on a creaking banister, he wondered briefly if perhaps the Joker had fallen through the hole. He sent his light in. Nothing but more rats.

Another hall on the second floor. He found a splintered door still held up by one hinge, its dusty fragments strewn inside a little room. Wally waved his penlight around. Old children's toys were scattered about, easily as old as the furniture downstairs. In one corner lay an old doll, a purple harlequin, dull with age and dust. Its porcelain mouth was grinning, and a wide crack ran down the side of its head.

He suppressed a shudder and swiftly backed out of the little room, reminding himself about the cops outside. He went further down the hall and found another staircase. The footprints went up.

The stairs were narrow, leading up to a small attic dimly lit by the amber glow of a flashlight. A sooty skylight hung overhead, intact despite its age and the dismal ruination of the rest of the house. And as the rest of the attic came into view, Wally found the Joker, sitting there on the floor, surrounded by stacks of boxes and piles upon piles of papers, contemplating a tattered old photograph.

But again Wally felt that something was terribly wrong. The Joker was ignoring his presence, despite the fact that the old stairs had creaked all the way up. He just kept staring at the photo, a three-inch black-and-white of some gawky-looking little boy. What the hell was going on? "Boss?" No response. "Boss, listen, we've gotta get outta here. There are cops crawlin' around outside." The Joker's eyes didn't waver from the photo. "Damn it, Joker, are you listening to me? Don't you understand we're hot?"

For half a minute longer the Joker stared at the photograph, then with perfect calm he gently slipped the photo into his vest pocket, and slowly picked himself up off the floor. "No, Wallace, I'm afraid it's you who doesn't understand," he said as he brushed the dust off his purple tailcoat. "I told you to wait outside." He was grinning now as he slowly stepped toward his henchman.

Wally started shaking, his forehead already wet with sweat. "Boss, please, I'm tryin' to tell you we're in trouble—"

The Joker's brow furrowed somewhat. "Wallace, Wallace, you don't have to explain. I understand, my boy, really I do." He pressed a reassuring hand on Wally's shoulder as the hireling inched away, backing into the banister. The Joker kept coming, pressing himself closer until his grin filled Wally's field of vision. His soft purple glove touched the back of Wally's neck. "Wallace, what is it? You look so pale. I'm worried about you, my boy. You desperately need some cheering up."

"Oh, no, please . . . no, no, no . . ."

Something pricked his neck. He tried to squirm free but the Joker was already stepping away from him. First Wally started to twitch, then thrash as his body went into sudden convulsions. His knees buckled and he smashed his face on the banister, splitting his lip. In seconds his motor control was gone, and he tumbled backward down the stairs, breaking bone and wood as he fell. He landed on his back, facing the laughing silhouette that watched him from the top of the steps.

The last thing Wallace felt as his eyes rolled up into his skull was the painful, uncontrollable urge to grin.

From above, it looked like a war zone.

The street below Grandvue Hospital swarmed with police, many of them occupied simply with redirecting traffic and keeping back the curious. Firefighters and paramedics sifted through the debris for victims of fallen masonry, gently loading them into waiting ambulances. Spotlights across the street shone into the gaping hole in the northwest corner of the third and fourth floors, where Gordon and his men surveyed the devastation.

Mingled with the rubble and ash were smears of bright red.

Batman could pick out Bullock's thick baritone over the other voices as he crept silently through the shadows outside. ". . . forty-three confirmed dead, including the woman driving by when the wall was blown out. Ninety-four injured, seventeen of those critical."

Gordon was scowling at the ceiling. Much of it had caved in, and he could clearly see the blackened ruin of the fourth-floor ceiling beyond it. "Has the rest of the building been evacuated?"

Bullock's jowls quivered slightly as he shook his head. "Not completely. Several patients in intensive care aren't ambulatory. Ride could kill 'em. Some docs insisted on staying behind to take care of 'em 'til they were strong enough to move."

"What caused it?" Batman asked as he stepped into the light.

Gordon and Bullock turned as one, the sergeant making a noticeable effort not to look startled. "Some kinda incendiary," Bullock said. "Took out the nursery and a pediatrics ward right below it."

Batman noted the pattern of destruction. "But the explosion took place in the nursery."

Bullock nodded. "Chemical residue on some shards of glass suggest the bomb was planted in a baby bottle. Witnesses confirm the blast occurred right after a nurse took in a cart for the two A.M. feeding."

Batman looked at Gordon. "I'll want some of the shards for analysis."

Gordon peered back at him through the smoke issuing from his pipe. "You'll get them. Parquette and Silva already took them downtown to the Department labs. I'll signal you the minute they're through."

"What do you have on the nurse?"

Bullock drew out a dog-eared notepad from his coat. "Cassandra Alvarez, thirty-seven. Registered nurse, twelve years, exemplary record. Well-liked by her co-workers. No criminal record. Died in the explosion."

The Caped Crusader dropped slowly to one knee, reaching out two gloved fingertips to the edge of the crimson puddle at his feet. The blood shone against the dark fabric of his gauntlet.

"I'll need her dossier," he said finally, "plus those of anyone else who might've had contact with the cart."

"I'll get right on it," said Bullock, and went back to coordinating the other detectives milling about the wreckage. Batman continued to stare at his fingertips as Gordon watched him intently.

"How many children?" he asked softly.

Gordon breathed out a cloud of smoke. "All twenty infants in the nursery died in the blast. Five of the kids in this ward were crushed to death when the ceiling caved in. The other three suffered second-degree burns and multiple broken bones, but they should make it."

"Children . . ." he whispered.

A draft was blowing into the room. Gordon thrust his hands deep into the pockets of his trenchcoat. "I don't mind telling you I'm scared. Few clues, no suspects, not even a motive . . . it's my worst nightmare come alive." He paused, frowning at the street. The last of the ambulance doors were slamming shut, sirens kicking in as they drove off to St. Matthew's, across town. Gordon listened as the whine faded into the distance. "This city's child mortality rate has gone through the roof in only a few weeks. Kids falling out of windows, drownings, gas leaks, fires. . . . Too many fatalities in a very short time. Now this."

"Our quarry's becoming more ambitious."

"Then I take it we've drawn the same conclusion."

"Probably. You believe in coincidence even less than I do. But we'll find him."

"You sound certain. I wish I could be. But my gut tells me we're going to see a lot more death before this is over."

"No." Batman closed his fist over the blood and stood up. And it seemed to Gordon suddenly that the figure beneath the flowing blue cape and cowl was no longer merely frightening, he'd become menacing. "No more deaths. Tell your men, Jim. Warn the public. We're dealing with a terrorist bent on mass infanticide. Do what you can to protect the kids." He turned back to the hole in the wall, his cape billowing as he strode toward it.

"What about you?" Gordon asked.

Batman stopped at the jagged edge of the floor, staring calculatingly at the blackened skyline of Gotham City.

"I'm going to bring him down."

He took hold of the line that waited for him outside the hole and vanished into the night like a dark wind.

He longed for sleep, yearned for the calm and serenity that came with blissful unconsciousness. Yet the solace he so craved somehow always eluded him, for in his most private moments he would lay awake remembering, always remembering, until he at last closed his eyes, only to find himself suffocating in his dreams.

He could still see Mommy walking into his room as he scratched contentedly away at his sketchpad. "Sweetie? Can I talk to you?"

He looked up at her. "Sure, Ma."

She glanced briefly at the cartoons flashing across the TV screen. His toys, of course, were scattered everywhere, and she smiled warmly when she spotted his favorite, Mr. Giggles, the old purple harlequin doll he'd kept since he was a baby.

Then she did something very odd: she sat down on the floor next to him. "So how was school today?"

"Z'okay," he said. "Mommy, are you awright?"

The grin spread across her face uncontrollably. "Just fine, sweetie. But you see, I've got a really big surprise, and I'm trying to think of a good way to tell you."

"What? What is it?"

"Well, you know that baby your friend Stevie's family just had?"

"Yeah."

"Well . . ." Mommy looked left and right, as if to make sure no one could overhear, then leaned real close and whispered, "We're gonna have one, too."

His eyes popped. "Aw, cool! Really? When? Can we go tonight? You got enough money?"

"Whoah, honey, take it easy." She laughed. "It isn't like buying a new TV. The baby's gotta grow first."

He frowned. "You mean like fruit?"

"Uhh . . . not exactly. It's a little different."

"I thought we hadda go to th' ospital."

"That comes later. We won't have the baby until next year, around the beginning of summer."

His face fell. "Aw, why so long?"

"I told you, sweetie, the baby needs to grow."

"Where?"

She took his hand and pressed it to her stomach. It felt warm. "In here."

He looked up at her doubtfully. "You sure?"

"Pretty sure."

"Wow." He sighed. "Can I pick if it's gonna be a boy or a girl?"

She took him in her arms and kissed him, then winked. "We'll see. But listen, sweetie, I'm gonna need a lot of help, and you've got be my special guy until the baby arrives. You think you can do that?"

"Sure. What do I gotta do?"

"Just stay close to me, and help me, and protect me, and keep me warm, and don't ever forget I love you very much."

"But what about Daddy?"

"He'll be helping, too, but he's gonna be working real hard at his job. So when you're not in school, I might need you to keep me company."

"Didja tell him yet?"

"Sure did. I just got off the phone with him." She pinched his chin. "He's pretty darn excited, let me tell you."

"Are you happy, Mommy?"

"Oh, you bet I am."

He looked down for a moment, as if thinking hard, then looked up at her again. "Me, too."

Then she hugged him again, for a real long time.

After Daddy got home from work that night, he took them all out to a restaurant. He kept kissing Mommy and asking her if she felt okay. Mommy just laughed and told him she was fine. It took him days to calm down a little, to

stop bringing home baby stuff and to quit running
around, as Mommy said, like a chicken with his head cut
off.

"See, sweetie?" She laughed. "This is how your father
acted before you were born."

Daddy looked up from the crib he was building and
scowled. "Hmph," he said, and dove back into the instructions.

But a few weeks later, Daddy lost his job, and nothing
was ever quite the same afterward.

It really wasn't so bad at first, but as time wore on, his
father found that no one would hire him, and he quickly
became more and more depressed. Then he would drink,
and the depression became anger, and he and Mommy
would start yelling at each other. Sometimes after a fight,
Daddy would storm out of the house, slamming the front
door, and she would sit alone in her room and cry.

Then one night the boy awoke to find Daddy sitting in
the dark by the bedroom window, head bowed, staring
vacantly at the harlequin doll he held in his lap, sounding as if he'd been crying.

"Just isn't fair, sport," he mumbled. "I mean, I've tried
so hard. So hard. I played the game their way. Two years
I've been dry. Why doesn't anybody understand? It was
only one drink, one stupid drink." Daddy looked up at
him, and in the pale moonlight shining through the
blinds, his eyes looked shriveled. His breath smelled of
whiskey. "But those guys, those guys, they're like wolves.
They watch you all the time, waiting for you to slip, then
they eat you alive." His hands worked Mr. Giggles,
wringing it, twisting it. "I can handle losing a job, but my
wife's pregnant, dammit! They didn't have to blacklist
me, too! They didn't have to take everything away!" Then
he started sobbing, and continued for several minutes.

"World hates us, sport, you know that? Oh, yeah, it
hates us. Bastards! It lets—it lets us pick ourselves up
from the sewer and build a decent life, and then it takes it
all away as if nothing matters! Nothing matters."

"Daddy . . ."

"Daddy? Daddy?" He started laughing as his fingers
continued to claw at Mr. Giggles. "Daddy. God, what a

*joke! Everything I've been doing to clean up my life is
somebody's joke!*

"Baby can't live, you know," he told Mr. Giggles. "Oh,
no, baby can't live if Daddy doesn't have a job. No job, no
money. No money, no food, no home, no life! Might as
well all of us be dead. Better off, better off in this sick,
sadistic world! Better off dead!"

Suddenly furious, Daddy flung the doll across the
room. The boy let out a strangled cry as, to his horror, Mr.
Giggles crashed against the wall, losing pieces of its porcelain head as it hit the floor. It landed face up and grinning, shafts of moonlight streaking across its painted
visage.

Shaken, his father got up suddenly and fled the little
room, bumping into things as he stumbled out the door.

Later still, the boy lay awake in bed, sweating, and
didn't fall asleep again for quite some time.

He never forgot what happened to Mr. Giggles.

Eight nights went by like slow torture, the longest quiet
time since the killing spree began. Batman had slept little since the Grandvue bombing, watchful for any more
unnatural child deaths, trying to find a pattern in those
that had gone before. To his disappointment, no pattern
emerged. The incidents seemed to have no common denominator.

Bullock's incendiary turned out to be a homemade
job. Any idiot with a chemistry textbook could've put it
together. Consequently, Batman had nine suspects in
the bombing, including the late Cassandra Alvarez, but
nothing he could find connected any of them with the
previous killings. Someone had gone to a great deal of
trouble to make the deaths seem unrelated.

He reached for his car phone as he sped south along
the Martin Luther King Drive. "It's me," he said. "Anything new at your end?"

"Nothing helpful," Gordon replied. "The tension
level's rising all over. You can feel it. Like the calm before the storm."

He'd felt it, too. "Who've you got at the orphanage
tonight?"

"McCord and Tabler. They check in every two hours, but the reports never vary. Situation negative." He was silent a moment. "I dunno . . . I keep thinking we may lose this one."

"Pessimism isn't like you, Jim."

"Maybe not. Damn arthritis is acting up again, and these cold nights don't help a bit. How the hell do you do it, anyway?"

"Mirrors. It's all done with mirrors."

"You're a real bastard, you know that?"

"Has Bullock finished pulling together that information on the victims' parents?"

"Not yet. He would've been done tonight, but there was some gang trouble in the Alley."

"The Alley?"

"Yeah. Real mess, too. It's all over now, but there was evidently a rumble shortly after ten P.M. Not enough that some nutcase is after the kids. They have to kill each other, too. Whole damn city's going to hell."

"G'night, Jim." Batman hung up and tightened his grip on the wheel. Cursing silently, he hit the accelerator and thundered down the drive. He thought about Leslie, besieged at the clinic with a sudden flood of cut-up, bullet-ridden teenagers.

A slight motion of his wrist against the wheel and the car suddenly darted into an oncoming exit like some angry black eel. Block after block became a blur through his windshield, and the smooth steel and glass of Gotham's midtown gave way to the decay and squalor of Crime Alley.

In the streets, all manner of nocturnal vermin fled at his approach, his headlights blazing like starving eyes as they cut through the night. One street near the clinic was unusually dark, the lamplights having been recently shattered, no doubt to cloak the rumble. Batman made use of the darkness and parked where the shadows were thickest. Blood and broken glass littered the street.

He got out and took in his surroundings, seeing them vividly despite the darkness, a setting burned forever into his memory. There on the corner beneath an undamaged lamp, the spot where he'd watched his parents die, the gunshots resounding eternally through his head.

Not far from there was where he'd met Jason, years later, as the boy was trying to boost his tires. Jason . . . whom he'd buried, as he'd buried his parents.

Jason . . .

Somewhere in the shadows, something moved.

Counting on the darkness and his cape to conceal him, Batman held very still and listened. A rustle on his right, coming from a narrow alley across the street. Two, maybe three people, heading toward the clinic. He caught a minute flicker of red in the shadows, reflected off the moonlight. A grim smile lifted the corners of his mouth, and he waited.

Presently, one of the shadows stumbled. The red flicker whispered angrily. "Yo, take it easy, idiot. You screw this up, I'll put you in the friggin' hospital myself."

"I can't see, man," the other said. "An' I'm tellin' you, I don't like this. The 'Man watches that place."

"The hell with him! And the hell with you if you got a problem! Go on, Gary, go home if you ain't with me. You, too, Rich. I don't need this garbage."

"That ain't what I meant, man," Gary whispered. "I just think we oughtta wait 'til the heat's down. We wait a week or two, we can waste 'em when nobody's lookin'."

"No!" the flicker said as they got closer to the light. "Tonight! I don't give a damn if the heat's on. We gettin' those punks tonight. You hearin' me?"

"*I* hear you, Sammy," Batman said aloud. "But I'll be damned if I understand."

Startled, all three stopped in their tracks. Gary dropped whatever he'd been carrying and it shattered loudly on the ground. There was a smell of gasoline.

Towering over them, the Batman stared at the remains of the Molotov cocktails and seized Sammy roughly by his jacket. "Are you out of your mind?"

"Go to hell, man," Sammy spat. There was hate in his eyes. Batman could feel it. The red-jeweled earring he wore as his badge of office glittered even more under the lamplight. His friends recovered quickly and had moved behind Batman, drawing out a couple of .38s.

Still holding Sammy, Batman glanced over his shoulder at them, his eyes narrowing dangerously.

"Just try it."

Rich's jaw worked nervously. Gary was already sweating. After a moment, they lowered their guns and dropped them on the sidewalk.

Batman turned back to Sammy. "Now what the hell's your problem?"

"You, man!" he shouted. "You're my freakin' problem! You and that kiss-ass treaty you made me agree to! Those lowlifes were just waitin' ta backstab us. They came into Darkangel territory and cut my people down, man, an' we hadn't done nothin'!"

"So now you're firebombing clinics, is that it? What else, Sammy? You blowing up babies in your spare time, too?"

Sammy laughed. "You crazy, man. You know that?"

Batman leaned into his face. "Yeah, Sammy, I'll tell you how crazy I am. Somebody's been killing kids in this city, and if I thought you, the other Darkangels, or any of the Overlords had anything to do with it, I'd make you wish you'd died in the rumble."

"Man, I had nothin' to do with that stuff! You got that? Nothin'!"

"Then why the Molotovs?" Batman shouted.

Sammy was seething. "Overlords came outta nowhere and killed three of mine, Bro! Andy and some o' his backstabbers got cut before the cops showed, so they took 'em to Old Lady Leslie's."

Batman kicked at the remains of the firebombs. "So now it's revenge? Even if it costs innocent lives? Dammit, Sammy, do you want a war on your hands? Is that what you're after?"

Sammy said nothing.

"Let's get something straight," Batman went on. "You guys aren't supposed to be part of the problem, anymore. You're supposed to be working toward the solution. You're in it together. If you can't handle that anymore, if you guys really want things to go back to the way they were before the treaty, you'll be drowning in blood before you realize what's happening."

Sammy glanced at his lieutenants, then he looked up at Batman. "So what're we supposed to do? Let 'em come back so they can do it again?"

"Nobody's saying that, Sammy. But think for a minute: Andy's always stuck to the treaty. He was eager to see the Alley change as you were. Why would he stop?"

"What're you sayin', that maybe we started it?"

"No, but this whole thing feels wrong. You guys had peace for close to a year and it was working! Whatever you think happened, there must be more to it. Give me a chance to find out before you start another war."

Sammy stared at him a moment longer, then turned and started to leave, Gary and Rich following close behind.

"One more thing, Sammy," Batman said, retrieving the fallen guns.

Sammy turned, arching an eyebrow at him.

Batman's look was ice. "Stay away from the clinic. Anyone messes with it, it's war with *me*."

Sammy grinned and threw him a mock salute. "Of course, Bro," he said, and disappeared with his friends down the street. Batman watched as they turned the corner, and tucked the guns into a belt pouch. Then with silent strides, he turned and walked toward the clinic named for his father.

It didn't matter how many times she took them in, cleaned them, comforted them, treated their addictions, or stitched them back together, she never got used to feeling their pain. Each new victim claimed a small piece of her, until she felt she had nothing left to give. Yet, somehow, she always found a little more.

She put down the stethoscope and rubbed her eyes. Four major operations in as many hours, patching up kids who seemed intent on maiming or disemboweling each other, stitching up stab wounds that looked more like perforations on flesh that still had baby fat—it exacted its price on her, and Leslie Thompkins, M.D., Director of the Thomas Wayne Memorial Clinic, still couldn't afford the luxury of tears. She'd merely gotten used to fighting them back.

Ambulances from St. Matthew's had already carted off the ones needing the most attention. It still left her with twelve patients convalescing in a recovery room designed to hold half that number. She'd sent home her assistant, Peter, after the fourth operation, and spent the last hour making sure her kids were stable. Only then would she let herself go to her office long enough for a cup of coffee.

To her dismay, she found it already poured, steaming from a cup on her desk.

"I thought you could use some," a voice said from behind her. She immediately whirled around, ready to swing at whoever had broken in. She stopped herself in time.

"Dammit, Bruce, can't you ever come here without scaring me half to death?"

Even under his cowl he managed to look mildly hurt, but only for a moment. "Sorry, Leslie. Stealth becomes so much a way of life after a while, sometimes it's difficult to stop." He smiled at her. "Drink your coffee."

"Don't order me around," she snapped, then returned the smile. "Where's my hug?"

Batman opened his arms as he moved toward her. They embraced each other warmly for a long moment. "How've you been?" he asked.

Clinging to him tightly, she found the strength to laugh. "Awful."

"Bad night?"

"Oh, God, the worst."

"I heard about the rumble. I would've been here sooner, but I've been on a case."

She let go of him and stepped back, putting her hand on his cheek. "I know. I've been following it in the news. It's terrible, Bruce. All those children. How can something like that happen?"

"If I could answer that I might be able to prevent it. But I can't."

"Can you stop it?"

"I'm trying. So far, I'm coming up empty. I can't even determine who the killer is."

"Then maybe it's over. Maybe he's left the city. It's been eight days—"

"I know. But I think he's just laying low, waiting us out, hoping we'll lower our guard so he can kill safely."

Leslie shook her head as she reached for her coffee. "I never believed it could get this bad," she whispered.

Batman collapsed into a nearby chair, his own exhaustion after a frantic night of following empty leads catching up to him. Mirrors indeed. "I used to say the same thing," he murmured. "But there's always a new horror. And the old ones never really go away."

Leslie lowered herself into her own chair, nursing her coffee with both hands. She tried changing the subject. "So what brought you here?"

"The rumble, originally," he said. "I thought perhaps I could help." Then he looked up at her, and couldn't help but smile. Everytime he saw her, Leslie looked a little thinner to him, her hair a little whiter, but the face was still very much as it had been twenty-five years ago when he'd first surrendered to her welcoming embrace. The same compassionate eyes reaching out to him as they did on that corner where his parents were murdered. She even still wore that same gold charm around her neck, designed to look like half a broken heart with the words, *I love you*, inscribed across it. And he realized then he couldn't remember ever seeing her without the pendant, as if she wore it constantly just for him. But of course that was absurd. She'd been wearing it when they met, and to this day its message went out to all the hurt and troubled kids who washed up on her doorstep.

"But the truth is, I missed you," he finished.

She reached out and touched his hand. "Thank you, Bruce. That's very sweet. How's Alfred?"

"Crusty as ever. He's been pestering me to get more sleep, as usual, but his latest trick is to bring me warm milk down in the cave."

Leslie laughed aloud. "He's a jewel."

Batman nodded. "That he is. I could never manage without him." He trailed off, staring vacantly at the viewing window across the room.

Leslie watched him over the brim of her coffee cup. "You've got something else on your mind."

"Hmm. Something."

"Want to talk about it?"

He looked at her. "What went down tonight?"

Leslie closed her eyes and shook her head. "A nightmare. Everything seemed to come apart at once, Bruce, and it was completely without warning."

"Sammy Levant implied as much."

"You spoke to him?"

"Yes." He hesitated. "I . . . bumped into him on my way here. He said the Overlords came out of nowhere."

Leslie's eyebrows furrowed. "I don't understand."

"The Overlords' attack. Didn't you just say it was completely without warning?"

"Yes, but I meant the Darkangels' attack, not the Overlords'."

Batman stared at her. "The Darkangels started the rumble?"

"No, no. The Overlords started the rumble, but it was in retaliation for Darkangel attacks on *their* territory."

He was silent for a moment. "How do you know this?"

"Andy Sabastian."

"He's awake?"

"No, he's under. He had severe lacerations on the face and a couple of pretty deep stab wounds in the lower abdomen. I got to hear his side of it before we operated, though. He felt betrayed."

"Like Sammy," Batman said quietly. "It doesn't make sense. Their gang mentalities aside, these are two basically intelligent, honorable kids. But one of them's got to be lying."

"That may be," Leslie said, "but you can't take this on, too."

"I'm going to have to. You said yourself, everything's coming apart at once. It's only going to get worse unless I get involved."

Leslie put down her cup and glared at him. "Bruce, you can't carry the weight of the world on your shoulders! You're not the Messiah."

"Would you have me walk away from it, then? Sammy was on his way to blowing this place up when I stopped him. Should I have turned my back?"

Leslie looked shaken. "I only meant—"

"I know what you meant," he told her softly. "But there's no one else to help them. And if no one does, they'll kill each other, you know that. I'll do what I have to. I'll do what I can . . . weren't those among your first words to me? Isn't that what you tell these kids?"

Leslie turned toward the window through which she could see into the recovery ward. "I guess you'll want to talk to Andy."

"Yes."

"He'll be under for quite some time. He needs to heal. Tomorrow night?"

"Fair enough. There's other work I need to get done, anyway. I'll have to go."

"I know." A tear was sliding down her cheek.

A faint smile creased Batman's face. He reached out and caught the tear on his gloved finger.

Leslie turned back to him. "What are you staring at?"

Batman's smile didn't fade. "Just remembering. You know, I watched you while you were going over your patients, your gentleness with them, the look on your face. You really care for each and every one that comes in here, don't you? Every one, as if they were your own."

She hesitated. "I cared about you, too, Bruce. I still do. When you were young I tried so hard to give you peace, to help you channel all that rage inside you. I'd hope to help you heal. But I never could."

Batman knelt down in front of her and took her hands. "Don't ever think that, Leslie, please. You saved me. I'm sorry if what I've become a frightens you, but if I hadn't had your love to hold me together when I needed it, who can say what I might have become?"

She looked into his eyes a moment longer and passed two fingers across his cheek.

"Then go. Do what you can."

He said his good-byes and walked out the front door, past the plaque with his father's name, and Leslie's, and went down the steps. He walked slowly across the silent street toward the Batmobile, melting once again into the shadows.

The light reached him first, a sudden flash from behind that annihilated the shadows and for an instant made the Alley bright as day. Then all at once he heard the blast, felt the shockwave and the burning wind and the rain of dust and fragmented brick, and found himself facedown in the street, while behind him the clinic died.

Ignoring the blood he tasted, he lifted his head and saw the flames erupting from the windows, hearing their crackle even over the ringing in his ears. For a moment he crouched frozen in the street. For only a moment.

Images raced through his mind: a medical warehouse exploding in Ethiopia, himself sifting through the wreckage, Jason's body lying broken and cold. . . .

"Leslie . . ."

The front door splintered as he kicked it in, a blast of heat catching him full in the face. He dropped down, keeping beneath the smoke, drawing his cape around him as he tried to see down the main corridor. Part of the roof had caved in, and a fallen beam blocked the recovery room like a huge torch. Impassable. Leslie's office door was open and unblocked.

He crawled in, only to find it in utter ruin. The viewing window had been blown in, showering the office with glass. The recovery room itself was an inferno. He couldn't even see into it, nor hear a single scream. This close, the flames had become a deafening roar.

Leslie was a bloody heap on the floor.

Jason's body lying broken and cold . . .

Batman crawled to her, tore off his glove, pressed his fingers beneath her left ear. Ignore the warm blood that slicks her neck. Find it. Find it.

It was there. The slight throb beneath the skin was faint. But it was there.

She was bleeding to death. From the look of it, she must have been standing by the window when the recovery room blew, and was thrown over her desk. God only knew how much glass had flown into her body. Some broken bones . . .

He tore his cape off at the neck and threw it over her. Then he reached beneath her, trying to be gentle, and lifted.

He stormed out the clinic through a cloud of black

smoke that poured from the door, holding tightly to his charge. Past the curb he fell to his knees, cradling her in his arms while the fire behind him raged on, consuming the remains of children who'd never had a chance.

People were gathering. He looked up at their faces, numb. "Help her," he pleaded. Then he froze.

Voices in the crowd became suddenly distant. Someone shouted to him something about having called an ambulance, but he scarcely heard it. Others moved in to help with Leslie, but he wasn't even conscious of his own movements as they helped him to his feet and guided him further from the fire. All he could see was the face staring at him from across the street.

Chalk-white and grinning, clad in purple from head to toe, the figure tipped his hat to him, revealing a wild mane of green hair before strolling off into the night.

And as Batman watched helplessly, feeling Leslie's blood flow down his arms, a growl began inside him that quickly rose into a feral scream.

"Jokerrrrrrrrrr!"

When Mommy came into his room the next day and asked him what had happened to Mr. Giggles, all he would do was shrug and say that it fell. Privately he was still shaking, feeling wounded, though it was a wound far deeper than any physical abuse his father might have inflicted, or desired to inflict. For that night Daddy had revealed himself, as if the funny and gentle man he'd known all his young life had been a lie, only to be supplanted by this nervous and hurtful thing that had apparently always lurked just beneath the surface. The sound of laughter in their house was gone.

Some nights later, the last fight erupted, and the worst. The screaming awakened him, the angry yelling back and forth, until he heard the sound of glass breaking and something heavy hitting the floor. Then silence, for what seemed like forever, and then his father raced into his room, turned on the light and, thinking him still asleep, began shaking him awake.

"Sport, wake up. C'mon, get dressed. We have to take Mommy to the hospital."

He sat up very suddenly. "She havin' the baby?"

His father didn't reply, just dug some clean clothes out of the dresser and tossed them onto the bed. "Put these on. I'll warm up the car."

The rest of the night felt more like a dream. His mother looked sick. Her face was white and clammy, and she spoke not a word as they drove to the hospital, though twice he remembered hearing a soft moan escape her lips, and suddenly he felt very afraid.

The emergency room lobby was crowded. Several people wore blood-soaked bandages on different parts of their bodies. A thin woman in the corner kept rubbing her arm and shivering, and a little boy a short distance away was curled up tightly in his chair, while his worried mother pressed a damp cloth to his forehead.

Nearly an hour went by before a doctor came out to talk to his mother. They wheeled out a table and lifted her onto it. His father could only stare after her as she disappeared into the examination room, then he buried his face into his hands, shaking.

Two hours later, the doctor came back out and took his father aside to talk to him. Daddy listened, whispered "Oh, God" once, and slowly turned to his frightened son as the doctor walked away.

"C'mon, pal. Mommy's gonna sleep here tonight."

"What about the baby?"

"She's not gonna have the baby anymore. Let's go home."

"No! I wanna be with Mommy!"

"Please, sport. We can't. She needs to rest now. We'll come get her tomorrow, I promise."

He started crying. "No, I wanna see Mommy . . ."

His father grabbed him and picked him up, holding him tightly to his chest as they rushed out of the lobby, the boy sobbing all the way home.

But true to his father's word, the next day they went back to the hospital and brought Mommy home, and though her skin was no longer clammy, she looked worse than she had the night before, and she cried almost constantly for several days, hardly speaking, staying in her bed the whole time. Only when he came to sit with her, sketching idly away at her bedside did she begin to feel a

*little better, smiling as she watched him. Eventually she
started talking more, and after a week or so, she got up to
get on with her life. But though his parents no longer
fought or argued as they had, and in time Mommy became less despondent, she never again took any genuine
joy in anything.*

*And one thing was becoming clear to him, and start-
ing to occupy his mind, both day and night. Daddy had
killed the baby.*

Gordon cursed when he saw the remains of the clinic, a
gutted ruin that left him with a sickening feeling of déjà
vu. He found Bullock sorting out the mess with Merkel
by the front steps. The pavement still glistened where
water hadn't puddled, though the firefighters had long
gone. A uniform was stretching yellow tape that read
POLICE LINE—DO NOT CROSS in front of the entrance.

"Fifteen dead," Bullock told him. "All kids. Incendiary, just like Grandvue."

Gordon sucked on his pipe. "Report said there were
only twelve kids in the building."

"Three more bodies were found in an alley down the
street. One of them was Sammy Levant. They were all
grinning."

Gordon looked at him sharply. "Shit. What about the
doctor?"

"She's in emergency at Saint Matthew's," Merkel
said. "She's in pretty bad shape."

"Is Batman still around?"

Bullock waved down a dark street with his cigar.
"That way. By his car."

"All right, keep me posted." Gordon headed down the
street, his eyes taking a moment to adjust to the change
in light, but he soon spotted the Batmobile's unique silhouette.

"Nothing about it pointed to him, Jim," creaked Batman's voice. He sounded terrible. At first Gordon didn't
spot him, then realized one of the doors was open, and
that he was sitting on the driver's side. "No clues, no

boasts, no calling cards. He struck anonymously, and I never once suspected. Now he's finished what he set out to do, and he can afford to rub my face in it. He's been manipulating me from the start."

"How so?"

"Don't you see? He's never worked outside his M.O. before. Always he's left a trail I could follow if I looked hard enough. It was a sick game to him. But this whole business was aimed at me, every aspect of it intended to manipulate me toward *this*. He even set the Darkangels and the Overlords against each other to draw me into Crime Alley. How could I be so blind?"

"You can't blame yourself for this."

"Who then? Can I blame him? He's insane." Batman rested his hand against the wheel and leaned forward heavily, shaking his head. "How do I put an end to it? Catching him is never a problem. But Arkham Asylum can't hold him, Jim. Neither can any other institution I can imagine. It's an exercise in futility. Lock him away, and sooner or later he's out again. And each time, the atrocity he commits is more insidious than the one before it, a vicious cycle that broadens geometrically, with no end in sight. *What do I have to do to stop him?*"

There were moments in his life when he truly amazed himself; he was quick to recognize genius, particularly when it grinned back at him in the mirror, and the artistic precision with which he executed each new enterprise always left him breathless, as it did his victims. For each death seemed like a new brushstroke on the masterpiece of his life, and what it would reveal to its spectators when he was done perhaps even he couldn't guess, nor find it within himself to care much, really. But nonetheless, Gotham City had proved to be a splendid canvas for his artistry, and though the poor fool might deny the charge vehemently, the Batman made a most inspiring muse.

Truth be told, the wretch had probably gone off the deep end after that last little bit of fireworks in Crime Alley. Everything had gone perfectly. Even the gang

fight his boys had managed to instigate had drawn in
the cowled chowderhead like a bat on a line. It was all
too rich.

Leaving the hotel out of which he'd been operating,
the Joker turned up the collar of his overcoat and
lowered the wide brim of his hat over his face. Where
were the boys? He did so hate to be kept waiting, particularly when he was eager to make himself scarce. Now
that Batman knew that he was the genius behind the
child-offings, he had to leave Gotham for a while to plot
anew. He'd considered his options and finally settled on
Metropolis as his next port of call. Perhaps he could
amuse himself fencing with that other imbecile for a
while.

But his ride was nowhere to be found. He'd be really
annoyed if it turned out they'd deserted him. He was so
looking forward to booting them out of the plane when
they were high enough. Now it appeared he'd have to
take a cab to the airport, and find some other diversion
to amuse himself during the flight. Life's little an-
noyances could really bring him down sometimes.

Halfway across the street, he heard thunder. Something that looked very much like a wide flat missile with
headlights was rocketing toward him. "Oh, drat," he
muttered, and started running toward an alley. He felt
the wind pulling at him as the Batmobile shot past.

Laughing uncontrollably, he drew out his Uzi as he
ran, paving his way through the alley with a spray of
death. A fence at the far end had a narrow gap in the
middle of it and he slipped through into an adjoining
alley, heading toward a nearby construction site. A couple of homeless people dove for cover from the gunfire.
He aimed at them cheerfully as he ducked behind a cin-
derblock wall.

Something like a vice clamped onto his arm, jostling
his aim, swinging him around. He lost his grip on the
Uzi and smashed face first into a brick wall. Fists were
suddenly slamming into him in rapid succession . . .

. . . and the Batman caught the Joker as the madman's spindly body went suddenly limp. It had happened
too quickly. Batman hadn't managed to work off a tenth

of the aggression he felt, and he'd hoped to make the
Joker feel every ounce of it before he lost consciousness.
Never mind. The police already had his henchman.
Enough that the monster was in custody again.

Or was it?

He looked at the Joker thoughtfully and then, throwing the maniac over his shoulder, Batman picked up the
Uzi and headed back for the Batmobile.

*He watched from one of the upstairs windows as his fa-
ther got out of his car and started coming up the front
walk. Everything was ready. Mommy would be at the su-
permarket for at least another hour. Right after she left
he'd started trashing the living room, throwing objects
and lamps everywhere, overturning furniture. That
would be enough to convince his father that something
terrible had happened. The rest . . .*

*The moment Daddy started up the walk, he ran into
his room and locked the door, then started wailing. The
room was dark, and he kept crying hard and loud,
screaming as if he were in agony. His father would walk
in, see the state of the living room, hear his son's distress,
and bolt upstairs. Already he could hear his father's
rapid footfalls on the staircase.*

*He kept crying and reached for the iron. He'd had it
plugged in and turned up full without any water for close
to an hour. The heat and smell filled the little room.*

*His father banged on the door loudly. "Son! Sport,
what's happened? Unlock the door!"*

*He only cried louder. The banging grew worse. His fa-
ther had started kicking in the door. A few more, and the
heavy door would break.*

*He yanked the plug on the iron and climbed atop the
dresser, watching as the door broke apart next to him. His
father's silhouette came into the room, then fell as the boy
brought the hot iron down with all his might on top of
Daddy's head.*

*His father screamed. The boy grunted and leaped onto
his back, bringing the iron down again. Something siz-*

zled. Again and again he hammered at Daddy, until the moaning and the thrashing stopped.

He never figured out how long he knelt there, mechanically pounding away. So many times while it was happening he kept expecting to wake up, that he no longer understood the passage of time. Only when he heard his mother's voice, as she screamed and screamed upon discovering him there, perhaps hours later, did the clock seem to start again. He looked up at her, his arms and front covered with blood, the gory iron still clutched in his tiny hands, and he smiled.

"S'okay, Mommy," he told her. "I kept my promise, see? He won't hurt you anymore. He won't hurt you anymore." But already he could tell something was terribly wrong. Mommy was shaking as she stood there, staring at him, terrified, tears streaming from her eyes, a low moan building in her throat. What was wrong with her? Couldn't she see everything was okay now?

"Whatsa matter, Mommy? I did it for you."

Again his mother screamed, an agonized howl that went on and on as she fled from him. He listened quietly as the sound receded out of the house and then was gone.

He leaned back against the dresser and looked over at cheerful Mr. Giggles in the corner, who still seemed happy despite the great big hole in his head. Then slowly, uncontrollably, he started laughing.

The cave.

A strange calm settled over him as he left the car and surveyed the cavern. The same calm, he reflected, that a baby must feel in the womb. Nothing outside exists. This is the whole of the universe.

Stalactites hung like jagged gray teeth from the ceiling, as if the cave were the maw of some great beast. If he listened very hard, he could hear the bats crying in the darker, deeper recesses. A shame about the bats, he thought.

He didn't bother removing the Joker from the Batmobile. There wasn't much point. He padded silently across the smooth floor, passing his many toys along the way, glancing briefly at the trophies near the far wall: the dinosaur, the giant penny, the huge grinning wild card hanging from the ceiling . . .

You see, Joker, here's my problem. I can't let you live anymore.

Grim-faced, he marched up the metal steps to the platform atop which his main console rested, and began tapping its keyboard before he could allow himself a chance to reconsider.

But neither can I live with the guilt of being your executioner.

He removed his glove and pressed his palm against the sensor. Immediately the lights in the cave shifted from yellow-white to a hellish red.

So the solution's very simple, really.

His screens lit up, each displaying the same message: "IDENTITY VERIFIED. AUTODESTRUCT READY. ENTER CODE."

I'm ending it here and now.

Batman tapped more keys, ignoring the sweat on his lip. The sound of metal slabs sliding and closing resounded through the cavern. The screens answered: "CODE VERIFIED. CAVE SEALED. AUTODESTRUCT ARMED."

For both of us.

He stared at the main monitor, heart feeling as if it would pound its way through his chest.

"INITIATE COUNTDOWN."

. . . and he saw Barbara, condemned to a wheelchair for the rest of her life because of a bullet the monster had sent blasting through her spine. And Jason, brutally murdered half a world away. Sammy Levant, grinning lifelessly from the gutter. Children all over Gotham dying horribly. A legion of grinning corpses paraded across his vision, and now Leslie—

His hand hovered over the last button, shaking.

Do it.

He felt her arms holding him for the first time, her voice echoing softly in his ear as he wept on her shoulder. "Come with me . . . I'll do what I can."

"INITIATE COUNTDOWN."

Do it.

"No!" he screamed, and smashed his fist into the screen. Glass shattered and sparks flew. Blood flowed from his broken hand. His eyes and teeth clenched in agony, though the pain had little to do with fractured bone.

"I can't," he whispered. "God forgive me, I can't. . . ." He turned away from the console and wept into his other hand, steadying himself against the platform railing. "I can't give him the final victory."

There was a tiny click behind him. Batman turned and saw the Joker standing next to the keyboard, his index finger still pressed against the destruct-engage.

"Then I'll just have to take it, old sport," he whispered softly.

"AUTODESTRUCT INITIATED. X-MINUS 59 SEC-ONDS."

Grinning, the Joker swung a metal pipe he'd procured, impacting solidly with Batman's jaw, sending him backward over the railing and down ten feet onto a steel worktable. The impact bruised his hip, but he managed to avoid landing on his broken hand.

Above him, the Joker leaped off the railing, his laughter echoing through the cave.

Batman got a leg up in time, caught the Joker in the abdomen as he fell, and swung hard, sending the maniac through the air and crashing onto the hood of one of the other cars.

Batman got into a crouch atop the table, his eyes flashing quickly up to the screens.

"X-MINUS 43 SECONDS."

He cursed. Brilliant idea, Batman, bypassing the abort command. The Joker looked hurt. The impact had jarred his back, judging from the way he squirmed atop the car. But it might mean Batman had a chance to save them both, if he could get them into the all-terrain vehicle, smash their way out . . .

His leg nearly gave when he leaped onto the floor. Hip was in worse shape than he realized. Forget it. Move.

The Joker was moaning. Nice sound. Batman grabbed him by the front of the shirt with his one good hand and dragged him off the car. The maniac struggled, trying to get some solid footing. *Not as injured as he wanted me to believe.* Batman pulled him closer. "Get this straight," he spat into the Joker's face, "We aren't dying in here."

"Oh, so fickle," the Joker admonished. Then he grinned. "I think I'm in love." Without warning he brought both arms up and smashed his fists into Batman's ears.

Batman recoiled, lost his hold. The Joker scrambled across the cave, searching frantically for a weapon among the trophies.

Batman watched him as his head cleared. Madman. The screens blazed: "X-MINUS 14 SECONDS." Damn him to hell. No time. But as he watched, a possibility came into his mind, and desperately his hand groped his belt, found his Batarang, and sent it whizzing across the cave. It caught the Joker near his left shoulder, its razored end sinking deep into the flesh beneath the collarbone. He screamed and fell to his knees beside the giant penny.

Batman rushed toward him as the seconds ran down, slamming his shoulder hard against the penny, grabbing the Joker even as it fell against the rocky wall and wedged itself there, holding steady at sixty degrees to the floor. Then the world began to shake and the sky began to fall, as carefully placed explosives throughout the cave split thousands of tons of stone loose from the bedrock beneath Wayne Manor, and the darkness descended.

The moment the chandeliers began to ring, Alfred knew. He started running through the old manor even as the tremor cut through it, feeling the rumble subside just as he reached his private office.

He found his personal elevator to the cave inoperable. Even the bookcase that camouflaged it refused to open. Rushing to his desk, he frantically powered up his personal computer and tried to link up with the cave mainframe.

"ACCESS DENIED," it told him.

Alfred muttered something very old and profane as he

tried the override, using his password. He tapped in, "FRIDAY."

After several torturous seconds, the screen responded. "HELLO, ALFRED. HOW CAN I HELP YOU?"

Alfred leaned forward. "LOCATE WAYNE," he instructed.

"UNABLE TO COMPLY. ALL PRIMARY SYSTEMS DOWN. 91% OF HIGHER FUNCTIONS DISABLED."

He hesitated. "SPECIFY CAUSE OF SYSTEMS FAILURE."

"IMPLEMENTATION OF AUTODESTRUCT PROGRAM."

He stared at the screen, his fears confirmed. "My God," he murmured. He leaned back in his chair and silently considered what to do next.

With his one good hand he fumbled for his utility belt in the darkness, drawing out a small cylindrical device. He pressed two switches on it, and there was light.

Batman's gamble had paid off. They were both alive, albeit trapped in a pocket of air. The penny, once wedged against the wall, had shielded them from the cave-in after he'd dragged them under it, although Batman couldn't be certain the giant coin's steel core would hold for any length of time under tons of rock. Still, for now at least, it looked secure, looming over them like a great copper lean-to.

How long had he been unconscious? An hour? Two, perhaps? Off to one side, the Joker lay on his back, his legs pinned by a large slab of stone. Batman found a soft spot in the opposite wall and inserted the dark end of the lighting device into it. Then he turned his attention on his foe.

"Before you say anything," the Joker said, wincing in pain, "I want you to know I don't think I'll ever understand what you see in all this cave nonsense."

Batman ignored him and checked out the slab. At least five hundred pounds, easily. At his best, he might manage it. But in his current shape, with a broken hand . . .

He put his shoulder against a convenient spot and heaved anyway. No luck.

"How touching," the Joker gasped. "But a moot gesture, old sport, unless you were planning to tunnel us out barehanded."

"How're your legs?"

The Joker grinned. "That's a joke, right? You loathsome monstrosity, I knew you had it in you." He winced again. The Batarang still protruded from his shoulder. The left side of his tailcoat was drenched with blood. Batman considered removing it, but it would probably only worsen the wound.

He stood up and looked around, listening. He could still hear dust falling. "We've got an air supply, at least for a while. Must be another cavity nearby."

"Comforting. I take it you'll be moving out soon? If not, call room service and tell them I demand another room." He laughed.

Batman turned to him. "Shut up."

The Joker only laughed harder.

"Stop laughing," Batman snapped.

"And what if I don't?" the Joker giggled. "What're you gonna do? Break my legs?" After that, he became hysterical.

Batman bent to one knee and hissed in his face. "I have a thousand other ways to add to your pain, Joker. Don't tempt me."

The Joker looked into his eyes and smiled affectionately, but he did stop laughing. Batman sat down against the wall and watched him silently.

"I don't suppose you have a deck of cards?" the Joker said.

Batman merely glared at him.

"Forget I asked."

"You're in such a talkative mood," Batman said slowly, "why not answer a few questions?"

The Joker made a sour face. "Oh, like what? What makes me tick? What is it that I really want? Won't I let you help me? Spare me, Bats. We've had this conversation before. Don't bore me again. It would really only drive me crazy." His face contorted. "Besides, why are you suddenly so relaxed? You're acting like you've got all the time in the world."

Batman shrugged. "I'm not bleeding to death."

"You're a very sick person, you know that, Bats? And I'm supposed to talk to you—?"

"All right, fine," he said, and suddenly leaned forward. "Then just answer me this: why the children, Joker? Why Leslie?"

"Bats, you know, you're a real turn-on when you're intense, anybody ever tell you that?"

"Answer me."

"All we need to do now is to get you to develop a slightly less perverse sense of humor."

"Why the children?"

"You know, I heard this story once—stop me if you've heard this one. Seems there was this traveling salesman selling semiautomatic whitefish door to door—"

"Why Leslie?"

"She was my mother!" the Joker shouted.

Batman stared at him, frozen. "What . . . ?"

The Joker wasn't smiling. "My mother," he repeated, more softly this time.

Batman's hand lashed out and gripped him by the throat. "You filthy, lying—"

The Joker chuckled breathlessly. "Oh, no, Bats," he said calmly. "I don't need to lie. I'm bleeding to death, remember? Besides, the truth'll hurt you far worse than my lies ever could."

Batman's teeth clenched. His hand tightened.

The Joker appeared unruffled. "Of course, if you strangle me now, you'll never hear the rest of it, and I know you, you cowled horror: that'll haunt you to your dying day—" His eyes rolled around at their surroundings, and he grinned. "—which is starting to look as if that may not be long after mine."

"I was ready to kill us both," he snarled.

"Oh, who're you kidding? Contrary to common belief, Bats, ready and willing are two entirely different things. When push came to shove, you just didn't have the stomach for it. Poor dear. You had such potential, too."

Batman loosened his grip and leaned back. He waited.

The Joker chuckled. "Ah, what a guy you are, Bats. My father was quite a guy, too, you know. But he didn't have to terrorize criminals to make it through the day. No, his wife and child were all the victims he needed. His outlook was simple: life was cruel. But it wasn't until years after I murdered him that I realized what an incredible genius he was."

Batman struggled to keep his voice level. "You mean, you . . . you killed your own father?"

"Well, I admit I may have been a little hasty, but I was only eight at the time and, well, you know how kids are. . . ."

"How?" Batman demanded softly. "How could you kill your own father?"

"Hmm . . . I think his causing my mother to miscarry while he was in a drunken rage might've had something to do with it. But who can say, really? Memories are such deceitful little buggers. They play little cat-and-mouse games with you if you aren't careful. But anyway, as I was saying, I was frightfully young when it all happened, and I suppose I did the dirty deed out of love for my mother.

"Oh, yes, Bats, don't you ever doubt it for a moment. I loved my mother with a vengeance (as I ended up proving quite literally when I brained the old man). She was my whole life, and I'd have done anything for her. Anything. And when the beast she married made her lose the baby, I killed for her."

He was silent a moment, his eyes becoming vacant as he shook his head and chuckled. "Women. Go figure them. Doesn't matter who they are. You give them what you know deep down they want, nine times out of ten they lose interest. I mean, do you understand them?"

Batman said nothing.

The Joker stared at him, breathing hard. *"She left me!"* he screamed. "I killed for her and she left me! She couldn't even bear to look at me, the deceitful cow! The cops and the doctors even helped her! They put me in a nuthouse for eight years, and she never once cared enough to find out about me. Never!

"Of course, by the time they let me out, I'd been filled up with so many of their drugs and rehab treatments, most of my memories became suppressed. Gone but not forgotten, as it were. They could only bury them, not purge them. And shortly after I got out, I came across an old Gotham City newspaper, and there she was, like a sign from God, on the front page. Different name now, but the same face, even after eight years. *My mother,* comforting this cute little rich boy whose parents had just been gunned down in the street." He locked eyes with Batman. "Can you, can you imagine for a moment what that did to me, to see her with another child? A stranger? After running away from me in *horror?* Do you have any idea of the pain in seeing her arms around him while that snot-nosed little brat cried on her shoulder?"

Batman went on staring, holding very still. The Joker's breathing was getting very ragged, his bloodloss becoming critical.

"After that it all came back to me. I followed her to Gotham City. . . . But you know, Bats, I actually tried to forget for a while, to get on with my life. . . . I watched from a distance, I waited, and I stayed away. . . . But then, of course, you and I met, and I think then I finally realized how right my father was . . . about everything . . . and I hated her for what she did to me . . . for having so much love and understanding to offer so many strangers over so many years . . . hundreds of children, maybe thousands . . . but nothing for her own son. Nothing for me! . . . And then the unkindest cut of all. . . . She befriended you. . . . *You,* the horror responsible for turning me into this . . . this *thing! How could she do that?*

"I got even, though. Didn't I, Bats? . . . First the brats, then her? . . . And what better way to get my revenge than to stick it to you at the same time, eh, old sport?"

His breathing was quite shallow now. He was slipping. Batman crawled over to him and pushed the hair out of his eyes. "Easy, Joker."

The Joker managed a ragged grin, then a painful, labored chuckle, then silence.

There was a low vibration building in the wall behind them, slowly rising to a deafening roar. Batman inched as far away from the sound as he could without leaving the Joker, and in short order a large portion of the wall collapsed around the jaws of some great metal beast with blazing yellow eyes. Batman squinted at it as the engine shut down and a man, wearing a hardhat and coveralls and carrying a medical bag, climbed out of the driver's compartment. "Are you all right, sir?"

"I'll make it, Alfred. You found us faster than I expected."

"No trouble, sir, once you activated your homing device." He reached for the light Batman had imbedded in the wall and handed it back to him. "And it was most fortuitous that the digging machinery was still in storage from when you first excavated the tunnel. My garden shovel was not quite up to the task. My word, sir, is that—?"

"Yes, it is," Batman said, staring down at the Joker.

"Is he dead?" asked Alfred, gazing at the still Joker.

"No," Batman said. "Not yet."

Alfred blinked. "I see. If I may say so, sir, your hand appears to be broken."

"It'll keep," he murmured, still staring at his old foe. The questions wouldn't stop echoing through his mind. How much of it was true? And how much a twisted fantasy? And more, could he live with the answers, if he found them? Or should he simply let it end here, forever entombed from human memory? It would be easy now, to walk away without a second glance. But the Joker had been right about one thing: he had no stomach for murder. Anyone's murder.

"Help me lift the stone off him, Alfred."

"Very good, sir," Alfred said, and looked around as he moved to the task. "Been doing a spot of redecorating, have you, sir?"

"Not now, Alfred."

Working together, they managed it, though the Joker's legs were a bloody mess. Alfred administered some quick first aid to stop the bleeding, and when it was done, Batman himself bent to lift the unconscious Harlequin of Hate.

Then he spotted something sticking out of the Joker's

vest pocket and took it out. It was an old black-and-white photograph of a small grinning boy. And as he stared at it, all the color suddenly drained from Bruce's face.

On a chain encircling the boy's neck was a pendant—the other half of Leslie's heart-charm. And the photo was just clear enough to make out the inscription:

best of all.

It wasn't until after he'd taken the Joker to the Arkham Hospital Annex that he spoke to Gordon and learned that Leslie was going to make it.

He went to the hospital as Bruce Wayne, and even so, her doctor allowed him into her room only reluctantly. She lay there in her bed, stitches everywhere, her silver hair a tangled mane. Bruce had to fight to control his anguish when he saw her.

She smiled at him when he approached and kept her voice very low. "Hi," she said weakly.

"Hello, Leslie. How do you feel?"

She made a slight movement that he took to be a shrug. "Painkillers help. I should be up and around in no time the doctor said. Doctor also said it looks much worse than it is. Stupid quack."

Bruce smiled.

Her finger brushed his hand. She felt the cast around it. "What happened?"

He shrugged uncomfortably. "Little accident."

"I'll bet." She paused. "You saved my life. Thanks."

Bruce's face fell. "I couldn't save the children."

"I know," she said. "You tried. I know you did. And I love you for that." The pendant still hung around her neck.

"Leslie . . . I have to ask you something."

"What is it?"

Bruce pulled the picture from his pocket and put it in her hands.

"Do you recognize this?"

Leslie looked at the photograph and breathed in suddenly. "Oh, my God . . ." she whispered.

Bruce leaned in closer. "Who is he, Leslie?"

She stared at the photo for a long time before replying. "When this picture was taken," she said slowly, "he was all the joy in the world to his parents. Then a terrible thing happened, and he was taken away. His mother almost killed herself after that, because she blamed herself for what had happened." She looked up at Bruce. "But she found a reason to go on, although she never saw him again. And she spent the rest of her life trying to atone for her weakness, and her failure."

"And the pendant?"

"I used to work in an orphanage, Bruce. I had dozens of those things made. I kept one half. The children got the other. All the children."

Bruce studied her face. "Was he your son, Leslie?"

Tears were streaming down her cheeks. "You're my son, Bruce."

Bruce bit his lip, then slowly bent down and kissed the top of her head. "Good night, Leslie."

Alone in his study, Bruce contemplated the photograph as outside his window, the sun went down and night threw its black cloak once again over Gotham City. And as he stared at the grinning face, he almost thought he could hear it laughing at him.

The Joker's Christmas

Karen Haber

T he big green iguana sat blinking placidly in the glass cage by the fireplace. A huge ribbon of green silk was tied in a bow at its neck. It was Christmas Eve, but the lizard didn't care. His beady eyes took in the festive preparations going on all around him without a glimmer of comprehension or interest. He crouched in his aquarium thinking slow lizard thoughts, dreaming of hot flat rocks and tropical nights.

"Jesus," Alfonso fumed. "Why did the boss adopt that thing as a pet?" He tapped his purple-enameled fingertips against the glass. The lizard didn't move. "Creepy. Why doesn't he just have the thing stuffed? Then at least we wouldn't have to feed it."

"Leave it alone," Franny said. Deftly she spun a silver ribbon around a large green box and whipped it into a fluffy bow. "Come help me finish wrapping these gifts, or they won't be ready. And you know how crazy *he* gets if we're not ready on time." She put the finishing touches on the glinting chartreuse package and leaned back to survey the effect, nodding her head until her green-and-black-frosted mane covered her eyes. "Not bad. I should go into packaging."

"Where is His Highness?"

"Upstairs, making sure everything's perfect for his outfit tonight."

Alfonso snickered. "Checking his list?"

"Twice." She smiled. Her mouth was a long red slash splitting a pale, thin face. "Glad I'm not on it." She went to work on another box.

"Don't be so sure of that," Alfonso said. He picked up a circular box and began wadding paper around it. "Remember Fat Louie's Thanksgiving bonus?"

"Yeah." Franny shivered. "Now *that* was ugly, wasn't it?"

"Took us weeks to clean up, too. And we had to replace all the wallpaper—twice."

"Don't remind me. I thought we'd never find the right shade of green Mylar. Still, the Boss usually doesn't kill anybody onstaff this late in the month. Hard to get replacements. Especially around the holidays."

"Good point. You hope." Alfonso managed to tie a crooked silver bow near the middle of the hatbox and tossed the finished package into a green sack by the door. Leaning back on his Cuban heels, he paused a moment to check his appearance in a pocket mirror. The reflection showed his square jaw, olive skin, dark eyes, and short bleached hair almost covered by a black beret. Not bad, he thought. But the room around him was something else.

Green. Everything was green. The tree was green. The lights that winked within its foliage were green. The green mylar walls were decked with boughs of green holly and green ribbons. To Alfonso, it was like standing in the middle of a giant dollar bill.

"Godrestyemerrygentlemenletnothingyoudismay—" The music poured out of the wall speakers, holiday carols set at manic fast-forward speed, sung by what sounded like crazed chipmunks and yodeling raccoons.

"Nice music," Alfonso said. He put away the mirror.

"Shhh. Here he comes! Quick, pile those packages into that sack." Frantically, Franny tossed him an armful of gifts. Alfonso slam-dunked them into the sack.

"And remember," she whispered, "chill out. He's really wired tonight."

A step in the hallway sent them scurrying like rabbits.

Then the door opened.

"Hey, Boss," Alfonso cried. "Haven't you heard that Christmas colors include a little red occasionally?"

The Joker gave him a cool stare. He was wearing a green silk smoking jacket lined in quilted plum satin. His hair was green. His skin was white as new-fallen snow. Or a corpse's inner arm. Only his lips, stretched over a ghastly smile, and around an expensive cigar, were red.

"I like green," he said quietly. Green fire danced in his eyes. "Any problem with that?"

"No, Boss," Franny whispered. "Love green!"

Alfonso turned as pale as the winter sky beyond the window. "Green is great," he said quickly. "Terrific color. My favorite."

The Joker's smile widened. His eyes gleamed with cheerful malice. "That's what I like to hear from my little helpers. You know how I thrive on agreement. Or, rather, how you do."

He chuckled and twirled the razor-tipped walking stick in his hand like a baton. "Now hurry, children. Idle hands are the devil's playground. Besides, I'd hate to have to punish one of you just because you made me late on Christmas Eve! I've got a lot of stockings to fill. So make sure those presents are wrapped and ready by the time I come back down. I'm almost finished donning my holiday apparel, but I wanted to see how you were getting along." He peered into the sack by the door. "Good. Almost done. I'll be back in five minutes. Be ready. Especially you, Franny. You may accompany me as Joker's little helper *numero uno*." He reached into his jacket, pulled out a short green velvet-and-ermine robe, and tossed it to her. "Get dressed."

She cast a desperate look at Alfonso. He grinned and made a slashing motion across his throat. Luckily, the Joker had turned away to straighten some green tinsel on the tree.

"Right away, Boss." She gathered up the costume and hurried into the bathroom to change.

The big green sleigh quivered on the loading dock as the engines flared to life: headlights came on like eyes opening in the dusk—green sodium eyes staring out over manic chrome grillwork in the shape of a grinning mouth.

"Gonna find out who's naughty and nice," the Joker sang. A curly green beard framed his smile. "Oh, I love the holidays," he said, fussing with the ermine cuff of his green velvet suit. "Hmmm, the stitching is crooked here. Guess I'll have to kill the tailor." He smiled cheerfully and blew a kiss to Alfonso on the dock below. At the touch of a button, the Joker's sleigh lifted off on huge airjets and took to the dark Gotham sky.

"Justhearthosesleighbellsjinglingringtingtingling-too . . ." the tapedeck sang at Mach 3.

"Franny, punch in the autopilot," the Joker said. "That green button there. I've already programmed it for tonight's run."

"Yessir."

Below, the lights of Gotham winked with Christmas color, blue and gold, red and green, yellow, white, a thousand earth-bound stars twinkling up at them.

The Joker raised a scornful eyebrow. "Garish display, don't you think? Excessive."

"I don't know—" Just in time, Franny saw the murderous twinkle begin to ignite in his eyes. "Oh, you're absolutely right, Boss. Tacky. Really." She nodded wildly until her green and black hair hung limply across her shoulders. "What's our first stop?"

"Commissioner Gordon's house." The Joker giggled. "He'll be out at the big Christmas gala at Gotham Country Club. And when he gets back, there'll be a big surprise waiting."

The big sled tilted down, cutting through the swirling snowflakes to land in front of a white, two-story colonial house.

"Commissioner Gordon! How will we get in?" Franny said. "The chimney's too small. . . ."

"Down the chimney? In this suit? Don't think like an amateur, Franny." Smirking, the Joker pulled an electric bolt-cutter from his pocket and handed it to her. "The red button controls the speed. Try maximum."

Obediently she pressed the snarling machine against the hinges. Sparks flew, and with a spectacular whoosh of air the front door gave way, falling backward as a high, thin alarm began to wail.

"A shame about those hinges," the Joker said, stepping inside the house. He put the electric bolt-cutter back into his pocket. "A smart cop like Commissioner Gordon should really know better than to have substandard hinges on his front door. Well, I'm sure he'll get them fixed soon. Bring the big square box, Franny."

She ran back to the sleigh and grabbed the gift sack. Which big box did he mean? She hunted furiously, tossing rejected packages over her shoulder onto the floor of the sleigh. She was halfway into the bag before she found the huge square box at the bottom. It was heavier than she'd expected. Teetering in her spike-heeled ankle boots, she hurried back to the house.

"B-boss?" The green bow on top of the box nearly blocked her vision. Franny staggered across the pinewood parquet floor into the formal dining area.

"Yellow wall-to-wall carpeting. I should have expected it." The Joker sniffed derisively. "And imitation Queen Anne. In mahogany veneer, no less. Well, what do you expect from the police? They never have any taste. I'm really doing Gordon a favor—once he opens this package he'll be eager to redecorate, hee-hee. Maybe I'll send him a few tips. Or some catalogues."

Franny put the gift down with a loud thump, scattering one of the twelve silver place settings on the highly buffed dining table.

The Joker smiled a sharp, dangerous smile and shook his head. Green curls danced along his jawline. "Not there, you pretty ninny! Under the tree. The tree! What's the whole point to this? Do you think I like wearing this false beard? Do you know how much ermine costs these days? My God, what does it take to get good help? Nobody understands an artist." He wrung his hands in mock despair. "Under the tree!"

"Sorry." Franny took up her burden once more and, wobbling, wove her way across the hallway and into the living room. She set the box down in front of the red-bedecked tree. She could hear a muffled ticking. It seemed to be coming from inside the box.

"Uh, Boss, what exactly are you giving Commissioner Gordon for Christmas?"

The Joker convulsed with laughter. "Ahahaha. What am I giving him? Oh, you are amusing, Franny. I knew you had hidden depths when I hired you. What am I giving him? What do you think? It's a bomb." The Joker wiped his eyes with a green silken handkerchief. "Bombs for Christmas. Isn't it brilliant? Give the gift that makes for lasting memories, I always say."

"Brilliant, Boss." Franny shivered and backed away from the box. Oh, why hadn't she become something nice and safe—say, a dental hygienist? Career decisions had never been her forte.

The house alarm shrieked defiantly, echoing down the long hallway leading to the front door. Franny's ears began to ring. She pulled off a green satin glove and nibbled on her green-and-purple-enameled thumbnail, staring all the while at the big, ticking green box.

"Aren't you worried that the cops will come?" she said.

"Of course not," the Joker replied cheerfully. "I want them to come. That's the entire point. Otherwise, they won't read my little note." He produced a folding tripod from his other pocket and set it up on the landing by the front door. Then he flicked an over-large playing card from a deck up his sleeve. It was a joker, in tones of green and white, with the words "Ho-Ho-Ho" in silver glitter ringing the boundaries of the card.

"You're leaving a card?"

"A holiday tradition, my dear. Greetings of the season. A master always pays attention to details. Remember that." He grabbed her sleeve and yanked her into the sleigh. "Come along. It's getting late, and I've got a lot of people on my list. We wouldn't want to deprive any of them, would we?"

The next stop was an imposing brownstone in the garden district of downtown Gotham. The sleigh settled quietly into the backyard, flattening a boxwood hedge and only just missing a red-metal swing set. The Joker rubbed his gloved hands together gleefully.

"City Council President Ruth Hays will come home to a holiday surprise," he said. "Come, Franny. Bring those two packages. Stereo bombs for an overachieving baby boomer."

With ease, he picked the backdoor lock and entered. The kitchen air was rich with cooking odors. The Joker closed his eyes in rapture. "Ahhh. Smells like the Christmas turkey is ready. Let's have a bite, shall we?"

"Boss, I don't think it's a good idea." Gingerly Franny balanced the two small boxes in her hands. She was eager to put them down and get away.

"I don't pay you to think, my dear." Reaching into the black-enameled microwave oven, he pulled a small bird out. "Ah, I see she's used a browning dish. Good. I do so dislike the look of pale microwaved meat. He tore at the drumstick, ripping shreds of meat away from the bone. "Mmmmm. Not bad." He chewed reflectively. "But a trifle underdone."

Franny set the boxes down carefully in front of the tiny tree by the white-tiled hearth and hurried back to the kitchen. Mouth watering, she watched the Joker finish his snack.

"Oh, sorry, dear. This is really much too rich for your simple tastes." He turned, picked up the remains of the turkey, and heaved it, browning dish and all, through the leaded-glass window and out into the yard. Glass tinkled as a shower of glittering shards rained down on the snowy ground, reflecting the neighbor's green and red Christmas lights as it fell.

"Why'd you do that?" Franny asked.

"Undercooked meat is dangerous," the Joker said. "Salmonella and all that. Besides, Ms. Council President Hays can always afford another bird." He pointed to a small video screen on the kitchen counter. "Turn on the set, Franny."

"TV? Shouldn't we be leaving?"

"Don't ask so many questions." The Joker's smile grew wider. Franny hurried to switch on the television. Squawking, it came to life in a blizzard of white and gray static.

"Try channel twelve. I like that newscaster—she always wears green."

Franny flipped channels until Venetia Fitter appeared: the anchorwoman of the Joker's dreams. Tonight

her pale hair was moussed into a series of frozen blonde
waves. She was wearing three shades of green silk. Only a
small red pin at her throat marred the purity of the effect.

"Good evening," Venetia said. "The annual Christmas Eve giveaway at Saint Michael's Church has gotten
a big turnout and—this just in. There has been an explosion at Police Commissioner Gordon's house. No inju-
ries. This is believed to be the handiwork of the Joker—
his usual calling card was found at the scene. A police
spokesman reports that a canister was recovered from
the debris and opened by the bomb squad. It contained a
message—which read: 'You'd better be good. Better not
cry. Better not pout, I'm telling you why. Santa Joker's
coming to town.'" She paused and looked offscreen as
though receiving additional information. A moment
later she was focused back on the camera. "Batman has
been summoned."

"Oh, good, good, goody!" The Joker clapped his hands,
dancing around the tiled kitchen with glee. "They got
my message. They know I care." His silver-tipped cowboy boots beat a manic tattoo on the kitchen floor. As he
capered, he pulled another joker card out of his sleeve
and slapped it down on top of the microwave. Still skip-
ping, he nodded toward the sleigh. "Come along, dear.
We've miles to go before we sleep."

Franny followed him out into the cold night. "Where
next?" she asked.

"That spoiled rich boy Bruce Wayne's appalling mansion." The Joker chuckled. "I'm an equal-opportunity
Santa—but I believe in giving it to the rich first."

Wayne Manor was dark and silent, a huge gray shadow
looming in the snowy night. The sleigh landed quietly
on the front lawn beside an enormous juniper bush.

"Looks like there's nobody home," Franny whispered.
She tugged nervously at her black and green bangs.
"What's with this rich guy? No lights? No plastic snow-
men on the front lawn? Oooh, this place gives me the
creeps."

The Joker nodded gravely. "And well it should, my
dear. Generations of do-gooders have lived here. Philan-

thropists." He shuddered. "It's a dangerous concept. Luckily, I think it's a dying one as well." He pulled his bolt cutter out. "This door appears to be thick. Well, these cutters should suffice."

He pressed the sawblades against the hinges and turned the machine on.

An alarm split the air, howling raucously. Its vibrations shook Franny down to her green-enameled toenails. Beside her, the Joker switched off the cutter and pocketed it.

"I-I d-don't l-like t-this," he said, oscillating to the alarm's rhythm. He stepped back out of range. "Wayne never did seem to have much of a sense of humor. Let's just leave the box and a card by the front door and go."

"F-fine w-with m-me," Franny said, vibrating like a cranberry in a blender. She put the gift down on the thick brown-rush doormat next to the Joker's greeting card, turned, and raced for the sleigh. The Joker was already strapped in his seat.

Once they were aloft, he switched on the radio.

"How are we doing?" he said, chuckling.

"—the Christmas Eve wave of vandalism continues as the Joker leaves unpleasant packages at the homes of some of Gotham City's best and brightest . . ."

"Hee-hee, I just love this season!" He kissed his wrists happily.

"Batman is reported to be hot on the trail of the Clown Prince of Crime."

Franny bit all the way through her thumbnail. Batman! Oh, why hadn't she become a hairstylist? She glanced uneasily at her boss. But he was hugging himself with joy.

"I should hope he's on my trail," the Joker said. "Otherwise, the Batdope isn't worth his cape." He turned off the radio. "Let's pay a visit to Mayor Gregson next."

The kitchen of Mayor Gregson's handsome duplex was alight, the tables covered with immaculate porcelain trays of party treats. Obviously the mayor was expecting guests.

"Hmm. Seems we were left off the guest list," the Joker said, peering through the window. "Must have been an oversight."

He knocked smartly at the backdoor. A butler in black coat and striped silk pants answered. He paused and looked them over.

"You *must* be the entertainment," he said. Each word was soaked through with condescension. "But you're way too early. Nobody is here yet. And doesn't Santa usually wear *red* and white?"

"There was a problem with the dye lot," the Joker said, winking. He patted the butler on the back. "Be a good boy, Jeeves, and don't breathe a word of our coming to anybody."

The butler remained mum as the Joker removed his hand and wiped off the dart he'd palmed. A rictus of ghastly mirth spread across the man's face and froze.

"Boss!" Franny scowled. "I thought we weren't going to kill anybody on this trip."

"I can't stand a critic," the Joker said. Gently, he set the corpse in place as a doorstop. "But come along, Franny. Don't dawdle. You know the drill by now. Put the present down by the tree. And yes, you may sample some of these treats. But be quick."

The Joker scooped up a salmon-colored canapé and took a bite. "Not bad. Not bad at all." Pulling a plastic bag out of his voluminous pocket, he began shoveling caviar-studded crackers and cheese bits into it. "Never know when you'll get hungry . . ."

"What are you doing?" a high-pitched young male voice demanded.

The Joker turned.

The voice belonged to a bespectacled boy of nine or ten. He had short, spiky brown hair and was wearing a faded black denim jacket with matching jeans. A small gold hoop pierced his left earlobe. He held a laptop computer dangling by its lid. "I asked you a question."

The Joker's smile broadened. "Go away, sonny, before you get hurt."

Franny came up behind the boy in the hallway. "You'd better listen to him," she said. "He doesn't like little kids. Get lost."

The boy lifted his nose higher and looked at them both with contempt. "You're the Joker, aren't you? Well, I'm Benjamin Gregson. The mayor's my uncle. And Batman's after you already. I saw it on the news. You'd better get out of here or—

"Or what?" The Joker's eyes twinkled murderously.

The boy faltered. Plainly, he was accustomed to adult attention and cooperation. "I-I'll call the police."

Still smiling, the Joker ripped the phone off the wall and tossed it to the floor with a clatter. "I doubt it," he said.

Benjamin Gregson watched him, pop-eyed. "You really are crazy, just like they said."

"They were right. They always are."

The boy backed away smack up against the dead butler. "Carlton! What happened to Carlton?"

"He's frozen with merriment of the season," the Joker said. He moved a step closer to the boy.

Benjamin scurried to the far side of the kitchen. A forced smile appeared on his face. "I'll bet you want to steal stuff, right? We've got lots of stuff here for you to steal."

The Joker watched him the way a cat watches a mouse. "Such as?"

"My uncle's got a new Rolex watch," the boy said eagerly. "It's under the tree in the red box. My aunt bought it for him for Christmas."

"Too gaudy. Besides, I already have five."

"There's the stereo: Blaupunkt—"

"Too bulky." The Joker took another step forward.

A fleeting look of fear crossed the child's face. "Um, well, what about my Nintendo?"

"I prefer American goods, whenever possible," the Joker said. "Last chance."

"My mom's fur coat?"

The Joker paused. "What color is it?"

"Russet mink."

"A shame." The Joker grinned with murderous glee. "I favor green. Oh well, I see our time's up." He grabbed for the child, clamping a hand on his windpipe and shaking him like a puppet.

"Boss, no!"

"Shut up, Franny. I'm not going to kill him. I'm just going to kidnap him. In case the Bat Bore gets too close. A hostage is always handy." Even as he spoke, the sound of footsteps on the roof betrayed the presence of another visitor. "There he is now, no doubt," the Joker said. "He'll probably try to come down the chimney. No imagination, that man. We'll just slip away. . . ."

"Not so fast, Joker." The Batman's voice was transmitted from above by some electronic device. "I've been monitoring the house for five minutes. The police are on their way."

"Swell," the Joker replied. "They'll get here just in time for the blast."

"You've planted another bomb?"

"Bravo, Mr. Ears." He shifted his hold on Benjamin to a hammerlock and applauded noisily. "You find it, you dismantle it, you own it. And the mayor's house—not to mention those of his neighbors—are saved. Otherwise, boom. Now, if you'll excuse us."

"You despicable maniac. Let go of the boy."

"Oh, that's out of the question. I've taken a real liking to young Master Gregson here." The Joker patted the child on the head benignly. "Maybe I'll return him in time for next Christmas."

"Joker—"

"You're forgetting that bomb, Batman. You've got five minutes."

Blowing a kiss upwards, the Joker scurried out the backdoor, Benjamin Gregson in tow, and Franny right behind.

"Oh, it's even better than I'd dreamed," he chortled. "Get in the backseat, kid, if you want to continue breathing."

The Joker hopped into the passenger seat up front. "Franny, let's head for City Hall."

"That's not on the list," she said.

"I'm feeling magnanimous—what can I say? It's Christmas." He flashed her a harsh green look. "Do it, or I'll let young Benjamin here drive, and you can ride outside."

"No thanks."

"I'd like to drive it," Benjamin piped up. "Can I drive it? Please? Can I?"

"Shut up, kid," the Joker snapped.

"I've got to go to the bathroom."

"Forget it."

"But I've got to go to the bathroom!"

Franny rolled her eyes at the Joker. "You were the one who wanted to bring him along."

The Joker glared at the boy. "Look, young man, we're halfway to City Hall. They've got bathrooms there."

"But you're going to blow it up."

"Yes, of course. But we'll let you use the little boy's room first. In the meantime, distract yourself. Play with your computer."

Benjamin smiled. "Okay. I've got a list, just like Santa."

"That's nice. Now be quiet."

"It's also a list just like my uncle's."

"I thought I told you . . . what did you say?" The Joker twisted around in his seat and stared.

"I've got my uncle's personnel files and database for the Gotham 500. I stole it the last time I visited him in his office."

"On that little machine?" The Joker shook his head in disbelief. "The bluebloods of Gotham? The City Hall files? Might I have a tiny peek?"

"I dunno." Benjamin leaned back, sullen. "Are you going to kill me?"

"No, of course not. Unless you'd like me to."

The boy nodded as though digesting the information. "Okay then," he said, much of his old confidence renewed. "I'll let you look. But it'll cost ya."

"Oh, this boy has a bright future. Maybe even in crime," the Joker chortled proudly. "A baby extortionist. How diverting. Very well, young man, how much?"

"You've got to let me drive the sleigh."

Franny turned and glowered at the boy. "I thought you had to go to the bathroom."

"Nah, that was just an escape ploy."

"Kid, you've been watching too many old movies." The Joker chuckled. "Well, it's Christmas. Why not?"

"Boss, I don't like it," Franny said. "He's a nasty little kid. I don't trust him."

"Silence. He is precisely the kind of child who plucks at my heartstrings. Come forward, Benjamin. Franny, get in back. We'll let Ben here drive for a while." He held

out a long green arm, reaching for the portable computer. "As long as he shows me those files."

"I dunno." Benjamin yanked the computer behind his
back. "I've got my own list. Let's go see what Sarah
Hartley's doing first. Peek in her windows."

"Aren't you a little young for that?" Franny said with
disdain.

"Hahaha. He's a menace," the Joker said. He laughed
wildly. "You must drive your uncle crazy."

"Yeah," Benjamin said. A sheepish grin lit his face.
"Whenever I'm around, he locks himself in his den."

"I'm not surprised. All right, Benjamin. First a peek
in Sarah Hartley's windows. Would you like to leave her
a bomb?"

Benjamin's face lit up with youthful malice. "Can I?"

"If you give me that computer file."

Franny snorted in disgust. "You deserve each other.
And Boss, we don't have that many bombs left. . . ."

"And if you're not careful, you'll be walking home,"
the Joker said. "Now get in back."

Pouting, Franny changed seats with the boy. She fas-
tened her green seatbelt tightly and closed her eyes.

"All right!" Benjamin said gleefully. "This is even
better than my mom's BMW."

"You mother lets you drive her car?" Franny said.

"No. I just wait until she's asleep and then I take it
out around the block. I even had a spare set of her keys
made."

"Fascinating, I'm sure," the Joker said. "Now push
this button to program our path. This is north, this is
south. There's a map over here. And if you don't mind,
while you're driving I'll just do a little light reading." He
grabbed up the laptop and began scrolling through its
contents. "Hmmm. Very interesting. I had no idea the
mayor had employed all your cousins."

"That's nothing," replied Benjamin. He pushed buttons at random. "He's got his girlfriend on the payroll
also. But my aunt doesn't know about her."

"A man of tradition," the Joker said, nodding sagely.
He opened his mouth to say more, but the sleigh dipped
suddenly and began a steep dive toward the Gotham
Central Post Office.

"Dammit, pull her up," the Joker said.

Benjamin pushed another button. The sleigh raised its nose and climbed sharply through the snow-laden clouds.

"Not that high—we're not pressurized."

"Boss, I'm getting carsick," Franny whined. "It's cold."

The sleigh tipped down again and began a series of roller-coaster loops.

"Wheee!" Benjamin shouted. "This is great."

"Get in back before you kill us," the Joker snarled.

"I don't wanna—"

"Get in back if you want to live to see eleven."

Eyes huge with fright, Benajmin abandoned the controls and dived onto Franny's lap.

"Oomph. Dammit, get off of me kid—Boss, he's feeling me up!" Franny slapped at his hands. "Stop it, you little creep. Oooh, Boss!"

"I'm busy, Franny. You have my permission to kill him if you'd like." The Joker punched in the autopilot, watching anxiously until the sleigh had resumed a smoother flight path skimming just over the rooftops of Gotham City. "Now then, young man . . ."

A blinding searchlight lit the interior of the sleigh with yellow glare.

"LAND OR BE BLASTED DOWN."

"The Bat Boob," the Joker said. He sighed. "In one of his ridiculous rubberband-propelled fliers, no doubt."

"Batman? Really?" Benjamin's voice was high with wonder. "Can I see him? Can I?"

"I'll do more than let you see him," the Joker said. "I'll let you meet him." He pushed a large blue button and the floor beneath the backseat shuddered.

"Boss!" Franny scrabbled out from under the boy and into the front seat.

"*This* is evil, young man." The Joker grinned maliciously. "Not just posturing and being a punk and wearing lousy clothing or even stealing computer files from your uncle. Here, I'll give you a first-hand demonstration." He pressed another button and the boy disappeared, seat and all, as a trapdoor sent him plunging down through the wintry air.

"Eyaaaaah . . ." said young Benjamin at the top of his lungs.

Franny watched him vanish into the cloud cover. "That little punk," she said with satisfaction. "I hope Batman doesn't catch him."

"Oh, I'm sure he will," the Joker said. "He's especially good at rescuing falling children and kittens from trees. But while he's preoccupied, we'll just change course and head for Mrs. Brinford's estate on the upper Gotham River."

The sleigh cut smartly through the growing fog. Sodium headlamps cast twin beams of green light into the murk ahead. It landed, with a bump, on the roof of the five-story postmodern Brinford villa. Below, the river flowed sluggishly, a dark gray ribbon dotted here and there by chunks of light gray ice.

"How do we get in?" Franny asked.

"Through the penthouse door, of course." The Joker climbed out of the sleigh and strode up to the glass-brick entrance. He rapped assertively. There was no answer. "Oh, well. Guess we'll just have to break in." He slapped a small piece of plastic explosive over the door lock and stepped back.

"Five, four . . ."

Franny gasped and ran for the back of the sleigh.

"Three, two . . ."

BOOM!

All that remained of the door was a few shards of wood hanging from the hinges.

"That explosive is two seconds too quick," the Joker said. He tapped his watch. "Remind me to reprimand Alfonso when we get back."

Franny peered out from behind a roof pipe. "Right."

"And just don't stand there. Get the gift—the one with the green arrows on the paper." The Joker sauntered into the penthouse.

A cowled and caped figure, midnight blue, stood waiting. Bat ears cast pointed shadows on the white wall behind him.

"There he is. I told you he'd come here," a familiar voice said.

Benjamin Gregson stood next to Batman, clutching the hem of his cape.

"I told you we should have killed that little creep,"

Franny wailed. She turned to flee, but a strong hand in a dark blue glove stopped her.

"I'll take that package."

"Oh, please, do," the Joker said. "I've been expecting this all night. How could you imagine I'd leave you off my gift list?"

The box ticked ominously.

"How long before this detonates?" the Batman demanded.

"Oh, that would be telling," the Joker said. He giggled madly. "But if I were you, I'd be more concerned about getting rid of that thing and keeping this fine young lad out of harm's way. We'd so hate to see anything ill befall him, wouldn't we, Franny?"

"Where's my laptop, Joker?" Benjamin cried. "You stole my laptop!"

"I'll give you your laptop, kid. And something else besides!" The Joker pulled the computer from his pocket along with a small, soft paper-bag, and tossed both at the boy.

The bag burst open upon impact, releasing a cloud of green gas. The boy sank to his knees, laughing madly. Behind him, Batman recoiled, wincing at the effect of the gas.

The Joker nodded, pleased. "I figured he'd be wearing some kind of filtering device so I gave the gas an extra punch."

"Boss, let's go," Franny whispered. "Before the gas gets us, too."

"Yes, of course, you're right. There's just no time to savor one's handiwork, is there?" He pushed her into the sleigh ahead of him.

"Where to?"

"Home, I think." He settled into his seat and with one quick move ripped off his false whiskers.

The sleigh rose smoothly into the dark sky, unpursued.

"That was a short run," Franny said.

"All good things must end." The Joker chuckled. He rubbed his chin, removing the last bits of the spirit gum he'd used to glue on the beard. "What a surprise for old Bats when he finds out that bomb is a dud."

"A dud?" Franny stared at the Joker in surprise. Was he getting soft in his old age?

"Oh, yes. It's the last thing he'll be expecting. It's packed with green talcum powder and a computer chip Christmas card that plays Silent Night backwards. Hahaha. It'll drive him crazy."

"But I thought—"

The Joker's look rebuked her. "Franny. After all, it *is* Christmas."

She nodded. Even the Joker got into the holiday spirit. Wait until she told Alfonso.

A loud ticking intruded upon her thoughts.

She whirled in her seat to see a small puce package sitting on the floor behind them.

"Boss, there's one gift left!"

"Eh? But that's impossible. I dumped the rest with that kid."

The Joker turned, glanced at the gift, and started cackling.

"Shouldn't we get rid of it?" Franny squealed. "What's so funny?"

"Hahaha. Maybe I didn't give the dud to Batman after all. And the joke's on me. Hahaha." The Joker clutched his stomach, howling with mirth, his knees drawn up to his chest.

Behind them, the ominous ticking stopped. Dead silence filled the cabin.

The Joker caught Franny's eye and he winked merrily.

"Then again," he said, "I could be wrong."

On the Wire

Andrew Helfer

In his dream, he could hear his beautiful wife humming to herself as she worked in the kitchen. Through his window, he could see his two children playing in the backyard. As he lounged in his Lay-Z-Boy easy chair reading the afternoon paper, a handsome Labrador retriever slept quietly at his feet.

The late afternoon sun shone through the window, bathing him and his surroundings in its golden warmth. He looked up from the paper a moment, his eyes scanning across the wood-paneled walls of the den. He sighed with satisfaction. This was his kingdom. His domain. Life was good. He was happy.

The soothing tones of his wife's voice wafted in from the kitchen, barely outdistancing the tantalizing scent of meat loaf. "Supper's ready, dear," she sang, and in response, he rose from the chair's plush embrace to join the rest of his family in the dining room.

As he walked through the foyer connecting the two rooms he passed by a mirror hanging on the wall. Absently, he glanced at his reflection—and stopped. Something was wrong. Moving closer, he studied the face in the mirror—a face that could only belong to him. Brilliant blue eyes. An aquiline nose. A head of thick blond hair, sweeping back over his forehead. A hard, square jaw; thin masculine lips, a tan; healthy complexion . . .

This was not his face.

His eyes widened. "This is not me," he murmured in disbelief. A finger tentatively poked at the freshly shaven cheek, while another pushed down on his lower lip, pulling it back to reveal an even row of pearly white teeth.

"Dear?" his wife called from the next room. "I said that supper was ready . . . Is everything okay in there?"

"Is everything okay?" he muttered to himself incredulously. "Is everything OKAY?" Someone had done something to his FACE, for god's sake! Someone had entered his kingdom and performed massive plastic surgery on him when he wasn't looking! Someone has stolen his very identity out from under him! Who was this freak in the mirror? Certainly not HIM!

He could feel his stomach begin to turn. A tightening sensation, down in the pit of his stomach. A rhythmic pulsating, an invisible hand squeezing at the bottom of his stomach, urging up the partially digested remains of his lunch. Despite it all, his eyes remained riveted to the horror that faced him in the mirror. Unable to turn away, he felt the hot acid rising up toward his throat. Nothing could stop it—

"Honey?" the voice behind him said, startled. On the cusp of release, his lips pursed tight to contain himself, he spun around. His wife . . . his beautiful wife stood before him, a five pound meat loaf laid atop the serving platter in her hands. She had a quizzical look on her face. "Are you all right—"

Something inside him clicked, and his world went green. He could feel his mouth open wide, feel his jaws unhinge, his face split, his body crack apart . . . and explode in a torrent of brilliant emerald bile. . . .

He awoke with a scream, his frail body jolting upright from the nightmare-soaked sheets. Beads of sweat dripped from his forehead, sliding down over his impossibly disfigured jawline. His lips trembled with fear. He felt his heartbeat thundering through his temples, and fearing his brain might suddenly explode from the pressure, gripped the sides of his head tightly. The strawlike texture of the hair there reassured him somewhat . . . but still, he had to be sure.

Weakly, he rose from the bed, and wavered through the darkness of the flophouse room toward a sliver of light in the distance. Recently, he'd taken to leaving the bathroom light on during the night. It was a beacon of something . . . something he couldn't quite pinpoint, but its presence had proved comforting to him of late.

A moment, and he pushed open the door. The bathroom mirror was first to greet him. He sighed a sigh of relief. His complexion was chalk-white again. His hair was green again. His lips were a familiar blood-red hue. His teeth . . . oh, his teeth. How beautifully yellowed and rotting they were. He smiled. And the smile grew wider, and wider, his lips pulling taut against his teeth, his jaw, until what was once a smile was now a sneer of monstrous proportions, a gaping half-moon shaped wound.

He turned the faucet on, splashed some cold water on his face to wash away the last lingering effects of his dream and turned back toward the bed outside.

Refreshed, he lay down on his back, eyes open in the darkness. Soon—in a week or two, when the heat had died down, he'd get out of this fleabag hotel, reconsider his alternatives, and, inevitably, begin plotting the next round in his ongoing war with the Dark Knight and humanity itself. But until then, he was stuck here, with nothing to amuse himself but a deck of cards, a primitive black-and-white television set . . . and his dreams.

God, it was depressing.

An hour passed. At 3:00 A.M., he gave up on the idea of sleep and turned on the television. His fingers tapped on the remote-control changer buttons with increasing frequency as the moments wore on, the pictures becoming a montage, then a blur of rapidly evaporating images—snippets of commercials, videos, reruns, and ancient movies. In the midst of it all, though, something had caught his eye—something that spurred his imagination. . . . He switched back and forth along the dial, searching for it. In a moment, he'd found it.

"Lonely?" A woman's voice said seductively. The screen showed a picture of a sinewy male yuppie sitting on a leather couch, his brow furrowed, eyes cast heavenward as he considered her question. "Meet interesting people just like you—right now!" The image was replaced by one of the same men dialing a telephone number. "Dial the Pleasure Line! Talk to men and women who want to talk to you! It's a great way to make friends, meet new and interesting people . . . and it's only one dollar a call! Don't miss out on any of the fun! Call now!" A number flashed on the screen. He committed the number to memory and, after turning off the television, reached for the phone.

Seven digits later, a tape-recorded female voice—one he recognized as the same as the voice on the television—came on the line. "Welcome to the Pleasure Line," it said. "Prepare to let it all hang out. Nothing's sacred, everything goes . . . for only twenty cents a minute."

The tape recording abruptly came to an end, and he found himself floating in an electronic void. There was no one else there . . . at least, no one else he could hear.

"Hello?" he said, rather meekly. No answer. He cleared his throat and said the word again, and again, but was greeted only by silence. Another bad idea, he thought to himself. Another buck down the drain. He made a mental note to find and blow up the company that ran this particular phone service, and was about to hang up when he heard the woman speak.

"Hi," she said, her slightly nasal voice full of hope and smiles. And that was all he needed. From the tone of that single word, his mind instantly assembled a full psychological and physical profile of the woman. He knew how she looked, how she walked, how she dressed. He knew about her dreams, her hopes, her fantasies—and knew she would tell them all to him soon enough. He would listen patiently to the fantasy, and then mercilessly squeeze the ugly reality out of her. He'd make her beg for him to stop. And he wouldn't.

She was perfect . . . the perfect toy. The perfect mouse. Soon, he would pounce upon his prey. But until then, he reminded himself, to prolong his pleasure he had to be on his best behavior.

"Why hello, young lady," he answered coolly, not betraying an iota of his secret knowledge. "What's your name?"

"Uh . . . Cathy. What's yours?"

"Call me . . . Jerome."

"Jerome . . . Jerome . . . you don't sound like a Jerome. Is that your real name?"

"No. Should that matter?"

"I dunno . . ." she said, thoughtfully. "But why not use your real name? It's only a name, after all. Lots of people have the same first name."

"Not the same as mine, my dear," he said, dropping in an element of mystery.

"Oh," she said, taking the hint. "Are you . . . famous? Are you not using your real name because I might recognize it?"

"Recognize . . . ?" he answered, feigning surprise. "Why . . . yes. But it's not you I'm worried about, dear Cathy. It's the others. The silent ones—the ones who listen in on the conversation of others and never say a word. They're out there, Cathy. I can feel them. What if I gave my real name and said some . . . personal things about myself. What if someone took down all those very personal facts of my life! It might very well ruin my career! Surely you can see the difficulty of my position here—"

"I didn't really think of it," she said, almost apologetically. "I didn't mean to force—"

"Someday, perhaps, I'll tell you who I really am. Perhaps. But until then, let's keep this on a pseudo basis, shall we?"

"Sure," she said, with obvious disappointment. "Whatever you want."

"But enough about me. Tell me about yourself, Cathy. Tell me everything—and start with what you look like. . . ."

"Well, I'd rather talk about—"

"Yes, yes . . . we'll get to me. But you first. Please. I need to form a picture. Just to get a sense of who I'm talking to."

"Well . . . I guess I'm pretty. Most people tell me I am, anyway. I'm five foot six, weigh one hundred and fifteen pounds, I've got blonde hair and blue eyes . . . and a pretty nice figure, I guess . . ." She paused, looking for something to cinch the visual impression. "There was this woman on the cover of last month's *Cosmo*," she said finally. "I guess I look like her . . . a little."

He took it all in for a long moment, savoring her mundane fantasy before beginning again. "Hmm . . ." he said. "You sound very attractive. Almost too good to be true, eh?"

She tittered nervously, confirming that it was. "Now it's your turn," she said. "Tell me about yourself."

He cleared his throat and began, recalling the nightmare image in the mirror. "I'm six foot one. One hundred and eighty pounds. Blond hair. Blue eyes. I've got a good solid build. I work out."

For a moment there was silence. "Really?" she said breathlessly, anxious to believe him.

"And . . . I wear glasses." he said. Throw in an imperfection or two, just to keep it honest. "I'm a little nearsighted."

"Oh, wow," she said. "I wear glasses, too! Isn't that neat?" She waited for his reply, but there was none forthcoming, so she pressed on. "What do you do for a living? I bet you're a doctor or a lawyer or something like that. You sound so smart."

"I'm a criminal, Cathy. A very smart criminal," he said. "So smart," he continued, "that you might say I've gotten away with murder." He felt a gleeful snicker coming on, and bit his lip hard to keep it down.

She began to laugh. "You're so funny! I love it!" The laughter subsided. "Come on. Really. What do you do?"

"Actually, I'm an entertainer," he responded. "A comedian. Of sorts. One of the highest earning funnymen in the business, I'd guess."

"Really?" she said. He could hear the awe in her voice. "That sounds sooo exciting!"

"It pays the bills," he said nonchalantly. "After a while, it becomes a job like any other—though I must admit the element of danger continually refreshes the experience."

"Danger?" she said. "What kind of danger? Like people booing? Or throwing tomatoes? How dangerous can being a comedian be?"

"It has its moments," he answered. "I cater to a very unusual crowd. Even though I know they enjoy my act, down deep they'd like to see me dead."

"I don't understand," she said, clearly mystified.

"It doesn't matter. Nothing matters right now—except you and me," he said, adding a little French twang to the last bit. God, he could be charming. He heard her giggle. She was flattered. "Now you tell me, Cathy—what do you do for a living?"

"Well," she said. "Nothing as exciting as all that. I work down in the financial district. I'm a receptionist at a stock brokerage company. Maybe you know it—Butz Brothers?"

He did know it. He remembered robbing that particular company about five years before. A pretty good haul. He'd selected it because he thought the name was funny. Any company named Butz deserved to be cleaned out. "I think I've heard of it," he said.

"It's pretty boring, and the pay isn't great. But I'm going to steno school at night, because I'd like to become a court reporter. . . ."

"Ah . . . we all have our dreams. . . ." he said wistfully. "Are those your dreams, Cathy? To become a stenographer?"

"No, silly," she answered, tittering. "What I'd really like to do is be a TV star. On the soaps. To have people know my face when they see me in the street. To have them ask for my autograph. To go to those parties you see on *Entertainment Tonight*. That would be cool." She paused, sensing she might have revealed too much, not realizing he already knew it all. "I bet you get to go to those parties, huh?"

It was time. He ignored the question. Instead, he posed another:

"Are you lonely, Cathy?"

"Me? No . . . of course not," she said, a hint of nervousness in her voice. "I've got lots of friends. And I'm dating three different guys right now. Nothing serious yet, but . . ."

"Cathy, why did you call this number?"

"Because I'm bored," she answered defensively. "Just for now. I couldn't sleep."

"If you couldn't sleep, why not call one of your friends? I'm sure THEY would understand your problem."

"But—"

Time to lunge. "No, Cathy," he said. "The simple truth of the matter is, you're lying. About everything. Well, maybe not about the job—that seems mundane enough—but everything else is a lie. The boyfriends. The description. It's all a load of crap . . . isn't it?"

Silence. "Isn't it?" he roared. He could almost feel her jump on the other end of the line.

"Yes," she said. He could feel all her energy, all her enthusiasm, drain out of her with that single word. She was beaten.

"You're fat, aren't you, Cathy?"

"Yes." Her voice was small. Almost inaudible.

"You're ugly, aren't you?"

"Yes."

"You have no boyfriends. No one pays any attention to you at all. You go to work everyday, ride the subways, walk the streets, take the elevator up to your office . . . but you're invisible. No one notices you. No one sees."

"Yes."

"And afterwards, you go home to watch game shows and soap operas and eat chocolate and junk food and get deeper and deeper into the lonely pit you call a life."

"Yes." She was whimpering now. Making soft snuffling noises as the despair took hold of her. He had her where he wanted her. Now it was time for the masterstroke.

"And you ask yourself—is this life worth living? And you think about the knife in the kitchen. About the pilot light on the stove. About the gas in the oven. About the pills in the medicine cabinet."

The line was silent. He continued.

"Go to the medicine cabinet. Get the pills and bring them back here. I'll wait for you. And along the way, stop in the kitchen. Turn on the gas."

Silence.

"It's the only way, Cathy. You know it. I know it. At least you'll have some company on the way down. Isn't that what you want?"

She cleared her throat. She was almost there. He clenched his fist in divine anticipation. One more insinuation—one more bit of gentle prodding—would send her toppling over the edge. Then she would be his. Then she would—

"Yo', dude!" a new voice suddenly interrupted. "Is this the party line or what?" It was a young voice—he couldn't have been over eighteen years old. But it was enough. In the midst of this, the most delicate of psychological surgeries, some cretinous, addled-brained punk had knocked over his instrument tray, and scattered his scalpels all over the operating theater. He might still complete the surgery—but he had to be quick about it.

"Get off the line, punk," he growled.

"You talkin' to me, dude?" the kid said defiantly. "What 're you, king of the phone company, or what?"

"Don't push your luck, punk," he answered. "Don't make me angry. We're in the middle of a conversation here. We don't want to be interrupted."

"Oh, yeah," the kid said. He could almost see him smirk. "A conversation. Right. Sure. That ain't no conversation, man. You're just playin' with the babe's head. Tryin' to screw her up. Make her cry. Why 'n't you leave her alone, dude. Why 'n't you just kill yourself."

"I can trace this line, punk," he said. He was bluffing and he prayed the punk wouldn't know it. What else could he do? "I can find out where you live. I can kill you. And your parents. Burn your house to the ground. Don't push me."

"You're full of it, dude," the kid answered. "Go ahead and trace it, if you can. I'm at a party right now, man—and I don't even know who's throwin' it! You killing anyone, it's gonna be the dudes who threw this bash!" The kid began to laugh, a slightly drunken hiccuping laugh. He was taunting him. It was infuriating.

"Final warning," he said, knowing that he'd already thrown down his last card. "Get off the line, or I'll—"

"I ain't talkin' to you anymore, creep," the kid said,

dismissing him. "Where's the babe? She still there?" He paused, waiting for her to respond. "Yo', babe! You still out there? Come on—I wanna talk to you."

From somewhere far off, he heard her again, emerging from the despair-filled corner he had backed her into. Her white knight had arrived to save her, and she was rushing up to meet him. "Hi," she said. Her voice was hoarse. She'd been crying.

"Hi, babe," the kid said. "My name's Ronnie. What's yours?"

"Cathy. Nice to meet you, Ronnie."

"Likewise," he said. "I just wanted to tell you that this dude is a psycho. A nut job. Any dude plays with someone's head like that, they gotta be a freak. Know what I mean?"

"I guess . . ." she said. She was coming back. It was over. He'd lost.

"You don't wanna even talk to a guy like him," the kid said. "Scary dude. He's probably sitting in some hotel somewhere, all by himself, like, gettin' off on all this."

"You think?" she said. He could feel his anger reach a new level. He wanted to break in on the conversation, wanted to tear the both of them up into tiny pieces—but he knew his power was gone—and that, for tonight at least, he was totally, utterly impotent.

"I know," the kid said. "Guys like that—they're losers."

"I guess you're right," she said.

"Lissen. I'm at a party over on Northside right now. It's pretty cool. Lots of beers, good music. We'll probably go till dawn. Why'n't you come on over? It'll be fun."

"Really? You think it'd be okay?"

"Sure. Got a pencil?" He was about to give her the address when she stopped him short.

"Wait," she said. "What about . . . *him*. I mean, he's probably still listening—if he hears the address, he could come over and—"

"Don't worry about it. He tries anything, me 'n' my buddies, we'll kick his butt. Might even do this party some good—it could use a little excitement. Matter of

fact," he continued, "if the psycho dude is still out there,
I'd like to extend a personal invitation to him. You come
on over, we'll give you a dose of some righteous hell."
After the kid gave the address to her, he prepared to sign
off. "You're sure you're coming?" he said. She sensed he
really wanted her to.

"Absolutely," she reassured him.

"Cool," he answered. "See you then." There was a
click, and the kid was gone.

The line fell silent. Still, he hadn't heard a second
click, one that would have signaled Cathy's departure.
Was it possible? Was she still there? Would he have yet
one more chance to turn the game around and pick up
where he'd left off? He pressed his ear hard against the
receiver, as though that might improve his hearing.

He heard her take a deep breath. "You're a bastard
. . . a sadistic bastard," she said in a measured, somehow
confident voice. "What did I ever do to you? I called this
line to have some fun! Because I wanted to be something
I'm not! I look at myself in the mirror everyday. I can see
what I am! I don't need a jerk like you to tell me. But
what the hell's wrong with playing some other part once
in a while?"

He was about to answer her, but the question turned
out to be a rhetorical one. A click, and she, too, was gone.
He was alone.

It was hopeless. He hung up the phone. He'd lost the
game. The goddamned surfer punk had done it. It was
all his fault. He wished he could shove his fist down the
punk's throat and tear out his beer-bloated teenaged
belly. He knew where they were. He had the address. He
wanted to go to that party so badly he could taste it.
Wanted to enter the house with his trusty Uzi in hand
and mow them all down. Let God sort out which one was
Cathy and which one was that damned punk.

But he knew he couldn't. He couldn't afford to be seen
on the streets. Not now. Not yet. They all thought he
was dead. If someone—a cab driver, a pedestrian, anyone—should identify him, the hunt would start all over
again. And he wasn't prepared for that. All he could do
was stay here. Sit in this hotel room, while the woman

whose life he'd come so close to destroying discovered the meaning of life all over again.

God, it was depressing.

Nothing had gone as planned. Not even the slightest thrill was afforded him by that humorless God upstairs. He couldn't do anything right. He closed his eyes tight in the darkness, feeling tears welling up inside him. His life was a waste. There was only one cure for it.

He reached under his bed and groped around between mattress and boxspring until he felt the cool polished wood handle in his hand. He pulled it out and held the gun gingerly.

He snapped off the safety. Pulled back the trigger. Heard it click into place. Pressed the barrel against his temple. Squeezed the trigger.

He heard the *pop!* sound as the rolled-up flag with the word "Bang!" on it unfurled and bounced against his head. It smarted. But it felt good.

He laughed himself to sleep.

The Fifty-third Card

Henry Slesar

POLICE NAB ARMORED CAR BANDITS

ARSON SUSPECTED IN WAREHOUSE FIRE

GOTHAM BANK ROBBERS ESCAPE BUT LEAVE LOOT BEHIND

22 DIE IN CRASH OF CHARTERED BUS

Commissioner Gordon scanned the front page of the *Gotham Gazette* with the grim satisfaction of a general studying the map of a battle zone. These communiqués from the front line didn't mean the endless war against crime was being won, but at least the forces of law and order were holding their own, and at a time when the Commissioner feared the possibility of an underworld blitzkrieg. The explanation for his concern was simple enough. Batman was on holiday.

Gordon didn't begrudge the Caped Crusader some respite from the combat zones of Gotham City. If anyone deserved some R and R it was that dedicated daredevil who had slammed the iron doors of justice in so many evil faces. In a way, the Commissioner welcomed the opportunity. While he freely admitted Batman's contribution to the low crime rate, there was no doubt in his mind that his capeless but competent police forces were capable of protecting the public, *without* the necessity of flashing the Bat Signal across the heavens of Gotham City.

Of course, it helped to know that master criminals like the Joker hadn't been heard from in weeks. And judging from the conventional caliber of crimes and disasters reported in the local press, it looked as if that Grinning Ghoul was still licking his wounds from his last encounter with Batman. With a sigh of relief, the Commissioner turned to the sports pages. His mood changed when he saw that Gotham's pitching ace, Les Kovacs, had been assaulted with four home runs by the Cubs the night before.

That was how his daughter Barbara discovered him, muttering into his morning coffee. She laughed when she learned the reason.

"Is *that* all?" she said. "I thought sure it was something in the headlines."

"I know, I know," he growled. "You expect me to go to pieces just because Batman decided to take some time off. You don't think I can keep this town under control without him?"

"I never said any such thing." She locked her arms about his neck and kissed his bald spot. "But I also notice," she said mischievously, "that you haven't told anyone about Batman's little vacation."

"No use tempting Providence," Gordon said. "Batman himself asked me to keep it quiet. He also said that he could still be reached in the case of a real emergency. He gave me a number to call, told me just to leave my name. Peculiar number . . . it has an area code I can't identify."

"But if I know you," Barbara said, flipping back to the front page, "you won't call him because of stories like *these*. It would have to be an atomic bomb threat or an invasion from Mars. . . ." But she was frowning over the paper now, and Gordon looked at her curiously.

"What is it? Read about someone you know?"

"No," she said. "Not personally. But these musicians who were killed . . . The Bobby Armstrong Band. They played at Kate Allenby's debutante ball, just a year ago. . . ."

"I don't remember reading anything about musicians."

"It's right here. The bus accident."

"Oh, that."

"Don't be so callous, Daddy." She scanned the story rapidly. "They went through a guardrail on the highway. All those poor broken bodies strewn among their instruments. It's just awful."

"I wasn't being callous, baby." He put his arm around her shoulder. "Life is full of accidents, unfortunately, and there isn't too much we can do about them. But crime is something we *can* do something about—which means it's time for me to get to that office."

He didn't give another thought to the dead musicians on his drive to Police Headquarters. There was too much else to think about, including his daughter's ill-concealed concern about his ability to handle the Batmanless days ahead. But it was almost a week since the Night Creature had appeared in his study to announce his departure, and no catastrophe had befallen Gotham City. With any luck, that odd telephone number in the Commissioner's wallet would never be used. . . .

There were two things Commissioner Gordon didn't know about that number. One was the fact that the "area code" was actually a United States satellite signal. The second was that any message reaching that number would be conveyed to the newly established Moonbase One, where a group of prominent investors had gathered to formulate a plan for private development of the moon's mineral wealth. "Batman" wasn't among them, but Bruce Wayne was. The caped figure was being lightly ironic as he told the Commissioner about his forthcoming "vacation." It may have been a holiday for Batman, but for Bruce Wayne it was strictly business.

Gordon had often wondered about the economics that allowed Batman to pursue his nonprofit career. Once he had even made a tentative suggestion about public funding, but Batman had disdained the idea. If Gordon had known his true identity, he would have realized that Bruce Wayne's fortune supported his crime fighting mission handily. But even crime-fighting was inflationary. The equipment in the Batcave alone, including its state-of-the-art supercomputer, was worth more than a hundred million dollars. Bruce Wayne had good reason to keep expanding his fortune. He was Batman's sole support.

There was the usual stack of messages on his desk when Gordon arrived, and the first three widened the slightly self-satisfied smile he had worn all morning. The crime laboratory had concluded that the warehouse fire had, indeed, been arson, and the second message told him that the owner had confessed to insurance fraud. The third message concerned the capture of the hapless bank robbers who had become too unnerved to take the loot with them. The fourth, however, wiped the smile from the Commissioner's face. It was an accident report that read:

Gas main explosion at Yacht Club social hall. Fourteen dead, all rehearsing musicians.

It was the last word that troubled him.

Musicians.

He was thinking about Barbara as he picked up the phone and called Matt Stampfli, the deputy assigned to the Accident Division. Matt wasn't there, however, so his assistant recited the meager details available.

"There was a big annual dance scheduled for tonight," he said. "The band rehearsed until about one-thirty this morning, and they were just about to break up when the explosion hit. None of them had a chance."

"And where's Matt?" the Commissioner asked. "Is he out there?"

"No," the assistant said. "Matt's at the auto shop."

"What the hell is he doing at the *auto* shop?"

"Well . . . something else came up. About that bus crash yesterday, the one that ended up in the ravine?"

"What about it?" Gordon asked, feeling a sudden chill.

"There was something funny about the brake linings of that bus. He wanted our guys in Auto to look them over."

Gordon said some religiously inspired words, but there was nothing reverent about the way he said it.

He tried not to let the information spoil his morning. The fact that thirty-six band players had died within thirty-six hours was a grisly coincidence, but no basis for panic. If the brakes of the bus *had* been tampered with, there could be more than one explanation, including insurance, as in the warehouse case. The alternative notion, that there might be some connection between the bus crash and the gas explosion—well, all right. Suppose there was some maniac out there who hated musicians? They'd catch the loonys and put him away. He shook the subject out of his head and picked up the next message. A man named John Burke had been shot and killed late last night for no apparent motive. Gordon checked out a later report, and was relieved to learn that Burke was a headwaiter. Not a musician.

There was a conference at the Mayor's office that afternoon, but Hizzoner didn't attend, being too busy politicking in this election year. Gordon did see District Attorney Tom Riggs and Milt Jaffe, Police Chief, and asked them about the two accidents. Riggs wouldn't commit himself, but Jaffe was his usual blunt self.

"Accident, my left eyebrow! Somebody clobbered those brakes, and I wouldn't be surprised if we came up with bomb fragments from that Yacht Club explosion. Somebody doesn't like two-step music. Some crazy rock-and-roller, probably."

"Don't listen to him," Riggs said. "Milt's got three teenagers."

"What have your boys got on this shooting last night?"

"The headwaiter? I've wanted to take a potshot at one of those snooty bastards myself."

"So far, nothing," Jaffe told the Commissioner. "Burke had no family, no friends outside the restaurant, lived alone. . . . It may have been just a random shot from a window or rooftop."

"That's all we need," Gordon said sourly. "A sniper on the loose."

His good mood of the morning was gone.

That evening, the Commissioner came home to find his daughter entertaining a yuppie assistant D.A. named Mark Something-or-Other, whose deference toward Gordon made him feel ancient. For Barbara's sake, he answered his questions with forced cordiality—until they got around to the subject of Batman.

"Some of us at the office were talking about him," Mark said. "You know, wondering whether this vigilantism was good or bad for Society . . ."

You could hear the capital *S*. Gordon bristled and started to explain about Batman's deputized status with the police, but the look on the A.D.A.'s face told him that he wasn't going to buy that rationalization. As far as Mark Something-or-Other was concerned, Batman served the law by breaking it, and maybe the Commissioner was making a mistake by encouraging this superhero approach to crime control. If Gordon had had a better day, he might have let the matter slide. Instead, he exploded.

"So you think we don't need 'superheroes,' huh? Then just who is going to handle the *supervillains?* Or hasn't that occurred to you?"

"I'm not saying Batman hasn't done some good," Mark said stiffly. "But personally, I think these 'supervillains' have been overrated. I mean, in terms of the overall crime problem. This Joker, for instance. He's done a great deal of damage, but he's never really *succeeded* in his grandiose schemes, has he?"

"Because Batman has always foiled him," Barbara said. "You have to admit that, Mark."

"Yet he's not behind bars, is he? The Joker is still on the loose, Batman or not." The look of smug triumph on his face raised the Commissioner's blood pressure ten points. But he saw the pleading look in Barbara's eyes, and decided to change the subject.

"Well, where are you two headed tonight? Movies?"

"Mark's taking me to the Comedy Corner. Jackie Jeeps is going to be there tonight."

When Gordon seemed unimpressed, Mark said: "He's one of those hot new stand-up comics."

"Too damn many of them right now," Gordon grunted. "And what I'd like to know is, why do so many comics have names that begin with *J?* Jackie Mason, Jackie Gleason, Jack E. Leonard, Joey Adams, Joe E. Lewis, Joe E. Brown, Jerry Lewis, Jerry Lester, Jimmy Durante, Jay Leno, Joan Davis, Joan Rivers . . ."

"You have a wonderful memory, Daddy," Barbara laughed.

"But you left one out," Mark said. "The Joker."

Gordon was asleep when he heard the front door open, and he automatically reached for the bedside alarm. He still hadn't broken the habit of monitoring his daughter's homecoming hours, even though she was old enough to set them for herself. He was pleased to see that it was still before midnight, until he heard the mumbling voices downstairs and detected a treble note of hysteria. Was Barbara crying? If it was a lovers' quarrel, it was none of his affair, he told himself. Yet, just the same, he slipped into a threadbare robe that should have been discarded five years before and padded quietly downstairs. He was just in time to hear the door close behind Barbara's date. When she saw her father, she went trembling into his arms.

"Oh, Daddy, it was horrible! It was just awful!"

"Jokes that bad, huh?"

"No! He was killed—murdered! Right on stage!"

He pushed her away and saw the unmistakable stamp of terror on her face.

"Jackie Jeeps," Barbara said. "The comedian. He was shot by someone in the audience! He just pulled out a gun and shot him!"

"Good Lord," Gordon said. "Did they get the assassin? He didn't get away, did he?"

"I don't think anybody even got a good look at him! He was all the way in the back, near the exit door. But he was laughing louder than anyone else. He was still laughing when he shot him!"

"You poor child. It's one thing to read about murder, but to actually witness it . . ."

"Mark and I were at a table in the front row. He was hit once in the chest and once in the head . . . there was so much blood! And there was that laughter—that terrible, eerie laughter."

Gordon held her close again, rubbing her icy hands. But he felt cold himself, even in the warm confines of his comfortable old wool robe. He couldn't help remembering Mark's last words before they left the house only two hours before. Joker begins with J. . . .

He expressed no theory about the murder at the office meeting the next morning. Nobody even mentioned the possibility of linkage until he dropped the hint himself.

The idea was quickly shouted down, although Riggs, perhaps out of professional courtesy, did admit there might be a vague pattern in the recent spate of violent deaths.

"Thirty-six musicians. A headwaiter. A stand-up comic. I suppose there's a bit of a connection. Gotham nightlife?"

Jaffe was as blunt as ever. "The Bobby Armstrong Band only played for society weddings and geriatric dances. Same goes for the Yacht Club bunch. I think you're barking up the wrong tree. If you ask me, it was one of Jackie Jeeps's girlfriends. He had one for every day of the week."

"How would you know that?" Gordon asked.

"I read it in Johnny Fisher's column, in the *Gazette*."

"Funny you mentioned Fisher," Riggs said. "I noticed somebody else wrote his column in today's paper. Said something about him being sick."

"What's that got to do with the price of tomatoes?"

"Sorry." Riggs shrugged, looking like a kid caught with jam on his fingers. "I kind of enjoy his stuff."

That afternoon, when word came that Fisher had died of a yet undiagnosed ailment, the Commissioner thought of Riggs's remark. The story made the *Gazette*'s evening edition, and Gordon read it curiously.

GOTHAM CITY, Sept. 4—Johnny K. Fisher, the syndicated gossip columnist whose "My Kind of Town" column has been a favorite of Gotham Gazette readers for the past five years, died at Gotham Hospital at two A.M. A spokesman for the hospital, Dr. Myron Buchalter, said that the cause of death was a toxic reaction, but its cause could not be determined until the autopsy was completed.

Thomas Brennan, editor of the Gazette, said that Fisher had fallen ill upon his return from an interview with some personality whose name Fisher had refused to divulge. The columnist had only stated that his interview would be a "first" for his column, and would have his readers GRINNING FROM EAR TO EAR.

The last five words weren't capitalized in the *Gotham Gazette*—only in Commissioner Gordon's mind.

*   *   *

Barbara fixed him a butterflied leg of lamb that night, with a side dish of ratatouille. It was his favorite meal, and she knew that something was wrong when he seemed unaware of what he was eating.

"Please talk to me, Daddy. Tell me what's bothering you."

"The letter *J*," he answered ruefully.

On the local news show that evening, there was the report of another murder on the streets of Gotham City, and she could hear her father breathe a deep sigh of relief when they announced the man's name. It was Rudolph Bottoms, and he was a professional gambler. An unpaid debt was high on the list of probable motives.

The next morning, the headline about the slaying was one of the smallest on the front page. There were two others in a bolder typeface.

CRUISE SHIP SINKS IN GOTHAM HARBOR

Four Crewmen Injured as Engine Room
Explosion Wrecks Docked Liner

"MISS WONDERFUL" CONTEST WINNER DIES IN RUNWAY MISHAP

Cindy Lou Skinner, 20, Suffers
Fatal Concussion in Fall

But it was a small detail in the subhead of the third headline that gave Commissioner Gordon his most unnerving moment of the new day.

GAMBLER SHOT TO DEATH ON BANK STREET

Rudolph Bottoms Rumored to Owe
$250,000 to Las Vegas Casinos

Earned Notoriety as "Black Jack" Bottoms

The letter *J*.

It was a tormenting, tantalizing detail, too obscure, too meaningless, too cryptic. Gordon knew there was no way he could inflict it as a "theory" on the various investigations now keeping his department busy. And to suggest a "Joker" factor was equally out of the question. No witness had actually seen the Grinning Ghoul, and what mad motive would the Clown-faced Killer have for wanting the death of these unrelated victims? Or was Gordon simply unable to find the relational factor?

He tried to stop thinking about it. He wasn't a detective; he was an executive, managing the affairs of the largest municipal police force in the country. There were plenty of good investigative minds working on the problem. Unfortunately, one of the best minds of all was not available. The mind within the Microchiroptera Mask of the Caped Crusader.

When he arrived at Headquarters, he assumed that it was the sinking of the cruise ship *Carib Queen* that created the crush in the pressroom; it was certainly the worst pier disaster in the history of Gotham City Harbor. But he soon realized that the media smelled a sexier story in the dramatic demise of a young woman only moments after she had been crowned for her beauty. How could it happen? Where did the blame lie? Who was responsible for the weak structure of the runway where she took her victory walk, the last steps of her life?

But the most alarming question Gordon heard from the shouting reporters was this one:

"Is it true the police are investigating the possibility of sabotage? That someone had *deliberately* weakened that runway?"

It was something Gordon himself wanted to know, and he made a personal appearance in Milt Jaffe's office to determine the facts.

"What's this all about?" he asked. "You really suspect foul play in this beauty contest business?"

A Detective First Class named Bernie Wang was in Jaffe's office, and there was nothing inscrutable about his expression. "Suspect, hell!" he said. "There's no question about it, Commissioner. Somebody rigged up that stage. Somebody wanted to mangle that poor kid and they did a very good job."

When Gordon saw his daughter that night, he felt still another kind of anguish. Cindy Lou Skinner had been very close to Barbara's age. If Barbara had entered that dumb contest—and God knows she had the looks for it!—she might have been the doomed winner of that deadly crown.

But he found that Barbara couldn't accept the idea of premeditated murder.

"The killer, if there was one, couldn't have *known* that girl was going to win, Daddy. So how could it be homicide?"

"Maybe the perpetrator didn't care who won, as long as the new Miss Wonderful was injured or killed."

"You mean it was just at . . . random? What crazy fiend would do that?" Even though Gordon didn't reply, Barbara guessed what was on his mind. "But that's ridiculous, Daddy! Why would the Joker do such a thing? He always had *some* method in his madness, didn't he?"

"Maybe we just can't read the pattern yet. Maybe he's trying to tell us something, in some bizarre, deadly code. . . ."

She watched as her father removed his billfold, almost absentmindedly. Aside from the currency, she knew its contents only too well. One credit card, rarely used. Two pictures of Barbara, one as a toddler. One photo of the mother she never knew, her smile heartbreakingly sweet in the summer sunlight. And now, one other item. A folded slip of paper bearing the number that would summon Batman back to Gotham City. . . .

When she saw Gordon return the billfold to his pocket, she said softly:

"Why not, Daddy? Why not call him?"

"No," Gordon said, shaking his head. "It's not the end of the world. People are killed every day in a big city, some accidentally, some on purpose. . . . That man deserves a couple of weeks of peace, doesn't he?"

"That's not your reason," Barbara said crisply. "You're not worried about Batman getting in some beachtime. How can he get a tan, anyway, in that mask of his?"

"I'm sure it's no joke to him, baby. Batman is human. He needs some rest. Besides, there's no real proof of any kind of . . . conspiracy."

"Well, I think it's nothing but pride—stubborn macho pride! You just don't want Batman to think you can't get along without him."

"I'm going to bed." Her father sighed. "Maybe the headlines will look better in the morning."

Commissioner Gordon's bedtime prayers were answered. There were one or two minor crime stories on the front page, but the main headline in the Gotham press was an upbeat one.

ENGLAND'S QUEEN ELIZABETH TO VISIT U.S.

Gotham City First Stop on Tour

"Isn't that terrific?" Barbara beamed. "Maybe you can pull a few strings at the Mayor's office so we can be presented to her."

"You know our Mayor," Gordon said, cheerful at last. "He'll use the visit to pick up a few more votes. That's all he cares about these days."

"And I suppose you're going to get all hot and bothered about Security."

"That won't be our responsibility alone. This is international stuff, baby. We'll do our part, of course, but it'll be the Feds calling the shots." He pulled her onto his lap, big as she was. "And what's so important about being presented to a Queen? Since you're already a Princess." He gave her a loud "smack" on the forehead, and Barbara laughed, pleased to see his new mood.

The messages on his desk tempered that mood only slightly. There was a barroom knifing, with the culprit swiftly apprehended. A fire in a movie house, with the projectionist sustaining third-degree burns. There was a wife-beating, a gas station robbery, and only one murder marked P.U.—Perpetrator Unknown. It was a woman named Lola L. Finch, 58, widowed, strangled in the hallway of her apartment building. There was something vaguely familiar about the name, but Gordon soon put it out of his mind.

There was a hurricane of activity at Headquarters that day, and as he correctly assumed, the royal visit was at the eye of it. The trip had actually been planned weeks before, but publicity had been kept to a minimum for security purposes. And, of course, the FBI and Secret Service had formulated a plan that gave Gotham's own police force an essential but secondary role in the proceedings. When he saw Jaffe, the Police Chief described the visit as a royal pain in the neck, but he didn't seem all that displeased about it. Between the recent series of disasters and unmotivated slayings, his men had been working long tours of duty. It was a relief to give them a benign assignment like crowd control.

Barbara was ecstatic. The Mayor, as her father predicted, didn't let the opportunity for political haymaking slip by. He quickly made arrangements for a reception at his Mansion, and concocted a guest list of Gotham's most influential people. Since there was an arctic zone between him and the Police Commissioner, Barbara had no hope of receiving an invitation. But then it turned out that Mark Something-or-Other was actually a scion of one of Gotham's most distinguished families, and they were on the A list. Cinderella was going to the Ball, and Prince Charming was going to be her escort.

Gordon was happy for his daughter, even if he still didn't approve of her choice of beau. He was also content not to attend the party, preferring a quiet evening in front of the television set, or rereading some old Dickens novel in his bed, under a thick comforter.

He chose the latter entertainment the night of the party, only he had a hard time choosing the Dickens novel out of the bound set his wife had given him on their leather wedding anniversary. The memory of that time made him decide to browse through another kind of volume: the scrapbook they had started together to commemorate the first years of their marriage. It had ended with Barbara's birth. Or rather, it had been the beginning of Volume Two, exclusively devoted to their daughter.

Gordon settled into his bed with the big book in front of him, and turned the pages.

There weren't many photographs. Gordon had always been camera-shy, so most of the snapshots were of his wife. She smiled in almost all of them, and not because she had been told to say "cheese." She had simply been a woman who smiled.

But what the book lacked in photographs it made up in souvenirs. There were dance programs, theater tickets, invitations, newspaper clippings. There were few items related to Gordon's career, since he didn't think police activities belonged in a family album, but if some item tickled his wife's fancy, she would include it. Like the news story about his participation in a police raid on a burlesque house (anything *didn't* go in those days). When the young officer had been assaulted by the self-styled Queen of Burlesque who called herself Lola Lollipop . . .

Gordon laughed as he looked at the faded clipping. Even now, decades later, he could recall the heavily painted face of the enraged stripper, whose ferocious attack had resulted in his first service wounds. Lola Lollipop! She had actually written him a letter of apology a year later, when she had abdicated her throne and married one of the arresting officers. What was his name again? Finch, wasn't it? Little Joe Finch, who barely made the minimum department height? And what was Lola, six feet, a hundred and eighty pounds?

Lola . . . Lollipop . . . Finch.

He stopped laughing and sat upright in bed, recalling where he had read that name so recently—in the crime diaries. It had been poor old Lola who had been strangled in the hallway of her apartment house. It was probably drug-related, according to the investigating officer, some neighborhood junkie who killed her for her welfare money. It was a reasonable theory, except for one troubling detail: there had been six dollars and change in Lola's purse. . . . A mugger, especially one desperate enough to kill, would have cleaned her out. . . .

"Damn!" the Commissioner said aloud, a strict upbringing making it the strongest invective he ever used.

"There's something here . . . Something I just can't see
yet. . . ."

There was a yellow pad in the night-table drawer beside his bed. He put it on his lap, and began a list of
Victims.

The Bobby Armstrong Band

The Yacht Club Orchestra

John Burke, Headwaiter

Jackie Jeeps, Comic

Johnny Fisher, Columnist

Rudolph "Blackjack" Bottoms

Cindy Lou Skinner, Miss Wonderful

Lola Lollipop Finch, ex-Stripper

He stared at the list. It wasn't complete. There had
been other victims of various crimes in Gotham City, but
these were the most unmotivated ones that came to
mind. Was there a Common Denominator among them?
Was it "show business?" Was there some mutual interest? Was it some kind of vendetta? And what was it
about the last entry, about Lola Lollipop, that had
tweaked his intuition?

Then he remembered.

Burlesque Queen.

That's how Lola had styled herself, as so many other
strippers had (when they weren't calling themselves
"exotic dancers" or "ecdysiasts.") Lola had been the
"Queen" of Burlesque. And what did they call the win-
ners of competitions like the "Miss Wonderful" pageant?

Beauty Queens.

Then Gordon remembered one "victim" he had neglected to list: the Caribbean cruise ship now resting on
the bottom of Gotham City Harbor.

The Carib Queen.

His heart was beginning to pound.

He went back to the head of the list and pondered the

death of thirty-six musicians and four strangers whose
names began with *J*.

John Burke, the headwaiter who had caught God's eye.
*What if he had been called "Jack?" Like so many
"Johns?"*

Jeeps, the stand-up comic, no longer vertical.
*He was "Jackie" and "Jackie" was a diminutive of
"Jack."*

Johnny K. Fisher, the columnist, now gossiping with
Gabriel.
Born "John" and possibly nicknamed "Jack?"

And finally, Rudolph Bottoms.
Better known as "Black Jack."

One, two, three, four Jacks.
Thirty-six players, four Jacks, and three Queens . . .

It was either a gruesome coincidence—or a ghastly
nightmare. Was someone playing a terrible game with
human lives? A demonic game of cards? Were there
going to be fifty-two victims shuffling off their mortal
coils? What was the object of the game? And who was
behind it?

The answer thundered inside the Commissioner's
brain until he thought it would burst. His worst fear
might be coming true, that the dreaded Joker was once
again dealing a hand of horror in Gotham City.

It was enough to give him a splitting headache, and
Gordon went to the bathroom medicine cabinet in search
of an analgesic. But as he lifted the little white pills to
his mouth, he caught a glimpse of his pale face in the
mirror, and it seemed to take on a life of its own as it
stared back and shouted at him:

"Only *three* queens, you idiot! Only three—*so far!*"

He dropped both pills and water glass into the sink
and scrambled for the phone, trying to control his suddenly palsied fingers. His instincts didn't fail him. He
remembered the number of the emergency line in the
Mayor's office, and a special operator told him to hang on
while the Mayor was located, but of course, he was

warned, Hizzoner was very busy at the moment, considering the reception that evening. . . . Gordon exploded angrily, saying *damn!* to the reception, and that he would rather speak to Chief Jaffe or the FBI or the Secret Service anyway and she damned well better hurry if she didn't want a royal assassination on her conscience. . . .

While he waited, listening to the arrhythmical drumbeat of his heart, Gordon tried to control his panic. It wasn't only the Queen's peril that was on his mind. His own daughter was in that danger zone, and who knows how many might die in an attempt to breach the security wall?

A voice on the phone.

"Mr. Mayor!" Gordon shouted. "Is everything all right? Has anything happened yet?"

"No," the Mayor said sourly. "And it looks like it's *not* going to happen. Lot of disappointed people around here. You calling to gloat?"

"What are you talking about?"

"About the Queen. She never made the party. Seems there was some kind of cabinet crisis back home, and she decided not to come. Lots of apologies, but that hasn't made all these spiffed-up ladies happy. They've been practicing curtsies all week. . . ."

The phone almost dropped from Gordon's hand. He wasn't sure if the Mayor heard his "Thank God!" If he did, he probably thought the remark was spiteful rather than relieved.

There was no way he could avoid explicating his theory to Barbara. When Mark Something-or-Other brought her home at three that morning, she wasn't nearly as despondent over Her Majesty's nonappearance as Gordon expected her to be. In fact, her mood was slightly giddy, a state he ascribed to champagne and the glitter of the occasion. It was apparently a little more than that, since she didn't stop talking about Mark, Mark, Mark until sleep overcame her.

But at Sunday breakfast, she listened to her father's "deadly deck" theory, and her mood turned solemn.

"Oh, Daddy," she said with a sigh. "You're not actually going to *tell* this to anybody? I mean, officially?"

"I know it sounds farfetched, Barbs. But think about it! What else would explain such a bizarre series of events?"

"Coincidence would explain it," she said. "I mean, these four 'Jacks' of yours . . . Well, lots of men are named John, it's probably the most common name in Gotham City. And a 'beauty queen' or 'burlesque queen' aren't really the same as . . . well, the Queen of England!" The recollection made her sigh even deeper. "Boy, Her Majesty doesn't know what she missed last night. Mark looked so *handsome* in that tuxedo."

Barbara went back to bed, leaving him with daylight doubts and the Sunday paper.

The front page was full of political news, including the cabinet crisis in Great Britain, but there were some human-interest items, too.

SHORTY DAVIS, 73, DIES IN CRASH

Decorated Pilot in both WWII
and Korean Conflict

Gordon read the story with only desultory interest. Davis had been killed in a privately owned single-engine plane. Davis's wife had been stunned by the crash, swearing that her husband always made an elaborate flight check before takeoff, and the skies had been friendly.

It was only while he was putting the dishes away that Gordon revised the headline in his own mind.

SHORTY DAVIS, ACE PILOT, DIES IN CRASH

Wasn't that equally accurate?

Davis was an *Ace,* and now he was dead.

If the brakes of a bus can be tampered with, why not the controls of an airplane?

Was Shorty Davis the first of *four* Aces that were marked for death?

Barbara's caution was proper, of course. It was a nebulous theory, and hard to prove, especially with the ambiguous terminology involved. But if he was right, there were going to be more deaths and more disasters, until all the Queens, Kings, and Aces in the deck were gone, leaving only the Joker to celebrate his victory over—what? The purposeless, senseless madness of it all was appalling, but that didn't lessen the danger or the urgency.

Gordon, despite the apron around his waist, his hands submerged in sudsy water, still looked like a heroic statue a sculptor might have entitled RESOLVE.

Let them laugh at him. Let them think he was as unbalanced as the Joker himself. He was going to put his reputation on the line.

The next morning, in the D.A.'s conference room, Gordon took a deep breath and plunged in.

Everybody listened respectfully to his "Deadly Deck" theory. Only one person smothered a chuckle. Mark Something-or-Other, obviously trying to make points with Barbara's old man, said he found the Commissioner's theory "interesting." But there was no doubt that the skeptical level around the table was very high.

"It's true that the Joker's committed some bizarre crimes in the past," Riggs said. "But let's face it, Commissioner. His pranks always had a punchline. He may have chosen peculiar means to get what he wanted, but he always wanted *something*."

"That's the truth," Milt Jaffe said. "And what does he get out of knocking off this imaginary deck of cards?"

"I can't answer that question," Gordon said miserably. "I wish I could. Maybe it has something to do with Monarch—"

"With who?" Mark asked.

"That was before your time," Jaffe grumbled. "Monarch was a playing card company that the Joker robbed. Only he didn't call himself 'the Joker' then."

"He made his escape from the Monarch factory by swimming through a pool of chemical waste. It turned his hair green and his skin that dead-white color—that's

why he looks the way he does. And that's why he decided
to become the Clown Prince of Crime."

Mark looked doubtful. "Are you saying this is some
kind of revenge against the company?"

"No way," Milt Jaffe said, the dead cigar dancing in
his mouth. "Monarch's been out of business for
years. . . . Anyway, even if this theory of yours is true,
Commissioner, what the hell could we do about it? How
would we know the 'card' he'll be after next?"

"We don't know," Gordon said miserably. "But at
least we can be alert. He may be after another 'Queen' or
ready to start on the 'Kings.' We're not expecting any,
are we?"

"As a matter of fact," the D.A. said casually, "we are."

"What?"

"Ever hear of King Harold of Lumidia?"

"I never heard of *Lumidia,*" Jaffe said.

"It's one of those emerging nations," Riggs said. "It's
only been in existence a year, and its history is pretty
bloody. This guy Harold took over the throne in some
kind of palace revolution, and now he runs the country
with an iron sceptre. He must have got jealous when he
heard that Queen Elizabeth decided to visit Gotham
City, so he decided to do the same."

"He'll have to change his mind," Gordon said firmly.
"This is no time for a King to visit this town!"

"How do you propose to stop him?"

"I don't know! I'll call the State Department," Gordon
said. "I'll try to convince them that there are . . . unstable elements at the moment, that it would be better to
postpone the trip."

"Of course, you'll have to convince them of the merits
of your 'deck' theory," Riggs said.

"Yes," Gordon said unhappily. "I suppose I will."

"Lots of luck," Milt Jaffe said drily. But he looked at
the Commissioner with something close to compassion.

Gordon felt ten years older when he returned home that
night and turned on the local television news.

He was saddened to realize that he was actually
hoping for a card-related crime, for a Queen to be vio-

lated, a King to fall, an Ace to be trumped. But there was nothing.

He was just about to turn off the Johnny Carson Show—another funnyman with a "*J*"—when the screen went dark and a special bulletin was announced. Gordon listened in disbelief, and knew there was no way he could sleep until he read the whole story in the early edition.

LES KOVACS, PITCHING ACE, DIES IN FALL FROM HOTEL WINDOW

The story was a lengthy one, but most of the columns were filled with biographical facts about Kovacs's colorful career in baseball. There was a knowing reference to his reputation for hard drinking, clearly implying that alcohol was responsible for his plunge from that twelfth-floor window.

The details were sparse. All the police could uncover was that Kovacs had encountered a stranger at the dimly lit hotel bar, and they had left together. The only description they had concerned his height—he was unusually tall. The reason for their departure was easy to determine, judging from the empty whiskey bottles and the playing cards scattered across the room. There was a winning poker hand left intact on a table. Three aces, a King, and a Joker.

The Joker must have been wild, Commissioner Gordon thought grimly. Very, very wild . . .

The following day was one of the most demeaning of his long career. His call to the State Department had resulted in a literal invasion of his office and his privacy. There were three grim-faced Secret Service operatives waiting for him, and with exaggerated courtesy they hustled him off to some safe house in Gotham where another trio of government agents grilled him for hours about his knowledge of Lumidia, King Harold, Asian and African politics, international terrorism, and the Joker.

He was sweating like a grilled criminal by the time they were through. When he was given a chance to explain his motives for wanting King Harold's trip postponed, it sounded feeble to his own ears. If anything, they were even more polite than before. They promised to relay his "interesting conjecture" to the proper authorities, and drove him home.

What happened in the next five days was perhaps the cruelest occurrence of them all.

Nothing happened.

There were crimes, of course. There were accidents, natural and unnatural. There were half a dozen violent deaths, none worthy of sixty-point headlines. A wife bludgeoned her husband with his own bowling ball. A bartender shot and killed a robber. A six-year-old found his father's gun and crippled a neighbor. And there was a double suicide, of Joel and Jerry Kronk, fifty-six and fifty-eight respectively, sole survivors of a 50's singing group.

Gordon didn't know whether to feel chagrin or relief.

On the sixth day, his heart sank, for three reasons:

HOTEL "QUEEN" DIES IN ROBBERY ATTEMPT

Hermione Langston, Owner of Posh
Atlantis-Regency, Killed by Jewel Thief

BERNIE BAKER DIES IN AUTO CRASH

Was Famed as Gotham's "Donut King"

ANOTHER ROYAL VISITOR FOR GOTHAM

Lumidia's Sovereign to Visit City

When he arrived home that evening, he found his daughter sitting quietly in the living room, listening to an old LP record, in a pensive mood that troubled him.

"I know," he said glumly. "You've seen the headlines. About the hotel 'Queen' and the donut 'King' and you think I'm going to start making a fuss about my 'Joker' theory again. Make a fool of myself like I did the last time."

"No, Daddy," she said quietly. "You see—I believe you!"

"You what?"

She looked at him with eyes that were narrowed by pain.

"I was so stupid not to trust you, not to *understand*. You've been right all along, and nobody was smart enough to recognize it. It's the Joker, Daddy, it is! He's playing this horrible game of death and laughing up his sleeve at all of us!"

"But—what made you change your mind?"

"This," she said, indicating the record jacket on the floor. She picked it up and looked at the liner notes. "I thought I'd heard those names before. It was on a quiz show, *Jeopardy,* I think. The Kronk Brothers. There used to be *four* Kronk brothers, and you can understand why they used a different name for their singing group."

She turned the album around, and gave her father a look at the title.

The Four Aces Sing Again.

Gordon came as close to tears as he had been since the death of his wife. He slumped onto the sofa and Barbara put her arms around him as if he were the child between them.

"I was so shaken up when I realized the truth," she said. "I've had such a hard time with Mark about this 'Deadly Deck' theory of yours. He just won't believe it; he keeps finding all sorts of reasons *not* to believe it, all having to do with 'statistics.' We almost broke up twice because of it."

He patted his daughter's hand. "You don't have to make any sacrifices, baby. I'm big enough to defend myself."

"Well, it wasn't *just* because of you," she said wistfully. "There *was* something else. His absolute refusal to admit that he might be in danger, too, because of his name . . ."

"His name?" Gordon said, surprised. "You mean *Mark's* name?"

"Yes!" Barbara smiled weakly. "I know you keep calling him Mark Something-or-Other, but he *does* have a name. It's Marcus King, Jr."

"King!"

"There are dozens of people named 'King' in Gotham City, of course, and there's no reason why he should be in particular danger from the Joker, not that he agrees that there *is* any—"

"So he's the son of Marcus King? The Department Store man?"

"That's right. And tonight, when I remembered about this old album and realized that the Joker has managed to wipe out four Jacks, and four Aces, and three Queens . . ."

"You haven't seen the news today, have you? It's *four* Queens. That self-styled hotel queen, you remember her. She was killed in what was called a 'jewel robbery.' And unless it's sheer coincidence, that monstrous maniac has already killed his first King."

Barbara gasped. "Who?"

"He's not genuine royalty. Only a poor man named Bernie Baker—they called him the Donut King. But genuine royalty is on its way to Gotham this minute. Maybe right into the jaws of death. The grinning jaws of the Joker!"

"Oh, Daddy—you don't mean that King from Lumidia? The one you tried to warn off?"

"My warning wasn't heeded," the Commissioner said bitterly. "And now the Joker's joke may become an international incident. . . ." He stood up suddenly, his wrath seeming to add inches to his height. "Only I won't let it happen! I'll set a trap for the Joker if I have to commandeer every man on the Force! If I have to call out the Army, the Navy, and the Marines! He isn't going to get away with it!"

"But what if they still don't believe you? If they won't give you the manpower you need?"

"I'll make them believe me, or they can have my job!"

"Daddy, please don't do anything you'll regret. I

mean—there *is* an alternative—there *is* something else you can do—"

He stared at her.

"You mean Batman, don't you?"

"Has anyone else ever been able to stop the Joker?"

"You don't think I'm . . . competent enough, to handle the situation without him."

"I didn't say that, Daddy."

"It's what you think. What most of the world thinks, I suppose. Only this time, I'm ready for him. I've figured out his game plan! I'm sure. I can stop the Joker before he takes another life."

The telephone was ringing. Barbara picked it up, and at first her face brightened as she heard the familiar voice on the other end. But then every muscle in her body seemed to liquefy. She sank into a chair, limp as a Raggedy Ann doll, and her alarmed father rushed to her side.

"What is it?" he asked. "What's happened?"

She stared at the telephone, unable to reply. Gordon snatched it out of her hand and bellowed into the mouthpiece.

"Who is this?"

"It's Mark, Commissioner. I didn't mean to do that to Barbara . . . but I just had to tell her . . . why I won't be seeing her this evening. . . . This horrible thing that happened. . . ."

"What happened? What is it?"

"My parents . . . both of them . . . They were driving upstate . . . A car ran them off the road . . . They were killed instantly. . . ."

"Good God," the Commissioner said. He wanted to say something properly sympathetic, but his mind raced forward to a question that had to be asked.

"The other driver . . ."

"He never stopped. He got away without a trace. But . . . my father lived long enough to say something about him." The voice choked for a moment, but Gordon demanded to hear the rest.

"He said something about a horrible face at the wheel . . . A horrible, white, smiling face . . ."

The Commissioner hung up slowly.

He didn't look at Barbara again. He simply removed
his billfold and found a folded slip of paper. Then he
picked up the phone once more and dialed an unfamiliar
area code.

There was both good news and bad news for the Gotham
City Police on the morning that Pan-Oceanic's Flight
101 touched down at Gotham City Airport.

The good news was that the crowd was small. Few of
Gotham's citizens were aware of Lumidia, to say nothing
of its newly crowned King Harold, and the Gotham press
had done little to enlighten them. There were no banner
headlines about the royal visit, no live television crews
to record the event, although there was one ENG truck
representing the local station. At best, the event would
result in a brief story at the bottom of page one, and a
two-minute segment on the local news with film of His
Majesty, uniformed and bemedaled, waving and grinning from the top of the ramp. There would be a few
lighthearted words about his mission; aside from the
usual loan request, Lumidia was anxious to learn about
American palm-oil processing. There were a lot of palm
trees in Lumidia.

The bad news was that Gotham City's protection was
drastically reduced that morning. Despite the small
turnout, Commissioner Gordon's anxiety had resulted in
the assignment of almost one third of Gotham's police
force to ensure King Harold's safety. Cops outnumbered
spectators, and when His Majesty descended from the
ramp of the jetliner, he saw almost nothing but a sea of
blue. Actually, King Harold was flattered. Never having
seen an American police uniform, he assumed this was a
military escort, and saluted Gotham City's Finest like
the general he had once been.

Among the waiting dignitaries, Commissioner Gordon was the most apprehensive. There were three distinct possibilities that morning, all of them unnerving.
If everything went smoothly, and there was no attempt
on King Harold's life, Gordon's elaborate precautions
would make him a laughingstock. If there *was* an attempt, and it succeeded, it would make the entire police

establishment of Gotham City look foolish and inept. Either way, his career would be over.

It was only the third possibility that would save the day. If the Joker played out his hand, if he tried to eliminate the last card in his Deck of Death—and failed. But could that Jeering Jester be stopped? Was even all this massed power enough to foil the brilliant madman who had already taken so many lives in his senseless game of 52 Pickup?

Gordon hadn't heard one word from Batman since his call to the U.S. Satellite Station. He had followed instructions and simply left his name with the operator, but there had been no response, no way of knowing if his message ever reached the Caped Crusader. Even if it had, there had been no opportunity to describe the problem, to tell Batman about the danger he anticipated at Gotham City Airport. Despite the battalions of police officers, Gordon felt very much alone.

He clenched his fists as he saw the Mayor turn to ask an aide if he had the Key to the City. It was a symbolic silver-plated key of exaggerated size, offered to every important visitor. The aide seemed flustered by the question.

"I thought you wanted it left in the terminal," he said. "Higgins said you called and told him to leave it at the POA message desk."

"I didn't phone Higgins or anybody else this morning!" Hizzoner said indignantly. "Now go get the damned thing right now!"

The aide went trotting off toward the terminal building, and Gordon felt a sudden twinge of alarm.

"Mr. Mayor!" he said.

But the Mayor, deliberately or otherwise, didn't hear him. He started to walk toward the red carpet being rolled out on the tarmac. Gordon hesitated, not sure if he should run after him, to query this odd detail about a telephone call he had never made. Gordon was hypersensitive to odd details these days. But it was too late. The Mayor, eager to be the first to greet the royal visitor, was already at the ramp, extending his hand toward King Harold and beaming so widely that the sun glittered off his gold front tooth.

Some instinct made Gordon turn and look back toward the terminal. He saw the Mayor's aide—he suddenly remembered that his name was Philpott—talking to an unusually tall, thin man in an airline uniform whose face was in shadow. The man handed Philpott the key and strode off unhurriedly in the other direction.

The Mayor was already making his welcoming speech into the microphone, in his usual jocular style. Nobody knew if King Harold got the point of his humor, but he kept on smiling just the same. The smile was even more dazzling as Hizzoner took the silver key from Philpott's hand and presented it to His Majesty with a nondeferential bow.

To Commissioner Gordon, the world seemed to be moving in slow motion. He watched the presentation of the key—and out of the corner of his eye, the tall airline employee strolling casually toward a small helicopter—and he knew exactly what was going to happen next. Like the trailer of a movie, he saw the bursting globe of orange flame, the showering debris of metal and flesh and bone, as the nitroglycerin-filled cylinder detonated with a deafening boom and, for King Harold, Hizzoner, and God knows how many others, the Key to the City became the Key to the Kingdom of God.

But it didn't happen that way.

As if from outer space itself, there came a whizzing, whirling, singing thread of steel. As supple as a cowboy's riata, as swift as a line cast by an expert fisherman, its barbed end caught the ring at the end of the key and whipped it out of the Mayor's grasp. Like a hooked salmon, the silver object sailed over a thousand startled faces, and before they saw the fisherman himself, a caped figure straddling the top of a light stanchion, the concealed bomb did what bombs are meant to do. It exploded—but harmlessly, in midair.

Gordon's heart bounced between throat and chest as he saw Batman drop nimbly to the ground, already reeling in the Batwire that had saved so many lives.

But his mission wasn't completed. From his vantage point atop the stanchion, Batman had witnessed what the Commissioner himself had seen, the exchange between the tall "airline employee" and the Mayor's aide.

He had recognized that a switch of keys had taken place, and that the man who had casually boarded the small copter was the perpetrator.

The rotor blades were already turning, and they could see the deathly white mask of his face through the cockpit window, fixed as always in a diabolic grin that not even failure could wipe away. Even though his assassination was foiled, the Joker would soon be free to continue his career of malevolent mischief.

Batman didn't accept defeat so readily. He raced across the tarmac at Olympic speed, but the whirlybird was already beginning its ascent. For a moment, it looked as if Batman had lost him; but then they saw the steel lariat streaking forth once more, like a strand of lightning traveling from earth to sky. They didn't realize that its grappling hook had caught the tail wheel until they saw Batman lifted into the air, suspended from the copter like a performer in an aerial circus.

It may have been the shouts from below that alerted the pilot to his unwanted passenger. He leaned out and glared at Batman, his green hair blowing wildly in the wind.

It was only too obvious what he decided to do next. He headed the aircraft toward the control tower of Gotham Field. He was going to lose his dangling stowaway by crushing Batman against the tower.

His first pass failed as Batman wrapped his powerful legs about the wire and swayed away from danger. But on the ground below, a horrified Commissioner Gordon knew that the Clown Prince of Crime had gravity on his side. Sooner or later, he would smash his archenemy out of existence. Gordon almost wished he had never sent the message that brought Batman to this encounter.

The second pass against the tower was more successful for the Grinning Ghoul at the controls. Batman managed to avoid its full impact, but his side thudded against the structure with an impact that could be heard on the ground. They groaned for him and then gasped as they saw his grip on the wire loosen. Then they cheered as Batman managed to regain his hold.

The third pass would be the fatal one; that was obvious. It was also obvious that the Joker was enjoying this game. He took his time, circling the tower, dipping the copter lower so that there would be virtually no way for Batman to escape a full collision with the building. There would be only one alternative—to release his hold on the wire, and die an ignominious death on the ground.

There was a terrible, almost eerie silence among the crowd as the copter completed its circle and headed for the structure, and Batman's death.

Then Gordon realized something. *The Caped Crusader was no longer caped.*

The significance of the fact only became apparent when there was a strange, rendering, sputtering sound over their heads. And then Gordon understood. Batman had thrown his cape into the rotor blades, and the blades had found it indigestible. The rotors had slowed and then stopped, and the helicopter was beginning to spin out of control. Now gravity was no longer on the Joker's side.

It wasn't on Batman's side, either. But now that the Joker was no longer in control, Batman could take a desperate chance. He swung on the wire toward the control tower, and let go. When he landed on his feet, there was a roar from the crowd, but it wasn't loud enough to drown out the explosion that shook the ground when the copter fell to earth.

A thousand feet raced to the site of the crash, and a thousand eyes saw the broken body of the pilot amid the flames that began to consume it.

It was the ultimate punchline for the Joker.

Death.

Commissioner Gordon wasn't sure how long he had slept. He had fallen across his bed, fully-clothed, when there was still daylight in his window. Now there was darkness, and a strange glow in the room. Then he realized that Batman was there, silhouetted against the moon, waiting silently for the Commissioner to wake from his much-needed sleep.

"Batman!" he said. "I was hoping I could see you—"

"I knew you would have questions," Batman said.

"What I really have is gratitude. The whole city is grateful for what you did today!"

"I'm not here for my medal," the Caped Crusader said somberly. "There were too many lives lost while I was away."

"You can't be everywhere at once. And God knows it took us long enough to realize what was going on. But how did *you* find out? You had no briefing at all!"

"I did have a briefing—from my new supercomputer. While I was away, it recorded every crime committed in Gotham City, and searched them for relational factors. The computer reached its own conclusion, Commissioner, just as you did. That someone was playing a deadly prank involving a deck of cards."

"Then it must have also guessed the prankster," Gordon said. "It could only have been one man."

"Yes," Batman said. "That was only too obvious—except for one factor. The Joker's motive."

"We'll never know it now. He's taken the answer to his grave. But at least that Grinning Devil is in Hell where he belongs, and that's far more important."

"I believe I know the motive," Batman said quietly.

"You *do?* You mean your computer—"

"No," Batman said wryly. "That's one thing about computers—they don't think as deviously as Man. I realized the truth only when I applied an old legal question to every crime involved. *Who benefits?*"

"But—nobody really benefited. The crimes were senseless!"

"It was senseless to kill thirty-six musicians. It was senseless to kill four men named Jack, four 'queens' and four 'aces.' It was senseless to kill three self-styled 'kings.' But if King Harold of Lumidia had died, wouldn't his death have benefited one person? *His successor?*"

The Commissioner's jaw went slack.

"I don't understand, Batman! Why would the Joker care who ran that little country?"

"The Joker didn't care," Batman said grimly. "But King Harold's would-be successor cared. He especially cared about making sure that nobody—absolutely nobody—would guess that he had anything to do with the assassination of his 'beloved' monarch. . . ."

The blood rushed out of the Commissioner's head.

"Good Lord! Are you suggesting that all these crimes were meant to cover up *one* crime?"

"That's what I'm suggesting, Commissioner."

"And that it *wasn't* the Joker behind it? That the Joker was just being framed by this—would-be King?"

"His name is Herbert," Batman said. "He's Harold's cousin, his only living relative. Or rather, his deceased relative. Because it was Herbert's remains that were cremated in that helicopter crash this morning."

"Batman, are you sure?"

"Herbert had been in this country for the past four years, earning himself a graduate degree in political science and playing on the college's basketball team. He was also a skilled mechanic, an amateur pilot, and a crack marksman. He was six-feet-five, very clever, very ambitious, and completely ruthless.

"But how did you know? What made you guess the truth?"

"Once the idea occurred to me, it was simple enough to track Herbert's movements from the day of the first murders. He could be placed at the scene of almost every crime. But there was also something else. . . ."

"I know what it was," Commissioner Gordon said. "Something that even that supercomputer of yours doesn't have. It was your incredible intuition!"

"No," Batman smiled darkly. "It was something that occurred to me about Herbert's master plan. He was eliminating the entire deck of playing cards. But he forgot that every deck has *two* Jokers."

Museum Piece

Mike Resnick

CATALOG

Special JOKER Exhibition in the Batman Hall of the Gotham Museum

(CATALOG NOTES BY RICHARD GRAYSON, ESQ.)

Exhibit 1:

Lethal 10,000-volt "joy buzzer" with which the notorious Clown Prince of Crime dispatched five different people, including two members of his own gang.

Exhibit 1A:

Rubber gauntlets and thick-soled rubber boots created especially for the Batman by Reuben Kittlemeier (deceased). By allowing the Joker to think him unprepared and helpless, the Batman was able to get close enough to arrest him while the electric charge passed harmlessly through the safely grounded crime fighter.

Exhibit 2:

This was a two-headed coin (note that both heads are defaced) that the Joker had manufactured during the brief period of time that he allied himself with Two-Face, another criminal kingpin. Two-Face was known to always flip a coin when deciding between mercy and brutality, or even committing a crime versus obeying the law, and the Joker managed to plant this coin on Two-Face's person so that he would always elect to follow in the Joker's criminal footsteps.

Exhibit 2A:

This coin seems identical to the coin in Exhibit 2, but there is one vital difference: this coin, created by the Batman, is weighted so that, when flipped in the air, it will always land on its edge. The coin, which the Batman managed to substitute for the Joker's coin, so unnerved Two-Face that he turned upon his former ally, and during the confusion the police, under the leadership of Commissioner James Gordon, were able to capture both villains.

Exhibit 3:

This is the automatic pilot mechanism from the *Pagliacci,* a blimp that the Joker loaded with a deadly gas and aimed at the Thomas Wayne Memorial Stadium during the fourth quarter of the Gotham Bowl on New Year's Day.

Exhibit 3A:

This is a child's bow and hunting arrow with which the Batman improvised his last-second response to the Joker's threat. The blimp, struck in midair, dispersed its gas over the sea, and not a single member of the crowd of 75,000 was harmed.

Exhibit 4:

This normal-appearing fountain pen actually releases an ultrasonic blast that temporarily paralyzes its victim, and was used on the Batman when the Joker disguised himself as an autograph seeker.

Exhibit 4A:

This is a mask of the Joker's first known murder victim, which the Batman wore beneath his cowl as a safety measure during that period of time when the Joker publicly threatened to reveal his secret identity. When he was momentarily overcome by the ultrasonic fountain pen (Exhibit 4), it was this mask that the Joker revealed beneath the Batman's cowl. The shock of seeing his long-dead victim caused the Joker to go into a near-catatonic trance, a condition that persisted until hours after the Batman regained consciousness and returned his archenemy to Arkham Asylum.

Exhibit 5:

Remains of exploding baseball, capable of killing everyone within a radius of fifty feet, which the Joker substituted for the normal baseball that the mayor was supposed to throw out on Opening Day.

Exhibit 5A:

This is a chemically treated catcher's mitt that the Batman, disguised as the catcher for the Gotham Giants, used to muffle the explosion just prior to apprehending the Joker.

Exhibit 6:

This earthen jar holds the contaminant with which the Joker planned to poison Gotham City's water supply.

Exhibit 6A:

These eyebrows, blue-tinted contact lenses, false nose, and blond wig formed the disguise the Batman used to impersonate the Joker's henchman while substituting half a gallon of perfectly harmless Vitamin C for the contaminant.

Exhibit 7:

Clipping of hair, purportedly taken from Robin's head. The Joker, aware that Robin had been called out of town on a case while the Batman was otherwise occupied, used this in an attempt to entrap the Batman by convincing him that Robin was his prisoner.

Exhibit 7A:

Electron microscope with which the Batman analyzed the clipping in Exhibit 7, and proved that the hair came from a dog infested with a certain species of flea that could only come from Olson's Kennel on the shore of the Gotham River. He relayed this information to the police, who, led by Commissioner James Gordon, broke into the kennel and captured the Joker's entire gang.

Exhibit 8:

Coffin used by the Joker when he faked his own death to gain access to the North Gotham Mausoleum.

Exhibit 8A:

Sound detector with which the Batman detected the Joker's heartbeat in the mausoleum where the criminal's loot from the Gotham Diamond Exchange robbery was hidden.

Exhibit 9:

Juggling balls filled with knockout gas, which the Joker used during his attempt to steal more than $200,000 of gate receipts from the Gotham Circus.

Exhibit 9A:

False clown nose worn over breathing filter by the Batman, who masqueraded as a Gotham Circus clown to apprehend the Joker.

Exhibit 10:

This mounted snake is a rare South African variety whose poison leaves victims with a grotesque smile on their faces. This is not the actual snake used by the Joker, but is a member of the same species. (Courtesy of Gotham Museum of Natural History.)

Exhibit 10A:

"Trump," the mongoose that Batman borrowed from the Gotham Zoo to dispatch the Joker's killer snake. ("Trump" is on loan from the Gotham Zoo. Please do not feed him or insert fingers into his cage.)

Exhibit 11:

This is the phony television camera the Joker used when masquerading as a member of the media during an inaugural dinner for the mayor. The small red button on the left fires the handgun that is hidden beneath the lens.

Exhibit 11A:

The lens from the Joker's false television camera (see Exhibit 11). The Batman, suspecting just such an attack, had Robin sneak into the Joker's headquarters and replace the original lens with this specially treated lens, which distorts the user's perceptions and causes him to fire eighteen inches to the left of his target.

Exhibit 12:

Membership card to the exclusive Gotham Millionaires Club, made out to one Joe Ker. With this card, the Joker gained access to Gotham's richest men and women, whom he planned to hold for ransom.

Exhibit 12A:

Gold-plated honorary membership card to the Gotham Millionaires Club, offered to the Batman by unanimous vote of the membership after the Dark Knight had foiled the Joker's scheme. He declined membership, and donated the card to the Gotham Museum.

Exhibit 13:

This final exhibit is the cannister of lethal gas with which the Joker planned to kill himself after his most recent capture by the Batman.

Exhibit 13A:

Laughing-gas cannister substituted for Exhibit 13 by the Batman, which left the Joker laughing all the way to Arkham Asylum, where he currently resides. It is rumored that he is laughing still.

Balloons

Edward Wellen

CRACKLE ...r shot the ...
shattering ...plode in the priva...

High above the stippled green that was a forest, a press helicopter intercepted the wind-driven ten-story-tall balloon.

The cameraman in the chopper had a pasty face, scarlet lips fixed in a face-splitting grin, and Astro-turf hair. As the chopper closed in, he used a helium tank to inflate a sausage balloon. Then he held up the sausage balloon to show lettering on it that read: SAY "CHEESE."

In the basket of the ten-story-tall balloon, Roman A. Clay, the billionaire publisher famous for his partying, motorcycling, and ballooning, stepped between the two lovely models who formed his crew, put his arms around their bare midriffs, and smiled for the camcorder poking out of the chopper.

The cameraman snapped a special cube into his fill light and triggered it. Superlight blinded Clay and his crew.

They felt a thump and a jerk, but could see only a dazzle of benday dots. Slowly vision cleared, and revealed that a grappling iron now linked their basket to the chopper.

The cameraman held up another sausage balloon. This one said: JOKER TOWING SERVICE.

Roman A. Clay turned almost as pale as the cameraman. He was at the tender mercy of the notorious, the nefarious, Joker. His first thought was to unhook the grapnel, release the gas in the bag, and drop the balloon into the forest.

But the Joker had traded the camcorder for an Uzi. So Clay made no move toward the grapnel. His hand, however, inched toward his cellular phone.

The Joker saw the tycoon's hand edge below the bulwark of the basket. The Joker signed to his pilot and the chopper slanted higher to let the Joker look down into the basket.

CRACK! The Joker shot the phone out of Clay's hand, shattering the phone in the process. Bits of high-impact plastic stung Clay and his crew, drawing screams from all three.

The Joker held up another sausage balloon: NAUGHTY, NAUGHTY.

Clay sagged against the railing. He looked over and down. All below was forest. The Joker had chosen the intercept point well. No one had witnessed the air piracy, no one currently watched the chopper tug the captive free balloon at a good clip off course and *against* the wind. All hope of rescue faded from Clay's mind. When Clay's balloon failed to keep its ETA, searchers would hunt for it tens of miles from where it supposedly went down.

Needing comfort himself, he tried to comfort his crew as, under the crazy gaze of that weird face with its implacable fixed grin, the chopper towed the balloon toward the unknown.

Ten hours later, Roman A. Clay's staff at his Gotham City estate began to worry. And as the hours passed, the wire services started to chatter bulletins. The network anchor people impressively intoned these bulletins. Roman A. Clay's balloon had vanished without a trace on its way home from a state fair in Kansas.

In his hideout, not all that far from the Clay estate, a jauntily bereted and besmocked Joker sang ad-libbed doggerel as he mixed oil colors on his palette.

>"Sweet Turpentine.
>For you I pine.
>Sweet Turpitude,
>O'er you I brood."

He grinned at the blank canvas. "Ready or not, here I come!" And he attacked it, splashing and daubing away with savage glee and wild intensity, getting more spatters and dribbles on his smock than on the canvas.

>"Oh, my darling, oh, my darling,
>Oh, my darling Adrenaline.
>You jump-start me and keep me going,
>that is why my eyes have this shine."

Sudden inspiration hit him midstroke and his brush dribbled a largesse of red over the chest of his smock unheeded. His face split in two. "I'll throw that bat a curve!"

From his penthouse patio, Bruce Wayne swept the night horizon with his restless gaze. Northward, the suburbs spread out in a lacy tracery of lights; eastward, the stars melded with the bold carnival lights of Cockaigne Island Amusement Park; westward, the river netted moonlight; southward, the great ocean luminesced.

Beautiful, all of it, but a long siege of idleness left him bored.

A cacophony of car horns and police whistles rose from the street into his consciousness.

He stepped to his telescope.

It showed him gridlock all around the base of the Tempo Triangle Building, the world-renowned landmark at the throbbing heart of Gotham City. Traffic had stopped. Pedestrians crowded in from all sides, jamming Tempo Triangle. Everyone gaped at the building-girdling array of lights that spelled out the moving headlines.

Wayne sharpened his focus.

THE JOKER HOLDS ROMAN A. CLAY AND CREW
FOR RANSOM. DEMANDS ONE BILLION DOLLARS.
IN TOTO. THE JOKER CHALLENGES BATMAN TO
RESCUE CLAY BEFORE AUGUST 1 DEADLINE. ON
THE DOT.

The Joker! Wayne's blood quickened, fizzing like
champagne. Didn't give him much time. August first
was only a week away. Didn't give him much time. But
the more pressure the better. Made him push the envelope of his abilities. This was the challenge Batman had
unconsciously been waiting for and he felt alive and pur-
poseful and in command.

Wayne sprang to his direct-line speakerphone. Almost as though Commissioner Gordon had been awaiting the call, the commissioner answered on the first
ring.

"C.G. here."

"B.M. calling. I assume your people are trying to
track down the person responsible for flashing the
Tempo Triangle Building message about Roman A.
Clay."

"'Trying' is the operative word. The news bulletins
and the ads are fed into a computer that switches the
pixels on and off to make the message seem to move from
right to left. The Joker has managed somehow to access
the computer and impose *his* messages."

"I see."

"Er . . ."

"Yes?"

"You're taking up the gauntlet?"

"I just now said 'yes.'"

A deep sigh. "That's a relief. I'm in constant touch
with Clay's staff. They're preparing to convert his assets
to cash—just in case. Bad business, this. Could send the
stock market into a tailspin."

Wayne listened but kept watching. New words crept
around the Tempo Triangle Building.

CAN YOU LICK YOUR OZ IN A CAT AMOUNT,
PARD? SEE YOU THERE.

"Talk to you later, C.G.," Wayne said absently, and punched off without looking away from the message that was slipping around out of sight.

He waited for more, but the Joker, too, seemed to have punched off. The display resumed its normal town-crying of the world's calamities.

Wayne replayed in his mind what seemed to him the key message.

CAN YOU LICK YOUR OZ IN A CAT AMOUNT, PARD?

He knew the set phrase to be: *lick one's weight in wildcats.*

Oz. was the abbreviation for *ounces.* He turned to the unabridged dictionary. *Ounce* also meant the mountain panther *(catamount!)* or snow leopard *(pard!)*.

But the Joker had written it *OZ*, without the period, as in the Land of Oz. And TOTO (pointing to Dorothy's dog) and DOT (pointing to Dorothy) both confirmed that interpretation.

Yet, how could the Joker be waiting to confront him in the Land of Oz when there was no such place? Oz existed only in fantasy!

Wayne sat down with pencil and paper. He set his mind in neutral and began doodling, letting the pencil tune into his subconscious.

OZ.

The Wizard of Oz by Lyman Frank Baum.

Baum—tree.

Can't see the forest for the trees.

Then, with OZ as his starting point, he found himself working both ways from it, upward and downward, in alphabetical order:

                    LW
                    MX
                    NY
                    OZ
                    PA
                    QB
                    RC

He stopped and focused on:

OZ
PA

Had Baum's Pa been the basis for the Wizard of Oz?

He shook his head. He was getting sidetracked. He widened his focus:

NY
OZ
PA

Sensing with rising excitement that he was on the right track, he reached for the atlas. He turned to the maps of the several states and studied the New York-Pennsylvania boundary. He found lots of trees and a Cat.

With a tight smile, he pressed the redial key on the direct-line speakerphone.

"C.G. here."

"B.M. again. I think you can tell the searchers to narrow the search to Cattaraugus County, right on the New York-Pennsylvania border, where New York's Alleghany State Park adjoins Pennsylvania's Alleghany Reservoir."

"How—?"

"Please just do it. I'll explain some other time."

Click.

As the hours passed, Wayne felt less and less sure of his deduction. When at last the phone rang, he turned to listen with an attitude more of bracing himself for bad news than of eagering himself for good news.

"C.G. speaking. Just as you predicted, B.M. A ground party searching the forests of Cattaraugus County came upon the basket and the deflated bag of the missing balloon. But no signs of the balloonists."

Wayne's satisfaction in having read above and below the Joker's lines—for that after all was the relationship of NY and PA to OZ—was fleeting. His face set grimly. "It was hardly to be expected that the Joker would abandon his captives after taking the trouble to snatch them."

"I guess not." A pause, then, "The Joker left a note for you, pinned to the bag."

"Read it to me, please."

"'Frankly, would I Ly, man?'" C.G. spelled out the *Ly, man.* "Do you know what he means by that?"

Wayne explained about Oz and Lyman Frank Baum.

"Oh."

Wayne smiled crookedly. "Well, at least we now know one thing."

"What's that?" C.G. asked eagerly.

"We know the one place where Clay and his crew are not."

Sound filtered down: the tread of many feet on boards, the cries of pitchmen, the squawk of sea gulls, the notes of steam whistles. The Joker felt restless. He gave his slight paunch a pat of disapproval and looked around at his henchpersons (he was an equal opportunity employer) with even greater disfavor. They were lounging and slouching altogether too comfortably in the dayroom of the hideout.

"Jane Fonda time."

Groans rose, only to subside in wave fashion as his maniacal gaze swept around, dipping to take in a rugged dwarf. Behind the fixed grin, the Joker frowned thoughtfully when his eyes rested briefly on his right-hand man Leo. They had not yet begun exercising; why would Leo be already in a sweat? Guilty conscience? The Joker programmed himself to watch Leo from here on out.

At the moment, however, on with the pep talk. "Let me remind you, the Clay kidnap is the least of our planned exploits. While the forces of"—he raised his hands to claw a pair of two-finger quotation marks in the air around the word *good*—"*good* believe we're just sitting on our behinds, waiting to collect the ransom, we'll be out there pulling other capers."

There came a hearty chorus of "Yeah, yeah!"

"So, what say, let's get in shape."

There came a muted chorus of "Yeah, yeah."

He cupped a hand behind an ear and said in a mild, questioning tone, "I don't *hear* you."

Leo led the roar of "Yeah, yeah."

They knew what to do. They moved the varsity-crew rowing machine out from the wall and took their places on the sliding seats.

"Okay, Metrognome."

The dwarf squatted at the coxswain's post and beat time on bongo drums.

The Joker himself stood alongside with a whip, cracking it to encourage the oarsmen and oarswomen at their sweeps. Occasionally the lash drew blood.

"Building up the old lats and pecs," he heartened them.

After the exercise period, Leo had so stiffened that he could hardly move and he breathed laboredly through his crooked nose. The Joker, however, though his face remained pasty, felt the glow of invigoration and was raring to go.

He and Leo left the hideout, and while Leo chauffered him in a Good Humor truck to a real estate office in Gotham, the Joker changed in the back, making himself up carefully in a three-piece suit to pass as a businessman.

Putting cash down, the Joker signed a long-term lease for an office suite of his choice in the financial district's ultramodern Phoebus Building. Within hours, his henchpersons had moved packing cases of equipment in.

By evening they were all set to pull the caper.

"But first to twist Batman's ears," the Joker said. And he punched a command into his computer, sending a signal to the program that ran the bulletin lights girdling the Tempo Triangle Building.

That done, he swiveled around to find Leo biting Metrognome's nails to the quick.

"What makes you so nervous, Leo?" he asked kindly.

Leo's voice came out scratchy with fear. "Boss, is it really a good idea to tip your hand?"

"Why not, when I hold all the aces?"

Leo had no answer for that; even if he had he wouldn't have dared voice it.

Bruce Wayne burned the message into his brain.

FACE-TO-FACE IN YE OLDE FUN MIRROR

He had no doubt it was from the Joker to him.

He waited for more, but the regular flow of news flashes resumed.

POWER BLACKOUT AT PHOEBUS BUILDING . . . TON OF COCAINE STOLEN FROM POLICE PROPERTY CLERK VAULT. FLOOR COLLAPSES; WHEN DUST SETTLES, POLICE DISCOVER HUGE HAUL SEIZED AND HELD FOR EVIDENCE HAS VANISHED ALONG WITH OTHER GOODIES . . . POWER RESTORED TO PHOEBUS BUILDING . . .

These he paid little heed to. They might command his attention later, but right now he needed to concentrate on the message and decode its meaning and purpose:

FACE-TO-FACE IN YE OLDE FUN MIRROR

The obvious thing to note was the "ye olde." Why this anachronistic form in an otherwise straightforward phrase?

What if it signaled a further anachronism in what followed? What if the *f* in "fun" were really the old form of *s*?

That would make it a *sun mirror*.

The bulletins he had ignored flashed to the forefront of his thinking. And all at once everything tied in.

The Police Property Clerk's Office, a one-story annex of Police Headquarters, stood in the shadow of the Phoebus Building. The Phoebus Building's solar panels, a solid array sheathing the slanted roof and the whole facade, generated more than enough power to service the Phoebus Building's needs; surplus energy went to Pro Edison, generating a nice profit.

Wayne swung to gaze at the Phoebus Building. At this hour of the evening, it thrust up like a dark finger with a light dusting of windowshine from nearby buildings. By day, the monolithic Phoebus Building would be one great glaring sun mirror.

* * *

Batman swung the Batmobile into the Phoebus Building's parking lot. At the one break in the solar paneling, the glass street-level entrance of the Phoebus Building, the nightman recognized him and buzzed him in.

"Batman! Who are you looking for?"

"Good question." Batman scanned the wall directory. His eyes lit up.

Joseph Kerr.

It was a short mental leap from that to *Joe Kerr* to then to *Joker.*

"Which elevator to Joseph Kerr and Company, on the eighty-sixth floor?"

The nightman took him up. As they rode, the nightman said, "I sure hope the power doesn't cut off again. It did, for about ten minutes, an hour ago."

Batman nodded. "I heard. I doubt that it will happen again."

His nostrils worked, smelling burnt wiring and cindered circuitry, even before the nightman had unlocked the door to the darkened suite.

The nightman flicked the lights on. His jaw dropped. "What did they do to the place?"

"What indeed."

A laser gun stood atop a desk shoved against the wall. The barrel poked through the wall. Batman's nose wrinkled. The laser gun smelled burnt out, as did its cable, which was plugged into an outlet.

Batman stepped lightly onto the desk and held his hands behind his back to keep from disturbing the gun's angle.

The Joker had punched a hole through the outer wall and through the solar paneling.

Batman peered through the gunsight. He stared down, down, down at the police annex. The crosshairs quartered a hole in the annex roof. At first glance, it appeared as though a giant drill had drawn a huge core sample up and out of the annex.

But what had happened, Batman saw, was that the laser beam had sliced through in an oval. The Joker had made the cut at a carefully calculated slant. The disk cut out of the roof landed on the ground floor to one side of the pallets holding the ton of cocaine. The disk cut out of the ground floor landed, with its precious burden, in— Batman shrewdly guessed—the open body of a truck waiting in the basement garage.

Batman rode down in grim silence with the nightman.

The nightman called after him. "Don't you want me to validate your parking?"

Batman shook his head without breaking stride.

In the corner of his eye Leo caught the Joker entering the room.

"Faster!" Leo barked at the assembly line.

The dust-masked crew stepped up its repackaging of the ton of cocaine.

Leo turned and feigned a start of surprise.

The Joker stretched his grin. "That's right, Leo, let me disturb you."

He looked at one of the new glassine packets labeled with the Joker brand name and with a saxophone *J* as logo. He gave a nod of approval. "I've just looked in on our guest. It's a broadening experience for Mr. Roman A. Clay."

The Joker's eyes glittered and he rubbed his hands together. "Speaking of broads, let's join the ladies, shall we?"

Leo shivered, but turned the supervising over to Metrognome, an even sterner taskmaster than Leo, and followed the Joker out.

Dr. Amicia Sollis was dining with Bruce Wayne out on the patio of his penthouse when the Joker's next message flashed.

CHASE YOURSELF ON THE LOOP-THE-LOOP

Alfred his butler called their attention to it, and Amicia joined Bruce at the telescope.

"Another challenge to Batman?" she asked.

He shrugged. "Perhaps."

"I wonder what Batman makes of it—that is, if he's watching at all."

"Oh, he's watching."

Amicia cocked an eye at him but said nothing.

"That's his job," he hurried to add. He grew thoughtful. "As to what he makes of it—well, what is there to make of it? We all know what a loop-the-loop is—a centrifugal railway."

"But we also all know that the Joker is not that simple." She frowned. "Could he be hinting that he's transferring his activities to Second City?"

Wayne looked jolted. "Because of the Loop, the elevated railway ringing Second City's business district?"

"Exactly."

Wayne felt a sudden emptiness. If it were true that the Joker was leaving Gotham to take up in Second City, that would remove the Joker from Batman's reach. Rather, for Batman would never falter in his grim pursuit of the Grin Reaper, it would force Batman far from his base of operations.

"Can't you think of any other possibilities?"

Amicia smiled. "Sure. Off the top of my head, *loop* could refer to one of the identifying characteristics— loops, arches, and whorls—that a fingerprint expert looks for; *loop* could mean the platinum bent at one end into a loop that a bacteriologist uses to transfer microorganisms with; *loop* could stand for the aerial maneuver of a stunt pilot." She shrugged. "Or it could be none of the above. With the Joker's crazy sense of humor, it could be a play on *loupe*—l-o-u-p-e."

Wayne narrowed his eyes. "The magnifying glass that a jeweler uses to examine gems?"

"Exactly." She stared at him. "You don't think—"

"I do. What more lucrative caper than a heist at the midtown Emerald Center? I'll bet that's next on his hit list." He moved to the phone. "I'll tell Commissioner Gordon my hunch and let him pass it along to Batman."

Amicia's eyes shone. "You and Batman make a good team—the man of thought and the man of action."

"Thanks." Wayne smiled as he went to the phone, but it was a twisted smile. He sensed that Amicia's eyes shone at the thought of the man of action. "I think I speak for Batman when I say you can consider yourself part of the team."

With Amicia present, the direct-line phone was out of sight. He picked up the everyday phone and dialed.

The Joker peered from around the corner of the block. The coast looked clear. Rush-hour traffic was long gone. The fire truck idling behind him would have clear passage to the tall building housing the Emerald Center. He eyed the green neon sign over the entrance to the great conglomeration of offices and stores devoted to emeralds and other gems:

EMERALD CENTER

He stretched his grin. "The center of EMERALD is *R. Are* you ready?"

Leo and Metrognome and the others chorused, "Ready when you are, Boss."

"Then let's go." He pumped his arm up and down to signal the driver of the fire truck. And as the truck swept by him around the corner, he hopped aboard. Like all the others, he wore full fireman's gear, but his badge read *Deputy Fire Inspector*.

The fire truck stopped directly in front of the Emerald Center and the Joker hopped off. He rang the doorbell.

He looked through the glass door and watched the nightguard hurry from a desk near the bank of elevators.

The guard stopped just inside the door and looked at the Joker questioningly.

The Joker shaped words with his lips without actually saying anything.

The guard strained to listen, but heard nothing.

The Joker again lip-synced silence.

In total frustration, the guard unlocked the door and poked his head out.

The Joker spoke boredly, as if this were all in a long day's work. "Surprise inspection. As you know, we spring these at random."

The guard did not say he didn't know. But then, he did not say anything. The Joker's hand clamped the guard's face.

The Joker nodded. "You guessed it. Lucky you, it's your turn." The Joker shoved the nightguard backward and stepped inside.

The other pseudofirepersons trooped in after him, a pair pausing to bind and gag the nightguard.

Two guards on duty in the building's security control room watched it all on the bank of monitors.

"Do you see this, Darrell?" Without taking his gaze from the screen, he reached toward the button that would alert police headquarters.

"I see it, Harvey." And as he spoke, Darrell grabbed Harvey's wrist.

Harvey turned his head and found himself looking into the mouth of the pistol in Darrell's other hand. "What—!"

Pulling Harvey by the trapped hand, Darrell swung him, castered chair and all, away from the control panel. Then he let go of Harvey, but covered him with the gun while they watched the screen showing the deputy fire inspector advance toward the control room.

Eyes and gun never leaving Harvey, Darrell buzzed the door open for the figure in the tailored fallout suit.

The Joker entered and took in the tableau. "Ah! All as it should be in the control room. Everything under control." Then he snapped his fingers and held out his hand to Darrell.

Darrell reached his free hand into his breast pocket and drew out a master key and a piece of paper filled with numbers. The Joker took them without stepping into the line of fire.

"All there, Boss. Got the last one just this afternoon, on one of the minivids I planted to tape the jewelers working their vault combinations."

The Joker said pleasantly, "That's right, tell all our secrets to our friend here."

Darrell reddened, then paled.

Moving smoothly, still staying out of the line of fire, the Joker slipped Harvey's pistol from its holster, then stepped back and held it idly. "Just to keep him from doing something foolish."

The two of them looked at Harvey while discussing him.

"Think he'd zip his lip if we cut him in?"

Darrell studied Harvey's sweaty face and imploring eyes. "I'm not sure."

"Then don't you think you'd better make sure?"

Darrell visibly nerved himself, then plugged Harvey between the eyes.

"Did you hit the master switch to shut off all the alarms?"

The Joker's question broke Darrell out of a trance. Darrell shook himself. "Haven't had a chance yet."

"Now's your chance."

Darrell moved jerkily to a switch and hit it. He turned to the Joker with a feverish smile. "Now you're all set."

"Not quite."

Darrell looked puzzled.

The Joker brought Harvey's gun up and plugged Darrell between the eyes. "I advised you to make sure. I like to practice what I preach."

He kicked each body to make sure no life stirred, then pressed Harvey's gun into Harvey's hand and left to get on with the heist.

The Joker and his crew rode to the top floor. Metrognome ran ahead opening doors with the master key and wedging them ajar, then wedged the stairwell door open and moved down to the next floor to do the same . . . all the long way to the ground floor. In one office, Leo found a copying machine and made copies of the list of combinations. These he distributed to the others, who split into teams and opened vaults and poured out all the gems onto the floor. Last came the hose team, who lifted down the pleated hose on the hallway fire stanchion and stretched it and turned on the water and sluiced the glittering litter out of the offices and down the hallway to the stairwell and waterblasted it all down.

So it went, the gems pouring into a great sieve Metrognome set up at the very bottom of the stairway. Every so often he had to scoop out buckets of gems and carry them out and dump them into the false body of the fire truck.

Finally, they were done; they were all on the ground floor, emptying the last of the gems from the sieve. Not quite done; before they left the thoroughly looted Emerald Center, the Joker turned Metrognome upside down to shake emeralds from his pockets.

As the fire truck pulled around the corner, Leo, acting as tillerman, had a bad shock. His last look back had shown him the Batmobile whizzing to a stop at the Emerald Center's entrance. Evidently Batman had just missed glimpsing the fire truck, or had not as yet made the connection, for there was no immediate pursuit and they made a clean getaway. But the close call left Leo shaken.

Dr. Amicia Sollis tried to console Bruce Wayne. "Don't blame yourself, Bruce. It's Batman's fault they got away. If only he had responded to word of your hunch sooner . . ."

It did comfort him that Amicia faulted not him but the man of action. But he did blame himself. If only he had slipped away from Amicia on some pretext, changed immediately to Batman without going through the rigmarole of getting Commissioner Gordon to get in touch with Batman, he might have reached the Emerald Center in time to foil the Joker. Instead, the Joker had made a mockery of him, stolen billions in gems, and left two good men dead.

"Listen to what just came in over the tips hotline, B.M., and see what you make of it." Commissioner Gordon played a tape recording over the direct line to Batman.

A hoarse, muffled voice said, "If a guy who could hand you the Joker was ready to deal for witness protection, would you—uh-oh." Then, more loudly, "Well, if a half hour is the fastest you can deliver a pizza, forget it." The sound of a phone slamming down. And that was it.

"Well, B.M.?"

Batman smiled grimly. "Sounds to me as if the subject

of the tip walked in on the tipster. Let's hope the Joker didn't hear him and he lives to call again."

"Exactly our thought."

"Sorry I can't be more helpful, C.G."

"Maybe next time."

"Maybe next time," Batman echoed.

The Joker put an arm around Leo's shoulder and grew fondly reminiscent, his eyes focusing on a time in the past.

"Once, years ago, this surly waiter slighted me, gave me really abominable service. Yet, when it came time to tip him, I pressed a G-note into his hand and closed his fingers on the money. Oh, what a lovely smile cracked his face as he bowed me out. Of course, when he opened his hot little hand after I had gone, it was empty. Same applies to Batman. He may come closer and closer till he thinks he has me in the hollow of his hand, but when he opens his hand I'm not there."

"You said a mouthful, Boss."

The Joker turned his grin on Leo. "Leo, let's go for a ride." He felt Leo stiffen under his enfolding arm, and from Leo there came the gurgling of stomach acid. The Joker gave him a reassuring pat. "For pizza, of course. What else?"

The moving sign around the Tempo Triangle Building carried a new unauthorized and unpaid-for message:

SHOT HAS HIS NUMBER ON IT: 037

Bruce Wayne scratched his head. He felt sure Joker meant the message for Batman's eyes—but what person did *his* refer to?

Did *037* tie in with Roman A. Clay in any way?

He passed the buck to his subconscious while he shaved for a dinner date with Amicia. Then, as he stared in the mirror, razor poised, he found himself mentally turning *037* over into its mirror image: *LEO*.

That could not refer to Batman; the Joker had no way

of knowing Batman's birth sign—and in any case, Wayne was a Gemini. Nor could it refer to Clay; Wayne had flown out to Clay's big birthday bash last April, which made Clay an Aries.

Again he bucked it to his subconscious. And again he froze midstroke.

Leo and *shot* meshed in his mind. *Leo* meant *lion*, and when the Gotham Zoo had built a modern cageless replica of the veldt, the abandoned old lion house had become a shooting gallery where addicts smoked crack and freebased cocaine.

He reached for the everyday phone to bring dilettante Bruce Wayne's deductions to Commissioner Gordon's attention, that Gordon might pass it on to Batman. He stopped himself. He would not make the same mistake twice. This time, no rigmarole. He wiped shaving foam from his face and transformed himself at once into the man of action.

Over his shoulder he told his gentleman's gentleman Alfred to convey Bruce Wayne's regrets to Dr. Amicia Sollis. Batman made for the Batmobile.

Too early? Or too late?

The place seemed deserted. Something had scared the regulars away.

Then his gaze picked out of the shadows their vile leavings—empty crack vials and reused needles, like medical waste washed up on one of Gotham's beaches. There was no smell of lion, there was smell of evil.

Not too early. Too late.

What at first seemed a black plastic bag of cans salvaged for refund proved a body.

Lightly, lest a secreted needle prick his finger, Batman frisked the body. Carefully, he fished out a wallet.

His penlight picked out a driver's license photo that matched the corpse's crooked-nosed face. The license gave the man a name: Larsen E. Oliphant.

LEO.

Batman did not know why, but he felt certain he had heard this man's voice on Gordon's tape. There was no way of proving that. One day, perhaps, forensics would be able to make a corpse's vocal cords tell how they sounded in life. But now the voice was still and the message forever untold. Batman shook his head.

Commissioner Gordon passed the autopsy results on to Batman.

"The man had a long record. It ground to a halt with a bad needle."

"You're saying he OD'd on cocaine?"

"That I am."

"Thanks, C.G."

"Any ideas, B.M.?"

"I'm thinking about cocaine."

"The Property Office heist?"

"That—and the word *cocaine* itself."

He rang off before Gordon could question him about what he had not yet gotten a good handle on.

JOKER TO BATMAN: LET'S SCHMOOZE

In spite of himself, Bruce Wayne almost laughed. But the Joker's jokes had a way of turning dead serious—with the emphasis on dead. So Wayne gave the message crawling around the Tempo Triangle Building serious consideration.

To schmooze was slang for to gossip or to chat. Schmoozing required a time and a place. Where and when were the Joker and Batman to meet for their schmooze?

Time weighed on Wayne's mind. Midnight tomorrow was the Joker's deadline for the ransoming of Roman A. Clay and the two models. According to Gordon, the billion dollars in cash had been raised and sat awaiting instructions for the drop. Could the "schmooze" be the Joker's way of calling for a meet to establish the conditions for the drop? Was Batman to be the intermediary? Or did the Joker hope to keep him on the sidelines by leading him to believe he would be the intermediary—while quite other measures went forward?

Wayne set his jaw. Batman would not be sidelined. He would go about his business. If the Joker wanted to "schmooze," the Joker would have to be more forthcoming with the particulars of where and when.

Amicia was secure enough in her own selfhood and sense of worth that she did not lay guilt on Bruce. She understood. She would have expected *him* to understand if circumstances had compelled *her* to break a date.

So they met again without strain—though a curious smile played around her lips as he wasted no time in picking her brains.

"What do fun mirror, loop the loop, and shooting gallery add up to?"

"Amusement park," she said, squeezing lemon into her tea.

"And with a ton of cocaine on the loose, what amusement park do you think of?"

"Cockaigne Island," she said, stirring in two spoonfuls of sugar.

"What can you tell me about Cockaigne?"

"On hot summer days, a million Gothamites head for the two-mile strip of beach and boardwalk, because it's jampacked with funhouses, bathhouses, freak shows, roller coasters, hotdog stands, and amusements of all kinds."

"I meant, what can you tell me about the original Cockaigne?"

She arranged her thoughts. "The notion of The Land of Cockaigne, or Cockayne"—she gave him both spellings—"goes back to a thirteenth-century French poem. Scholars link the name to the Latin word *coquere,* from a word meaning 'cake,' so that 'The Land of Cockaigne' means 'The Land of Cakes.' It's a fantasy place, a land of plenty, where the rivers ran with wine, the houses were made of gingerbread and barley sugar, the streets were paved with pastry, and shops charged nothing for their goods. Buttered larks fell from the sky and roast fowl walked around, like Li'l Abner's shmoos, begging to be eaten—"

They looked at one another.

LET'S SCHMOOZE.

A chill traveled Wayne's spine. Joker was inviting him to Cockaigne Island Amusement Park. Wayne smiled grimly. Well, they would see which one was the shmoo.

The Joker was testing his skill at the shooting gallery booth on the boardwalk. He knocked down every duck as it passed. Then he took out a hand mirror, pointed the rifle backward over his shoulder, and popped the toy balloons of a kid strolling by behind him.

The kid cried.

The Joker giggled. Then for a fleeting instant a lost look came into his eyes. "I was once that little kid." Then he giggled again and the lost look was as if it had never been.

He glanced across at the photo booth. On sudden impulse, he said, "I'm feeling sentimental. I'd like a group photo as a souvenir. We won't have time later—we'll be too busy collecting the ransom, and then right after that we'll be splitting up. So let's take it now."

The Joker and Gang crowded into the tiny booth for a group photo. Then, yielding to the clamor of his henchpersons, the Joker posed alone for a portrait.

He settled himself, reached out to the button, then shook his head. "No, that's my good side." He faced the other way, *then* pressed the button.

An hour before midnight, a salt wind blew in from the darkening sea. Taking over as people drifted toward the subway entrances and bus stops, sea gulls and pigeons marched and countermarched upon the damp boardwalk, pecking up crumbs of popcorn and taffy and cotton candy. A few diehard loners and couples patronized the attractions or huddled on benches. To the one or two people who noticed Batman at all, he was only another shadow.

The Joker, however, wore infragoggles and spotted Batman upon his arrival at the amusement park. The infragoggles let him follow Batman's movements easily.

From his vantage point atop the loop the loop, where he was making last-minute adjustments, the Joker gave Metrognome the high sign.

Metrognome, got up as a Gypsy fortune-teller, beckoned Batman into the tentlike booth emblazoned MME DIVINA REVEALS YOUR FATE.

Batman entered warily and quickly pierced the fortune-teller disguise. When he had untied and ungagged the Emerald Center nightguard the man had told him one of the assailants was a dwarf fireman. Batman waved away a palm reading.

"Do you have a message for me from the Joker?"

The phony fortune-teller took the joker from a deck of cards and handed it to Batman.

Batman had to bring the card near the hanging light bulb to make out the handwritten message on the face of the card.

MEET YOU IN THE MIDDLE OF NOWHERE.

He turned to ask the fortune-teller what that meant but the fortune-teller had slipped out the back.

Batman left the booth—and bumped into Dr. Amicia Sollis.

"Batman!"

"Amicia!"

"You know me?"

Batman quickly recovered. "You're Bruce Wayne's friend." He looked around. "Is he here with you?"

"No, but I suspect he's somewhere about. At least, this is where I think he dashed off to."

"What are you doing here?"

"I wasn't about to let you two have all the fun."

"It could be dangerous."

"Isn't that what this place is all about? Danger is part of the fun."

Under his mask Batman made a face but he said nothing.

A calliope started up near the entrance to the Tunnel of Love.

Amicia cocked her head. "That's odd. Why would that start up when nearly everything else is closing down?"

Batman nodded absently. "Interesting, but I have a more pressing puzzle." He showed her the joker bearing the message MEET YOU IN THE MIDDLE OF NO-WHERE.

Amicia nodded absently. "Interesting, but the calliope is very suggestive. In Greek myth, Calliope, meaning 'Beautiful Voice,' was Orpheus's mother. You'll remember that Orpheus went down to Hades to bring his dead wife Eurydice back from the grave. He won Pluto over by playing the lyre, and Pluto let Eurydice follow him out as long as he didn't turn around till he reached the surface. But at the last instant he looked back to make sure she was right behind him—and she became a ghost again."

"Um," Batman said distractedly. His glance had fallen on a pitch still open across the way. It was one in which the sucker paid to toss small footballs through miniature goalposts.

His eyes lit up. "Of course! The middle of NOWHERE is *H*!"

He strode toward the football-tossing booth and heard Amicia's hasty heels behind him on the boardwalk.

The pitchman held out a pair of little footballs. "The dashing gentleman and the fair lady wish to try their skill? Ten throws for a dollar."

Batman snorted. "Skill!" He said over his shoulder to Amicia, "It's supposed to be a test of skill, but it's really a grift. The sucker has no chance to win the tawdry merchandise offered as prizes." He leaned over and reached below the counter. "See, the gaff is a hidden lever that narrows the goalposts so the football can't pass through." He worked the lever several times, then straightened and turned to confront the pitchman and modestly accept Amicia's plaudits and then get on with the business of meeting the Joker.

But they were gone. He just caught sight of the man hurrying Amicia into the Tunnel of Love.

The calliope stepped up its steam-whistle melody as if to keep pace with Batman's heart. By the time he reached the Tunnel of Love, the train of swan cars was already vanishing into the tunnel. Batman just made the last car.

Before the train took a curve, he made out the only others aboard—a silhouetted couple in the lead car. He recognized Amicia's profile, and now had recognized the man's.

The Joker!

As he caught sight of them again on the straight-aways, they seemed a pair of lovebirds, and he felt something like jealousy. But quickly he told himself their closeness was one enforced by the Joker.

Batman made his way over the swaying jouncing cars toward the front of the train.

Just as he set himself to pounce on the Joker, the lights went out and the train slowed.

When they came on again, the Joker was gone and the train picked up speed.

Batman climbed in beside Amicia.

"Are you all right?"

Her eyes shone, and when she spoke he was glad to see it was with excitement rather than fear. "Yes! Where did he go to?"

Before Batman could answer, the train gave a lurch and they were in darkness again.

"I think the Joker's switched us onto another track," he said when he got his breath back.

"Then that was really the Joker?"

"Yes. I should've known better back at the football pitch. That's where we were supposed to schmooze. But he saw you with me and was quick to take advantage. Now I have you to look out for."

"Don't worry about me. I can take care of myself."

Another lurch ended the argument. The train swerved into a lighted patch.

He saw a row of wooden duck cutouts off to one side of the track and it hit him that the swan train was heading through the shooting gallery. He and Amicia were to be targets.

Just in time he winged out his bulletproof cape, shielding the two of them from the Joker's deadly marksmanship. They rode through the fire, Amicia none the worse for the ordeal, Batman sustaining bruises from bullet impact.

But the ordeal was not over. The train picked up speed again, making it too dangerous to jump off even if the narrow tunnel had permitted. They had perforce to ride on.

Again, a lurch. They had not long to wonder what track the Joker had switched them onto. The train broke out into the open and they found themselves heading upward.

They were on the Loop the Loop.

Batman was all too aware that they were not belted in or harnessed. But centrifugal force should carry them safely through the overhead curve. Unless the Joker slowed or stalled the train at the top. Batman prepared himself for that eventuality.

He drew the hook-end of his coiled steel line from his belt and held it ready, giving himself lots of slack. He was aware of Amicia watching him and he spoke honestly to her. "I think the Joker means to pull another one on us. Put your arms around my neck."

"This isn't the Tunnel of Love," Amicia said. She gave a forced laugh. "Sorry, I'm just trying for lightness. I'll hang on."

She locked her arms around his neck. He sensed she was trying to keep it from being a choke hold.

He craned to see ahead and spotted the block the Joker had put across the rails at the very top. Just before the car hit the block, Batman swung the hook at a crosstie. He had only one shot at it, so it had to be good.

It seemed to catch and he had no choice but to act on the belief that it had caught. He thrust himself and Amicia out and away from the swan car. By the time they swung back the car had plummeted past them. He lowered them more slowly to the ground.

While he unhooked himself from the line, Amicia loosened her clutch to stand on her wobbly own. As much to keep her from dwelling on the death they had escaped and get her out of more harm's way as to summon help, he asked her to find a phone and bring Commissioner Gordon up to date. Gordon would know what to do.

Alone, he went to track the Joker to his lair.

By now, the boardwalk was for the most part dark. Everyone, even the gulls and pigeons, had gone. But one attraction remained lit: the funhouse with its sideshow.

"Step right up, friend," the barker said. He tore a ticket off a coil. "This one's on the funhouse."

The Joker.

Batman recognized him even though he had disguised himself once more.

"Joker, you'll have to answer for what you did."

"What I did is a question?"

Batman longed to wipe the smirk off the Joker's face. But before Batman could move to capture him, before the Annie Oakley wafted to the ground, the Joker had backflipped from his stand and vanished inside.

Batman followed swiftly, looking out for traps.

He strode past the human oddities on display, glancing at them only just enough to make sure none was the Joker in disguise. He knew the fat man and the Siamese twins had put themselves on show, still he did not like to stare.

He had to stare at the bat with a human head that confronted him—then saw it was himself made squat in a mirror. He had come to an array of fun mirrors that formed a dead end.

Yet the Joker had passed this way. At least one of the mirrors had to be a door.

"Batman!"

Amicia's voice, outside. He turned from the mirrors and dashed past the sideshow to the entrance.

"What is it?"

"Oh, there you are. The commissioner has already sealed off the boardwalk. But he says he can't move his SWAT teams in as long as the Joker holds Clay and the two women as trump cards."

"I understand. It's just as well. This is between Batman and the Joker, and I don't want innocent blood shed. But it goes against my grain to let him get away with the ransom, the cocaine, and the jewels. If only I could locate and free the hostages . . ."

He turned to look within. This time he let his gaze linger on the human oddities. Even if they did not find *him* something out of the ordinary, it seemed very strange that they had not reacted at all to what had been happening under their eyes.

They stood hardly moving, eyes open but unfocused. Now that he took a good look at them he saw they were drugged.

He saw more. The fat man was not a simple fat man. His banner said BALLOON MAN. And the Siamese twins were lovely enough to be models.

Batman sprang onto the platform. Close up, the features islanded in the moon face were Roman A. Clay's. The Joker had dosed him with steroids and pumped him full of silicone. The models, if Batman had to guess, were joined by Crazy Glue.

He called down to Amicia. "Get back to Gordon. Tell him to send ambulances. We have the hostages. I'll stand guard here till help arrives."

She stared a moment while it dawned on her, then turned and ran.

After medics had taken Clay and the models away, Gordon was ready to move his people in.

But Batman stopped him. "Please keep everyone away. This is between Batman and the Joker."

Gordon hesitated, then nodded. "As you wish. You've earned the right." He took Amicia's arm and gently led her out of the funhouse.

Batman waited a moment, then drew a deep breath and moved to the mirrors.

The first he tested gave to his touch. It pivoted, and he slid through a space.

And found the Joker's loot.

Boxes of packaged cocaine labeled Cotton Candy and crates of jewels labeled Ice Cream.

But no Joker.

Batman searched the place, though there seemed no space for the Joker to be hiding in.

Somehow, the Joker had found a way out.

On one wall hung a gaudy painting signed Joker. In spite of himself, Batman had to admire the Joker's artistry. Batman looked more closely at the abstract painting. It wasn't a canvas. The Joker had framed his paint-spattered smock. Batman had to smile.

All business again, Batman swung the frame away from the wall. An opening, the Joker's way out. With a grimace, Batman let the frame swing back into place.

He tensed, sensing movement behind him.

A mirror was pivoting and a figure was trying to slip out. Incredibly, the Joker *had* been hiding in here all along. For some reason, now that he had all but made his getaway, he had got stuck in the doorway.

Batman said, "Not so fast."

The figure remained helplessly reflected in the mirror.

The Joker, all right.

But when Batman moved in to collar him, he was not the Joker. He was a dwarf made up as the Joker and elongated by the fun mirror.

"I'm not the Joker, I'm not the Joker," he screeched. "I'm Metrognome. The Joker got away. I only wanted a few jewels."

And it was the jewels, more than a few, that had trapped him in the doorway, for his pockets bulged with them.

The Joker had escaped.

Maybe next time.

Jangletown

Elizabeth Hand and Paul Witcover

The package had reached him through the usual channels. It contained a small diary, the pages filled with a cramped, unruly script. There was no name to identify an owner, and the first pages had been torn out, so that the text began in midentry, dateless—flipping ahead a few pages he saw that none of the entries were dated.

The note accompanying the diary, written in green ink, was not signed or dated either. It did not need to be. He'd been expecting a communication of some sort for days now. With a sigh, he settled more comfortably into the black leather chair, had another swallow of the hot and bitter coffee, and, as directed by the note, began to read from the beginning.

. . . but sit, man, waiting for the J to hit. Outside the big bad city, Love Me Avenue. Gotta be in the right frame of mind for that scene, no lie. Need the Doctor for that. So backpack between my legs I leaned back against one greasy, pissed-on wall checking it all out: homeboys roaming in tight packs, junkies on the nod, jittery crackheads, stumblebums seeking handouts, busloads of paleface tourists like flocks of sheep ready for shearing. And cops just itching to open fire, got that look of hate and terror in their eyes to remind me of home and Dear Old Dead Old Dad. Headphones blasting Rictus, "Serene Disdain"—oh, yeah, it was starting to come together, my own private MTV! Dude slinked over mouthing, "Sense? Sense?" And I had to laugh, 'cause like all of a sudden it's jangle time, I mean the Doctor is IN, and that's all the sense I need.

Dude gave me a wink as I slipped by. "Man, you lookin'?"

"I'm *cookin',*" I said with a giggle, a little too loud. Couple of cops started over in slow motion, but by then I was out of there, on the street, safe.

Even cooking with J took some long seconds to plug in. Saturday night on Love Me Avenue, Jangletown, U.S.A. The poxy brain of Gotham in its perpetual grand mal seizure, neurons blazing like Chinatown fireworks to the tune of Live Girls and the strobing blues and reds of police cars and ambulances, sirens wailing, people wailing louder, stench of hot dogs and stale sweat and automobile exhaust trapped and festering at the bottom of these dead canyons sunk beneath a smog so foul and thick it's like living underwater. No, they will not find me here.

Day and night the smoke goes up from this island pyre to sting the eyes of angels. Do they weep? I sometimes wonder. Once, sick and feverish, I dreamed of angels gazing down, lovely faces lost in light, wings spread wide as clouds. Oh how I longed to join them, but then the fever broke. I never saw them again until the Doctor took me by the hand and showed me how to look. Now it's angels everywhere, man. But they're above this city like nowhere else. Here I'll find the one I seek, the prince of angels I glimpsed so long ago in a fever dream. I saw him again in Dear Old Dead Old's eyes, and it made me smile like the promise of a punchline as I pulled the trigger, jingle, jangle, jongle.

Rictus could not keep up with the Doctor. As I changed tapes, a voice at my shoulder grated, "Man, you got a crash?"

The dude from the Port Authority. Blue jogging suit; leather medallion of Mother Africa in purple, green, red, and white. I frowned, stepped away, ready to merge with and into the chaos of the street, janglewise.

"Hell, no one want to mess with you, boy. Yeah, you cookin' all right. But you be hurtin' soon, I see that. You call this number. Ask for Panic; that's me."

A slip of paper in my hand, and the dude was gone. Panic—like where do they get these names? Cranked some Ozone and let the flow sweep me where it would.

Panic: he knew that name. Part-time dealer in flesh, full-time in drugs. His kind were common as cockroaches and more difficult to exterminate.

Jangle: he knew that name, too. AKA Doctor and/
or J. Streets had been flooded with the drug over the
last few months; it had appeared out of nowhere in
tiny patches no bigger than a thumbprint, patches
emblazoned with crazy patterns, drunken mandalas
of violet and green and crimson that just so happened
to blend in perfectly with the current rage for face tat-
toos.

Gotham seemed to be a test area; other cities had not
yet reported substantial quantities of the drug. It was a
personal challenge, of course, these punks poisoning his
city, out to make their reps over his dead body like
gunfighters in the Old West. Sometimes he could hear
their laughter echoing even in this dark and peaceful
refuge.

But jangle was no joke. A cocaine derivative, like
crack, cut with the usual strychnine but also spliced
with a designer drug he hadn't been able to isolate, a
subtle psychedelic that induced hallucinations of a para-
noid nature as the dosage increased . . . which it always
did. Withdrawal saw to that. Euphoria, fantasies of
power and control, mystical delusions capable of reaching an intensity that in extreme cases (and they were all
extreme cases, sooner or later) erupted into full-blown
psychosis. And to judge by what he'd read so far, the
author of this anonymous diary was reaching the breaking point.

. . . but then it only took a second. Me, dazed and hungry by the dawn's
early gloom, the Doctor O-U-T and a dirty drizzle falling from a dirty sky
as I searched for a cozy corner where I could slap on some J in peace
and quiet, just enough to bring me down light as a feather. Had the
news buzzing in my ears, President declares war on drugs ha-ha, no
reports of suburban murders but then Mom worked nights and wouldn't
be home for another hour or so.

Next thing I knew I was on my butt watching a couple kids dive down
the subway with my backpack, my headphones bouncing along behind. I was too wasted to do anything but lay there while the street
Samaritans howled helpfully. Fortunately there were no cops around, so
I got to my feet and split though the cramps had started and I knew I
wouldn't get far.

I made it around the corner and halfway down the next block before my guts came boiling up in my throat. I barely had time to drop to my knees in the gutter. I wondered if I was dying and more than half hoped so. I'd always come down nice and slow before, easy does it, softened the crash with a nice fluffy pillow. What an idiot to keep all my stash in one place! I deserved to suffer, man.

And I did, lying there I don't know how long, an hour maybe, knowing if I didn't move it was just a matter of time before the cops found me on their next sweep of the Avenue.

Then came the miracle. Through my misery I felt a flutter of fingers deftly peeling the useless dose from my neck and replacing it with a fresh one. And oh, man, this was some pure stuff, I mean jangle with a capital J. In seconds I felt the cool and fiery rush enter my blood, saw behind my blinded eyes the intricate dance of light and shadow that forms the substance of this world and glimpsed once more in the dirty clouds, infinite hierarchies of angels, angels orchestrating our destinies with delicate strokes of their glittering wings, each bright feather keen as a razor blade.

"Don't freak," admonished the childish voice of my savior. "We gotta split. Come *on.*" And pulled me to my feet. "You okay?"

With an effort I blinked away the angels, saw a face scarcely less beautiful: high cheekbones, smooth skin so pale it seemed a hard look might leave a bruise, eyes wide and piercing blue, short hair colored and shaved in swirls as though tie-dyed except for a sheaf of white-blond bangs flopping over one eye. A tattooed Mandelbrot Set flared across his neck like the badge of some exotic clan, concealing from all but practiced eyes a jolt of J. Torn T-shirt, dirty jeans, purple All-Stars with bright green laces. I guessed he was no more than thirteen; two years my junior in all but the ability to survive on Love Me Avenue. "Way rad tattoo," I said.

"Name's Toddy," he answered. We fell into step with that weird synchronicity of thought and action that springs up between two users, as though the drug made us brothers.

"Mine's Galen," I replied. I had a feeling we were going to hit it off. I was warping out on the J. Without Toddy there I would've freaked for sure. "Galen Starling."

He giggled as we dodged through the crowded street, straights giving us glances of disgust and annoyance as they hurried to their nine-to-fives.

"Panic's gonna *love* that," he promised, an hysterical edge to his voice. While Toddy was calming me, I had the opposite effect on him. He absorbed my high like a jangle vampire.

Panic. That name sounded familiar, but it wasn't until Toddy had led me down a dizzying maze of streets and alleys to a building of bricked-and boarded-up doors and windows in a neighborhood that looked as if a war had swept through only yesterday that I remembered the slip of paper still in my pocket.

"What's this place, Toddy?"

"Home," he said, flashing me a grin perfect as an angel's wing. "It's cool—come on."

And with that, he scurried past the warped boards blocking the front door, leaving me alone on the empty street with no idea where I was or how'd I'd gotten there. My backpack was gone; the cops were probably after me by now. I didn't have a friend in the city but Toddy, and Toddy had jangle. I followed him in.

"Toddy?"

It took me a second to adjust to the gloom. What light there was came from candles and single bulbs dangling from extension cords high overhead. Portions of the walls and ceiling had fallen, giving the place a bombed-out look. A few kids my own age or younger were eyeing me sullenly from the shadows, boys and girls, black, white, brown, yellow.

"Well if it ain't Mister Independent," a voice rasped to my left.

I turned, saw Panic approaching with one arm draped about Toddy's shoulders, the other kids following. He was dressed in the same blue jogging suit as the night before, leather medallion jouncing upon his ample chest. Toddy was munching a candy bar, gazing up at Panic with a pure affection that made my skin crawl. I felt as if the ghost of Dear Old Dead Old had crept back to haunt me.

"Hey, boy, you're way ahead of schedule! Knew I'd be seeing you, but not so soon."

"I got robbed," I said glumly, shrugging.

"Now ain't that a shame!" Panic grinned like he knew all about my misfortunes. "Toddy tell me you need a place to stay."

I nodded, wary.

"Talkative, ain't you. What's your name?"

"Galen Starling."

Panic whooped. "Christ Almighty, where *do* you white folks get them names?"

I burned. "It's Gaelic."

"Oooo. Sound like a damn bird to me. Well, my name's Gaelic, too. It means, 'Watch your step, wiseass.' Know what I think? You that kid I heard about on the TV this morning. That right?"

I shook my head, mouth so dry the words came out whispered. "No way." I would have run, but the others were crowding me in.

He eyed me shrewdly. "Yeah, right. Well, you can crash here, I got plenty of room, plenty of everything, right? Only you gotta help out, everyone lends a hand when Uncle Panic's got work to do. Errands, you know? Deliveries, got some important people we can't keep waiting, need some smart kids, fast kids. You smart, Galen? You fast?"

I grinned then, J screaming through my brain like a missile. Fast? I'd show him fast.

So the mysterious author had a name at last. He fed it into the computer. Seconds later, the information flashed onto the screen.

Galen Starling, 15, wanted in connection with the murder of his stepfather. An unusual name, Starling . . . Cross-references to the child welfare files—a few minor drug offenses, petty theft, then buried in a footnote an allegation of sexual abuse leveled against the stepfather by one of Galen's neighbors, never followed up.

Between bureaucratic ineptitude and the tender mercies of the Panics of the world, what chance did kids like Galen have? It made him sick and angry; kids always hit him the hardest. His own childhood had been stolen—he knew better than most what it was like to be young, alone and afraid, with nobody to turn to, nobody to trust. Sometimes he wondered if that was what kept him going after so many failures, so many deaths he'd been powerless to prevent, had in a sense contributed to if not caused outright, part of him dying again each time. God, the blood on his hands! He was sick to death of the whole damn mess, but it was too late now, he'd lost too much to turn back, given up his soul piece by piece and become just another of Gotham's lurid fever dreams in the process. No, there was nothing to do but finish what he'd started. Or be finished by it. And never let them see the hurt and frightened boy he still, deep down, knew himself to be, whether kneeling on the dirt sidewalk watching his parents' lives bleed away or cradling in his arms the broken body of the brave boy he'd loved like a son.

*   *   *

Toddy's always asking how come I write so much in here. Hell, I don't know. I thought I might show it to Mom someday, let her know what it was like for me being alone so much of the time with Dear Old Dead Old while she was busy playing Angel of Mercy at the hospital. But I've torn all those pages out. Burned them. I mean, what's the point? That's all history now that he's dead. But the funny thing is, I can't quit writing. It's in my blood, I guess. Like jangle.

For sure Mom wouldn't recognize me these days. I got my hair cut and dyed and a tattoo like Toddy's; man, we cruise Love Me Avenue like a couple of Siamese twins! Purple All-Stars with green laces to show we're Panic's boys. But me and Toddy are gonna save us some money and split. Clear out where Panic'll never find us. I mean, it's too late for me; my father messed me up good before jangle came along to finish the job. But it breaks my heart to see the same thing happening to Toddy. He's still a kid, man. It isn't right, it just isn't right.

This is my favorite place. On the roof at night with a jolt of J leaking its slow magic into my blood and all of Gotham lit up like a Christmas tree. Nothing can touch me up here. I'm free, I can feel the angels so near I can shut my eyes and feel their wings brush my face. They're out there, man, all around me, calling me. Now and then a gunshot comes like an urgent summons and it's all I can do to hold myself back: the ledge beckons, my spirit soars as though I could fly! Sometimes I know that if I jumped I wouldn't fall, they would fold me in their wings and take me up to where the prince of angels lives. He gazes down on us with a secret smile and Gotham City throws back his warped reflection. I would go in search of him but the thought of Toddy keeps me here. Who'd take care of him if I was gone?

Then like an answer, a writhing shape appears against the sky—the image of a giant bat cast upon the clouds like some demonic brand. Its immense wings seem to beat tirelessly to hold itself in place. And though I know it's just an illusion caused by the motion of the clouds, a chill creeps across my bones as if death's shadow has touched me . . .

. . . knew it was bad this time cause the street names had changed: Love Me Avenue now Street of Chance, the letters in Chance writhing to spell CHANCRE and then CANCER, scarlet claws curving up from the C and R to reach for me. I yelled, dodging the claws.

"What the hell you doing, Galen? You want to freak the customers?" Toddy hissed, pulling me after him into an alley.

"Bad scene, bad scene," a voice crooned, laughing, from the street.

I slumped against the crumbling brick wall, let myself slide to rest on my haunches. I pressed my forehead against my knees and shivered.

"What is it, man?" demanded Toddy, nervous now for real. "C'mon, it's just the Doc running down, we'll get you stitched right back up, it ain't nothing really—"

I nodded, got myself together.

"S'alright," I said. I made a face like I was fighting nausea, but it wasn't that, really; unless you can figure that something like a scorpion burrowing through your brain could make you feel nauseous. I looked up at him: poor pretty Toddy, thirteen and lying to the cops that he was sixteen, lying to the marks that he was twelve. "Toddy, you ever felt bad on J?"

He dug the lavender toe of his sneaker into the rubble and twisted it, kicking up gravel and broken glass. "Bad? Yeah, sure, I felt bad. I feel bad right now, man, you're breaking my heart. C'mon, fer crissakes! Panic's gonna kill us if we get picked up by the cops—"

He pirouetted, shading his eyes with one hand as he peered out into the street. Something going on out there, motors running but not moving, that same voice chanting *bad scene bad scene* like he was making it happen by mouthing the words.

I stood, pushing Toddy so that he whirled glaring and then grinning to see me up again. "Hey, lookit that, huh?" He whistled, pointing out the alley. "You ever see a car that big?"

I looked. "Hell, I never saw a *plane* that big!"

We stepped out of the alley, Toddy tripping ahead of me in that lightfoot clumsy-pretty way he had, like a puppy dancing on its hind legs. A couple of girls in white lace and rubber went by chirping at the little blond kid staring big-eyed at a limousine that practically covered the whole block, poison green with purple accents, tires with hubcaps so clean the streetlights burned off them, the whole thing not only longer but bigger, more massive, taller than any limo I'd ever seen.

"Hey mister!" Toddy yelled, tossing his head so that his bangs flopped into his eyes. Little boy lost, oh, boy: I could see it now. "Hey mister, can I ride in your big car?"

A gloved hand stretched from the window, slowly, the glove that same glowing violet as the trim on the limo, brass buttons—hell, *gold* buttons—catching the light and winking.

The arm kept coming, the fingers twitching, beckoning Toddy, Toddy sliding warily now up to the curb, trying to see inside. I glimpsed a face, a woman's I thought, backstreet angel powdered pale like last year's vampire queens, mouth too heavily lipsticked but grinning so broadly that I looked behind me to see if she meant someone else—

But no one was there. In fact the street, crowded seconds before, was nearly empty. No, she meant me.

The hand stopped an inch from Toddy's face, seeming to stretch an improbable length over the sidewalk. The few passersby hurried on or else slowed to watch, snickering, as Toddy moved closer, until the hand gently cupped the back of his head. I watched, helpless; and yeah, jealous, too. And not just because here was a mark in a fancy car. There was something else, something about that ghastly face that drew me: like seeing someone you recognize from a dream. I took a step, near enough to see that nestled between those gloved fingers something glistened, something small and brightly colored, purple and green and red.

"Toddy—" I warned, doubtfully; but then the hand grabbed him by the neck. Toddy began to cry out and then stopped. A blissful expression crept across his face. The hand withdrew. Toddy just stood there, smiling a little, a sort of dopey smile. I could see a new little tab like a violet tick feasting amid the swirls of his face tattoo.

Behind me someone laughed. I stooped and threw a bottle at a guy standing there. I turned back to the limo, ready to lam another one through the window at the bitch inside.

Only it wasn't a woman. It was a man, and he was laughing, too.

"Just *keeping tabs* on him!" he wheezed between fits of giggles.

"Hey," Toddy began again, but doubtfully. He glanced up at me, shoving the hair from his eyes, then, wondering, touched the jolt on his cheek. I shook my head and tugged at his jacket.

"Come on, Toddy. Bad news—"

A man so tall he'd had that limo built around him; a man so rich he could afford it. And that face! Not a mask, not a transvestite either. Just that ghastly expression, Bette Davis eyes and Dawn of the Dead mouth, hair the color of sour apples swept back from a dead white forehead. The rest of him slung into a jacket and trousers the same unsettling hues as his car. Poison green and violet.

Poison scene. Violent. Bad scene bad scene . . .

The mocking angel in the car leaned out the window, streetlamp snaking a yellow line down his arm.

"Why aren't you in school, sonny?" he crooned; then cackled, so long and loud that I heard all around us a noise like a bunch of pigeons taking flight. But it wasn't pigeons, it was that block clearing out so fast it'd make your head spin.

"Toddy," I whispered, but Toddy wasn't listening to me anymore. He was beside the limo, standing on tiptoe to peer inside the open window—the car was that big. The freakish angel inside giggled helplessly, staring down at that small gold head with its rainbow swirls, the smear of dirt on the back of his neck where Toddy never bothered to wash. One gloved hand reached to gently stroke his bangs, then yanked, hard.

"Damn!" Toddy skipped backward, rubbing his head. But when he saw the freak was laughing he laughed, too, took a step forward, eyes already slitted with that conspiratorial look he got, the look we all got when we'd found a rich mark. But when I saw those emerald eyes gazing down at him I went cold. Because I'd never seen a look like that anywhere before, except in the first seconds when the jangle hit and I saw the angels, ravening angels sparking the Gotham night: and now here was one in front of me.

I stepped forward. "Hey, man," I said, trying to sound cool but I knew it came out a whine. "Got room for me, too?" 'Cause suddenly more than anything, more even than I was scared for Toddy, I was terrified the car would pull off and I'd never see that man again, never be able to find him.

His eyes flicked from Toddy to my face, lingered there thoughtfully as he toyed with an ascot loosely knotted about his neck. Black, red, green, purple: lurid colors fitting his delirious elegance, and where had I seen them before? I tried to look unconcerned, squinted to see what was beside him in the limo, but made out nothing. Only that his other hand, the hand that rested on his violet-draped knee, twitched endlessly, fingers drumming some intricate tattoo upon the seemingly empty air. Without thinking I moved a little closer to the car, until I could see that he flipped repeatedly through a deck of cards, shuffling one-handed the way I'd seen the sharps do it on Fleece Street. But never cards like these. Even in the shadows I could see their designs glowing spectrally, some kind of luminous paper I guess, and the figures on them seemed different from the usual array, Jack, Queen, Joker, King.

The emerald angel suddenly stopped shuffling, glanced down at the card facing upward on the deck. He sighed, shaking his head, and glanced out the window.

"Oh, dear," he murmured. His gaze met mine, bottle-green eyes only a shade paler than his hair and so full of sorrow I imagined he might weep despite his leering grin. "Not today, young man, I'm afraid you can't come today. You see, it's not in the cards: not yet. And I do so like to give people what they want. . . ."

His gaze darted to my temple, where the tab of spent jangle clung like soiled confetti. "But soon," he whispered. "I promise, soon. . . ."

Beside me Toddy fidgeted, his eyes glazing over as he swayed slightly. Finally he shoved me back against the curb. "Hey, c'mon Galen, you heard him—"

I bit my lip in disappointment as the limo door *shushed* open and Toddy disappeared inside, tossing me a final grin so delighted I had to smile back. Poor Toddy! He really *was* excited to be riding in a big car. Next to that lean tall figure he looked truly childlike, princeling for a day.

The man stretched his arm to tap once upon the driver's window. The limo's purr grew louder, became a throaty growl. A sheet of black glass began to slide up, cutting off Toddy's rapt face and tossing back my own thwarted reflection. Scant inches from the top it stopped.

"Here—" Green eyes etched through the window slit as two long white fingers, delicate and faintly trembling, held out a card like a radiant token. "Maybe next time, surely next time . . ."

The limo slipped away, leaving me gaping as the noisy tide of punks and janglies and chattering whores swept back to claim the street. Someone jogged my elbow; I kicked out defensively at a slack-jawed junkie staring with empty black terrified eyes at what I held.

"J-j-j-j—" he stammered. I pushed him away and started for the corner. There, safe in the crowd waiting to cross Love Me Avenue, I finally inspected what the angel had given me. Not a regular playing card at all: a fortune card, a tarot card I guess, livid figures rising dead-eyed from narrow coffins scattered crazily about a gray expanse of shattered stone and concrete. Above them all hovered the grisly form of a grinning green-haired angel, beryl wings curving to end in spikes of red and violet, white hands dropping brilliant shards of light. Purple, emerald, argent, scarlet discs like rain, like jewels; like jolts of jangle. And beneath it, tipsy block letters that spelled

THE LAST JUDGEMENT

It was only later, teeth chattering as my heart made its first run heavenward in Panic's gallery and I glimpsed his medallion hanging from a nail, that I remembered where I'd seen those colors before.

The man reading lifted his head, slowly; stared into the surrounding darkness as though he too glimpsed the colors there, and remembered where he had last seen them.

His fist opened, then clenched shut as he tried to keep his hand from shaking, tried to contain the rage building inside him. He pried the next page open, swearing as it crumbled at his touch, and continued reading.

Three days since I've seen Toddy. I tried asking back at Panic's about the guy in the car but everyone just looks at me like I'm crazy, or maybe like they're crazy and don't want me to find out.

Even Panic. "Where's your fair-haired boy, Starling?" He sat counting plastic bags full of iridescent jolts, a spangled mountain growing in front of him. "I ain't seen him for a while."

"I don't know." I'd hesitated to tell him about the man in the limo, but now I did, leaving out the part about the card he'd given me. Panic stopped counting, stopped doing anything. He didn't even look at me, just stared at the blank crumbling wall in front of him.

When I finished he said, "You say you don't know who it was."

I nodded. He turned to me then. His eyes were bleak, and I could tell it was an effort for him to smile. "Well, that's good, that's a good thing now. Now here—"

He handed me a Baggie, more J than I'd ever had in my hands at once, not excepting all the times me and Toddy had run it for him to Haggard Square and Nam and Gotham's other war zones. "Go ahead, take it," he urged, his eyes desperate. "Now go have some fun, have yourself a **big** time, forget all this crap. Toddy'll turn up. You'll see."

"You don't even care!"

"If I didn't, would I be giving you all this J?"

I eyed the Baggie in his hand. That much jangle would kill. Suddenly I wondered if Panic wanted me dead.

"No, no," he said quickly, seeing my fear. "It's a new batch, understand? Stepped on harder than usual—more money that way. The big man wants his profits, you know?"

I took the bag and split, not sure how much I believed Panic's story. For sure I didn't trust him, though.

Hell, I'll find Toddy myself; tune in with J and sniff him out. I'm not going back without him.

. . . angels everywhere they are guarding the city they are watching me waiting for me they have my father's face and my mother's eyes there are two I can see now they face each other across the canyons they strive endlessly and I am trapped between longing longing to be with them. . . .

* * * *

I found Toddy. What's left of him. Wandering down by the Canal. I saw him from behind and knew it was him, I yelled and shouted but he never turned around, finally I ran up to him and hugged him, nearly tackling him. He still never turned around to look at me so I pulled him up and looked at him.

When I saw his face I thought I'd be sick, he was just grinning, this awful smile. I said, "Hey, glad to see me or what?" But he never said anything. He just smiled, he never stops smiling now, like the man in the crazy sedan, he just smiles and won't say anything, not what happened, not what he did to him, he doesn't say anything at all.

I brought him back to Panic's. I didn't know what else to do, where else to go.

Panic had a sickly smile when he saw me coming, my arm around Toddy's shoulders. "You found your friend," he said. For a minute I thought maybe he was relieved, relieved to see me, relieved to see Toddy and think maybe everything was gonna be okay, it was just another mark in a fancy car.

Then he saw Toddy's face. "What's he smiling at?" Panic hissed. Kids scrambled to get out of his way as he stormed across the room, hitting one of those trailing lightbulbs so the whole place was filled with spinning shadows. "What's he laughing at, WHAT'S SO GODDAMN FUNNY?"

I started crying then. 'Cause like I walked the whole way across Gotham, from the Canal to here, practically carrying Toddy sometimes, and he never said a word, he never said a goddamn thing. "I don't know!" I shouted, shoving Toddy so he stumbled and then caught himself and stood between us, me and Panic, grinning that horrible empty grin. "Something happened, he did something to him—"

"*Who* did?" Panic yelled. It was like he'd gone crazy too, only crazy-scared. He grabbed me by the shoulders and shook me, saying over and over, "Who did it? Who?" until finally I spat out, "*You* know who! The guy in the limousine, that crazy guy, the one they say controls the J—"

He let go of me then and stepped back a little breathlessly, like I'd kicked him. "Who told you that? No one knows that, no one knows for sure, no one's supposed to say . . ."

His words trailed off. He stared at Toddy standing there, swaying a little like he was held up by wires. Then, before I knew what happened, Panic lunged at him. There was this flash of something in the air, and I heard one of the other kids cry out. Then Panic moved on, he crossed the room and hunched over a stack of Baggies. For a second Toddy stood there in front of me, still grinning; only now it was like he had two smiles, one on his face, another a brilliant slash of red across his throat. As I watched his head lolled back, until I was left with only that other grin. Without another noise, he toppled to the ground at my feet.

I went crazy then. Going after Panic, who was shaken enough to try and hide from me before he figured out it was him with a knife against one berserk kid with nothing. Then it was me running, kicking over stacks of jangle and yanking the lights out until the place was stone dark and one of the other kids hissed across the floor for me to follow her, she knew a way out.

I did, and she did. So now I'm here in the rain by Haggard Square, nothing but a pocketful of jolts and my notebook and a stolen pen. Toddy's dead and I know who's next, oh, yeah, I do, only no one's gonna track me down. I'm gonna freak him, that blood-soaked angel, I'm gonna give him something to laugh about, 'cause maybe he thinks he's gonna find me but it ain't gonna be like that. I'm gonna find *him*. He's somewhere in this sewer city and I'm gonna track him down, I'm gonna make him show me what it is he knows and I don't, I'm gonna make him tell me what the point is, what he's laughing at, what the punchline is. I'm gonna find him if it kills me.

The man lifted his head, stared into the surrounding darkness. His body shook with grief and rage. For a moment he could not go on, remembering. But that was long ago and this was a different boy. Then he turned the page and softly swore, as if hardly surprised to see the elegant script, the ink so thick and green it seemed to writhe across the page like some hothouse growth— toxic, evil and alive. It was a hand he knew well, a poison that never lost its sting but only added to the venom in his veins. Perhaps one day his tolerance for it would disappear like hope or happiness and he would die like all the others. Perhaps he would even welcome that end.

But not yet. Not while he could still hate, still hurt, still hear the horrid laughter and feel the loss as if it had happened only yesterday.

It did not take long for the boy to come here, the runaway named Galen Starling. But then I wanted to be found, nearly as much as he wanted to find me.

"A pretty name, Galen. Does a starling sing? Does it have a sweet voice?"

He stood, dumbstruck, in the middle of the chamber. I could see he was trying not to look impressed but oh! these youngsters, they wear their hearts in their eyes, haven't you noticed that, Gentle Reader? But I digress—

"What did you do to him?" he croaked at last, tearing his eyes from the images on the walls. His clothes were soaked from the passage through the tunnel and he shivered. I motioned him nearer to me where I sat alone in the center of the room. I had sent the others away, stupid thugs, this boy would appreciate my artistry more than they did. He was a dreamer.

"I did what I always do: I gave him what he wanted. I always give the people what they want. Jangle, for instance; and other things." I gestured at the walls. "Do you like my pictures?"

He crossed the room slowly, rubbing his arms as he stared at the photographs, averting his eyes from some, his gaze lingering upon others as he read the legend beneath each.

"Now that's a particularly good one there, Galen—'A Stitch in Time Saves Nine.' I had the devil of a time getting a needle through some of those spots!"

He gagged, turned to glare at me. "You're crazy, you're really crazy—"

I stood and crossed the room to join him. He shuddered as I casually draped my arm around his shoulder, but didn't pull away; no, he was a curious young man, eager to learn; a little bird striving to fly with eagles. "Here, Starling, look at this one—"

"No!" He surprised me then, he turned on me. His eyes were burning, he must have taken more of the drug on his way down. "Why—why do you look like that?"

"Like what?" I leered. I guided him away from the photos—he was not as astute a critic as I had hoped—and brought him to the center of the room, to the sofa there. "Have a perch, Starling." Oh, I do so love to play with them first!

"That smile," he whispered, sitting. He seemed more in awe of me than afraid, and—dare I say it?—quite entranced with what he saw. Meeting the Prince of Darkness on his own turf, et cetera. I decided to entertain him for a few more minutes. I took out my cards and began to shuffle them. "Why do you smile like that?" he demanded.

I glanced at the top card, then up at him. "This smile? Why, don't you recognize this, Starling? It's the smile on the face of the tiger. . . ."

As he stared at me I turned the card over, held it so that he could see the figure of the young violet-clad boy walking blissfully along the edge of a cliff, his eyes cast skyward as one foot strays into the empty air. "Oh, dear," I said, and let the card fall to rest upon his knee. "That's rather a bad one under the circumstances, Galen: The Fool. Delirium and madness. Thoughtless decisions. A sensitive soul led astray by bad companions."

He tried to run then, poor thing, but I clamped my hand around his neck and brought him to me.

"But why—" he whispered; that was before he began to scream. "Who are you?—"

"I am your heart's desire, Galen," I crooned, flipping one last card from the deck as it fell to the floor. Another bad card, Death grinning from a dark sedan. It was the last thing he saw before I started.

The young body he found in the vacant subway tunnel was spattered with paint: yellow, green, and red. There was an *R* carved upon the bright red breast. White makeup caked a tattooed face. The hair was dyed a sloppy green, the lips shone red. The arms were spread as though in flight; his feet had left the floor. The grin was so wide it had split the skin. The eyes would see no more.

Plucking from between stiff fingers the folded paper left for him to find, the man turned from the broken boy and read the Joker's note. Soft mocking laughter filled the room like poison flames inside his head.

"Birds of a feather die together," was what the Batman read.

About the Authors

EDWARD BRYANT has been one of the most heralded writers and critics of science fiction, fantasy, and horror for more than two decades, his short stories "Stone" and "giANTS" having each won the Nebula Award. His books include *Phoenix Without Ashes* (with Harlan Ellison), *Cinnabar,* and the short story collection *Among the Dead and Other Events Leading Up to the Apocalypse,* among others. **DAN SIMMONS** is the author of five novels: *Song of Kali* (winner of the World Fantasy Award), *Carrion Comfort, Phases of Gravity, Hyperion,* and *The Fall of Hyperion* (coming in March 1990 from Doubleday Foundation). Winner of *Twilight Zone* magazine's Rod Serling Memorial Award for best new writer in 1982, he currently resides in Colorado.

JOEY CAVALIERI lives in New York City.

GEORGE ALEC EFFINGER's stories and novels have made his name significant in the science fiction field for nearly twenty years. Author of *When Gravity Fails, A Fire in the Sun,* and the forthcoming Doubleday Foundation novel, *The Exile Kiss,* he most recently won both the Hugo and Nebula awards for Best Novelette for his story "Schrödinger's Kitten."

KAREN HABER, while having started her career as a non-fiction writer, has written stories for *The Magazine of Fantasy and Science Fiction, Full Spectrum 2,* and *Women of Darkness.* She is married to Robert Silverberg, with whom she currently edits the original anthology *Universe* and was coauthor of the first volume in the Doubleday Foundation series *The Mutant Season.*

ELIZABETH HAND is the author of the forthcoming Bantam novel *Winterlong*. Her short fiction has appeared in *Pulphouse, Full Spectrum 2, Twilight Zone,* and *The Year's Best Horror 1988.* She reviews books regularly for the *Washington Post Book World* and is a Contributing Editor for *Science Fiction Eye* magazine. She is at work on her second novel, *Aestival Tide,* and lives in Rockport, Maine. **PAUL WITCOVER**'s fiction has appeared in *Isaac Asimov's Science Fiction Magazine, Night Cry,* and *Twilight Zone.* He recently completed his first novel, *Piggydossum,* and is at work on a biography of Zora Neal Hurston. He lives in New York.

ANDREW HELFER has been a comic book editor for DC Comics for several years, guiding the adventures of such characters as Superman, Green Lantern, and Justice League America. His writing has included the series *Deadman, The Shadow,* and the recently completed miniseries *Justice Inc.* (illustrated by our cover artist Kyle Baker). In addition to his full-time job, he is also a writer for the "Superboy" syndicated television series. He lives in New York City.

EDWARD D. HOCH, born 1930, is one of the most prolific short story writers in history, with over 800 published works of mystery, science fiction, and horror to his credit. President of the Mystery Writers of America in 1982, he was also the winner of the organization's Edgar Allan Poe Award in 1968.

STUART M. KAMINSKY is well known for his tales of 1930s Hollywood and is the author of the Toby Peters and Porfiry Petrovich mystery series. *A Cold Red Sunrise,* the latest novel in the Rostnikov series, won the Edgar Award for Best Novel in 1988. Born in 1934, he is Professor of Radio, Television, and Film at Northwestern University.

JOE R. LANSDALE is best known as a writer of horror and suspense, with dozens of short stories to his credit. His work has appeared in *Twilight Zone, Mississippi Arts and Letters,* as well as the *Shadows* and *Black Lizard Anthology of Crime* collections. His novels include *Dead in the West, The Nightrunners, The Drive In* and *The Drive In 2.* In 1989 he was nominated twice for the World Fantasy Award, for Best Novel *(The Drive In)* and Best Short Story ("The Night they Missed the Horror Show" from *Silver Scream*). He lives with his wife and children in Nacodoches, Texas.

ROBERT R. McCAMMON, a native of Birmingham, Alabama, has published nine novels of horror and dark fantasy, including *Swan Song, The Wolf's Hour, They Thirst,* and *The New York Times* bestseller *Stinger.* His short fiction has been adapted for television, his World Fantasy Award-winning story "Nightcrawlers" appearing as an episode of the 1980s revival of *The Twilight Zone.*

WILL MURRAY, in addition to being the current pseudonymous writer of Richard Sapir and Warren Murphy's *Destroyer* action series for New American Library, also scripts the *Destroyer* comic series for Marvel Comics, is the Boston Correspondent for *Starlog* magazine and has written numerous radio scripts for *The Adventures of Doc Savage* for National Public Radio.

MARCO PALMIERI's story "Best of All" marks his writing debut. A native New Yorker, he currently lives in Brooklyn with his roommate Doris and their cat Lestat, where he is finishing work on a novel.

GARFIELD REEVES-STEVENS is a Canadian-born writer whose previous novels include *Bloodshift, Dream-*

land, Children of the Shroud, and *Nighteyes.* Now a California resident, his new novel will appear in 1990 from Doubleday Foundation.

MIKE RESNICK has published over 200 novels under various pseudonyms and is one of the most popular fantasy and science fiction writers of recent years. His work includes the Galactic Midway, Ganymede, and Velvet Comet series, and "Kirinyaga," which won the 1988 Hugo Award for Best Short Story.

ROBERT SHECKLEY is the author of over ten science fiction novels and more than a dozen short story collections. His short story "Seventh Victim" was the basis for the 1965 film *The Tenth Victim,* starring Marcello Mastroianni and Ursula Andress.

HENRY SLESAR has been writing for print and television for decades, thirty of his stories having been adapted by Alfred Hitchcock for the original *Alfred Hitchcock Presents* television series. An executive in the advertising field for many years, he has written hundreds of short stories and received the Edgar Award twice, in 1960 and 1972.

S. TEPPER usually writes fantasy and science fiction.

MARK L. VAN NAME is a full-time freelance writer from North Carolina. **JACK McDEVITT,** also a long-time freelance science fiction writer, is the author of two novels, and won the 1987 Philip K. Dick Special Award for his first novel, *The Hercules Text.* His latest novel is *A Talent for War* and his short story "Whistle" appeared in *Full Spectrum 2.*

EDWARD WELLEN's writing career began in 1952 and in the years since has published one novel and more than 250 short stories, mainly in the fields of fantasy and science fiction. He has taught writing through the mail for Writer's Digest and continues to write freelance. He lives in New York.

F. PAUL WILSON, born in 1946, is the author of such horror novels as *The Tomb, The Keep* (made into a film by the same name by *Miami Vice* creator Michael Mann), and *Dydeetown World*. Winner of the 1979 Prometheus Award, he is also a full-time physician in New Jersey.

About the Editor

MARTIN H. GREENBERG is the editor or author of over 300 books, the majority of them anthologies in the science fiction, fantasy, horror, mystery, and western fields. In addition to editing *The Further Adventures of Batman,* he has collaborated editorially with such authors as Isaac Asimov, Robert Silverberg, Gregory Benford, and Frederik Pohl. A professor of political science at the University of Wisconsin, he lives with his wife and baby daughter in Green Bay.

DON'T MISS
THESE CURRENT
Bantam Bestsellers

BANTAM
SHOP·AT·HOME
C·A·T·A·L·O·G

Special Offer
Buy a Bantam Book
for only 50¢.

Now you can have Bantam's catalog filled with hundreds of titles plus take advantage of our unique and exciting bonus book offer. A special offer which gives you the opportunity to purchase a Bantam book for only 50¢. Here's how!

By ordering any five books at the regular price per order, you can also choose any other single book listed (up to a $5.95 value) for just 50¢. Some restrictions do apply, but for further details why not send for Bantam's catalog of titles today!

Just send us your name and address and we will send you a catalog!